MARVEL ACTION

CAPTAIN MARVEL

Ghost in the Machine

Look at Meme Now!

Writer: Sam Maggs
Pencil Layouts: Mario Del Pennino
Inks: Isabel Escalante
Colorist: Heather Breckel
Letterer: Valeria Lopez

Game On!

Writer: Sam Maggs
Artist: Sweeney Boo
Colorist: Brittany Peer
Letterer: Valeria Lopez &
          Nichelle Vidales

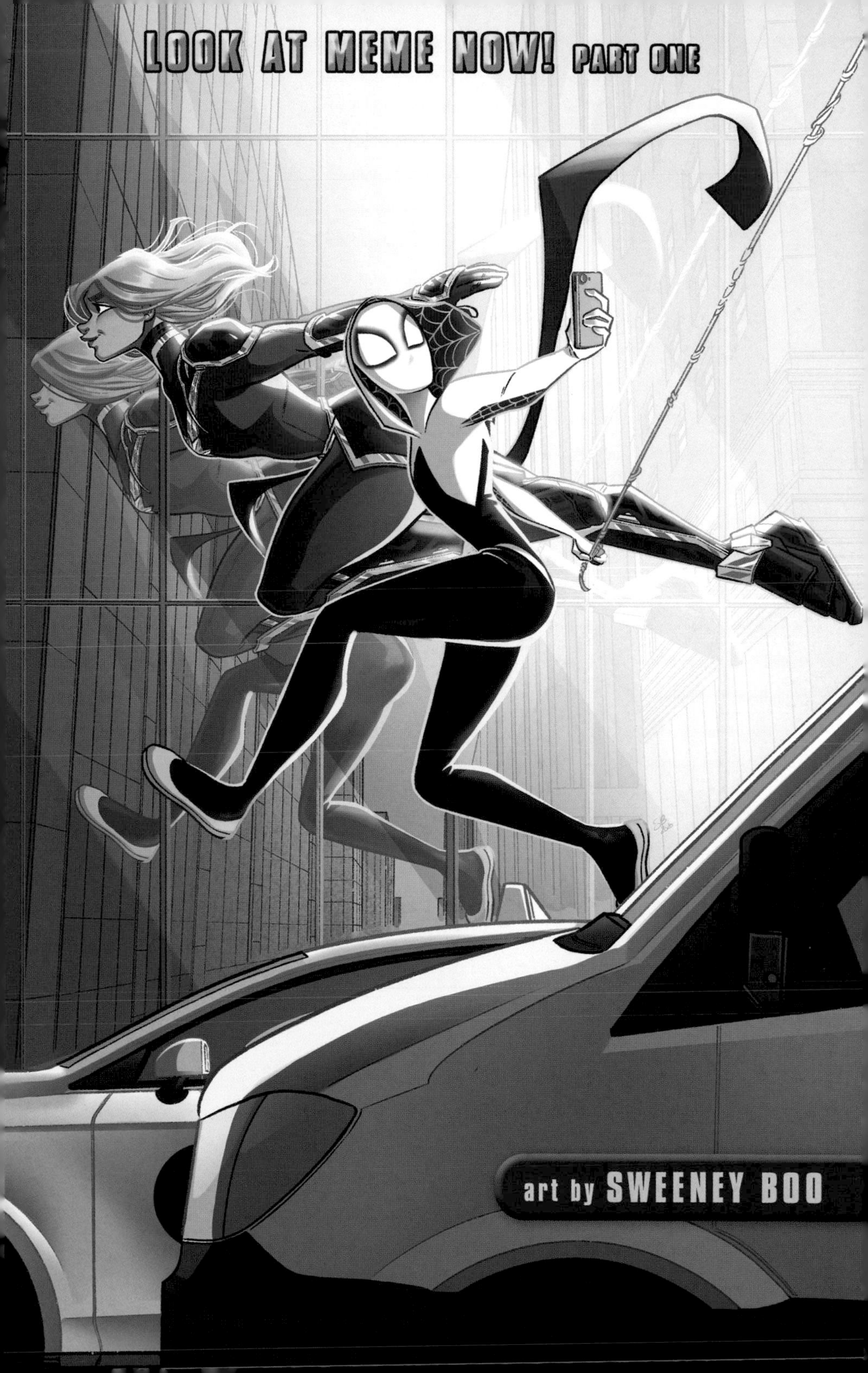
LOOK AT MEME NOW! PART ONE
art by SWEENEY BOO

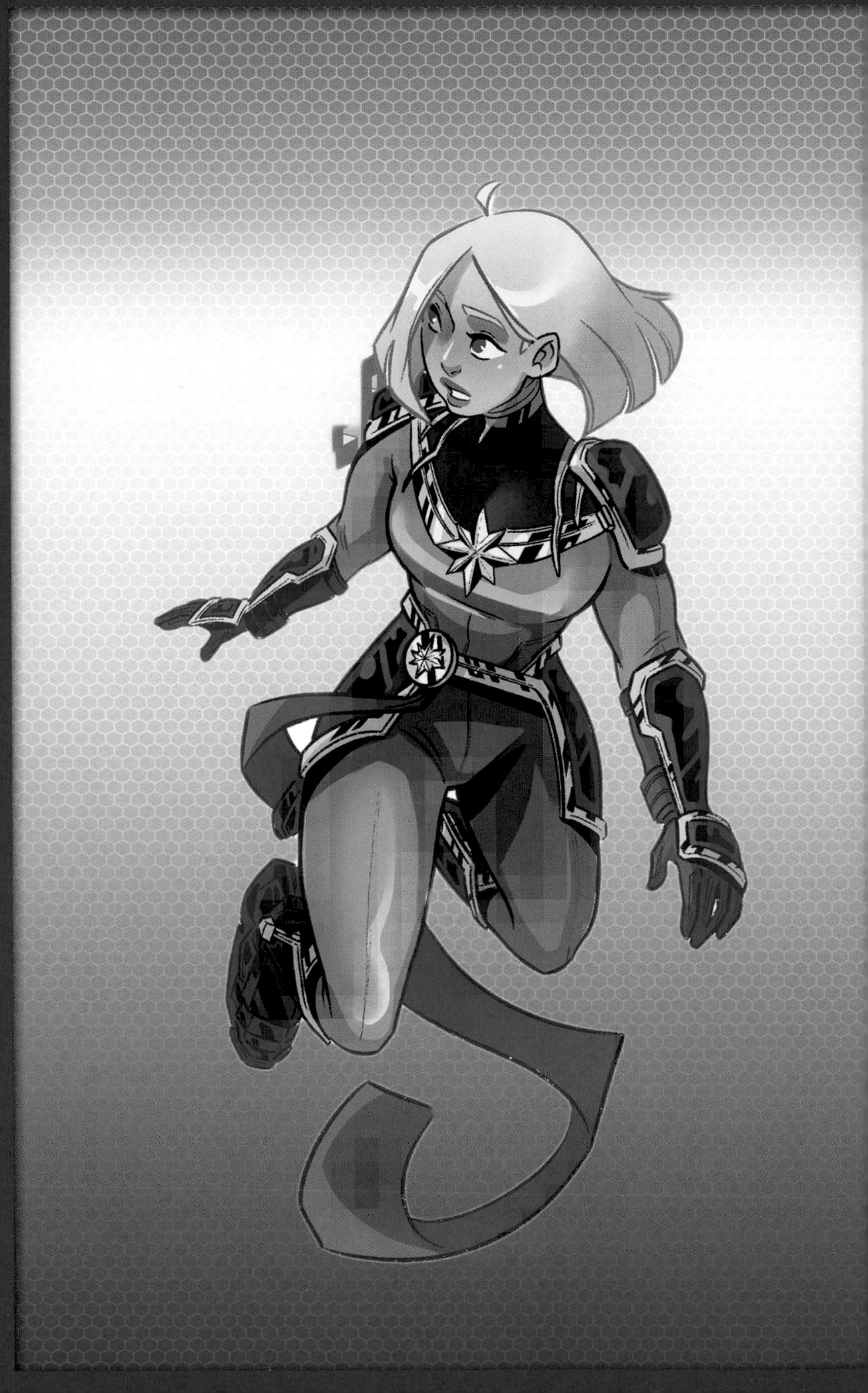

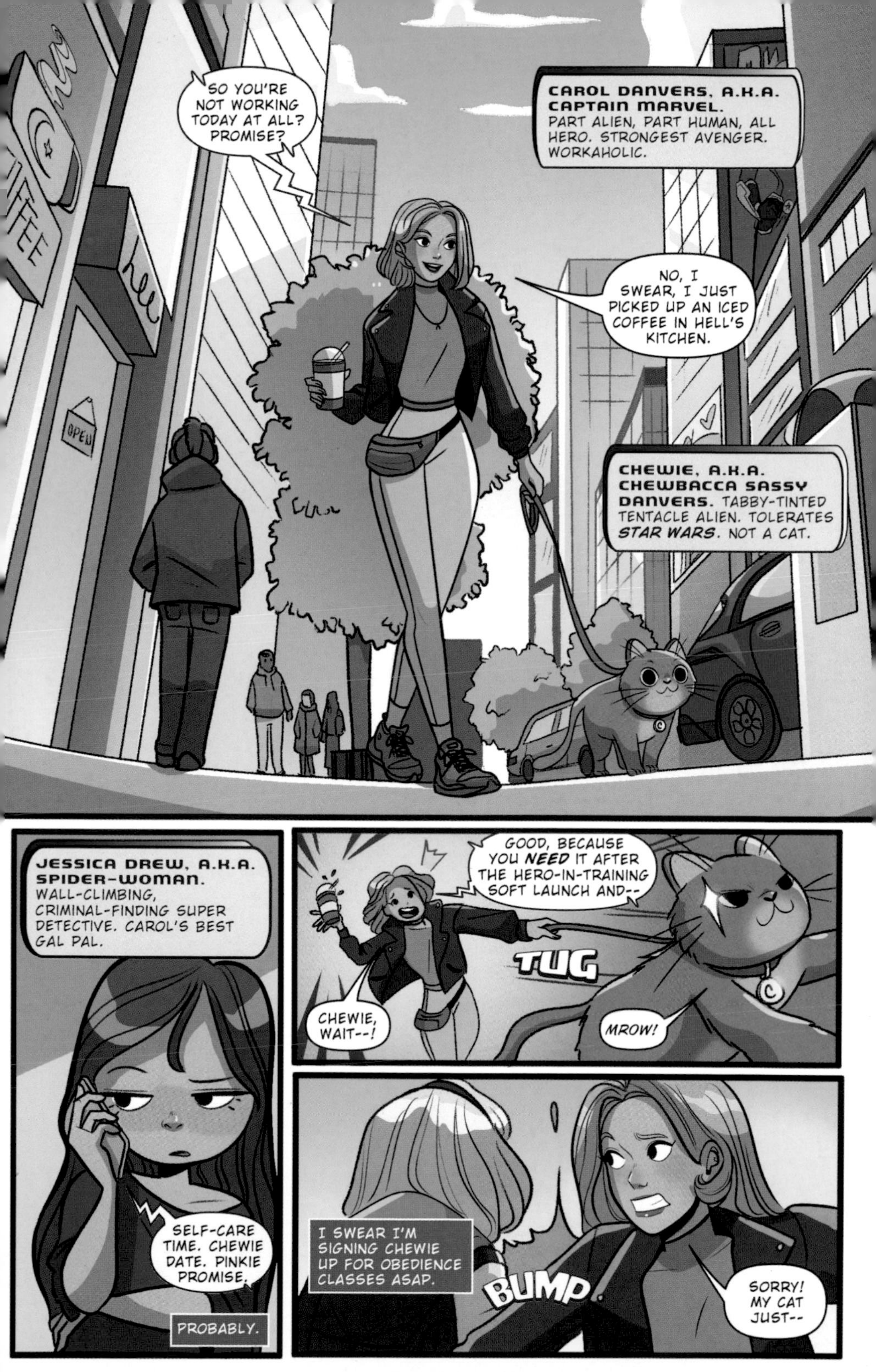
SO YOU'RE NOT WORKING TODAY AT ALL? PROMISE?
CAROL DANVERS, A.K.A. CAPTAIN MARVEL. PART ALIEN, PART HUMAN, ALL HERO. STRONGEST AVENGER. WORKAHOLIC.
NO, I SWEAR, I JUST PICKED UP AN ICED COFFEE IN HELL'S KITCHEN.
CHEWIE, A.K.A. CHEWBACCA SASSY DANVERS. TABBY-TINTED TENTACLE ALIEN. TOLERATES *STAR WARS*. NOT A CAT.
OPEN
COFFEE
JESSICA DREW, A.K.A. SPIDER-WOMAN. WALL-CLIMBING, CRIMINAL-FINDING SUPER DETECTIVE. CAROL'S BEST GAL PAL.
SELF-CARE TIME. CHEWIE DATE. PINKIE PROMISE.
PROBABLY.
GOOD, BECAUSE YOU *NEED* IT AFTER THE HERO-IN-TRAINING SOFT LAUNCH AND--
TUG
CHEWIE, WAIT--!
MROW!
I SWEAR I'M SIGNING CHEWIE UP FOR OBEDIENCE CLASSES ASAP.
BUMP
SORRY! MY CAT JUST--

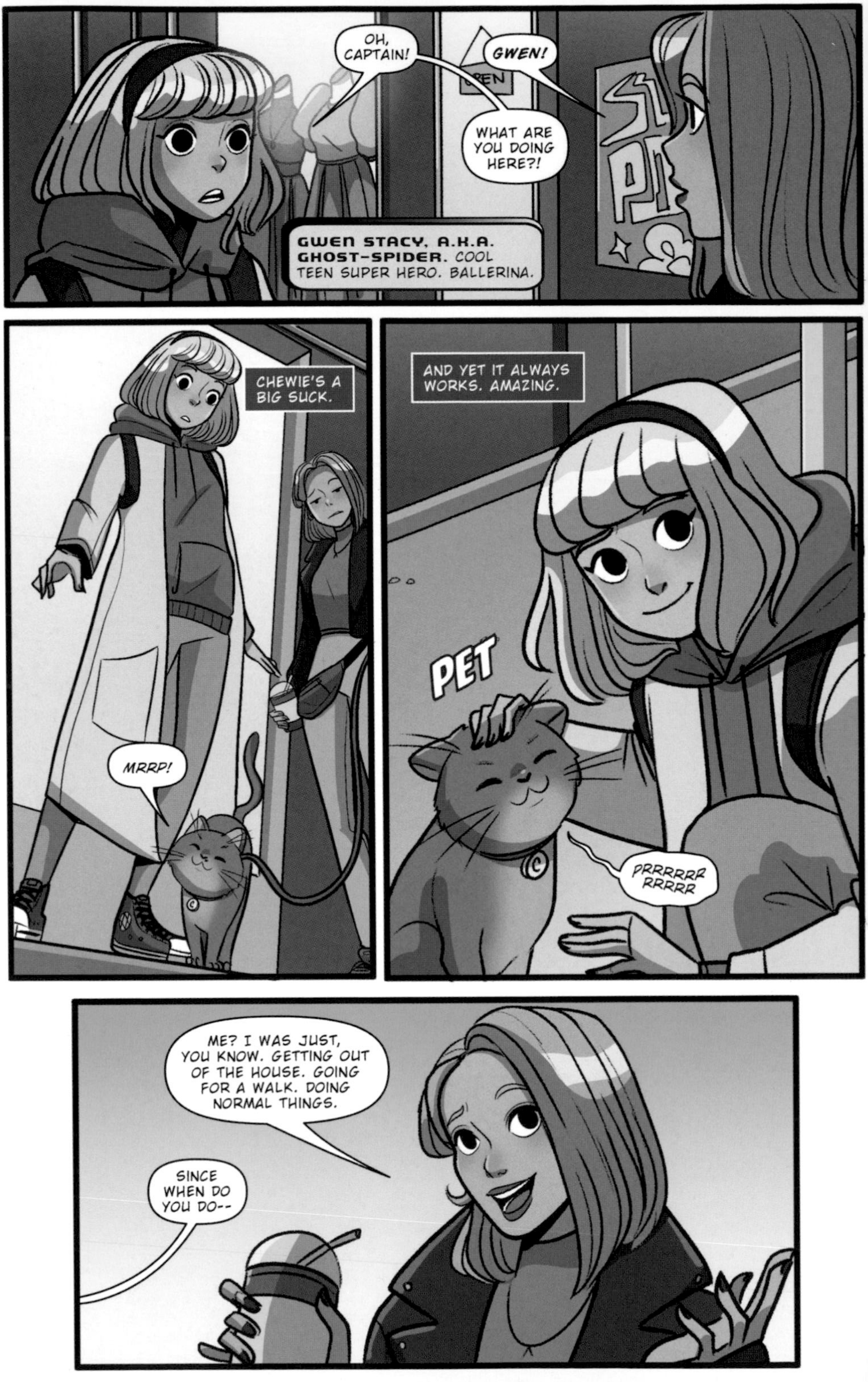
OH, CAPTAIN!
GWEN!
WHAT ARE YOU DOING HERE?!
GWEN STACY, A.K.A. GHOST-SPIDER. COOL TEEN SUPER HERO. BALLERINA.
CHEWIE'S A BIG SUCK.
MRRP!
AND YET IT ALWAYS WORKS. AMAZING.
PET
PRRRRRR RRRRR
ME? I WAS JUST, YOU KNOW. GETTING OUT OF THE HOUSE. GOING FOR A WALK. DOING NORMAL THINGS.
SINCE WHEN DO YOU DO--

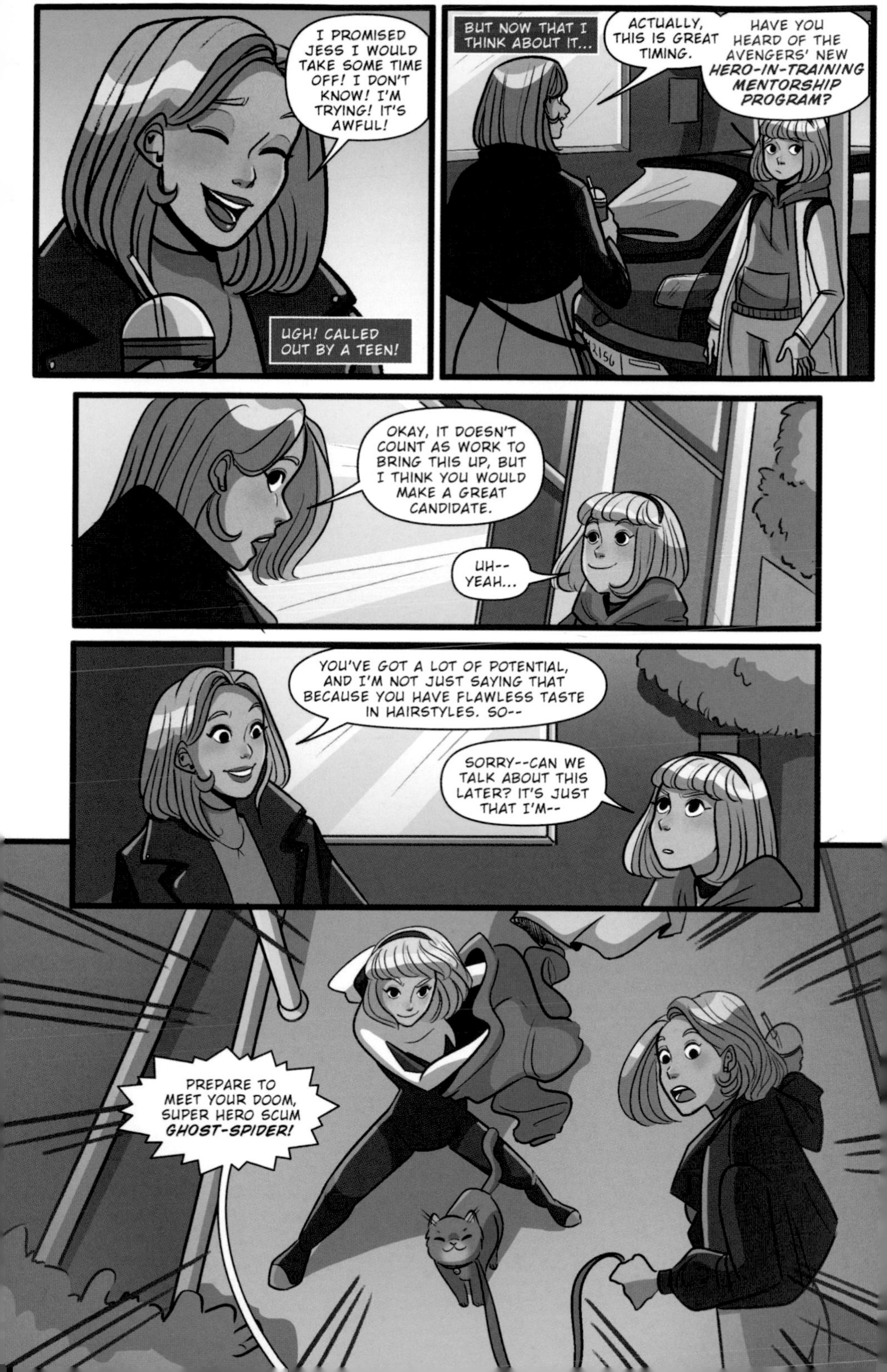
I PROMISED JESS I WOULD TAKE SOME TIME OFF! I DON'T KNOW! I'M TRYING! IT'S AWFUL!
UGH! CALLED OUT BY A TEEN!
BUT NOW THAT I THINK ABOUT IT...
ACTUALLY, THIS IS GREAT TIMING.
HAVE YOU HEARD OF THE AVENGERS' NEW ***HERO-IN-TRAINING MENTORSHIP PROGRAM?***
OKAY, IT DOESN'T COUNT AS WORK TO BRING THIS UP, BUT I THINK YOU WOULD MAKE A GREAT CANDIDATE.
UH--YEAH...
YOU'VE GOT A LOT OF POTENTIAL, AND I'M NOT JUST SAYING THAT BECAUSE YOU HAVE FLAWLESS TASTE IN HAIRSTYLES. SO--
SORRY--CAN WE TALK ABOUT THIS LATER? IT'S JUST THAT I'M--
PREPARE TO MEET YOUR DOOM, SUPER HERO SCUM ***GHOST-SPIDER!***

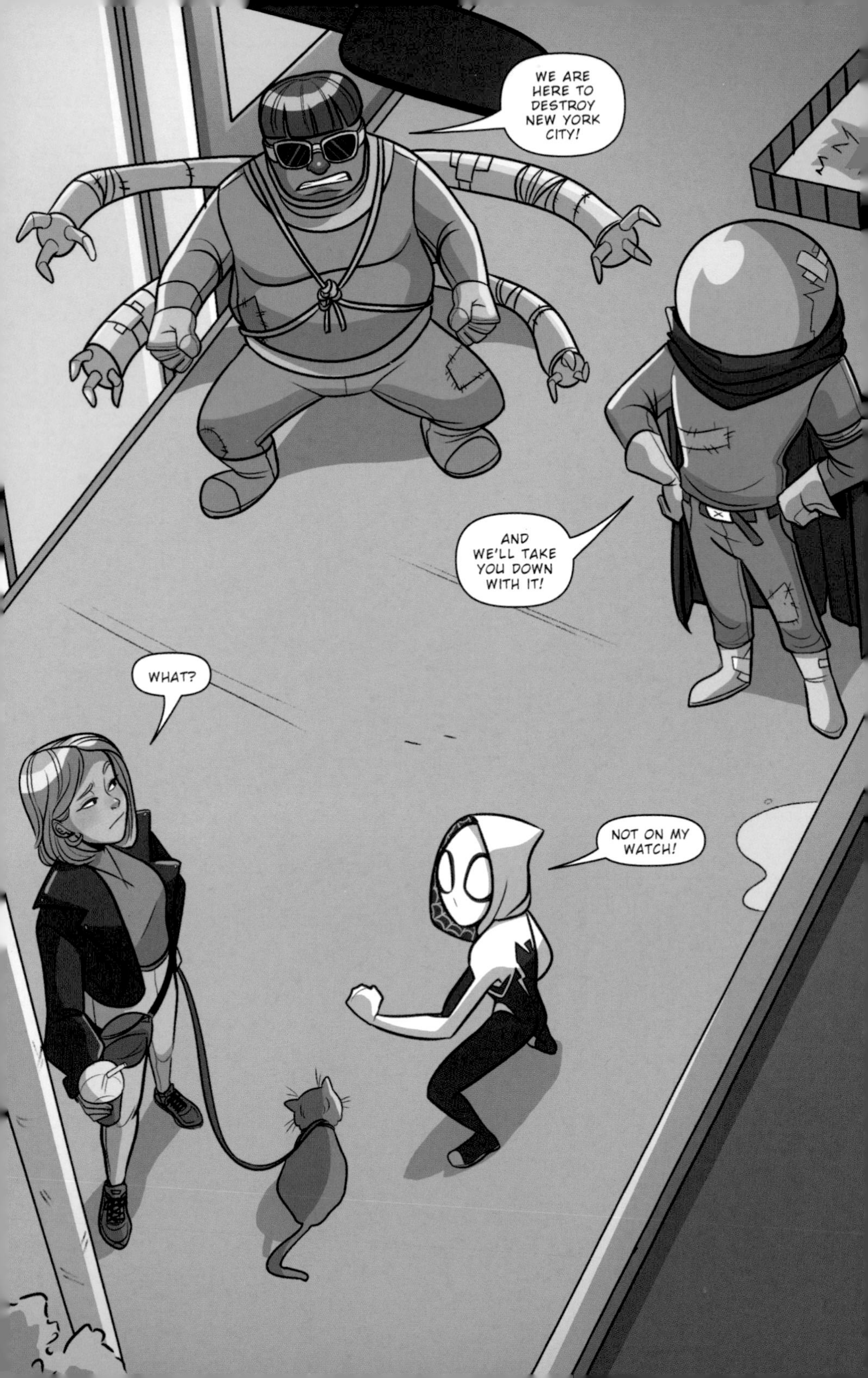

WE ARE HERE TO DESTROY NEW YORK CITY!
AND WE'LL TAKE YOU DOWN WITH IT!
WHAT?
NOT ON MY WATCH!

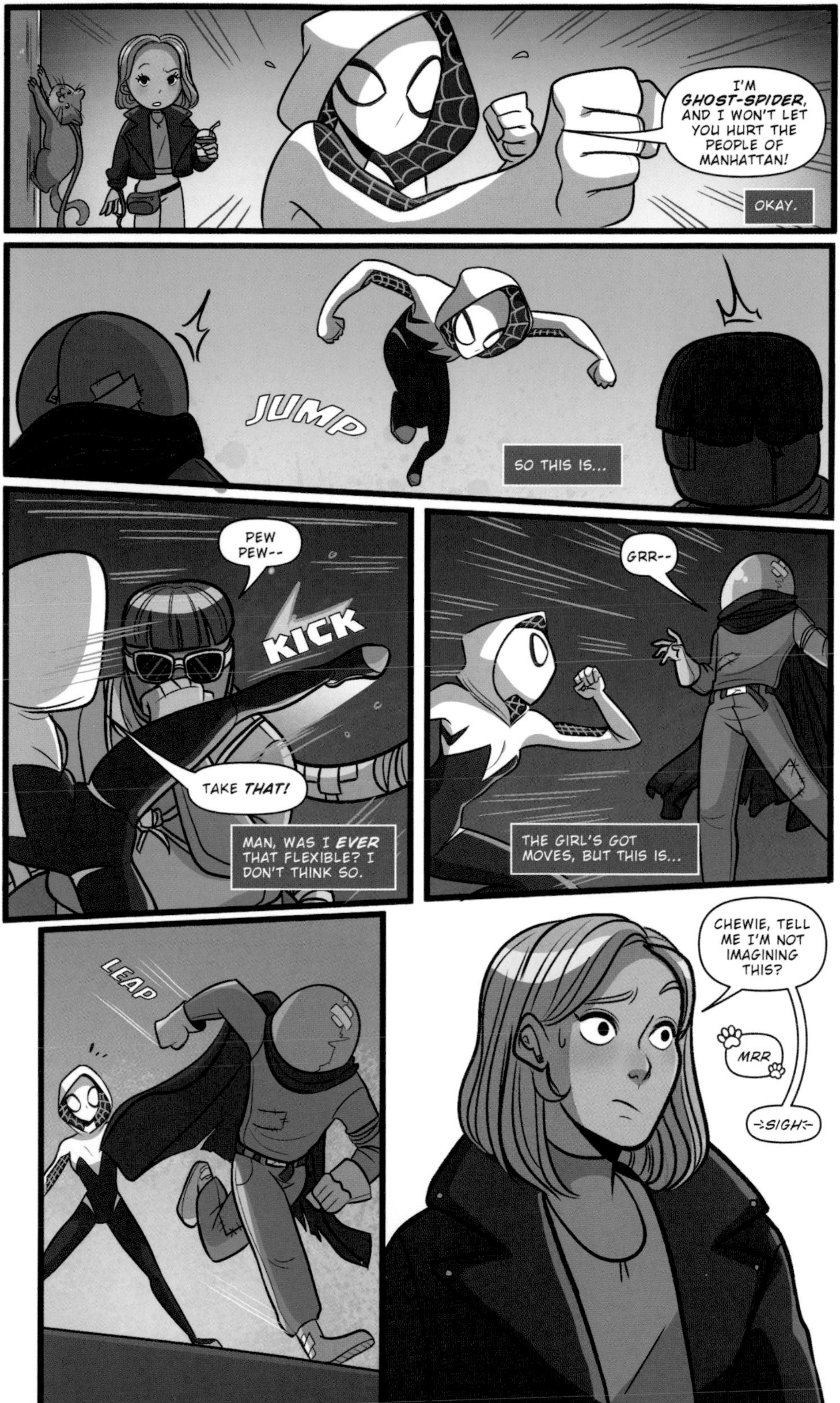
I'M GHOST-SPIDER, AND I WON'T LET YOU HURT THE PEOPLE OF MANHATTAN!
OKAY.
JUMP
SO THIS IS...
PEW PEW--
KICK
TAKE THAT!
MAN, WAS I EVER THAT FLEXIBLE? I DON'T THINK SO.
GRR--
THE GIRL'S GOT MOVES, BUT THIS IS...
LEAP
CHEWIE, TELL ME I'M NOT IMAGINING THIS?
MRR
SIGH

ALL RIGHT. IF THIS IS HAPPENING, IT'S TIME TO DEAL WITH IT. AND FAST.

DON'T YOU DARE TELL JESS.

RRR?

I AM *GHOST-SPIDER*, FIGHTER FOR TRUTH AND JUSTICE, AND I WILL ALWAYS PROTECT NEW YORK CITY!

UH--

OH, NO--

GWEN, ON YOUR SIX!

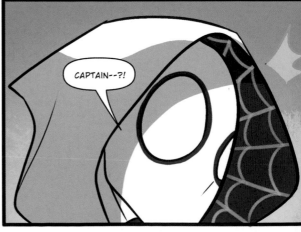

CAPTAIN--?!

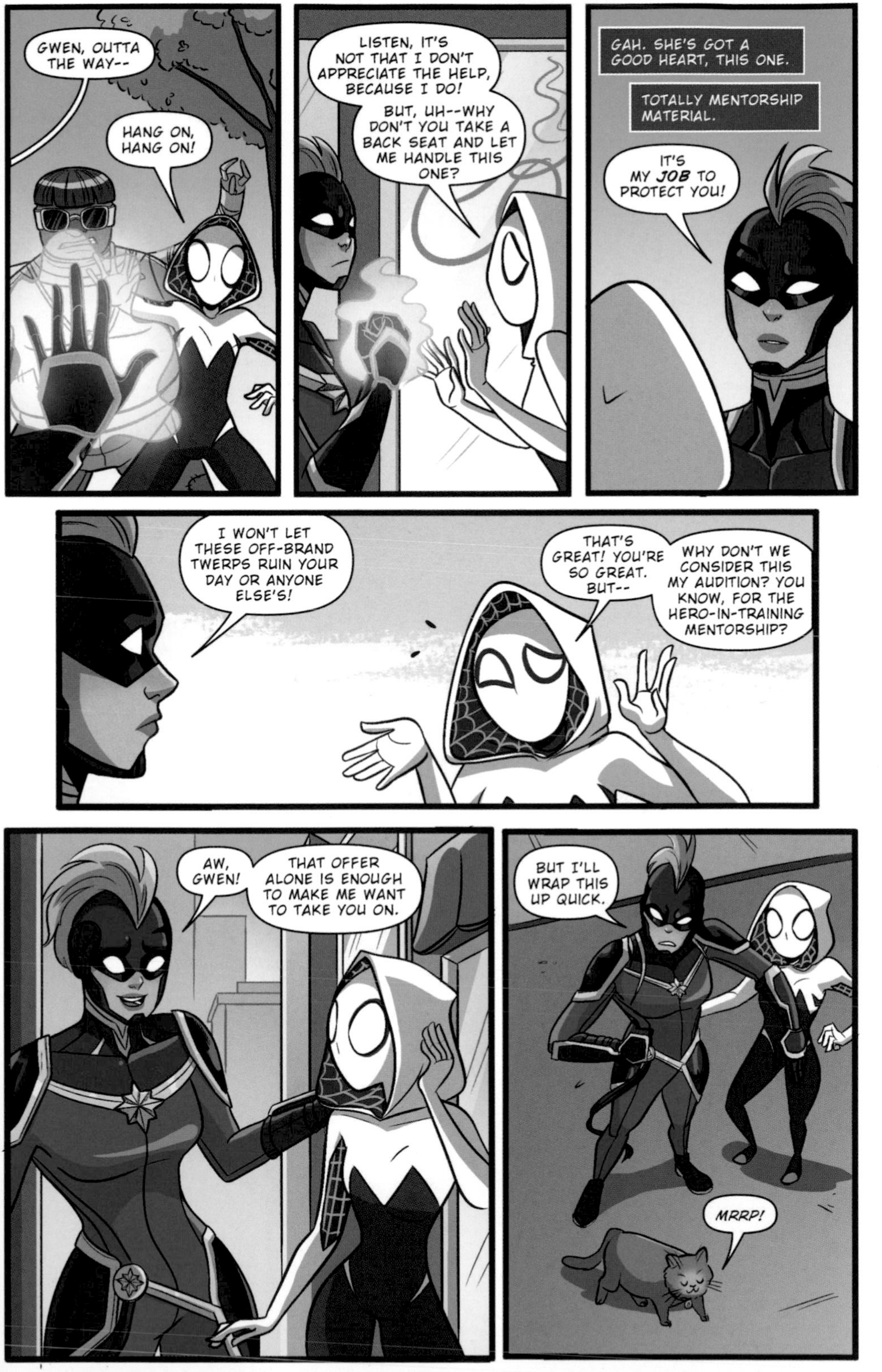
GWEN, OUTTA THE WAY--
HANG ON, HANG ON!
LISTEN, IT'S NOT THAT I DON'T APPRECIATE THE HELP, BECAUSE I DO!
BUT, UH--WHY DON'T YOU TAKE A BACK SEAT AND LET ME HANDLE THIS ONE?
GAH. SHE'S GOT A GOOD HEART, THIS ONE.
TOTALLY MENTORSHIP MATERIAL.
IT'S MY JOB TO PROTECT YOU!
I WON'T LET THESE OFF-BRAND TWERPS RUIN YOUR DAY OR ANYONE ELSE'S!
THAT'S GREAT! YOU'RE SO GREAT. BUT--
WHY DON'T WE CONSIDER THIS MY AUDITION? YOU KNOW, FOR THE HERO-IN-TRAINING MENTORSHIP?
AW, GWEN!
THAT OFFER ALONE IS ENOUGH TO MAKE ME WANT TO TAKE YOU ON.
BUT I'LL WRAP THIS UP QUICK.
MRRP!

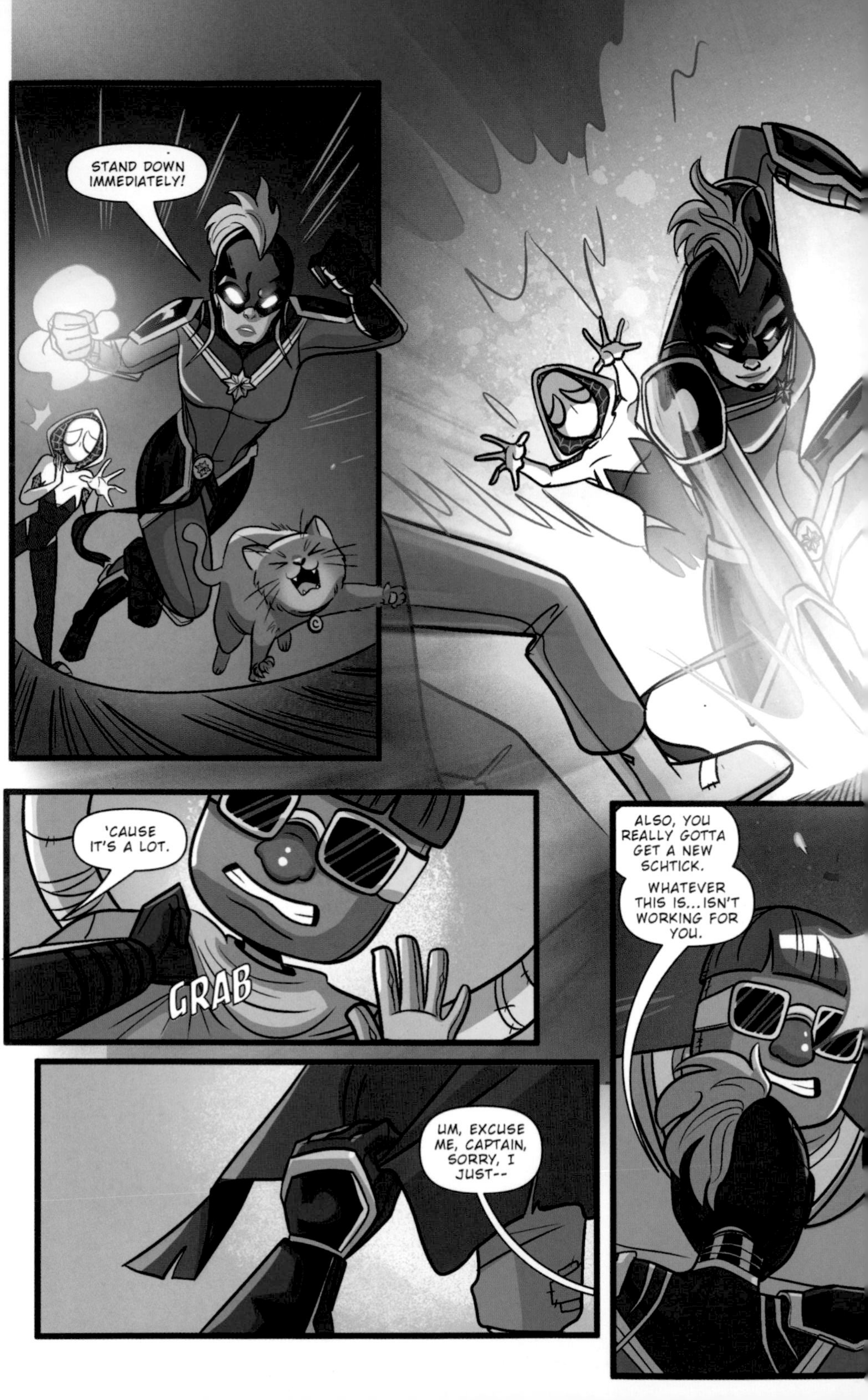
STAND DOWN IMMEDIATELY!
'CAUSE IT'S A LOT.
GRAB
ALSO, YOU REALLY GOTTA GET A NEW SCHTICK.
WHATEVER THIS IS...ISN'T WORKING FOR YOU.
UM, EXCUSE ME, CAPTAIN, SORRY, I JUST--

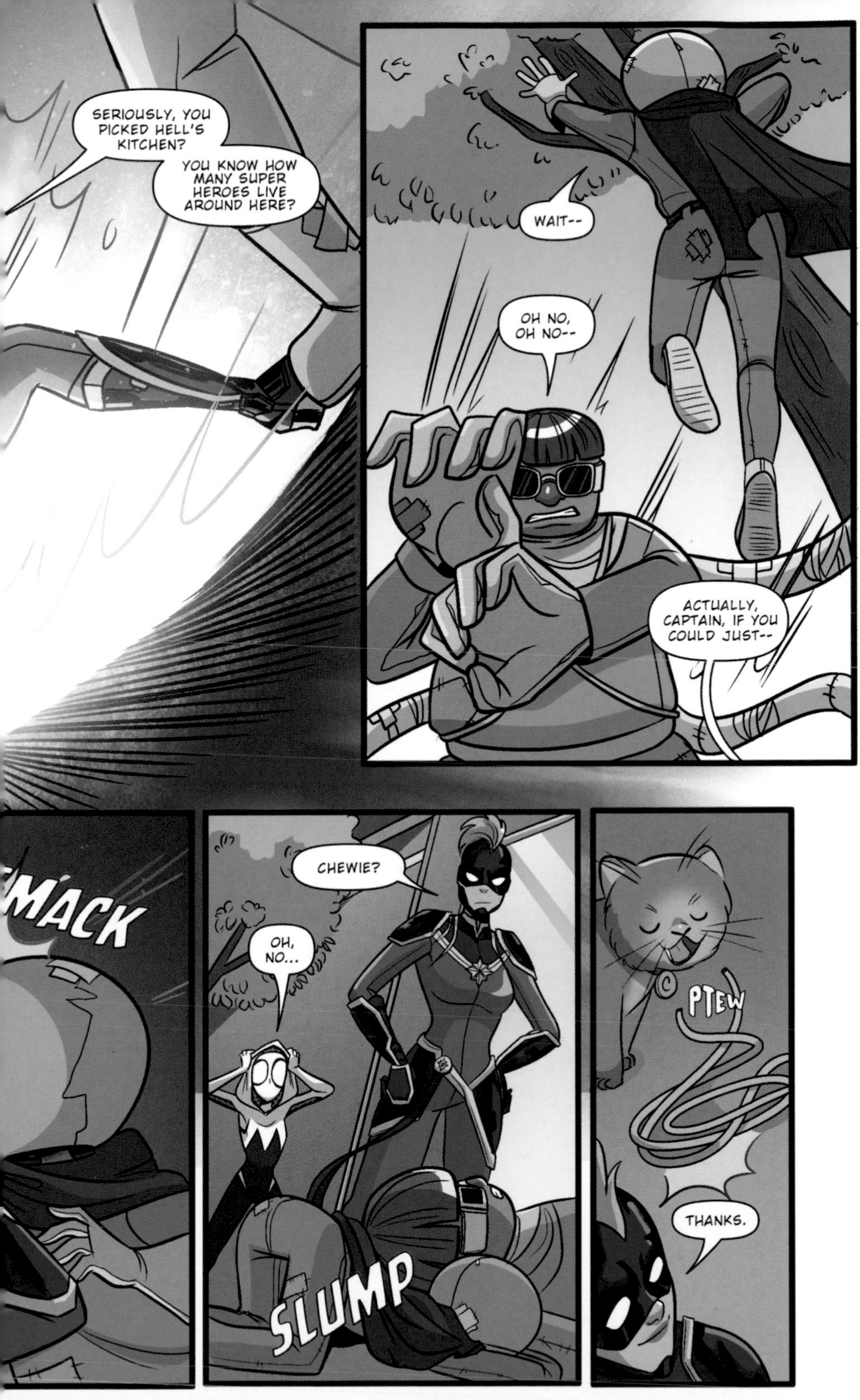
SERIOUSLY, YOU PICKED HELL'S KITCHEN?
YOU KNOW HOW MANY SUPER HEROES LIVE AROUND HERE?
WAIT--
OH NO, OH NO--
ACTUALLY, CAPTAIN, IF YOU COULD JUST--
MACK
CHEWIE?
OH, NO...
SLUMP
PTEW
THANKS.

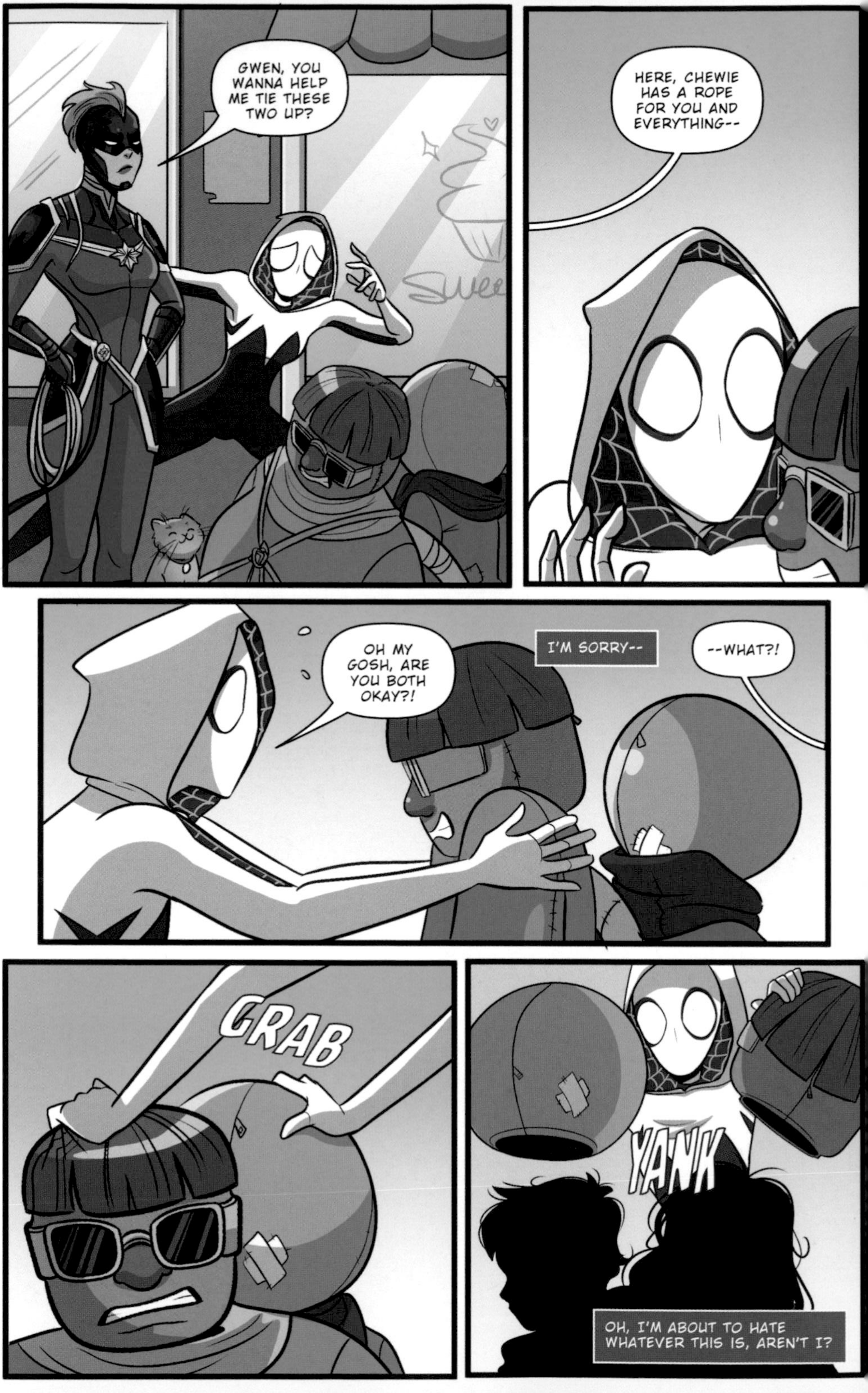
GWEN, YOU WANNA HELP ME TIE THESE TWO UP?
HERE, CHEWIE HAS A ROPE FOR YOU AND EVERYTHING--
OH MY GOSH, ARE YOU BOTH OKAY?!
I'M SORRY--
--WHAT?!
GRAB
YANK
OH, I'M ABOUT TO HATE WHATEVER THIS IS, AREN'T I?

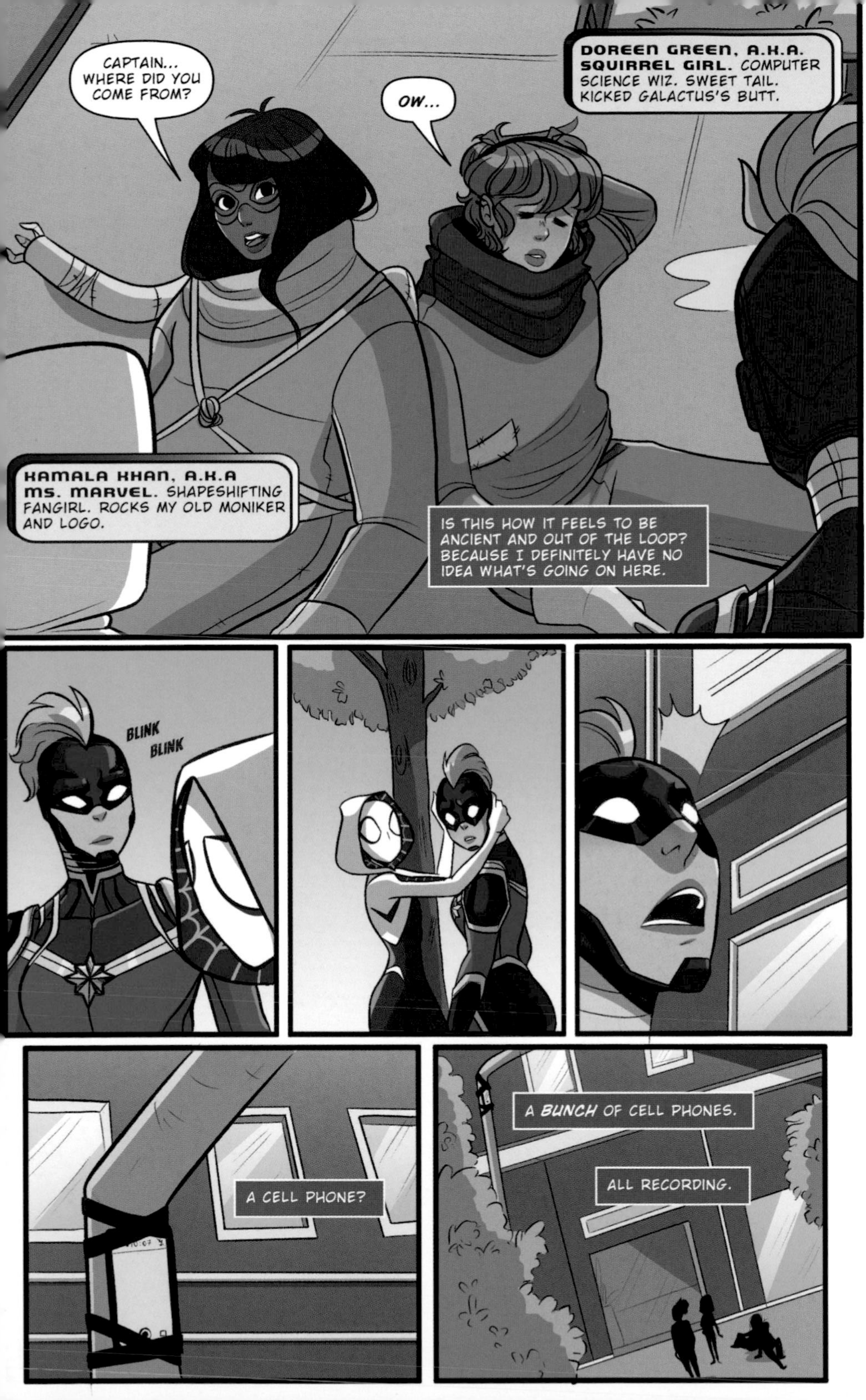
CAPTAIN... WHERE DID YOU COME FROM?
OW...
DOREEN GREEN, A.K.A. SQUIRREL GIRL. COMPUTER SCIENCE WIZ. SWEET TAIL. KICKED GALACTUS'S BUTT.
KAMALA KHAN, A.K.A MS. MARVEL. SHAPESHIFTING FANGIRL. ROCKS MY OLD MONIKER AND LOGO.
IS THIS HOW IT FEELS TO BE ANCIENT AND OUT OF THE LOOP? BECAUSE I DEFINITELY HAVE NO IDEA WHAT'S GOING ON HERE.
BLINK
BLINK
A CELL PHONE?
A *BUNCH* OF CELL PHONES.
ALL RECORDING.

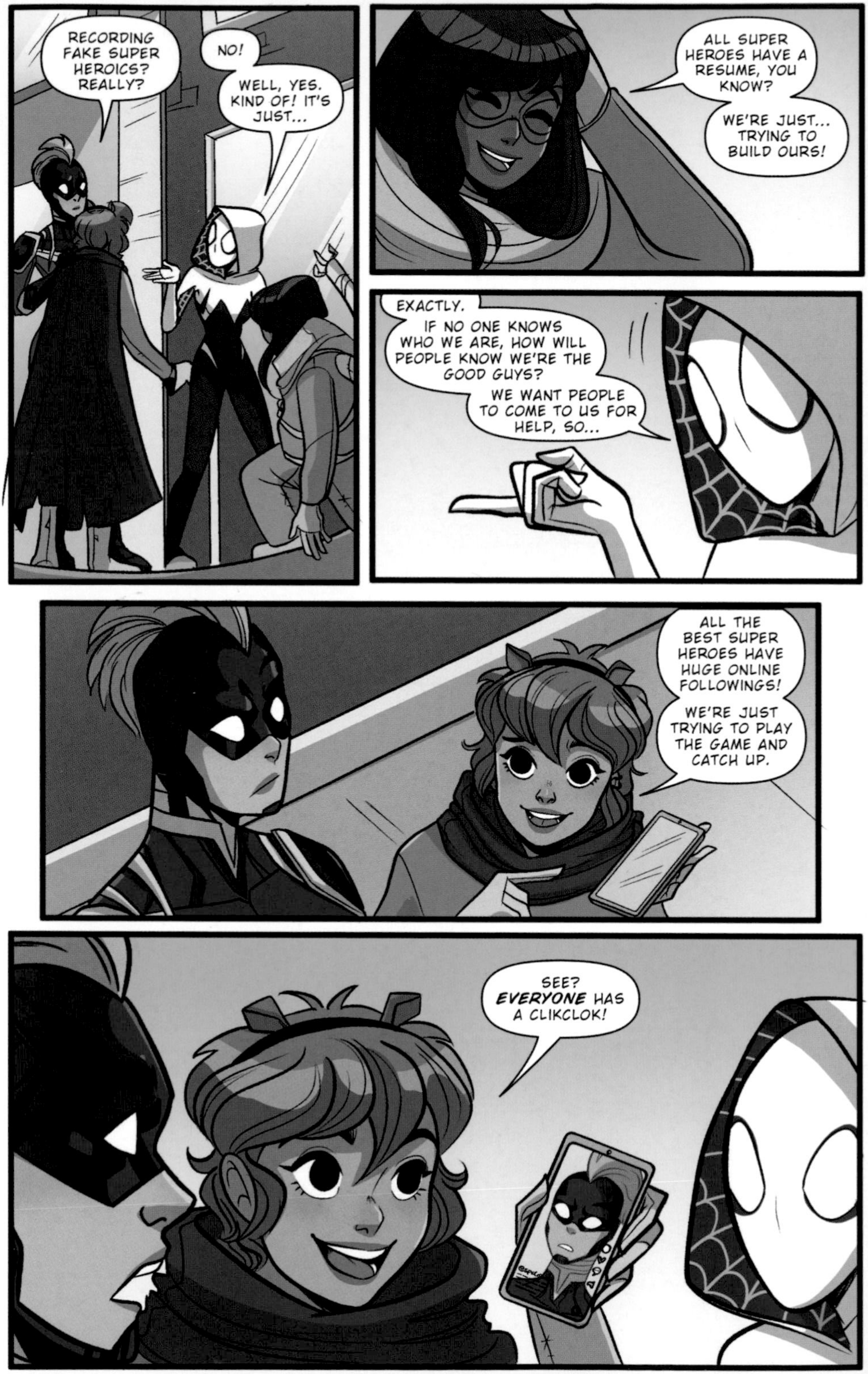
RECORDING FAKE SUPER HEROICS? REALLY?
NO!
WELL, YES. KIND OF! IT'S JUST...
ALL SUPER HEROES HAVE A RESUME, YOU KNOW?
WE'RE JUST... TRYING TO BUILD OURS!
EXACTLY.
IF NO ONE KNOWS WHO WE ARE, HOW WILL PEOPLE KNOW WE'RE THE GOOD GUYS?
WE WANT PEOPLE TO COME TO US FOR HELP, SO...
ALL THE BEST SUPER HEROES HAVE HUGE ONLINE FOLLOWINGS!
WE'RE JUST TRYING TO PLAY THE GAME AND CATCH UP.
SEE? *EVERYONE* HAS A CLIKCLOK!

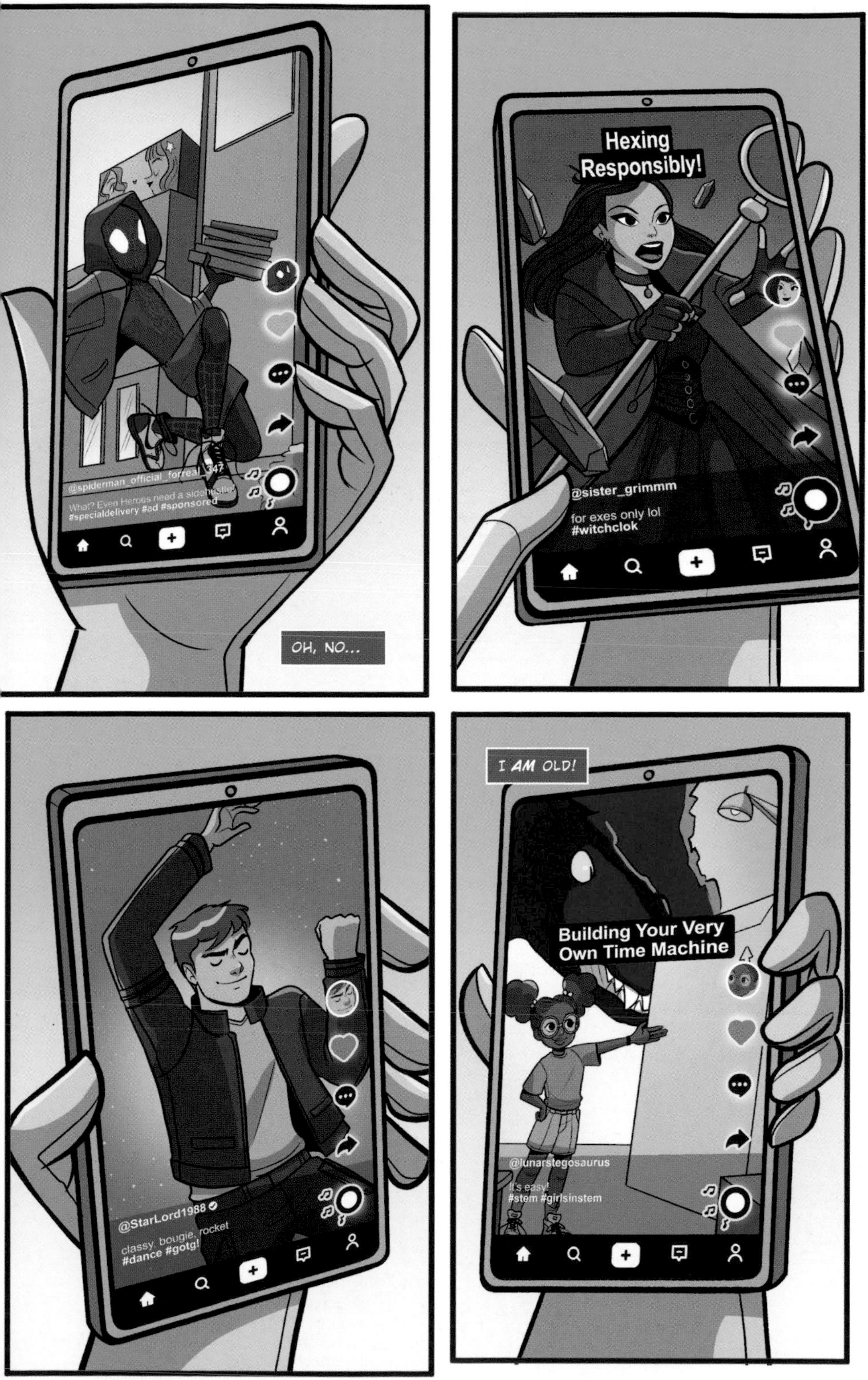
@spiderman_official_forreal_347
What? Even Heroes need a sidehustle!
#specialdelivery #ad #sponsored
OH, NO...
Hexing Responsibly!
@sister_grimmm
for exes only lol
#witchclok
@StarLord1988
classy, bougie, rocket
#dance #gotg!
I AM OLD!
Building Your Very Own Time Machine
@lunarstegosaurus
It's easy!
#stem #girlsinstem

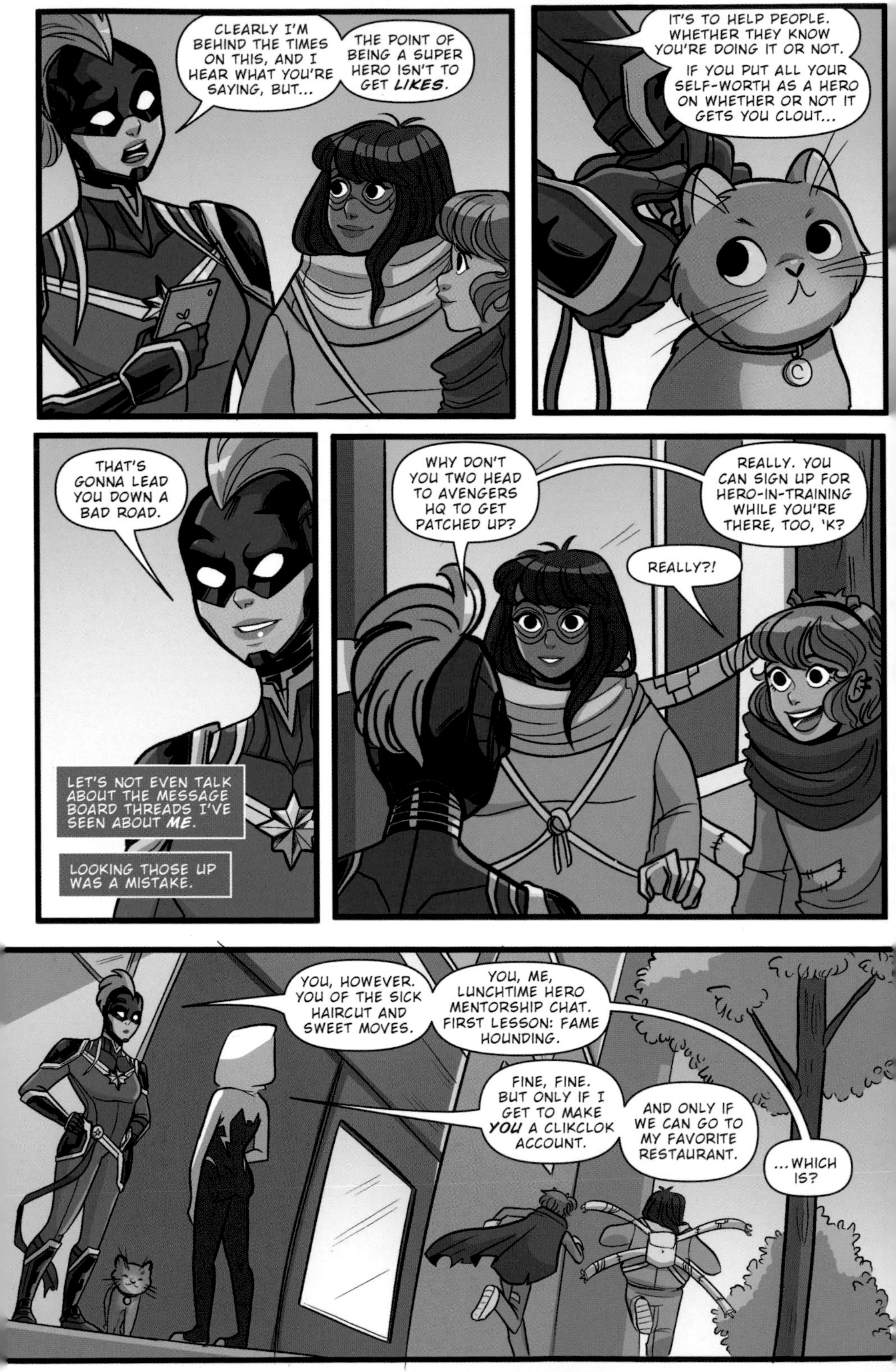
CLEARLY I'M BEHIND THE TIMES ON THIS, AND I HEAR WHAT YOU'RE SAYING, BUT...
THE POINT OF BEING A SUPER HERO ISN'T TO GET *LIKES*.
IT'S TO HELP PEOPLE. WHETHER THEY KNOW YOU'RE DOING IT OR NOT.
IF YOU PUT ALL YOUR SELF-WORTH AS A HERO ON WHETHER OR NOT IT GETS YOU CLOUT...
THAT'S GONNA LEAD YOU DOWN A BAD ROAD.
LET'S NOT EVEN TALK ABOUT THE MESSAGE BOARD THREADS I'VE SEEN ABOUT *ME*.
LOOKING THOSE UP WAS A MISTAKE.
WHY DON'T YOU TWO HEAD TO AVENGERS HQ TO GET PATCHED UP?
REALLY. YOU CAN SIGN UP FOR HERO-IN-TRAINING WHILE YOU'RE THERE, TOO, 'K?
REALLY?!
YOU, HOWEVER. YOU OF THE SICK HAIRCUT AND SWEET MOVES.
YOU, ME, LUNCHTIME HERO MENTORSHIP CHAT. FIRST LESSON: FAME HOUNDING.
FINE, FINE. BUT ONLY IF I GET TO MAKE *YOU* A CLIKCLOK ACCOUNT.
AND ONLY IF WE CAN GO TO MY FAVORITE RESTAURANT.
...WHICH IS?

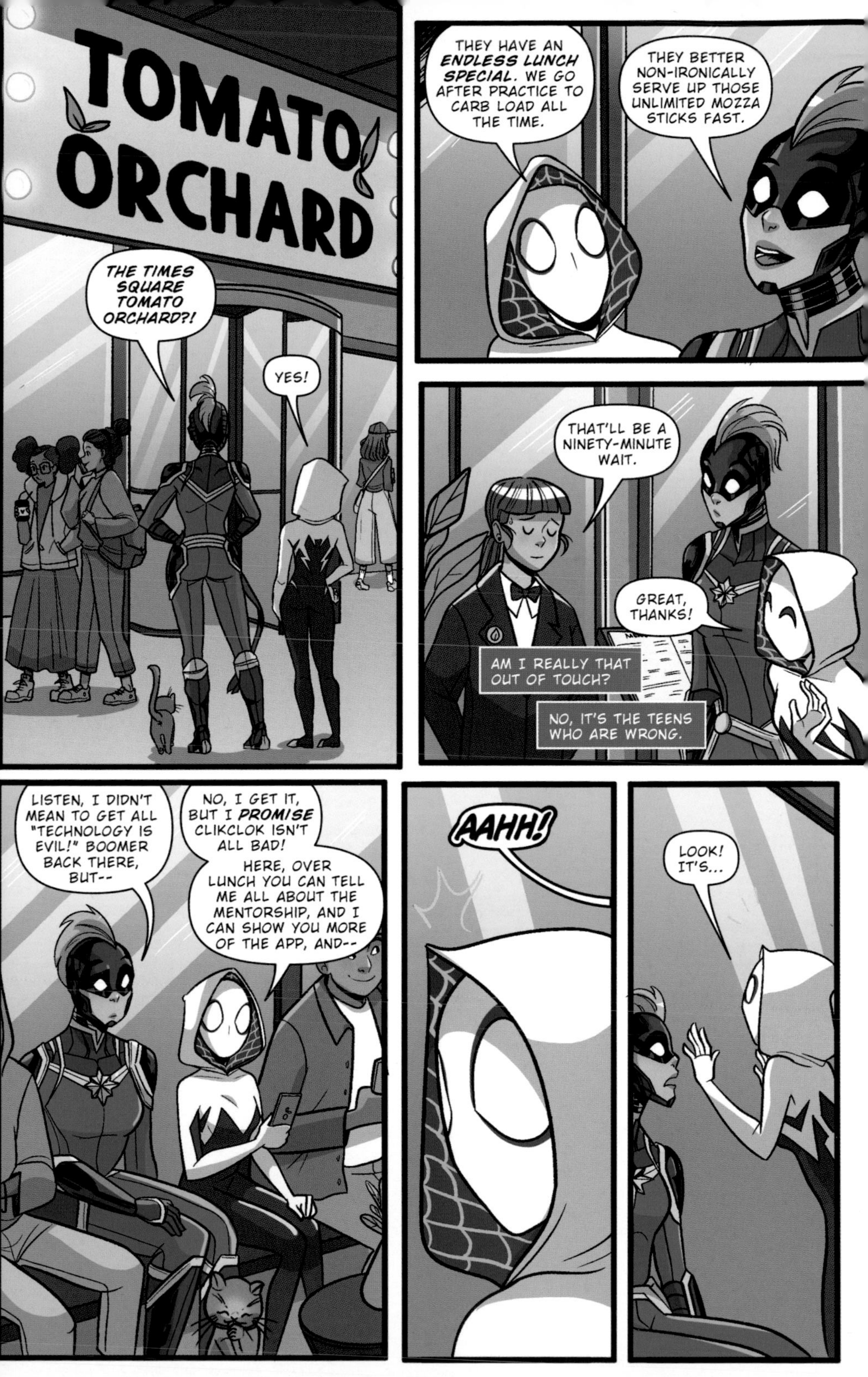
TOMATO ORCHARD
THE TIMES SQUARE TOMATO ORCHARD?!
YES!
THEY HAVE AN *ENDLESS LUNCH SPECIAL*. WE GO AFTER PRACTICE TO CARB LOAD ALL THE TIME.
THEY BETTER NON-IRONICALLY SERVE UP THOSE UNLIMITED MOZZA STICKS FAST.
THAT'LL BE A NINETY-MINUTE WAIT.
GREAT, THANKS!
AM I REALLY THAT OUT OF TOUCH?
NO, IT'S THE TEENS WHO ARE WRONG.
LISTEN, I DIDN'T MEAN TO GET ALL "TECHNOLOGY IS EVIL!" BOOMER BACK THERE, BUT--
NO, I GET IT, BUT I *PROMISE* CLIKCLOK ISN'T ALL BAD!
HERE, OVER LUNCH YOU CAN TELL ME ALL ABOUT THE MENTORSHIP, AND I CAN SHOW YOU MORE OF THE APP, AND--
AAHH!
LOOK! IT'S...

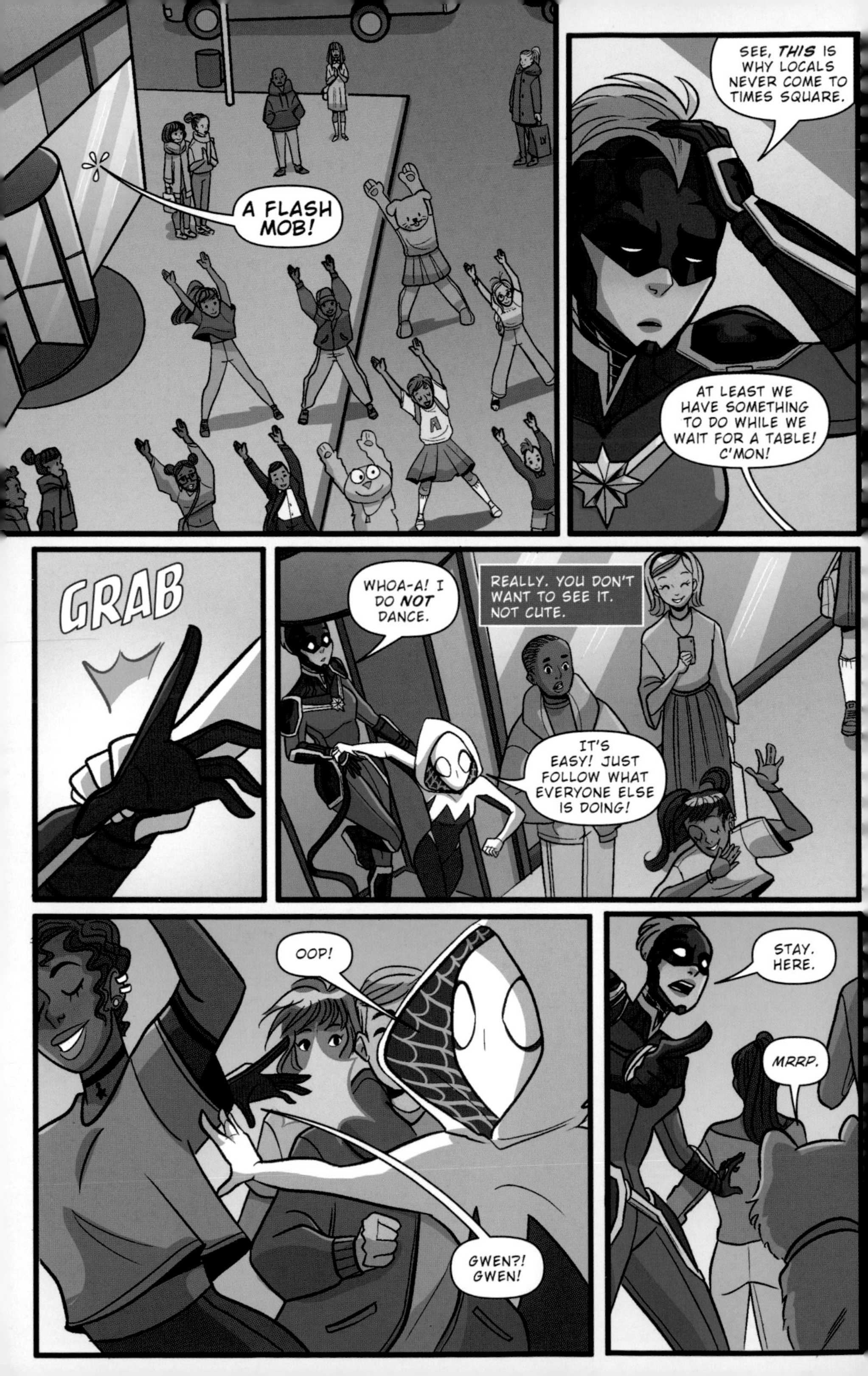
A FLASH MOB!
SEE, THIS IS WHY LOCALS NEVER COME TO TIMES SQUARE.
AT LEAST WE HAVE SOMETHING TO DO WHILE WE WAIT FOR A TABLE! C'MON!
GRAB
WHOA-A! I DO NOT DANCE.
REALLY. YOU DON'T WANT TO SEE IT. NOT CUTE.
IT'S EASY! JUST FOLLOW WHAT EVERYONE ELSE IS DOING!
OOP!
GWEN?! GWEN!
STAY. HERE.
MRRP.

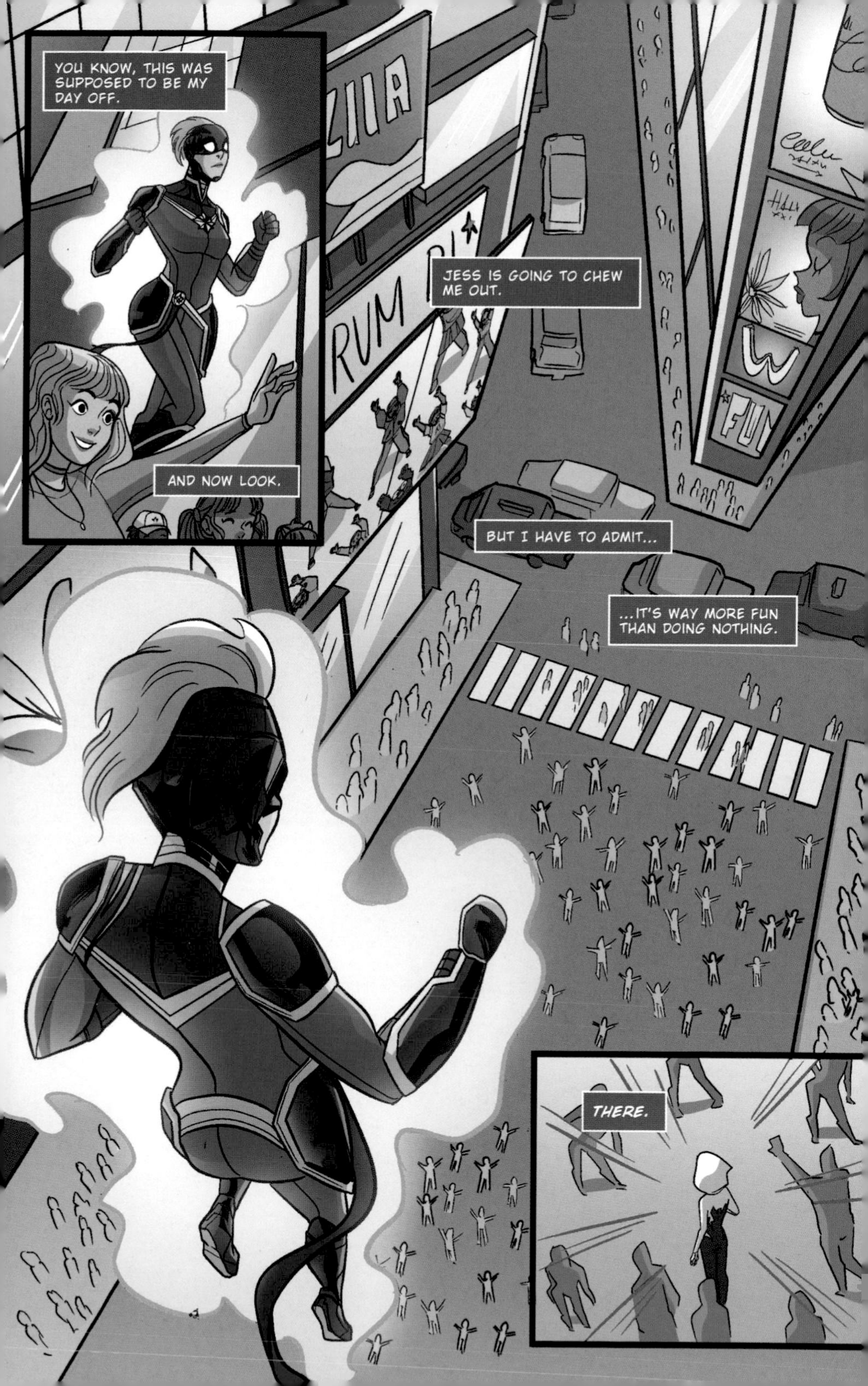
YOU KNOW, THIS WAS SUPPOSED TO BE MY DAY OFF.
AND NOW LOOK.
JESS IS GOING TO CHEW ME OUT.
BUT I HAVE TO ADMIT...
...IT'S WAY MORE FUN THAN DOING NOTHING.
THERE.

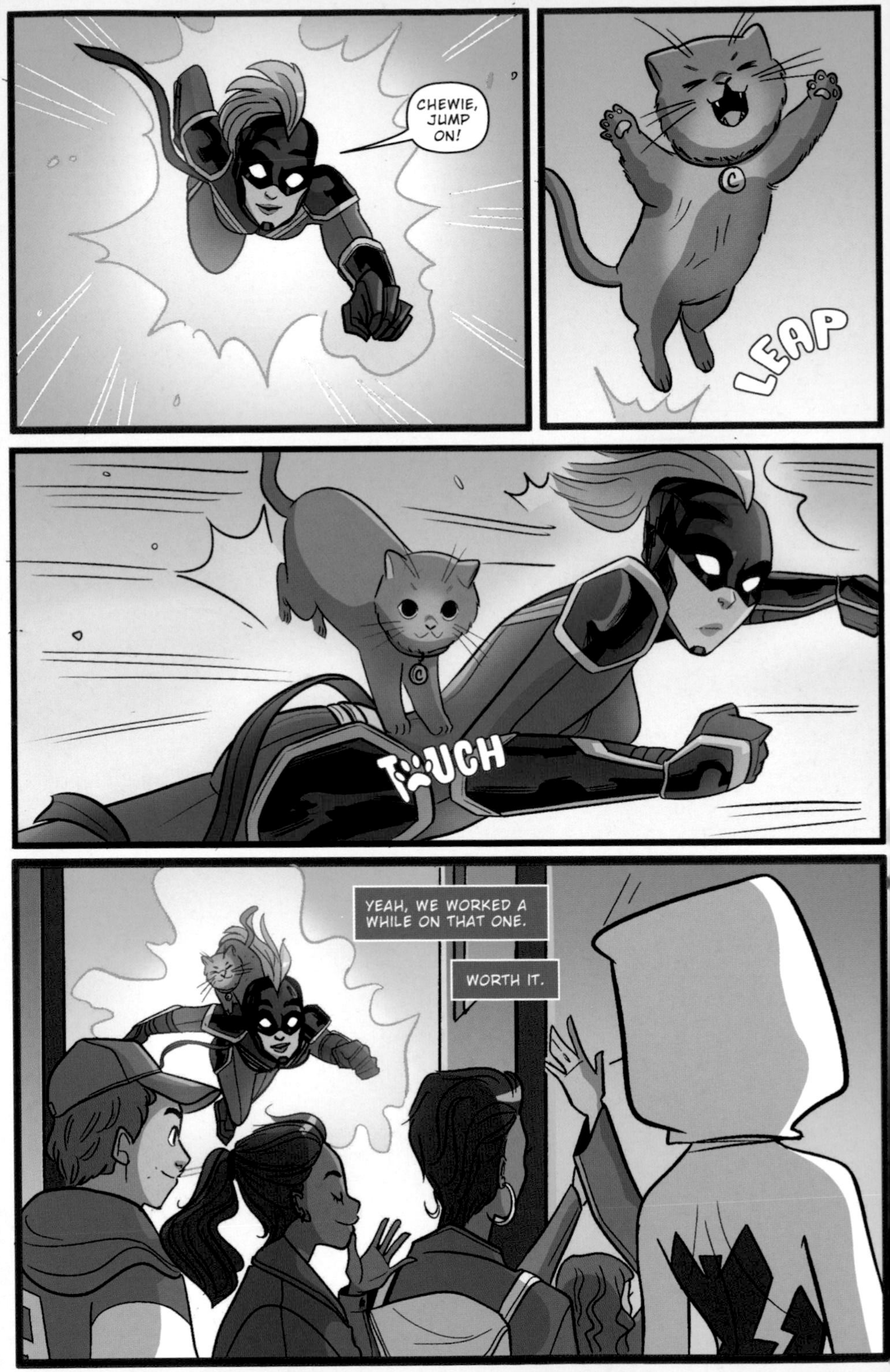
CHEWIE, JUMP ON!
LEAP
TOUCH
YEAH, WE WORKED A WHILE ON THAT ONE.
WORTH IT.

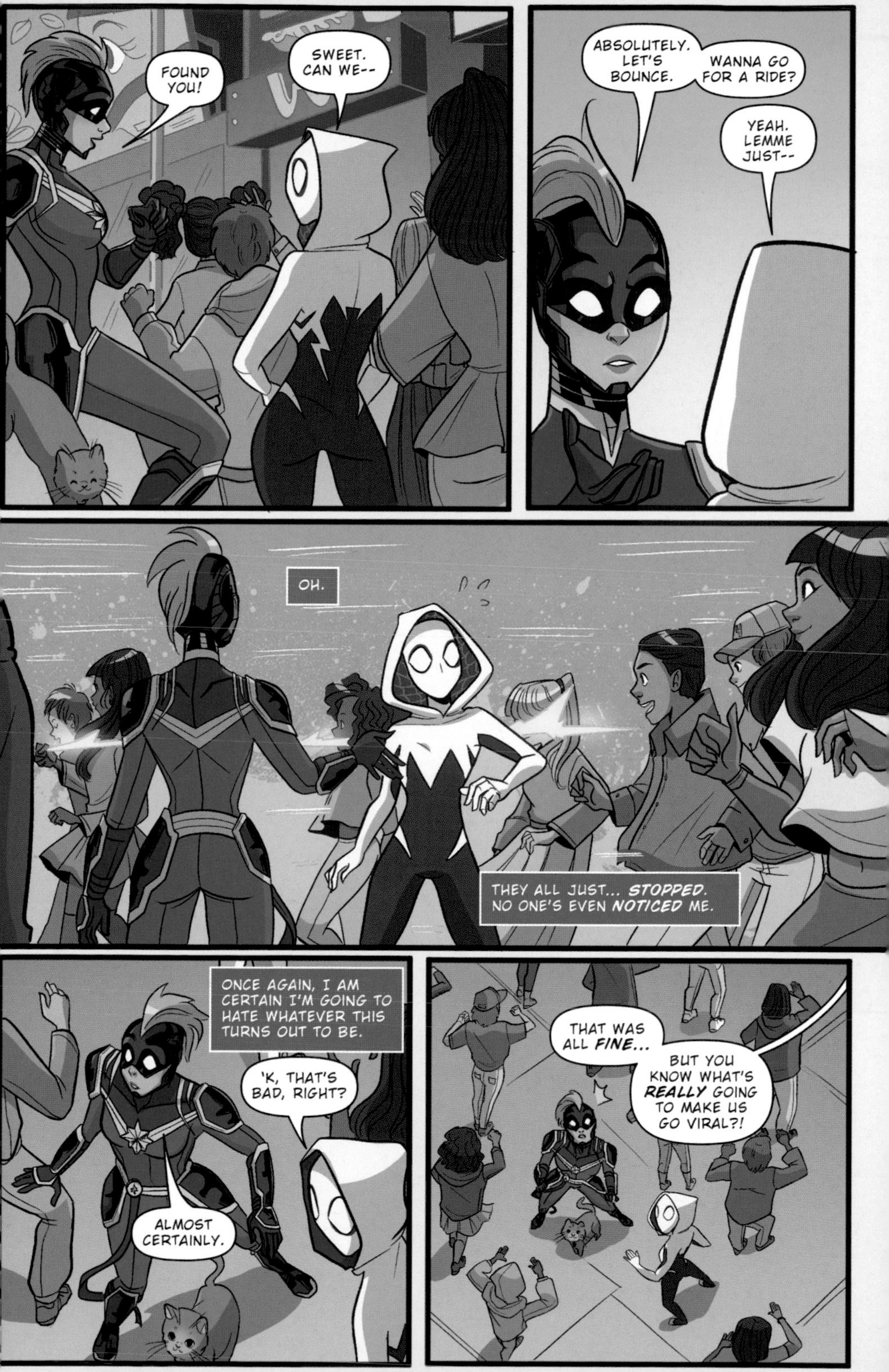
FOUND YOU!
SWEET. CAN WE--
ABSOLUTELY. LET'S BOUNCE.
WANNA GO FOR A RIDE?
YEAH. LEMME JUST--
OH.
THEY ALL JUST... STOPPED. NO ONE'S EVEN NOTICED ME.
ONCE AGAIN, I AM CERTAIN I'M GOING TO HATE WHATEVER THIS TURNS OUT TO BE.
'K, THAT'S BAD, RIGHT?
ALMOST CERTAINLY.
THAT WAS ALL FINE...
BUT YOU KNOW WHAT'S REALLY GOING TO MAKE US GO VIRAL?!

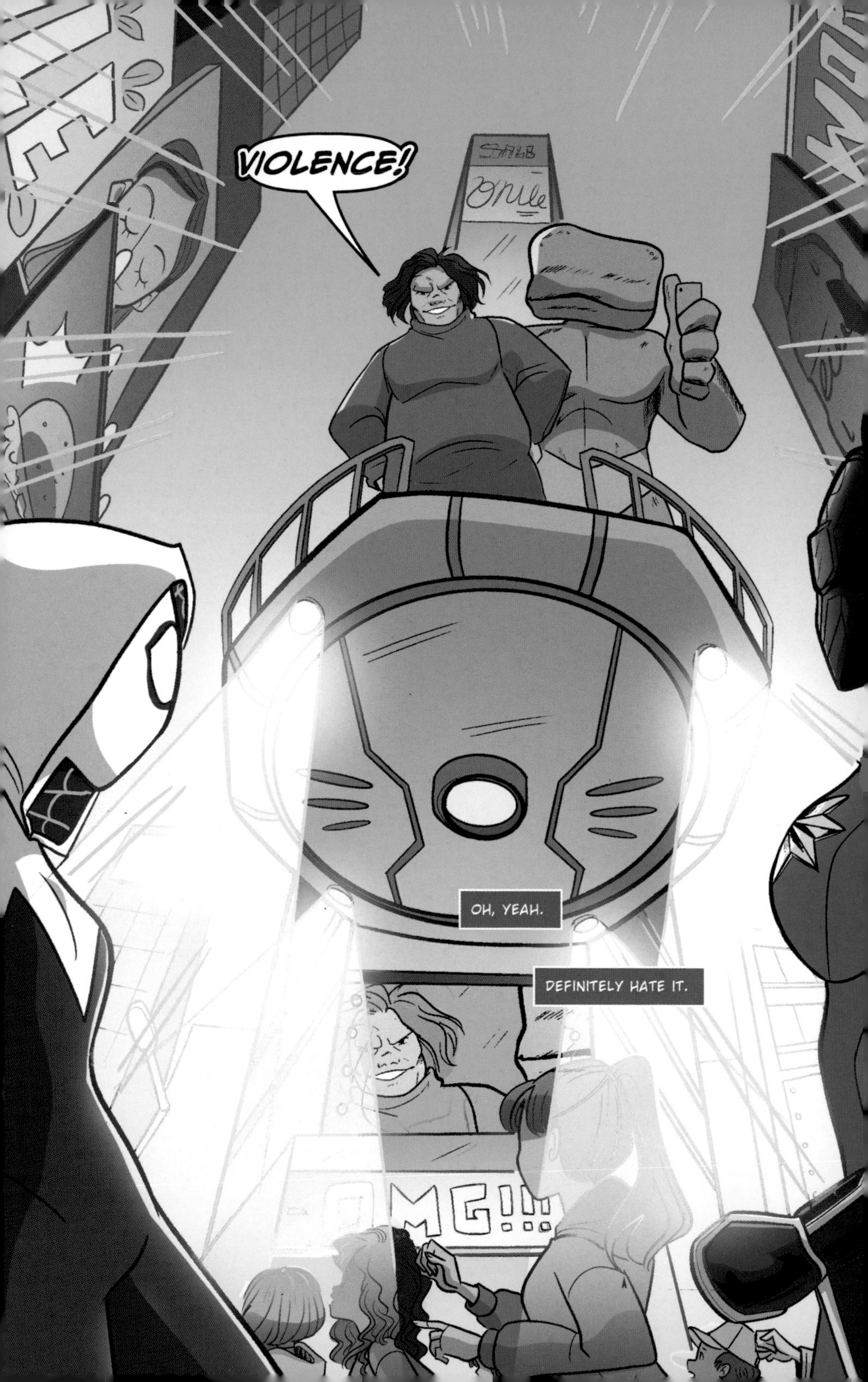
VIOLENCE!
OH, YEAH.
DEFINITELY HATE IT.
OMG!!!

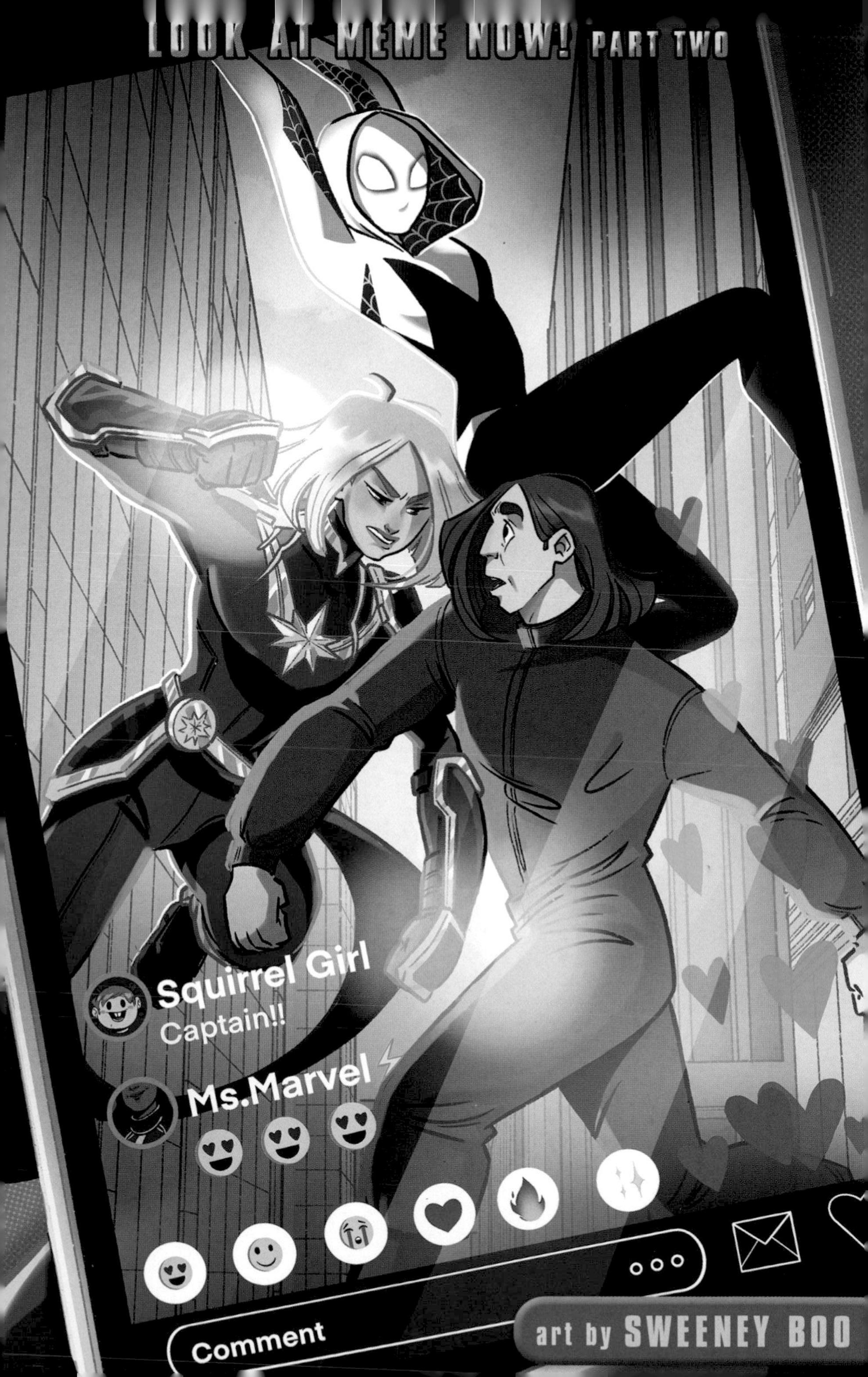
LOOK AT MEME NOW! PART TWO
Squirrel Girl
Captain!!
Ms.Marvel
Comment
art by SWEENEY BOO

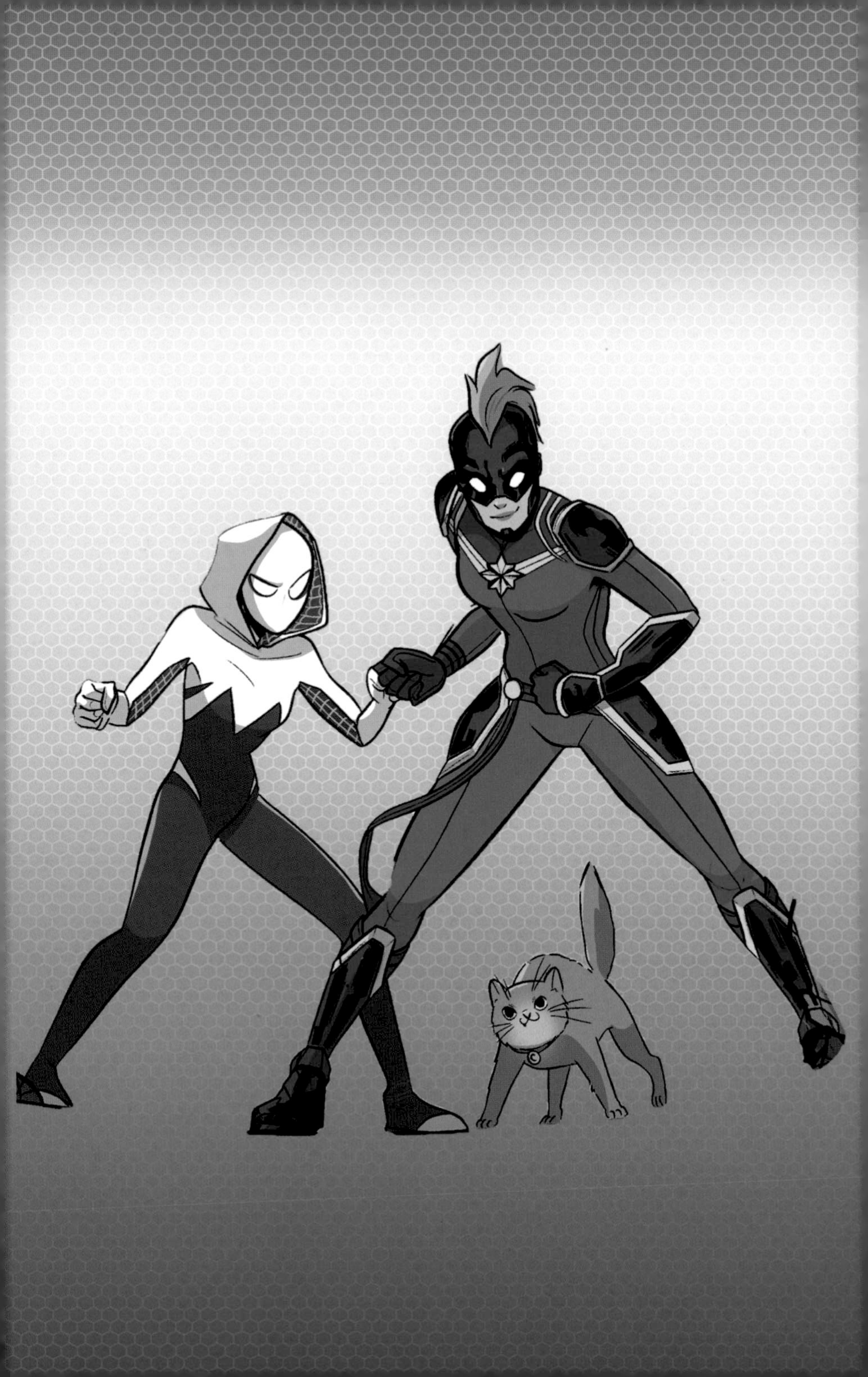

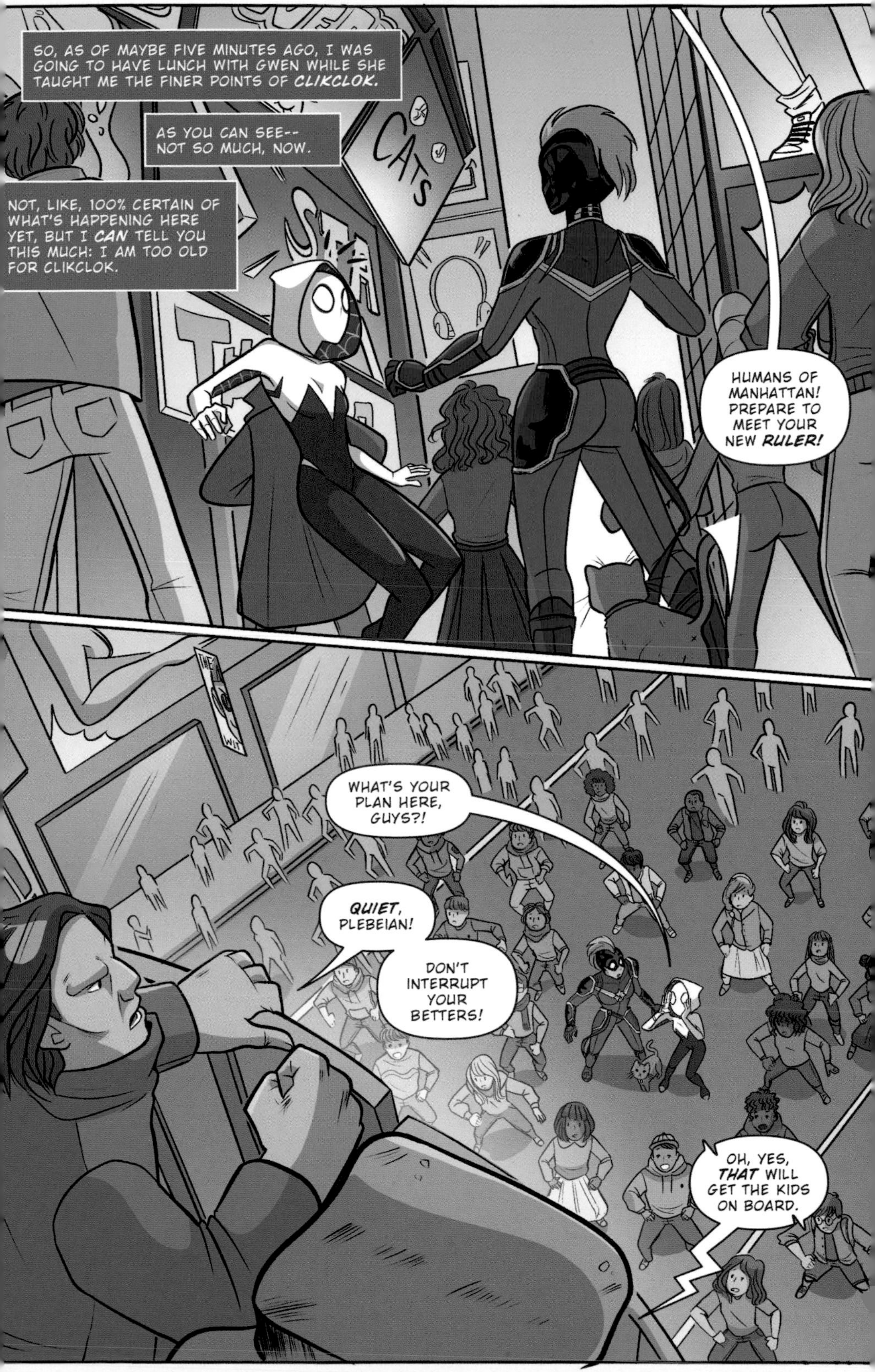
SO, AS OF MAYBE FIVE MINUTES AGO, I WAS GOING TO HAVE LUNCH WITH GWEN WHILE SHE TAUGHT ME THE FINER POINTS OF *CLIKCLOK.*
AS YOU CAN SEE-- NOT SO MUCH, NOW.
NOT, LIKE, 100% CERTAIN OF WHAT'S HAPPENING HERE YET, BUT I *CAN* TELL YOU THIS MUCH: I AM TOO OLD FOR CLIKCLOK.
CATS
HUMANS OF MANHATTAN! PREPARE TO MEET YOUR NEW *RULER!*
WHAT'S YOUR PLAN HERE, GUYS?!
QUIET, PLEBEIAN!
DON'T INTERRUPT YOUR BETTERS!
OH, YES, *THAT* WILL GET THE KIDS ON BOARD.

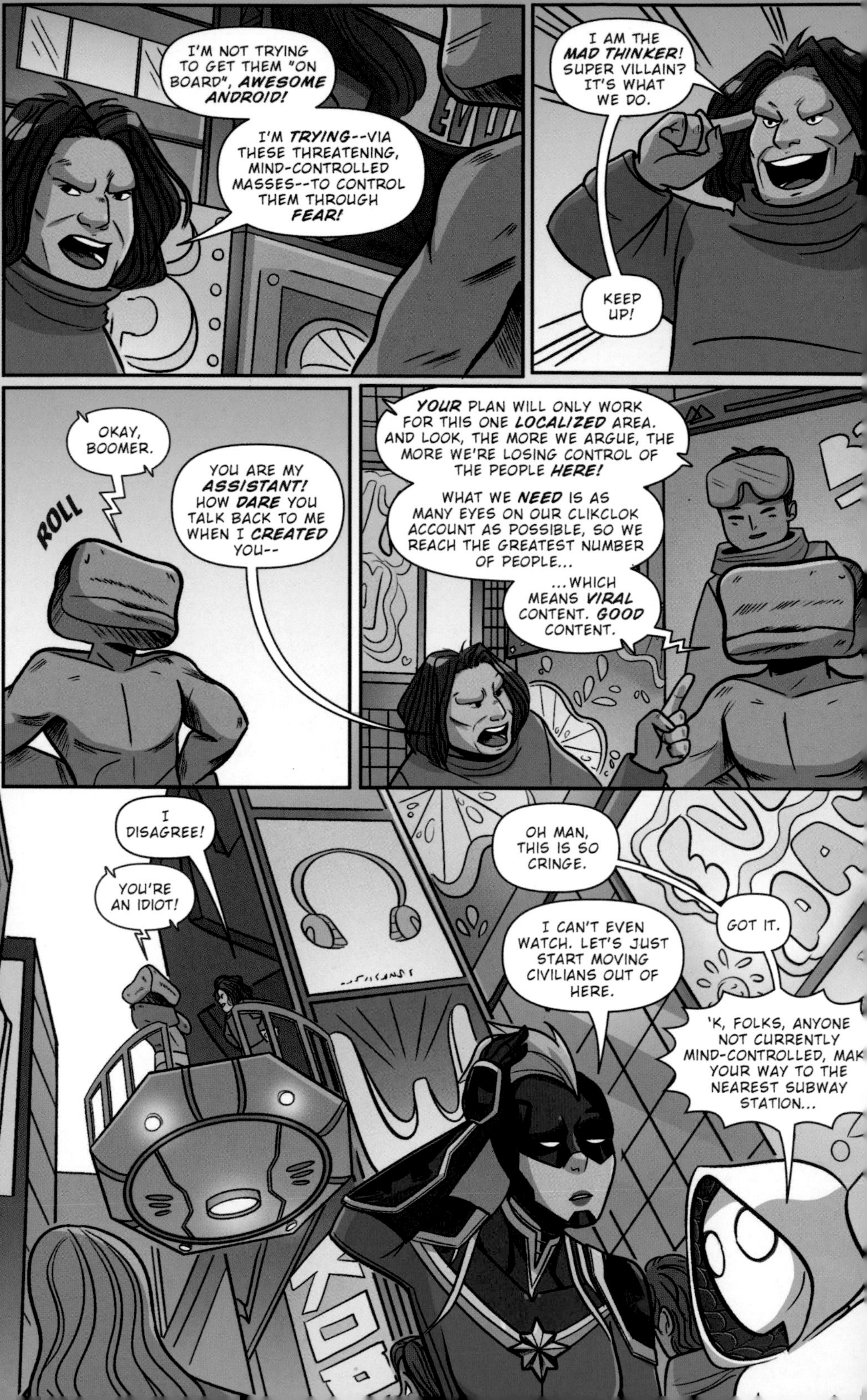
I'M NOT TRYING TO GET THEM "ON BOARD", AWESOME ANDROID!
I'M TRYING--VIA THESE THREATENING, MIND-CONTROLLED MASSES--TO CONTROL THEM THROUGH FEAR!
I AM THE MAD THINKER! SUPER VILLAIN? IT'S WHAT WE DO.
KEEP UP!
OKAY, BOOMER.
ROLL
YOU ARE MY ASSISTANT! HOW DARE YOU TALK BACK TO ME WHEN I CREATED YOU--
YOUR PLAN WILL ONLY WORK FOR THIS ONE LOCALIZED AREA. AND LOOK, THE MORE WE ARGUE, THE MORE WE'RE LOSING CONTROL OF THE PEOPLE HERE!
WHAT WE NEED IS AS MANY EYES ON OUR CLIKCLOK ACCOUNT AS POSSIBLE, SO WE REACH THE GREATEST NUMBER OF PEOPLE...
...WHICH MEANS VIRAL CONTENT. GOOD CONTENT.
I DISAGREE!
YOU'RE AN IDIOT!
OH MAN, THIS IS SO CRINGE.
GOT IT.
I CAN'T EVEN WATCH. LET'S JUST START MOVING CIVILIANS OUT OF HERE.
'K, FOLKS, ANYONE NOT CURRENTLY MIND-CONTROLLED, MAK YOUR WAY TO THE NEAREST SUBWAY STATION...

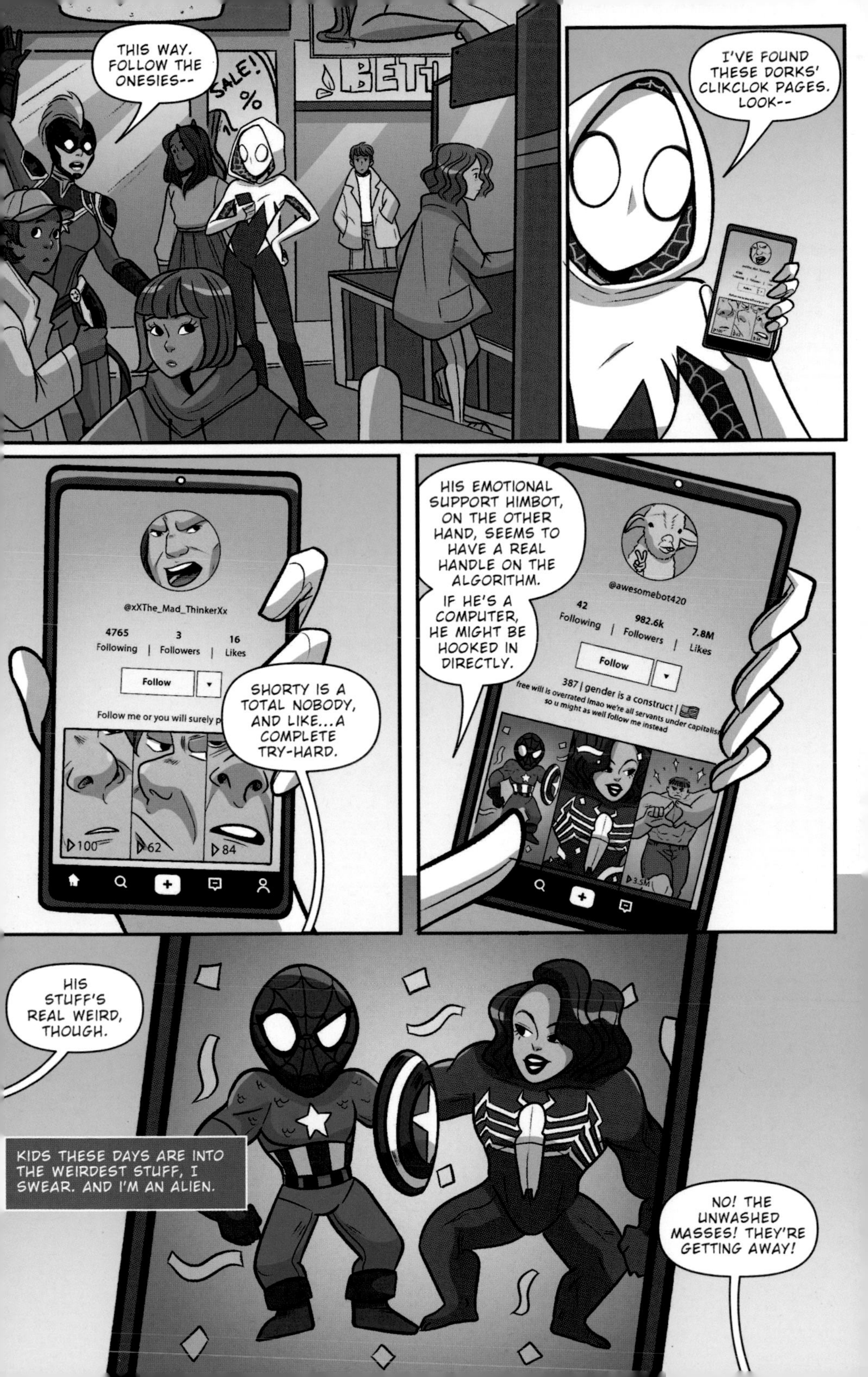

THIS WAY. FOLLOW THE ONESIES--
SALE! %
I'VE FOUND THESE DORKS' CLIKCLOK PAGES. LOOK--
@xXThe_Mad_ThinkerXx
4765 Following | 3 Followers | 16 Likes
Follow
Follow me or you will surely p
100
62
84
SHORTY IS A TOTAL NOBODY, AND LIKE...A COMPLETE TRY-HARD.
HIS EMOTIONAL SUPPORT HIMBOT, ON THE OTHER HAND, SEEMS TO HAVE A REAL HANDLE ON THE ALGORITHM.
IF HE'S A COMPUTER, HE MIGHT BE HOOKED IN DIRECTLY.
@awesomebot420
42 Following | 982.6k Followers | 7.8M Likes
Follow
387 | gender is a construct |
free will is overrated lmao we're all servants under capitalism
so u might as well follow me instead
3.5M
HIS STUFF'S REAL WEIRD, THOUGH.
KIDS THESE DAYS ARE INTO THE WEIRDEST STUFF, I SWEAR. AND I'M AN ALIEN.
NO! THE UNWASHED MASSES! THEY'RE GETTING AWAY!

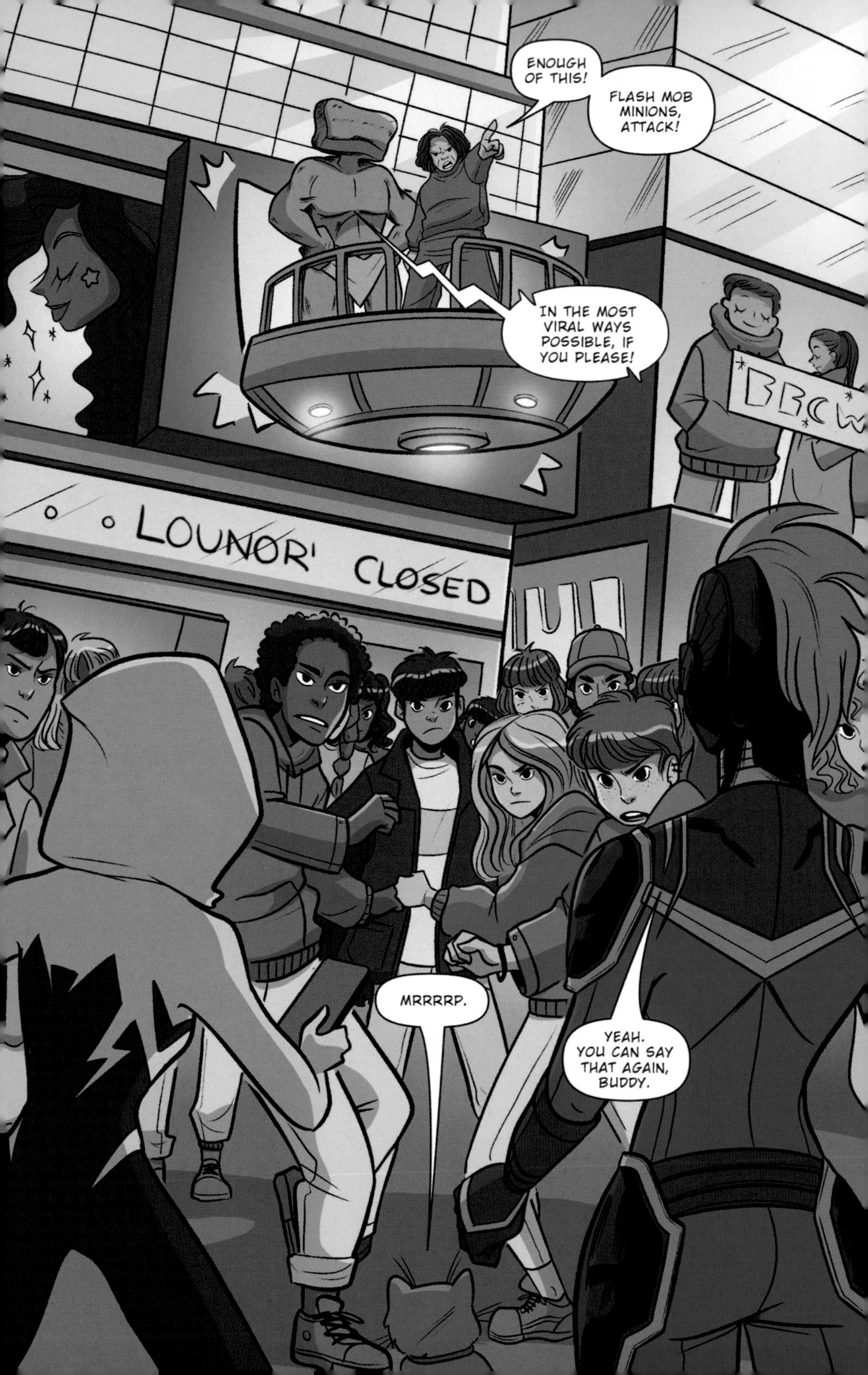
ENOUGH OF THIS!
FLASH MOB MINIONS, ATTACK!
IN THE MOST VIRAL WAYS POSSIBLE, IF YOU PLEASE!
CLOSED
MRRRRP.
YEAH. YOU CAN SAY THAT AGAIN, BUDDY.

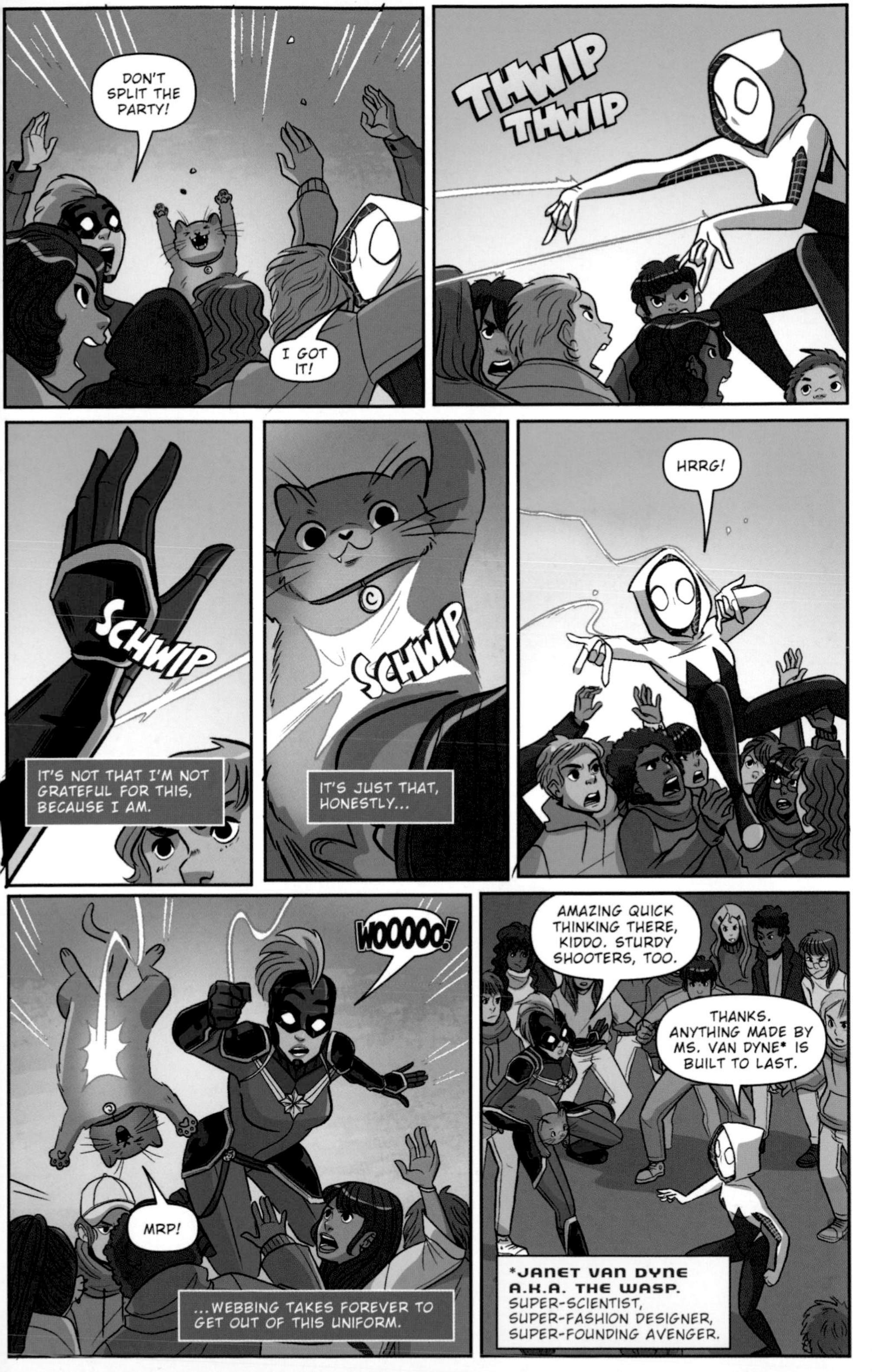
DON'T SPLIT THE PARTY!
I GOT IT!
THWIP THWIP
SCHWIP
IT'S NOT THAT I'M NOT GRATEFUL FOR THIS, BECAUSE I AM.
SCHWIP
IT'S JUST THAT, HONESTLY...
HRRG!
WOOOOO!
MRP!
...WEBBING TAKES FOREVER TO GET OUT OF THIS UNIFORM.
AMAZING QUICK THINKING THERE, KIDDO. STURDY SHOOTERS, TOO.
THANKS. ANYTHING MADE BY MS. VAN DYNE* IS BUILT TO LAST.
*JANET VAN DYNE A.K.A. THE WASP. SUPER-SCIENTIST, SUPER-FASHION DESIGNER, SUPER-FOUNDING AVENGER.

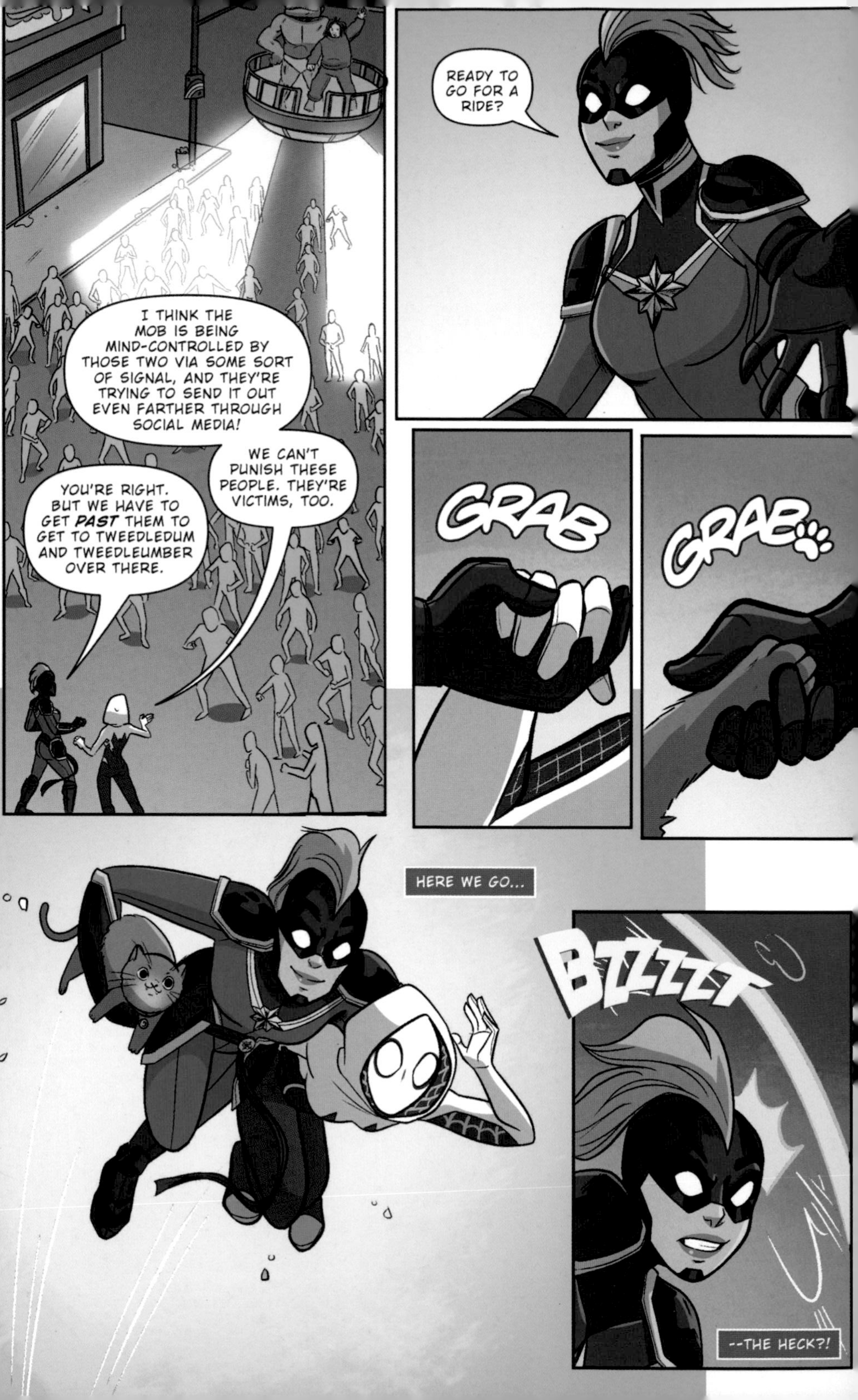
I THINK THE MOB IS BEING MIND-CONTROLLED BY THOSE TWO VIA SOME SORT OF SIGNAL, AND THEY'RE TRYING TO SEND IT OUT EVEN FARTHER THROUGH SOCIAL MEDIA!
WE CAN'T PUNISH THESE PEOPLE. THEY'RE VICTIMS, TOO.
YOU'RE RIGHT. BUT WE HAVE TO GET *PAST* THEM TO GET TO TWEEDLEDUM AND TWEEDLEUMBER OVER THERE.
READY TO GO FOR A RIDE?
GRAB
GRAB
HERE WE GO...
BZZZT
--THE HECK?!

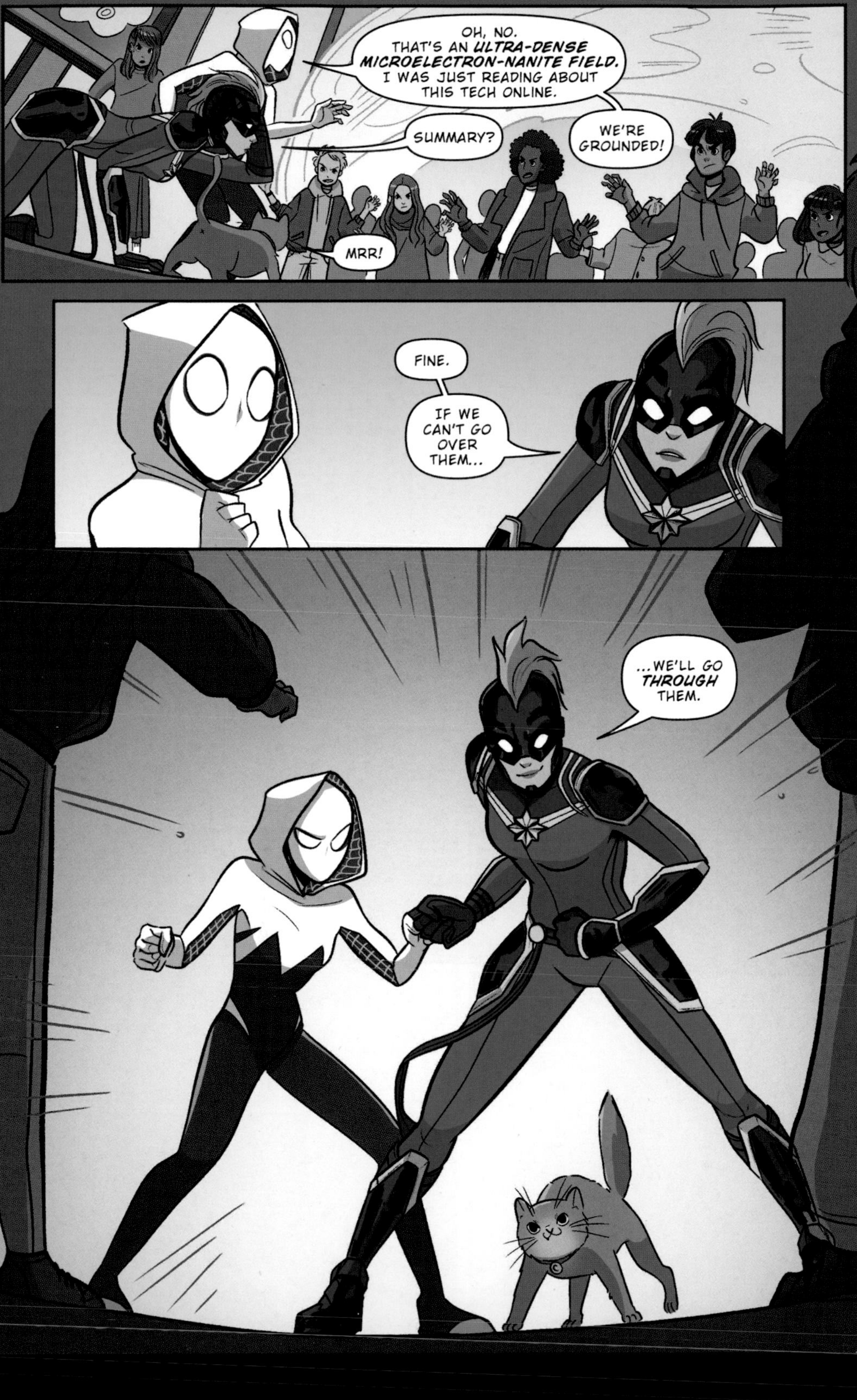
OH, NO. THAT'S AN ULTRA-DENSE MICROELECTRON-NANITE FIELD. I WAS JUST READING ABOUT THIS TECH ONLINE.
SUMMARY?
WE'RE GROUNDED!
MRR!
FINE.
IF WE CAN'T GO OVER THEM...
...WE'LL GO THROUGH THEM.

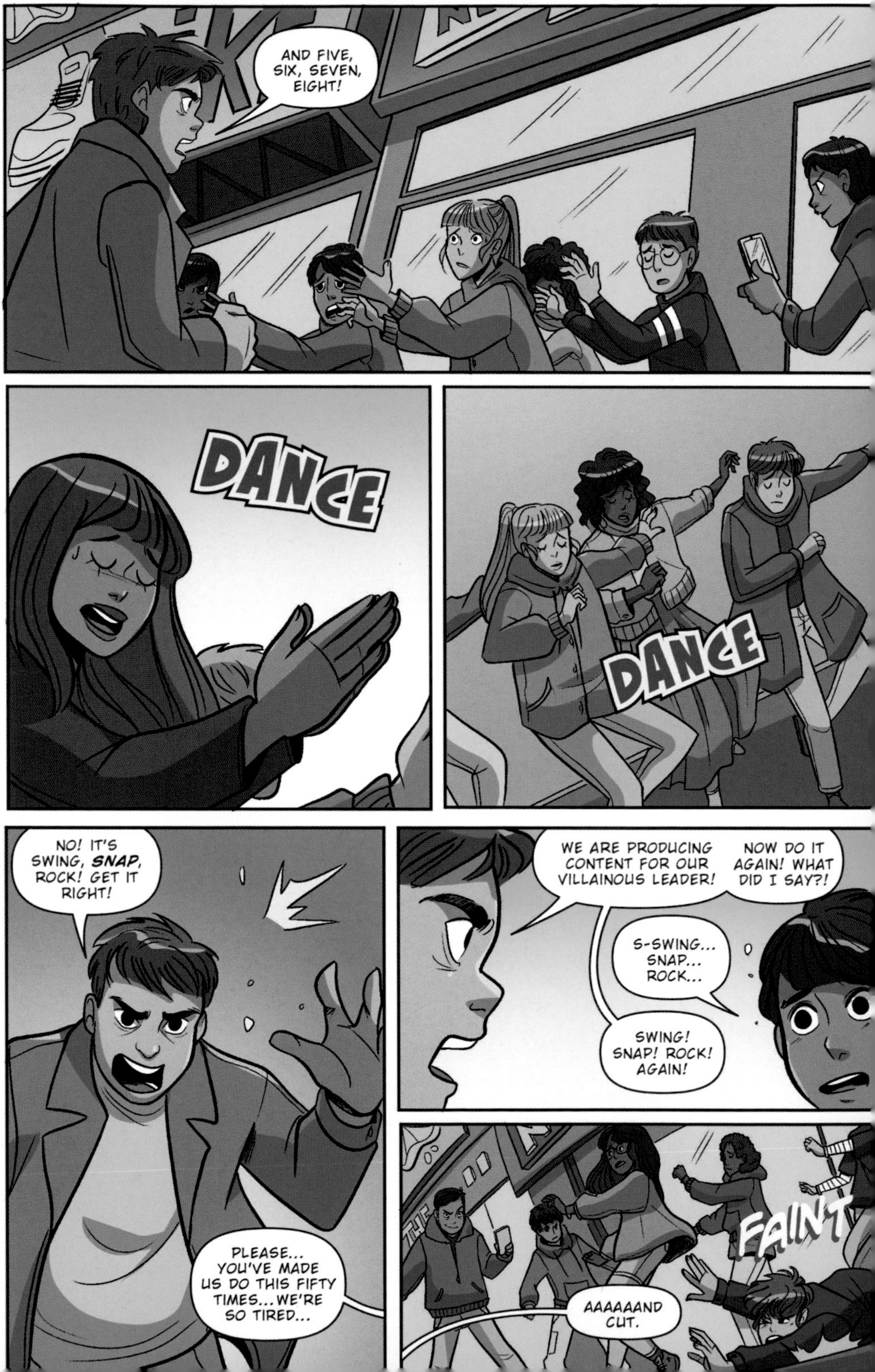
AND FIVE, SIX, SEVEN, EIGHT!
DANCE
DANCE
NO! IT'S SWING, SNAP, ROCK! GET IT RIGHT!
PLEASE... YOU'VE MADE US DO THIS FIFTY TIMES... WE'RE SO TIRED...
WE ARE PRODUCING CONTENT FOR OUR VILLAINOUS LEADER!
NOW DO IT AGAIN! WHAT DID I SAY?!
S-SWING... SNAP... ROCK...
SWING! SNAP! ROCK! AGAIN!
FAINT
AAAAAAND CUT.

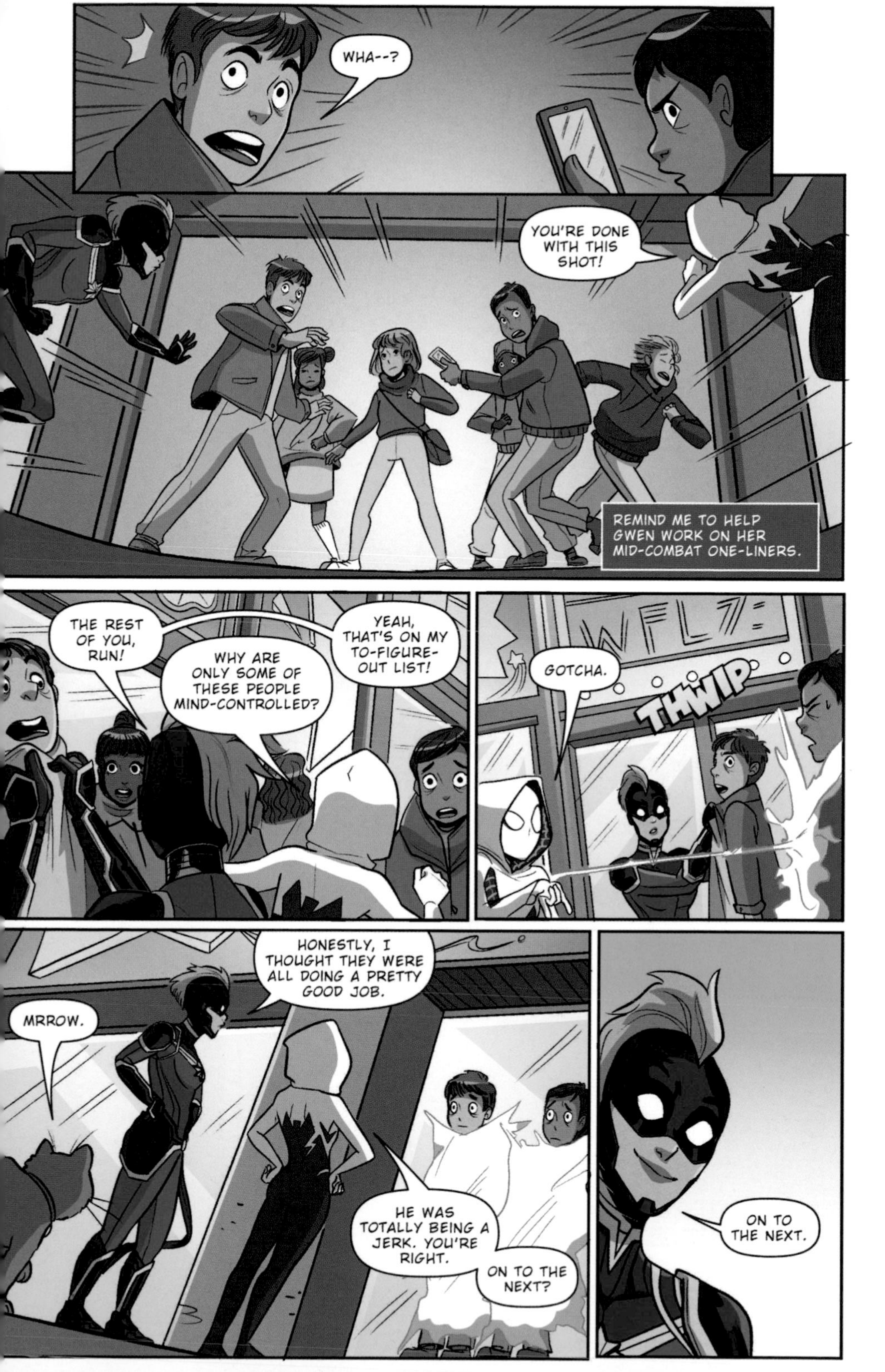
WHA--?
YOU'RE DONE WITH THIS SHOT!
REMIND ME TO HELP GWEN WORK ON HER MID-COMBAT ONE-LINERS.
THE REST OF YOU, RUN!
WHY ARE ONLY SOME OF THESE PEOPLE MIND-CONTROLLED?
YEAH, THAT'S ON MY TO-FIGURE-OUT LIST!
GOTCHA.
THWIP
HONESTLY, I THOUGHT THEY WERE ALL DOING A PRETTY GOOD JOB.
MRROW.
HE WAS TOTALLY BEING A JERK. YOU'RE RIGHT.
ON TO THE NEXT?
ON TO THE NEXT.

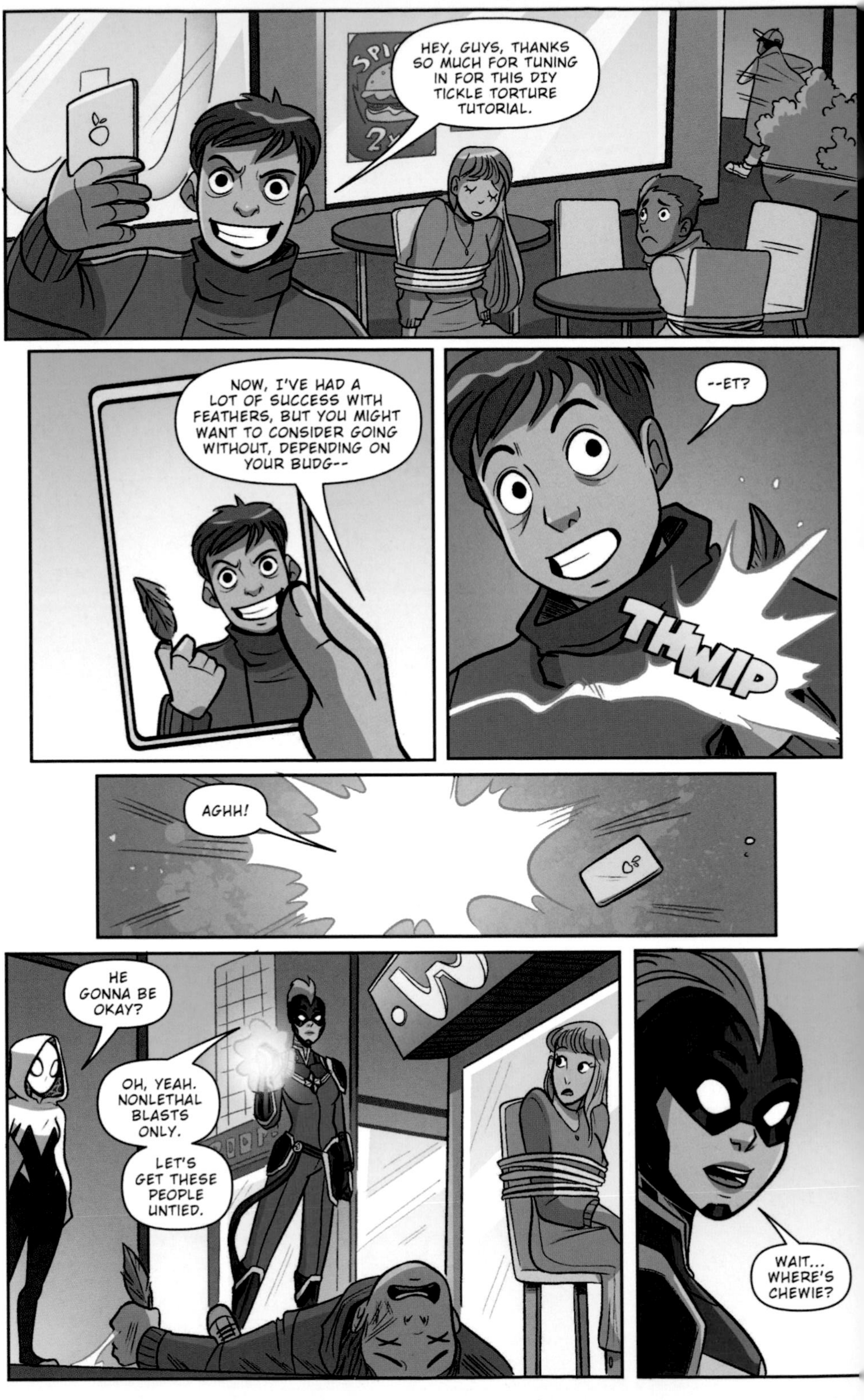
HEY, GUYS, THANKS SO MUCH FOR TUNING IN FOR THIS DIY TICKLE TORTURE TUTORIAL.
NOW, I'VE HAD A LOT OF SUCCESS WITH FEATHERS, BUT YOU MIGHT WANT TO CONSIDER GOING WITHOUT, DEPENDING ON YOUR BUDG--
--ET?
THWIP
AGHH!
HE GONNA BE OKAY?
OH, YEAH. NONLETHAL BLASTS ONLY.
LET'S GET THESE PEOPLE UNTIED.
WAIT... WHERE'S CHEWIE?

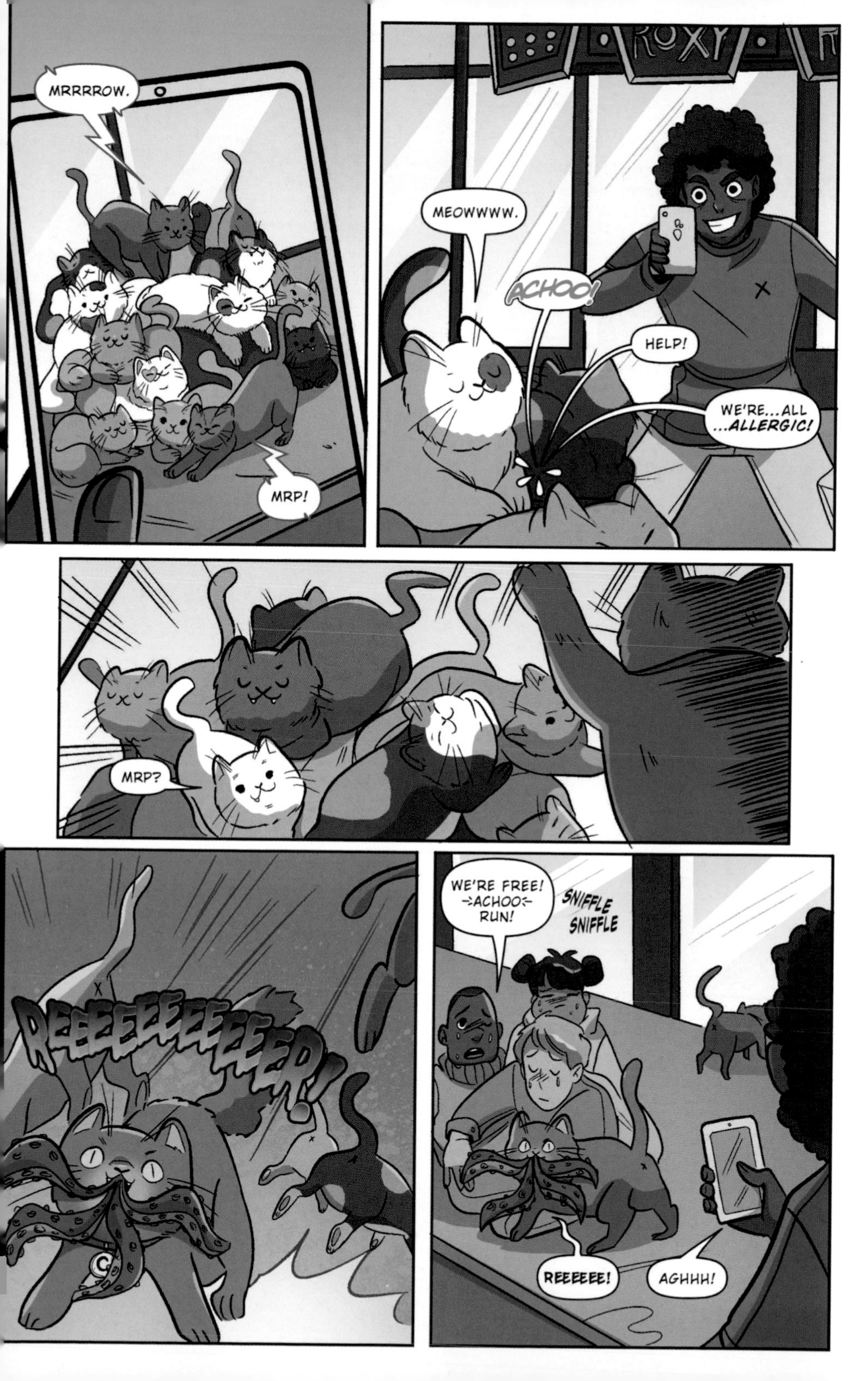
MRRRROW.
MRP!
ROXY
MEOWWWW.
ACHOO!
HELP!
WE'RE...ALL ...ALLERGIC!
MRP?
REEEEEEEEEEEP!!
WE'RE FREE! -ACHOO- RUN!
SNIFFLE SNIFFLE
REEEEEE!
AGHHH!

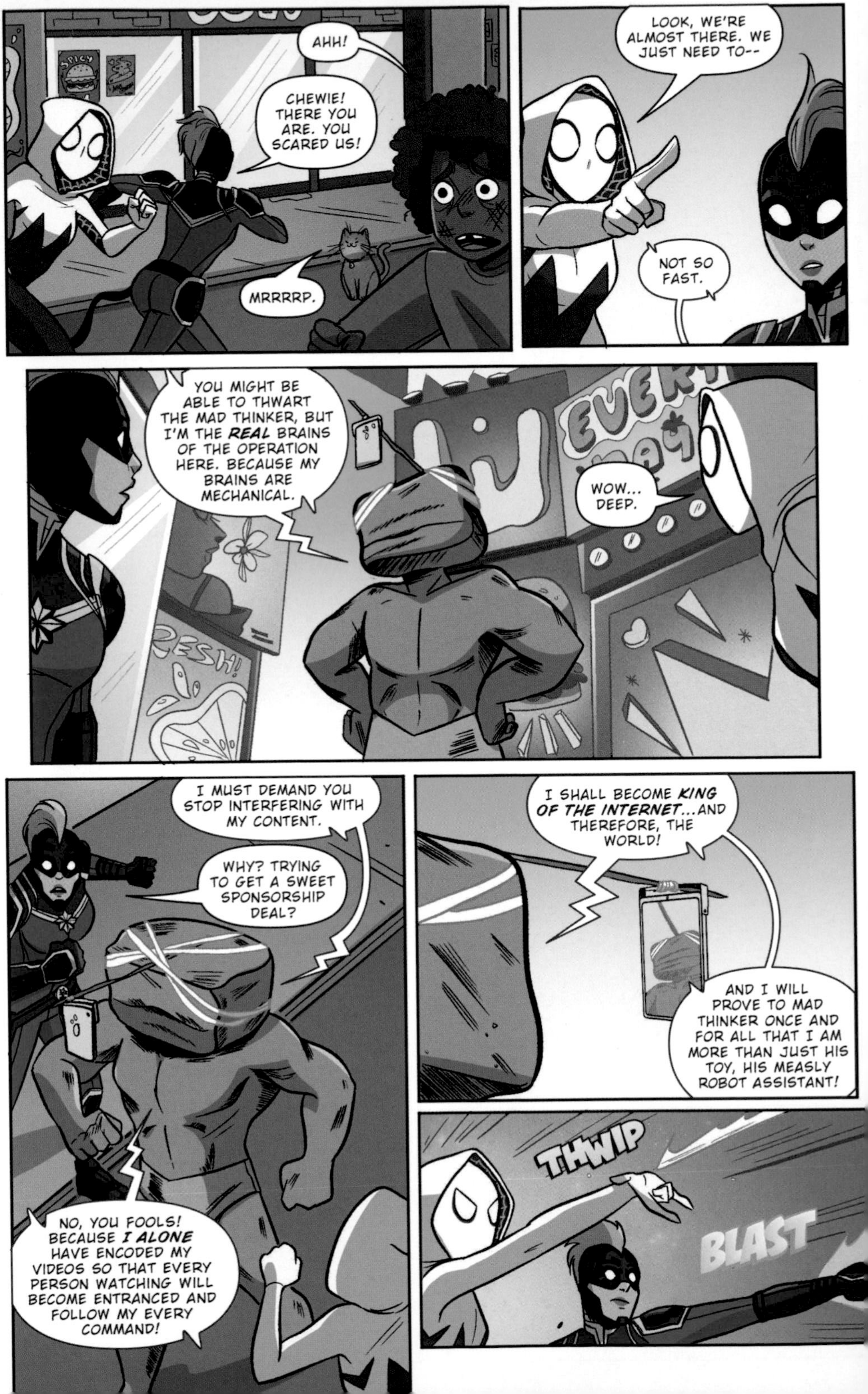

AHH!
CHEWIE! THERE YOU ARE. YOU SCARED US!
MRRRRP.
SPICY
LOOK, WE'RE ALMOST THERE. WE JUST NEED TO--
NOT SO FAST.
YOU MIGHT BE ABLE TO THWART THE MAD THINKER, BUT I'M THE REAL BRAINS OF THE OPERATION HERE. BECAUSE MY BRAINS ARE MECHANICAL.
WOW... DEEP.
I MUST DEMAND YOU STOP INTERFERING WITH MY CONTENT.
WHY? TRYING TO GET A SWEET SPONSORSHIP DEAL?
NO, YOU FOOLS! BECAUSE I ALONE HAVE ENCODED MY VIDEOS SO THAT EVERY PERSON WATCHING WILL BECOME ENTRANCED AND FOLLOW MY EVERY COMMAND!
I SHALL BECOME KING OF THE INTERNET...AND THEREFORE, THE WORLD!
AND I WILL PROVE TO MAD THINKER ONCE AND FOR ALL THAT I AM MORE THAN JUST HIS TOY, HIS MEASLY ROBOT ASSISTANT!
THWIP
BLAST

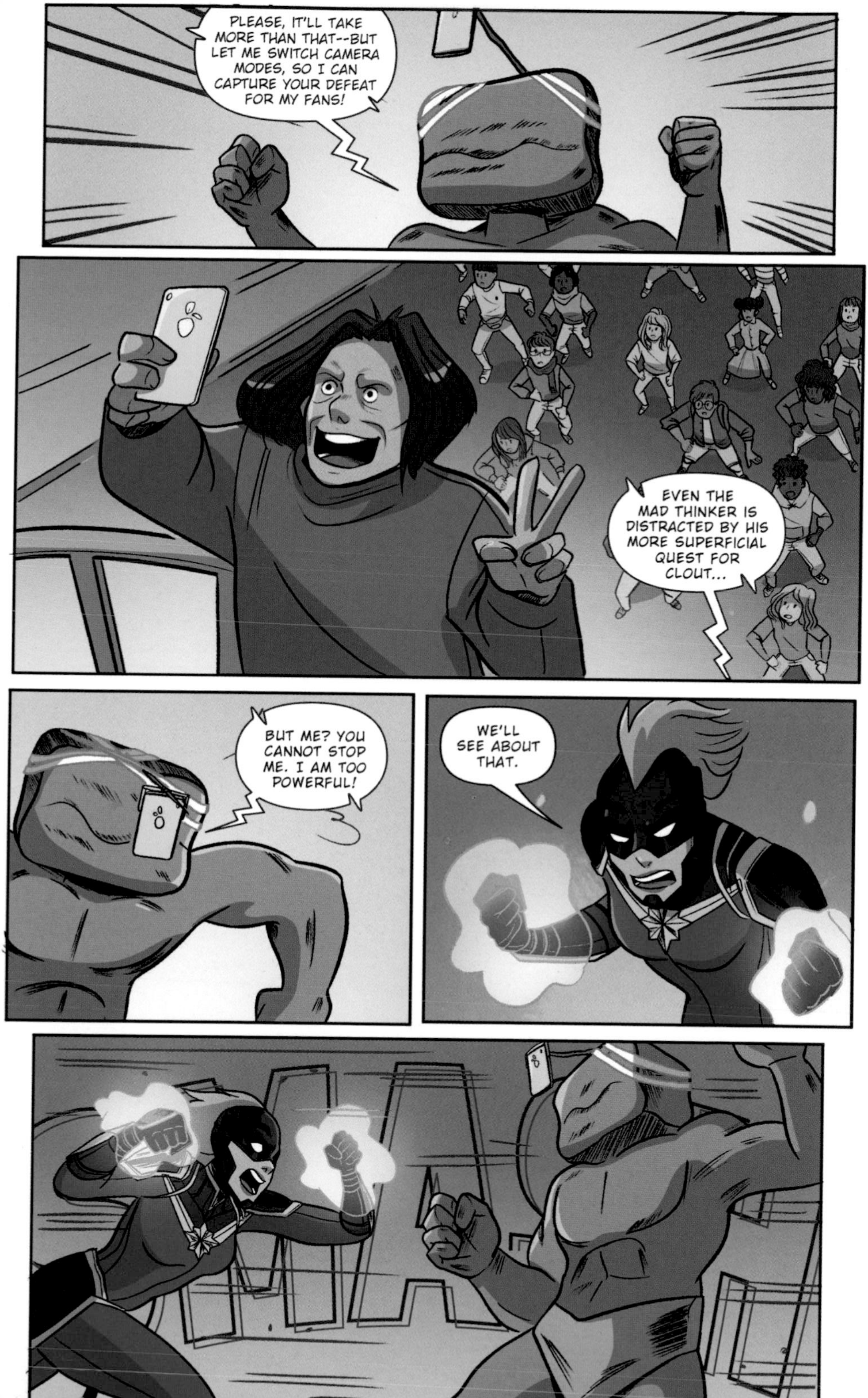

PLEASE, IT'LL TAKE MORE THAN THAT--BUT LET ME SWITCH CAMERA MODES, SO I CAN CAPTURE YOUR DEFEAT FOR MY FANS!
EVEN THE MAD THINKER IS DISTRACTED BY HIS MORE SUPERFICIAL QUEST FOR CLOUT...
BUT ME? YOU CANNOT STOP ME. I AM TOO POWERFUL!
WE'LL SEE ABOUT THAT.

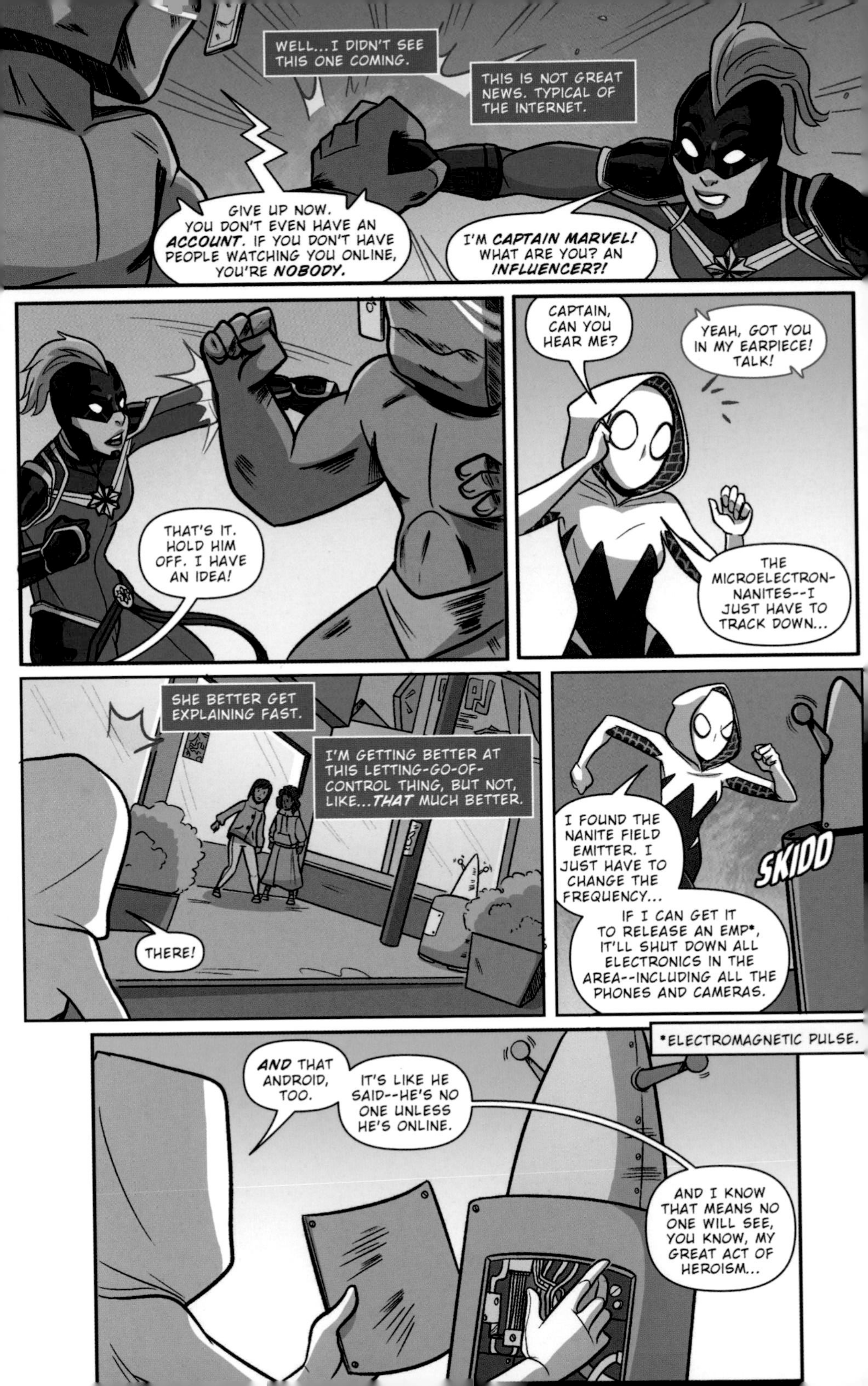

WELL...I DIDN'T SEE THIS ONE COMING.
THIS IS NOT GREAT NEWS. TYPICAL OF THE INTERNET.
GIVE UP NOW. YOU DON'T EVEN HAVE AN ***ACCOUNT***. IF YOU DON'T HAVE PEOPLE WATCHING YOU ONLINE, YOU'RE ***NOBODY***.
I'M ***CAPTAIN MARVEL!*** WHAT ARE YOU? AN ***INFLUENCER?!***
THAT'S IT. HOLD HIM OFF. I HAVE AN IDEA!
CAPTAIN, CAN YOU HEAR ME?
YEAH, GOT YOU IN MY EARPIECE! TALK!
THE MICROELECTRON-NANITES--I JUST HAVE TO TRACK DOWN...
SHE BETTER GET EXPLAINING FAST.
I'M GETTING BETTER AT THIS LETTING-GO-OF-CONTROL THING, BUT NOT, LIKE...*THAT* MUCH BETTER.
THERE!
SKIDD
I FOUND THE NANITE FIELD EMITTER. I JUST HAVE TO CHANGE THE FREQUENCY...
IF I CAN GET IT TO RELEASE AN EMP*, IT'LL SHUT DOWN ALL ELECTRONICS IN THE AREA--INCLUDING ALL THE PHONES AND CAMERAS.
*ELECTROMAGNETIC PULSE.
AND THAT ANDROID, TOO.
IT'S LIKE HE SAID--HE'S NO ONE UNLESS HE'S ONLINE.
AND I KNOW THAT MEANS NO ONE WILL SEE, YOU KNOW, MY GREAT ACT OF HEROISM...

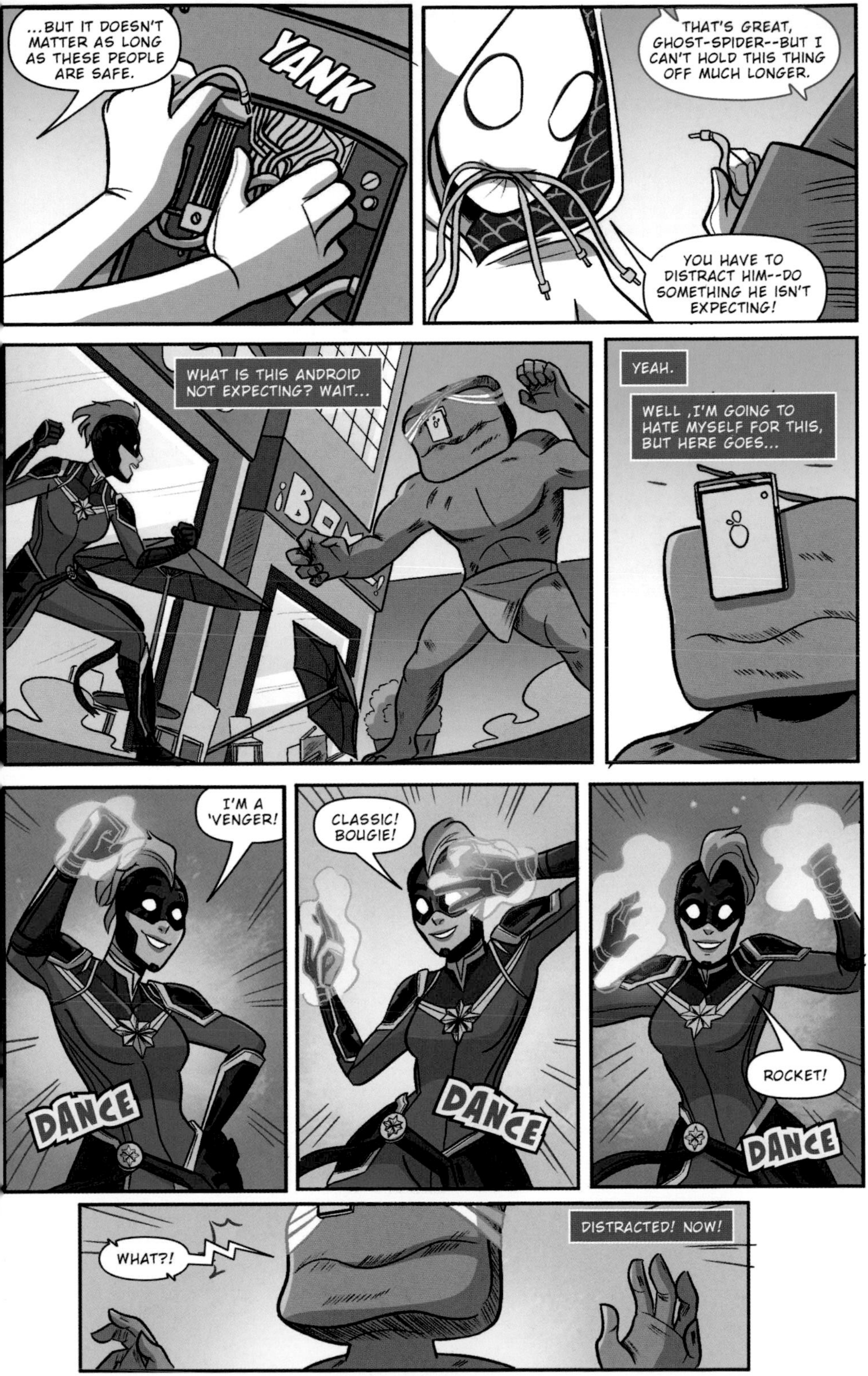
...BUT IT DOESN'T MATTER AS LONG AS THESE PEOPLE ARE SAFE.
YANK
THAT'S GREAT, GHOST-SPIDER--BUT I CAN'T HOLD THIS THING OFF MUCH LONGER.
YOU HAVE TO DISTRACT HIM--DO SOMETHING HE ISN'T EXPECTING!
WHAT IS THIS ANDROID NOT EXPECTING? WAIT...
YEAH.
WELL ,I'M GOING TO HATE MYSELF FOR THIS, BUT HERE GOES...
I'M A 'VENGER!
DANCE
CLASSIC! BOUGIE!
DANCE
ROCKET!
DANCE
WHAT?!
DISTRACTED! NOW!

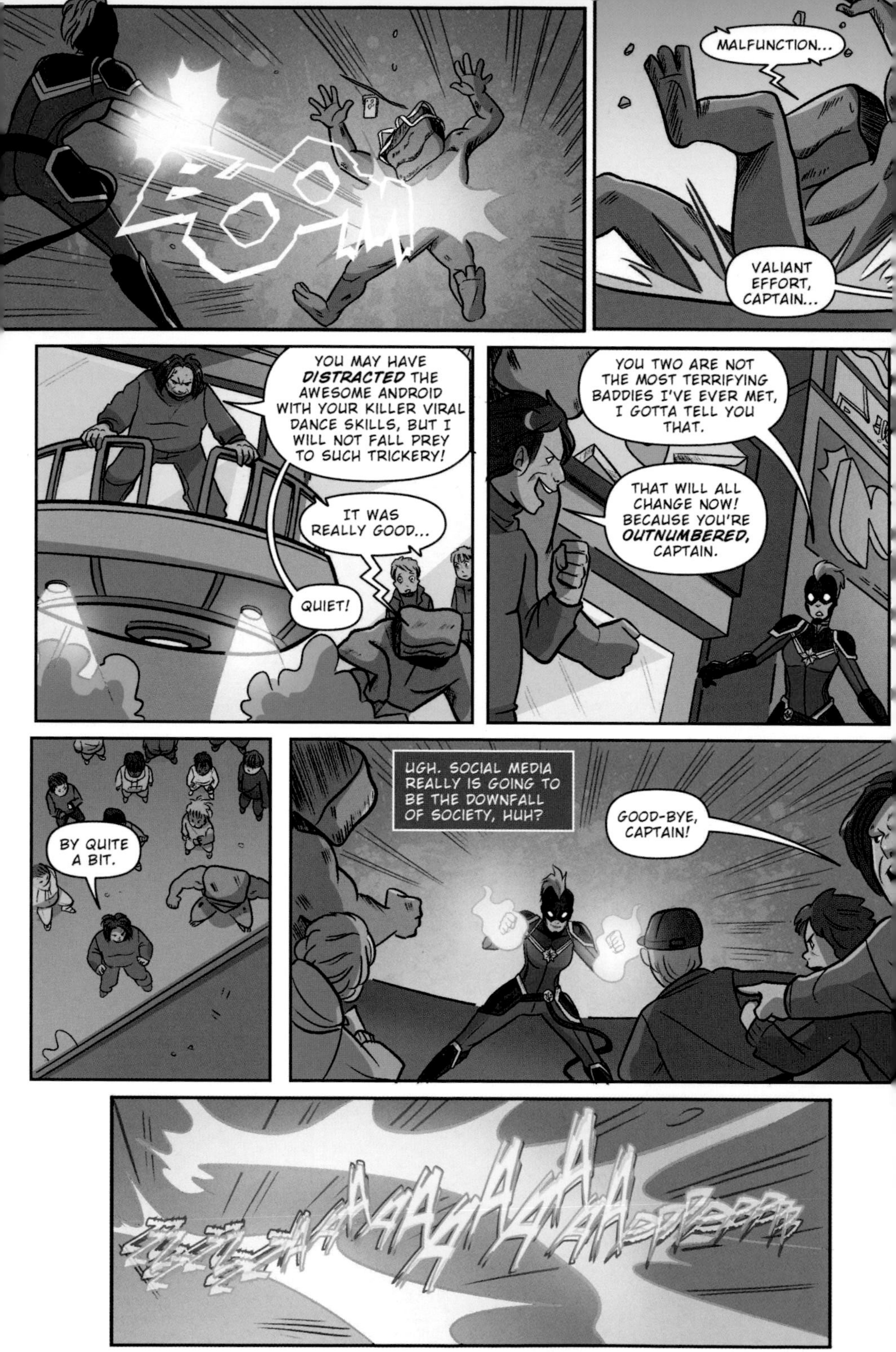
MALFUNCTION...
VALIANT EFFORT, CAPTAIN...
YOU MAY HAVE DISTRACTED THE AWESOME ANDROID WITH YOUR KILLER VIRAL DANCE SKILLS, BUT I WILL NOT FALL PREY TO SUCH TRICKERY!
IT WAS REALLY GOOD...
QUIET!
YOU TWO ARE NOT THE MOST TERRIFYING BADDIES I'VE EVER MET, I GOTTA TELL YOU THAT.
THAT WILL ALL CHANGE NOW! BECAUSE YOU'RE OUTNUMBERED, CAPTAIN.
BY QUITE A BIT.
UGH. SOCIAL MEDIA REALLY IS GOING TO BE THE DOWNFALL OF SOCIETY, HUH?
GOOD-BYE, CAPTAIN!

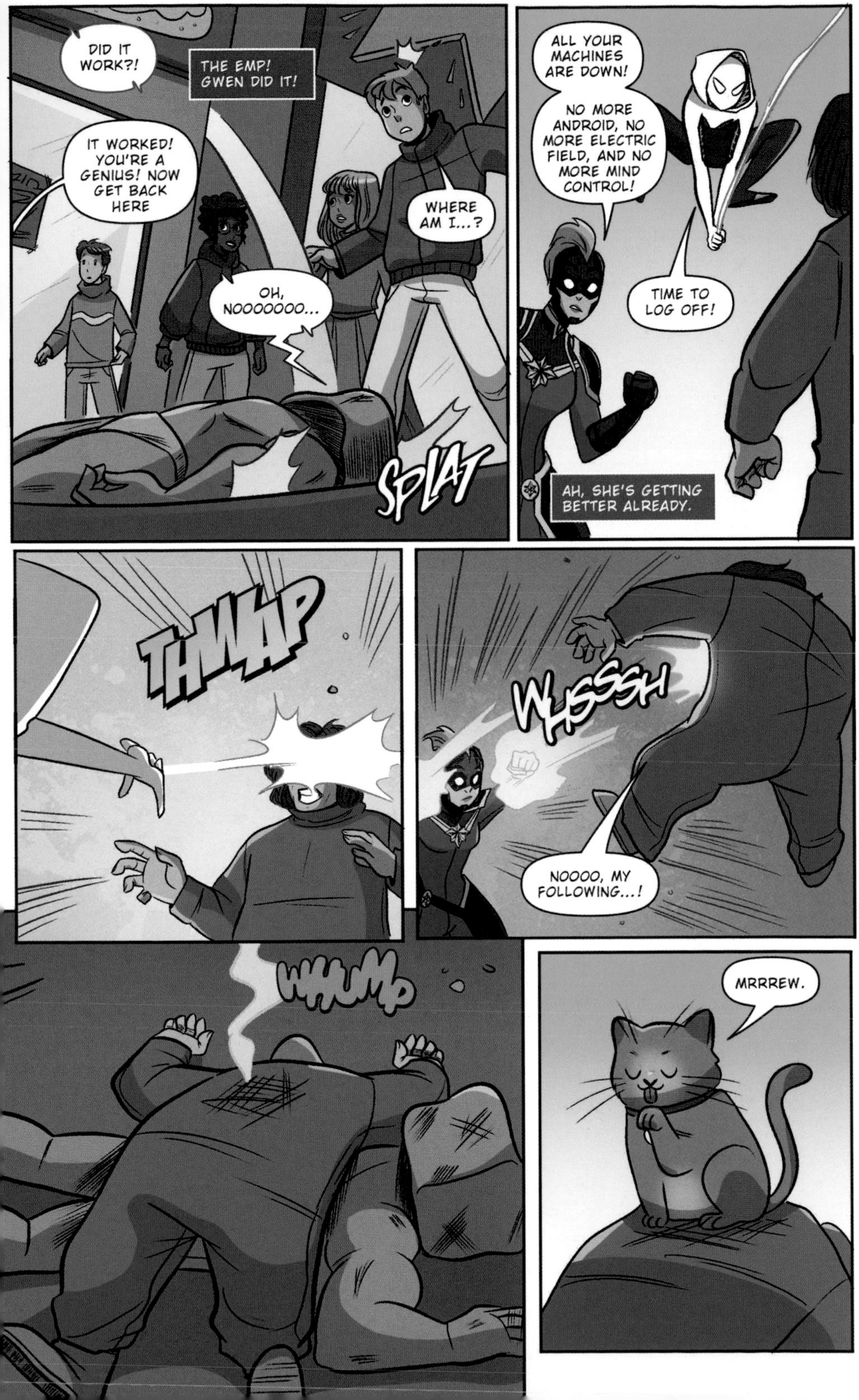
DID IT WORK?!
THE EMP! GWEN DID IT!
IT WORKED! YOU'RE A GENIUS! NOW GET BACK HERE
WHERE AM I...?
OH, NOOOOOOO...
SPLAT
ALL YOUR MACHINES ARE DOWN!
NO MORE ANDROID, NO MORE ELECTRIC FIELD, AND NO MORE MIND CONTROL!
TIME TO LOG OFF!
AH, SHE'S GETTING BETTER ALREADY.
THWAP
WHSSSH
NOOOO, MY FOLLOWING...!
WHUMP
MRRREW.

NICE ONE, GHOST-SPIDER.

NO NO, IT WAS ALL YOU, CAPTAIN MARVEL.

MEOW.

OKAY, AND YOU TOO, CHEWIE.

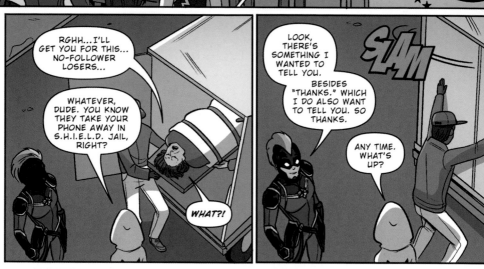

RGHH...I'LL GET YOU FOR THIS... NO-FOLLOWER LOSERS...

WHATEVER, DUDE. YOU KNOW THEY TAKE YOUR PHONE AWAY IN S.H.I.E.L.D. JAIL, RIGHT?

WHAT?!

LOOK, THERE'S SOMETHING I WANTED TO TELL YOU.

BESIDES "THANKS." WHICH I DO ALSO WANT TO TELL YOU. SO THANKS.

ANY TIME. WHAT'S UP?

SLAM

I KNOW SETTING OFF THAT EMP MEANT NO ONE SAW YOUR BIG HEROICS.

BUT YOU SAVED THOSE PEOPLE. *THEY* KNOW WHAT YOU DID. AND THEY'LL SPREAD THE WORD.

I THINK YOU MIGHT HAVE ENDED UP IN A LOT OF THESE SHOTS ANYWAY. YOU MIGHT WANT TO CHECK YOUR FOLLOWER COUNT.

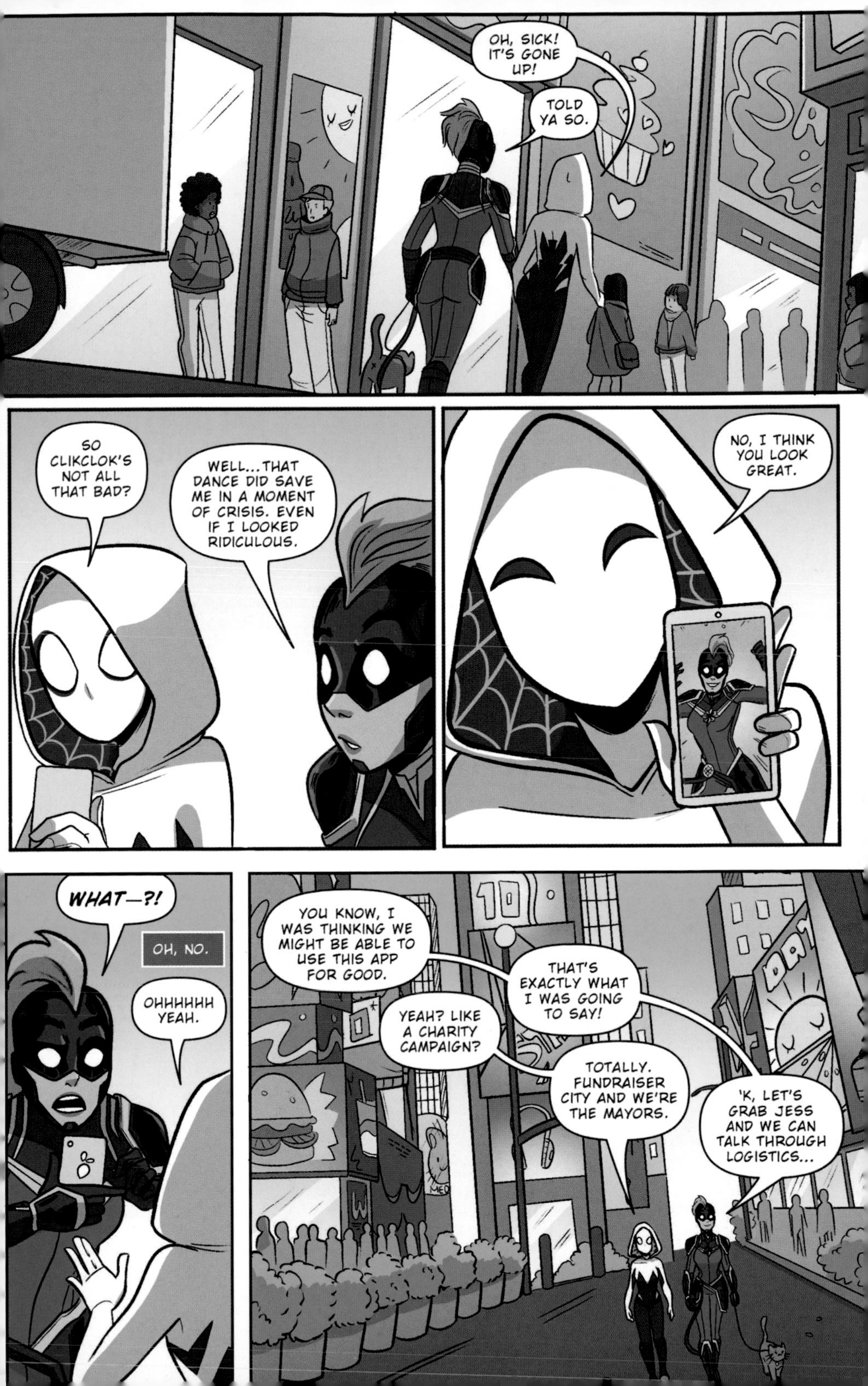
OH, SICK! IT'S GONE UP!
TOLD YA SO.
SO CLIKCLOK'S NOT ALL THAT BAD?
WELL...THAT DANCE DID SAVE ME IN A MOMENT OF CRISIS. EVEN IF I LOOKED RIDICULOUS.
NO, I THINK YOU LOOK GREAT.
WHAT—?!
OH, NO.
OHHHHHH YEAH.
YOU KNOW, I WAS THINKING WE MIGHT BE ABLE TO USE THIS APP FOR GOOD.
THAT'S EXACTLY WHAT I WAS GOING TO SAY!
YEAH? LIKE A CHARITY CAMPAIGN?
TOTALLY. FUNDRAISER CITY AND WE'RE THE MAYORS.
'K, LET'S GRAB JESS AND WE CAN TALK THROUGH LOGISTICS...

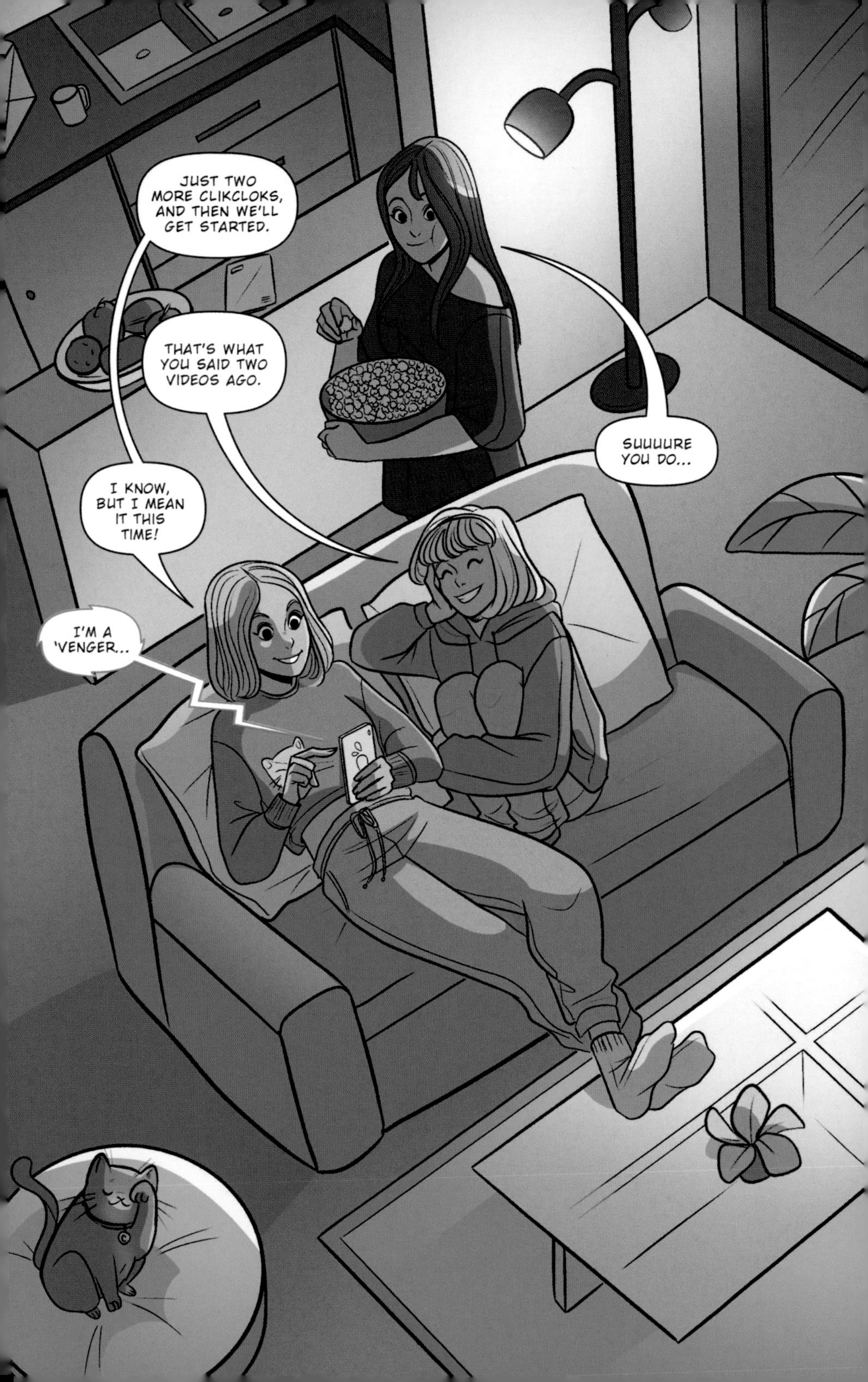
JUST TWO MORE CLIKCLOKS, AND THEN WE'LL GET STARTED.
THAT'S WHAT YOU SAID TWO VIDEOS AGO.
SUUUURE YOU DO...
I KNOW, BUT I MEAN IT THIS TIME!
I'M A 'VENGER...

GAME ON! PART ONE

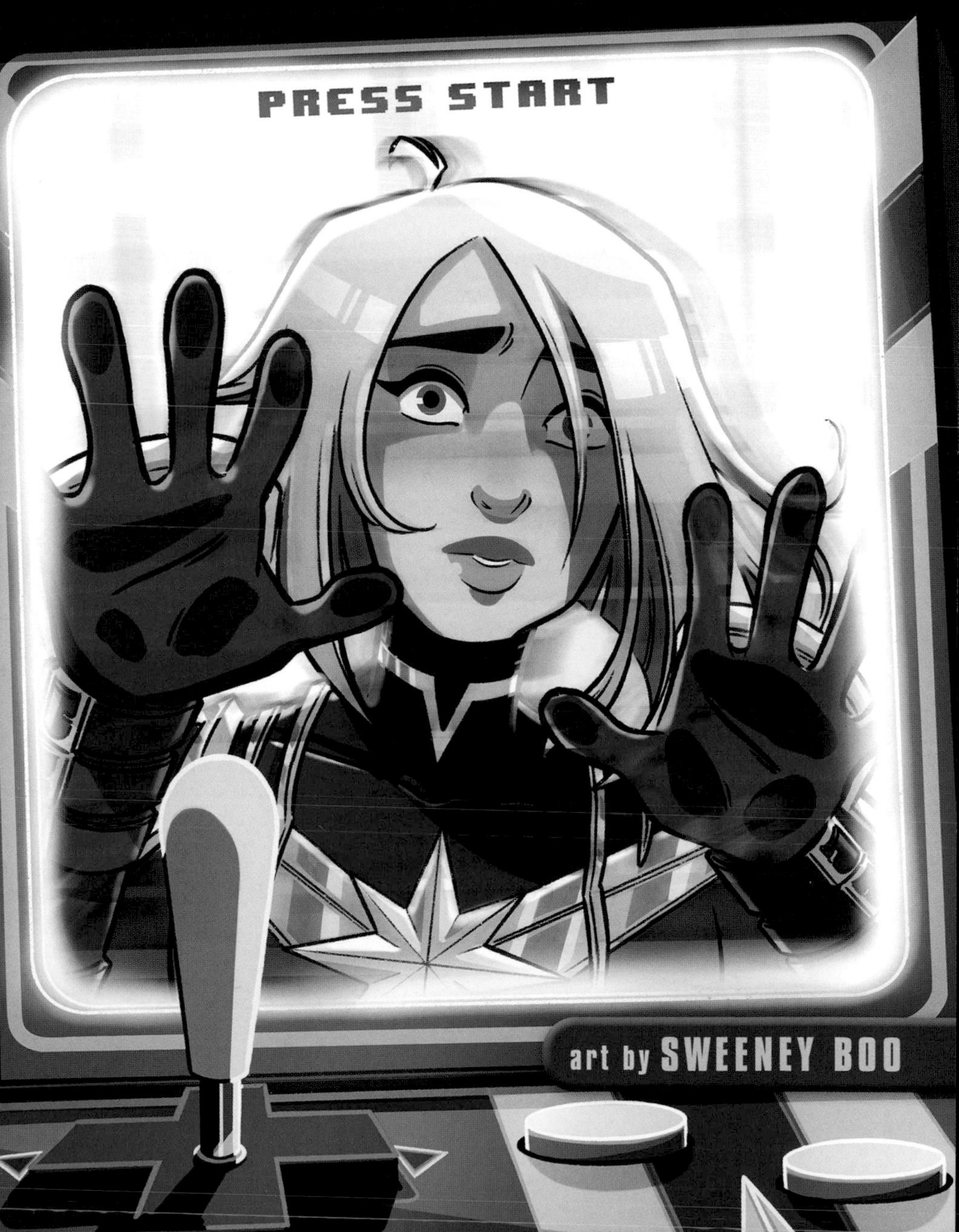
PRESS START
art by SWEENEY BOO

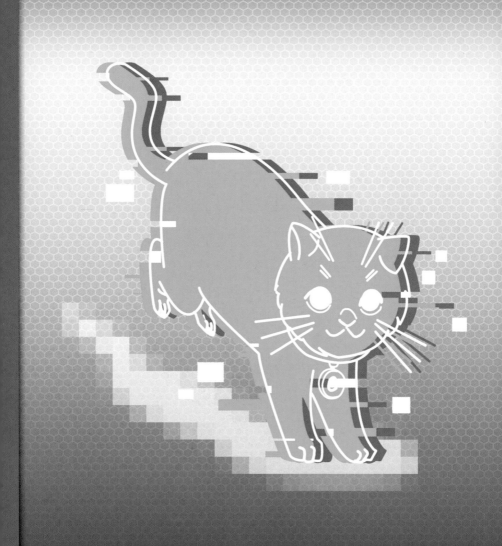

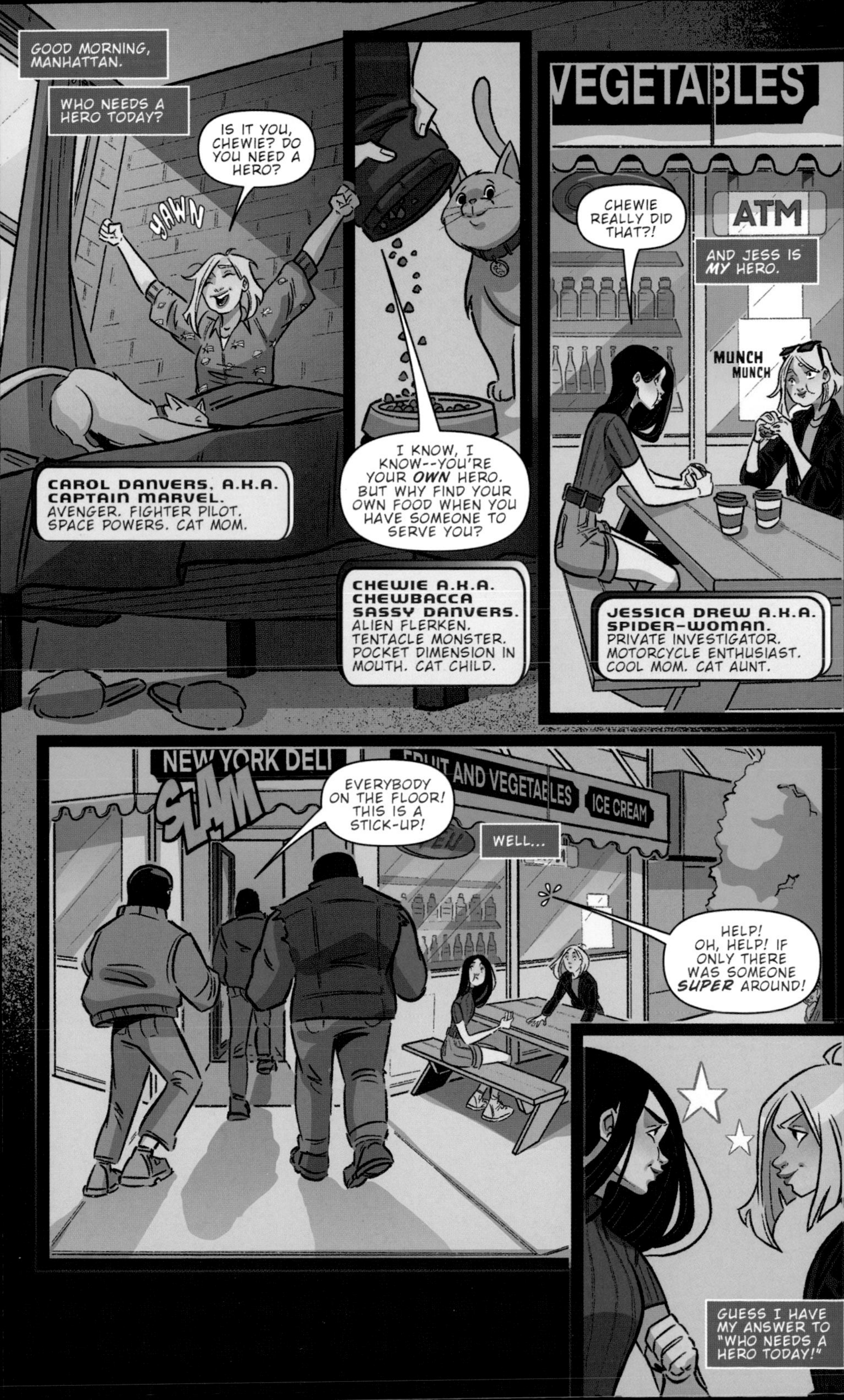
GOOD MORNING, MANHATTAN.
WHO NEEDS A HERO TODAY?
IS IT YOU, CHEWIE? DO YOU NEED A HERO?
YAWN
CAROL DANVERS, A.K.A. CAPTAIN MARVEL. AVENGER. FIGHTER PILOT. SPACE POWERS. CAT MOM.
I KNOW, I KNOW--YOU'RE YOUR OWN HERO. BUT WHY FIND YOUR OWN FOOD WHEN YOU HAVE SOMEONE TO SERVE YOU?
CHEWIE A.K.A. CHEWBACCA SASSY DANVERS. ALIEN FLERKEN. TENTACLE MONSTER. POCKET DIMENSION IN MOUTH. CAT CHILD.
VEGETABLES
ATM
CHEWIE REALLY DID THAT?!
AND JESS IS MY HERO.
MUNCH MUNCH
JESSICA DREW A.K.A. SPIDER-WOMAN. PRIVATE INVESTIGATOR. MOTORCYCLE ENTHUSIAST. COOL MOM. CAT AUNT.
NEW YORK DELI
FRUIT AND VEGETABLES
ICE CREAM
SLAM
EVERYBODY ON THE FLOOR! THIS IS A STICK-UP!
WELL...
HELP! OH, HELP! IF ONLY THERE WAS SOMEONE SUPER AROUND!
GUESS I HAVE MY ANSWER TO "WHO NEEDS A HERO TODAY!"

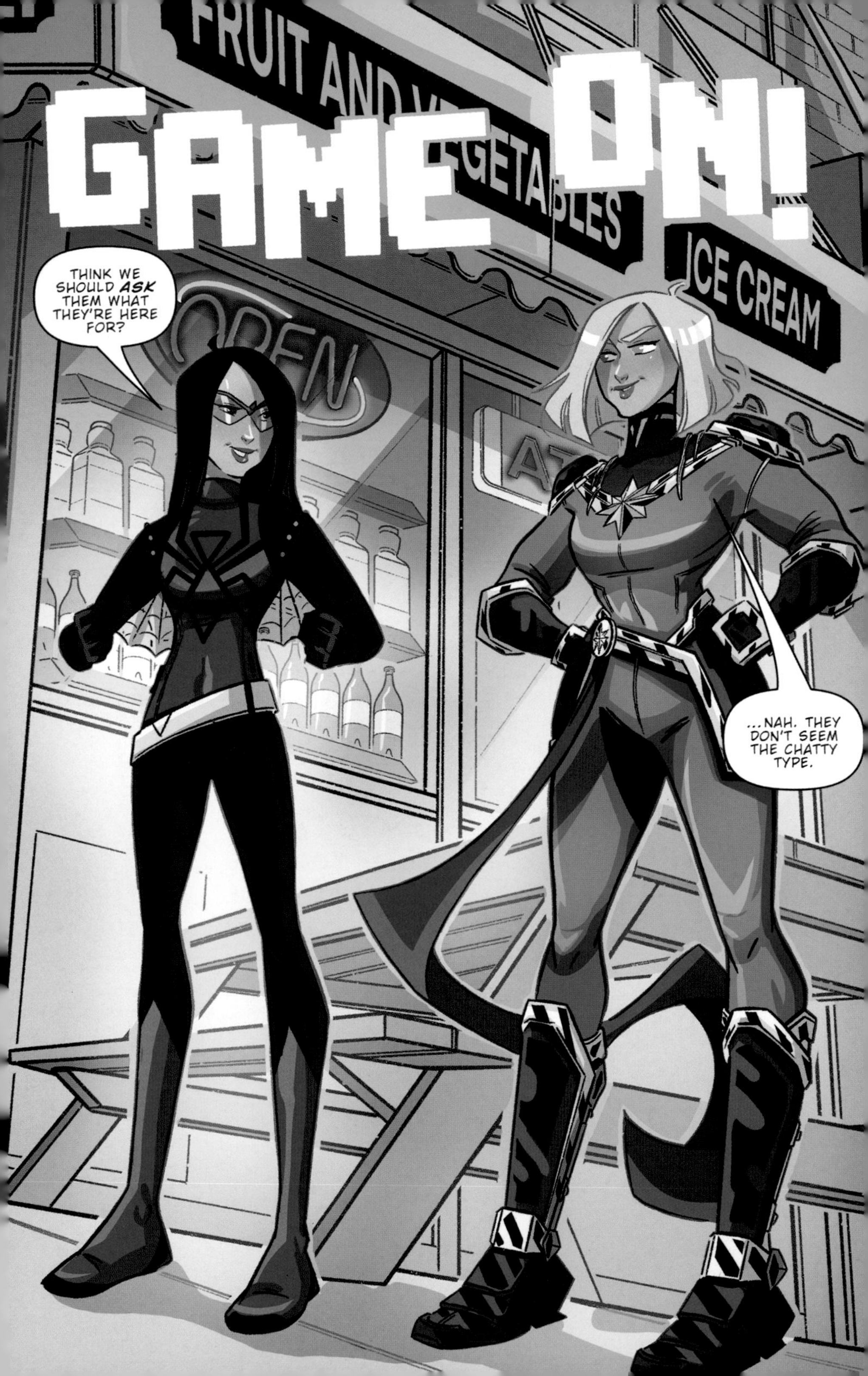
GAME ON!
FRUIT AND VEGETABLES
ICE CREAM
OPEN
THINK WE SHOULD ASK THEM WHAT THEY'RE HERE FOR?
...NAH. THEY DON'T SEEM THE CHATTY TYPE.

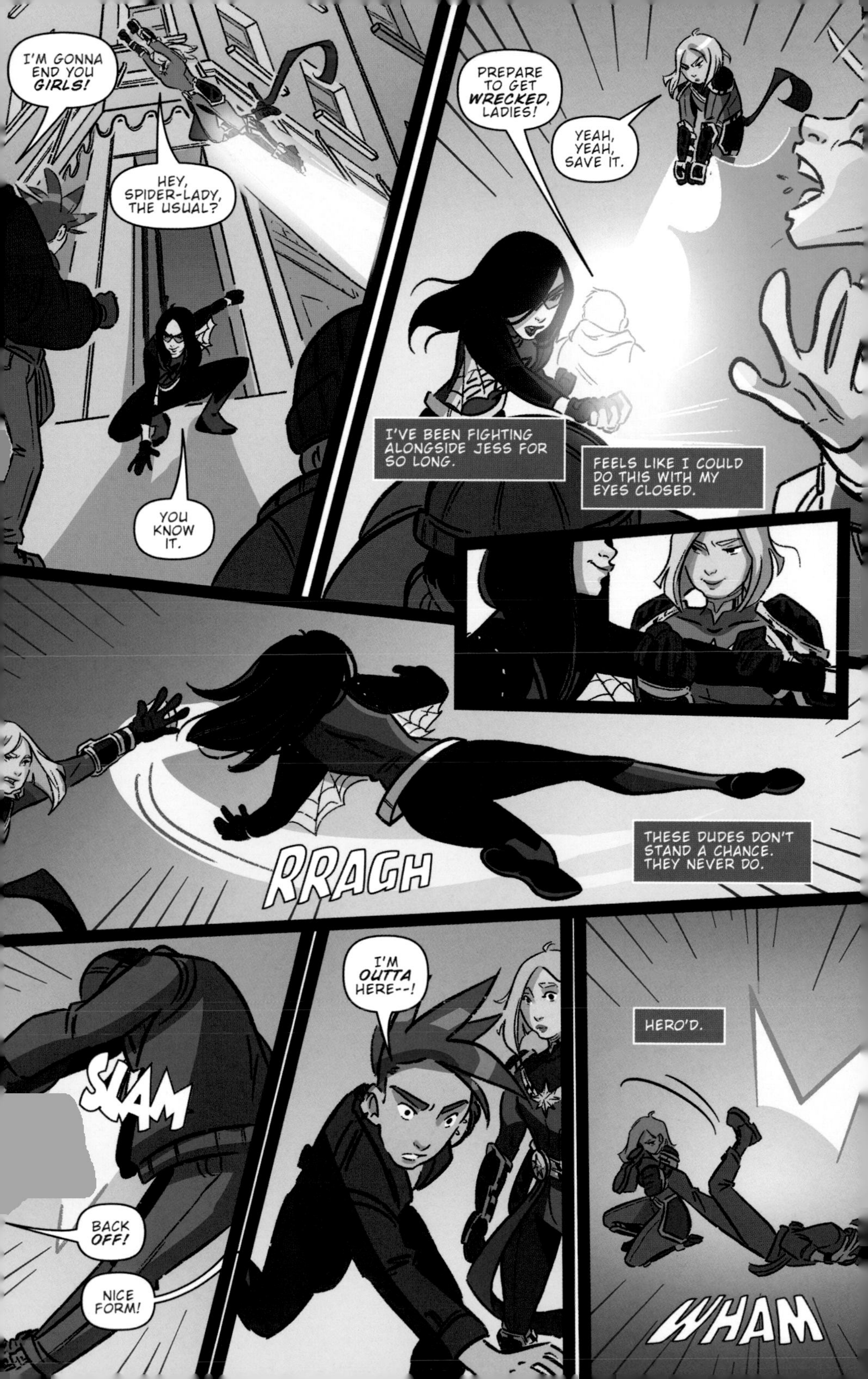
I'M GONNA END YOU GIRLS!
HEY, SPIDER-LADY, THE USUAL?
YOU KNOW IT.
PREPARE TO GET WRECKED, LADIES!
YEAH, YEAH, SAVE IT.
I'VE BEEN FIGHTING ALONGSIDE JESS FOR SO LONG.
FEELS LIKE I COULD DO THIS WITH MY EYES CLOSED.
RRAGH
THESE DUDES DON'T STAND A CHANCE. THEY NEVER DO.
SLAM
BACK OFF!
NICE FORM!
I'M OUTTA HERE--!
HERO'D.
WHAM

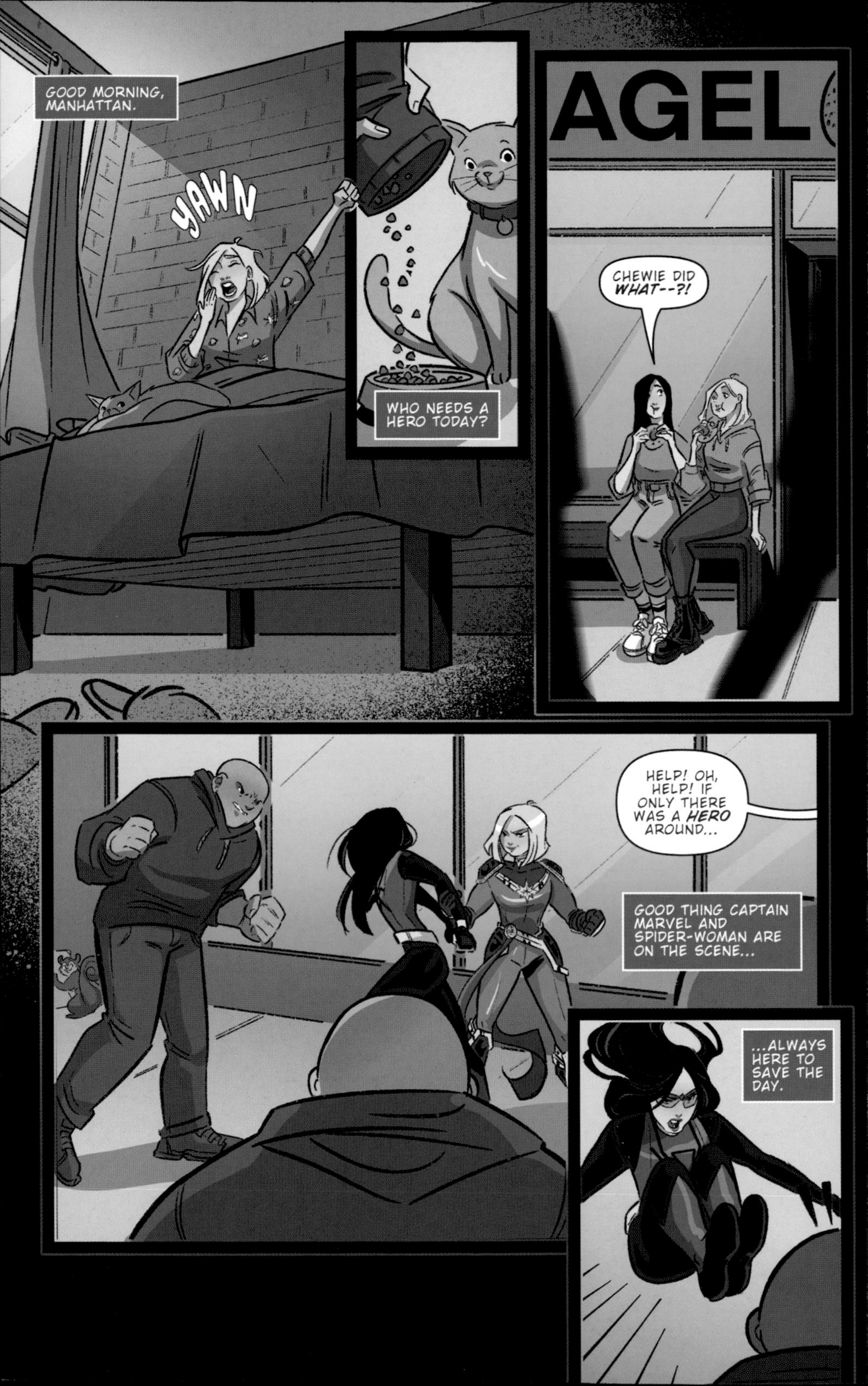
GOOD MORNING, MANHATTAN.
YAWN
WHO NEEDS A HERO TODAY?
AGEL
CHEWIE DID WHAT--?!
HELP! OH, HELP! IF ONLY THERE WAS A HERO AROUND...
GOOD THING CAPTAIN MARVEL AND SPIDER-WOMAN ARE ON THE SCENE...
...ALWAYS HERE TO SAVE THE DAY.

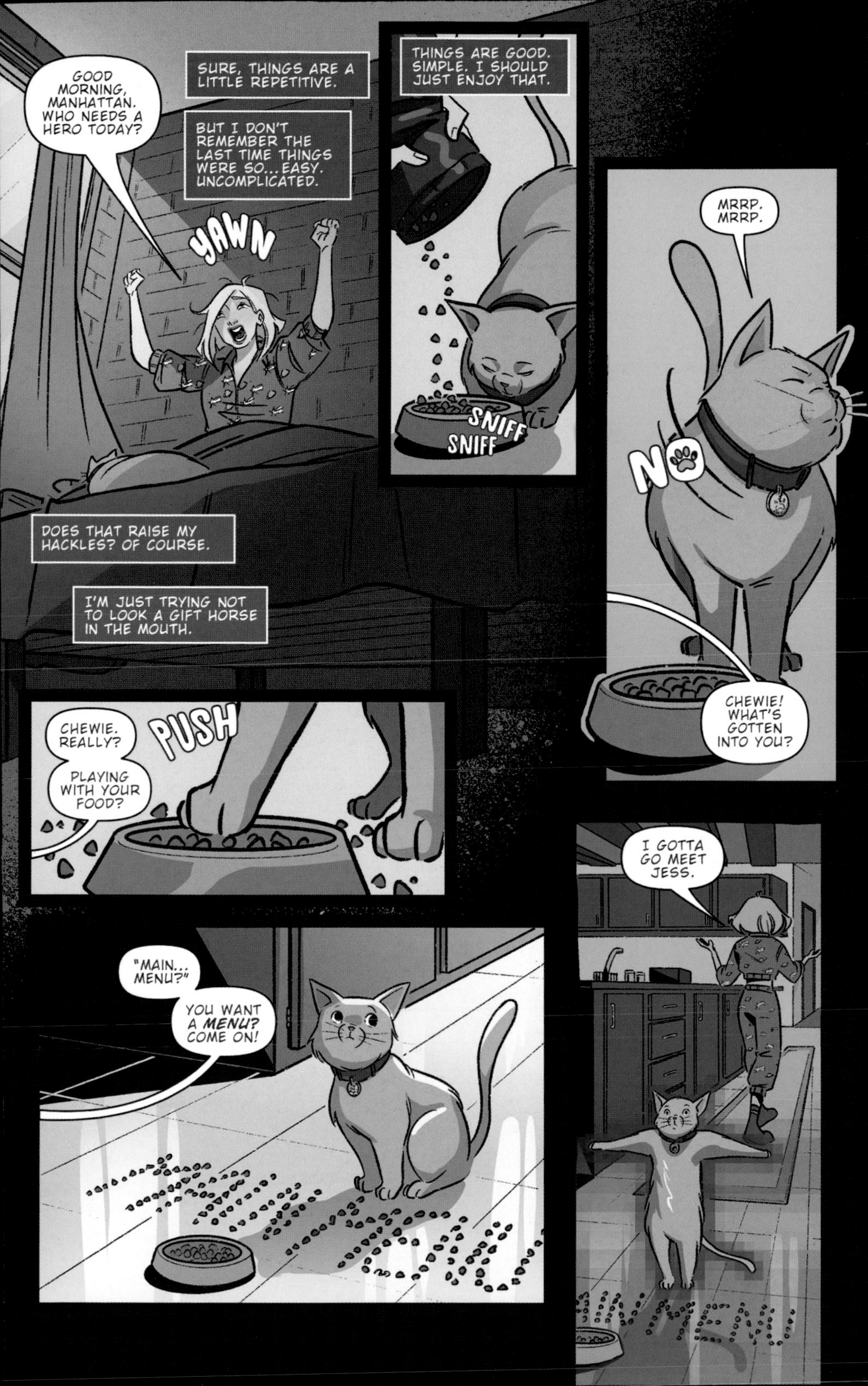
GOOD MORNING, MANHATTAN. WHO NEEDS A HERO TODAY?
SURE, THINGS ARE A LITTLE REPETITIVE.
BUT I DON'T REMEMBER THE LAST TIME THINGS WERE SO... EASY. UNCOMPLICATED.
YAWN
THINGS ARE GOOD. SIMPLE. I SHOULD JUST ENJOY THAT.
SNIFF
SNIFF
MRRP. MRRP.
NO
CHEWIE! WHAT'S GOTTEN INTO YOU?
DOES THAT RAISE MY HACKLES? OF COURSE.
I'M JUST TRYING NOT TO LOOK A GIFT HORSE IN THE MOUTH.
CHEWIE. REALLY?
PLAYING WITH YOUR FOOD?
PUSH
I GOTTA GO MEET JESS.
"MAIN... MENU?"
YOU WANT A *MENU?* COME ON!

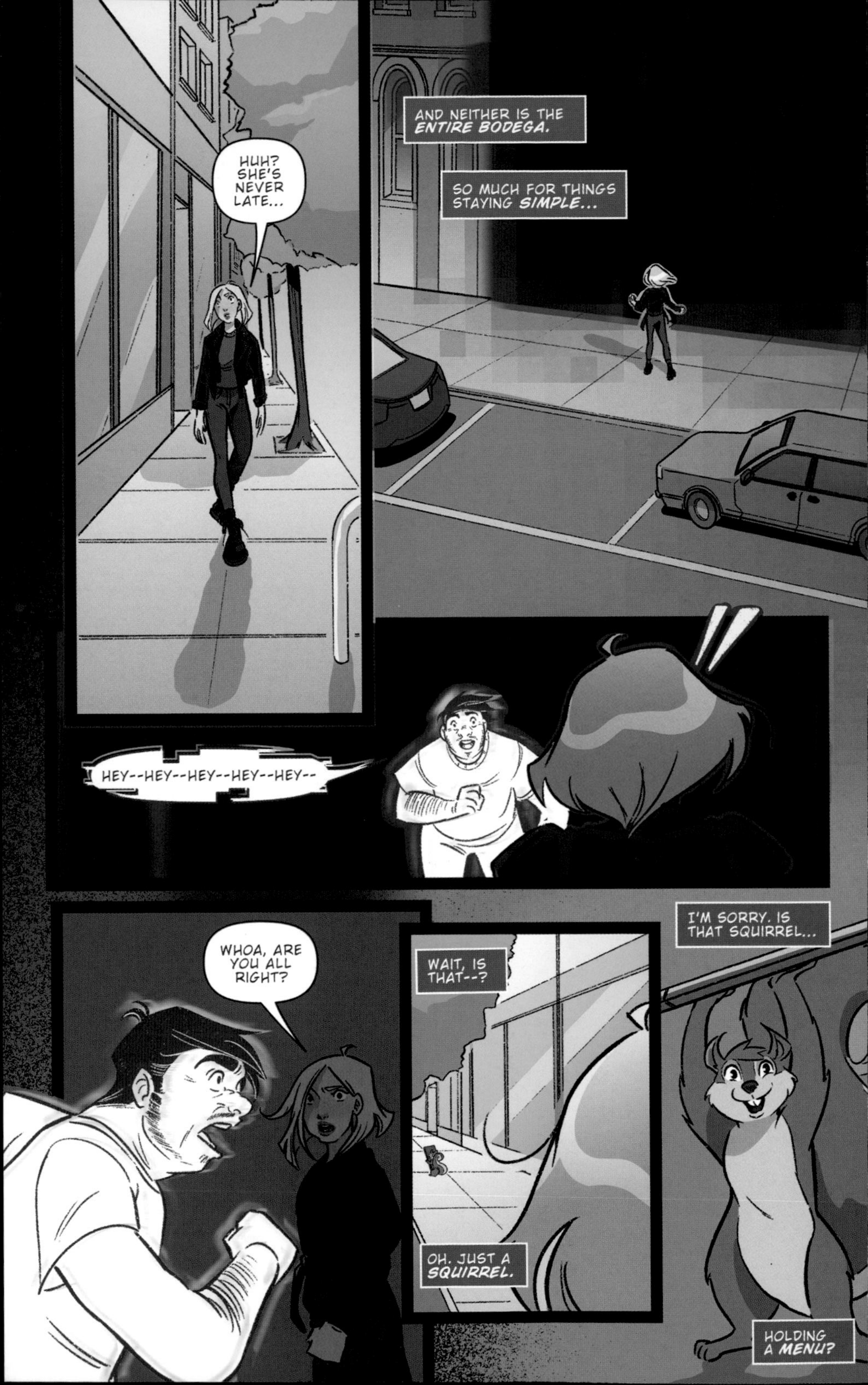
HUH? SHE'S NEVER LATE...
AND NEITHER IS THE ENTIRE BODEGA.
SO MUCH FOR THINGS STAYING SIMPLE...
HEY--HEY--HEY--HEY--HEY--
WHOA, ARE YOU ALL RIGHT?
WAIT, IS THAT--?
OH. JUST A SQUIRREL.
I'M SORRY. IS THAT SQUIRREL...
HOLDING A MENU?

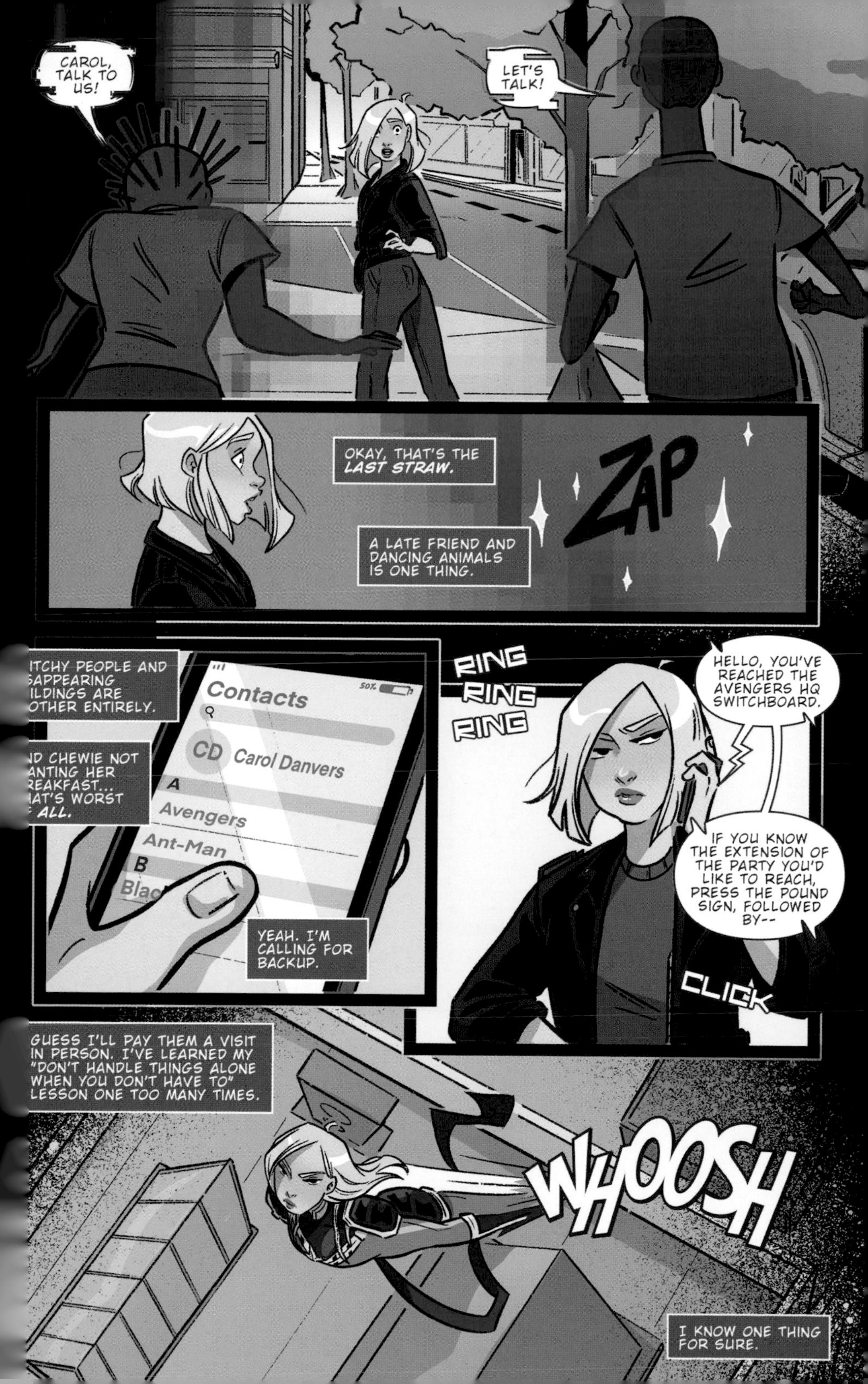
CAROL, TALK TO US!
LET'S TALK!
OKAY, THAT'S THE *LAST STRAW.*
ZAP
A LATE FRIEND AND DANCING ANIMALS IS ONE THING.
ITCHY PEOPLE AND SAPPEARING ILDINGS ARE OTHER ENTIRELY.
ND CHEWIE NOT ANTING HER REAKFAST... HAT'S WORST *ALL.*
50%
Contacts
CD
Carol Danvers
A
Avengers
Ant-Man
B
Blac
YEAH. I'M CALLING FOR BACKUP.
RING
RING
RING
HELLO, YOU'VE REACHED THE AVENGERS HQ SWITCHBOARD.
IF YOU KNOW THE EXTENSION OF THE PARTY YOU'D LIKE TO REACH, PRESS THE POUND SIGN, FOLLOWED BY--
CLICK
GUESS I'LL PAY THEM A VISIT IN PERSON. I'VE LEARNED MY "DON'T HANDLE THINGS ALONE WHEN YOU DON'T HAVE TO" LESSON ONE TOO MANY TIMES.
WHOOSH
I KNOW ONE THING FOR SURE.

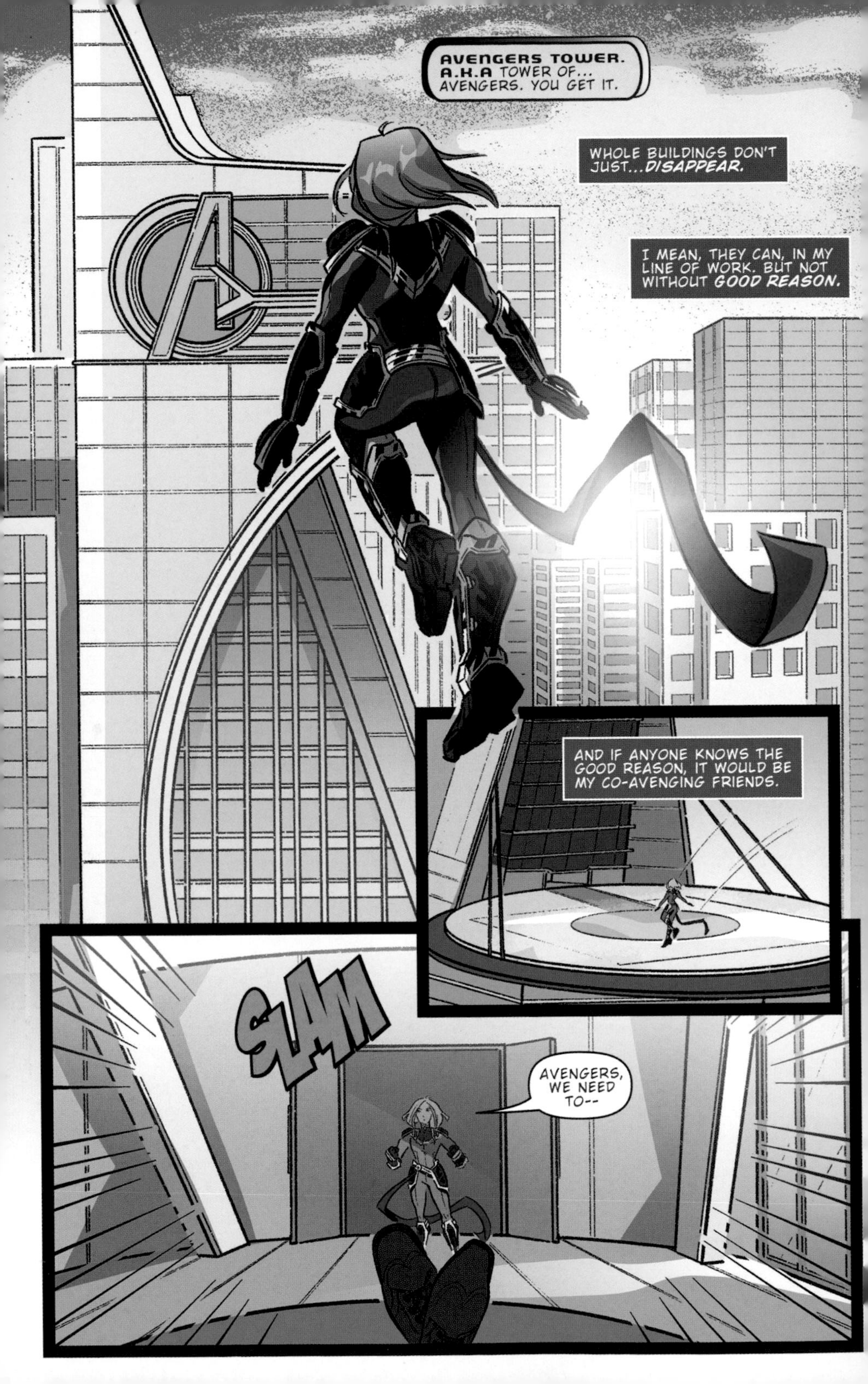
AVENGERS TOWER. A.K.A TOWER OF... AVENGERS. YOU GET IT.
WHOLE BUILDINGS DON'T JUST...DISAPPEAR.
I MEAN, THEY CAN, IN MY LINE OF WORK. BUT NOT WITHOUT GOOD REASON.
AND IF ANYONE KNOWS THE GOOD REASON, IT WOULD BE MY CO-AVENGING FRIENDS.
SLAM
AVENGERS, WE NEED TO--

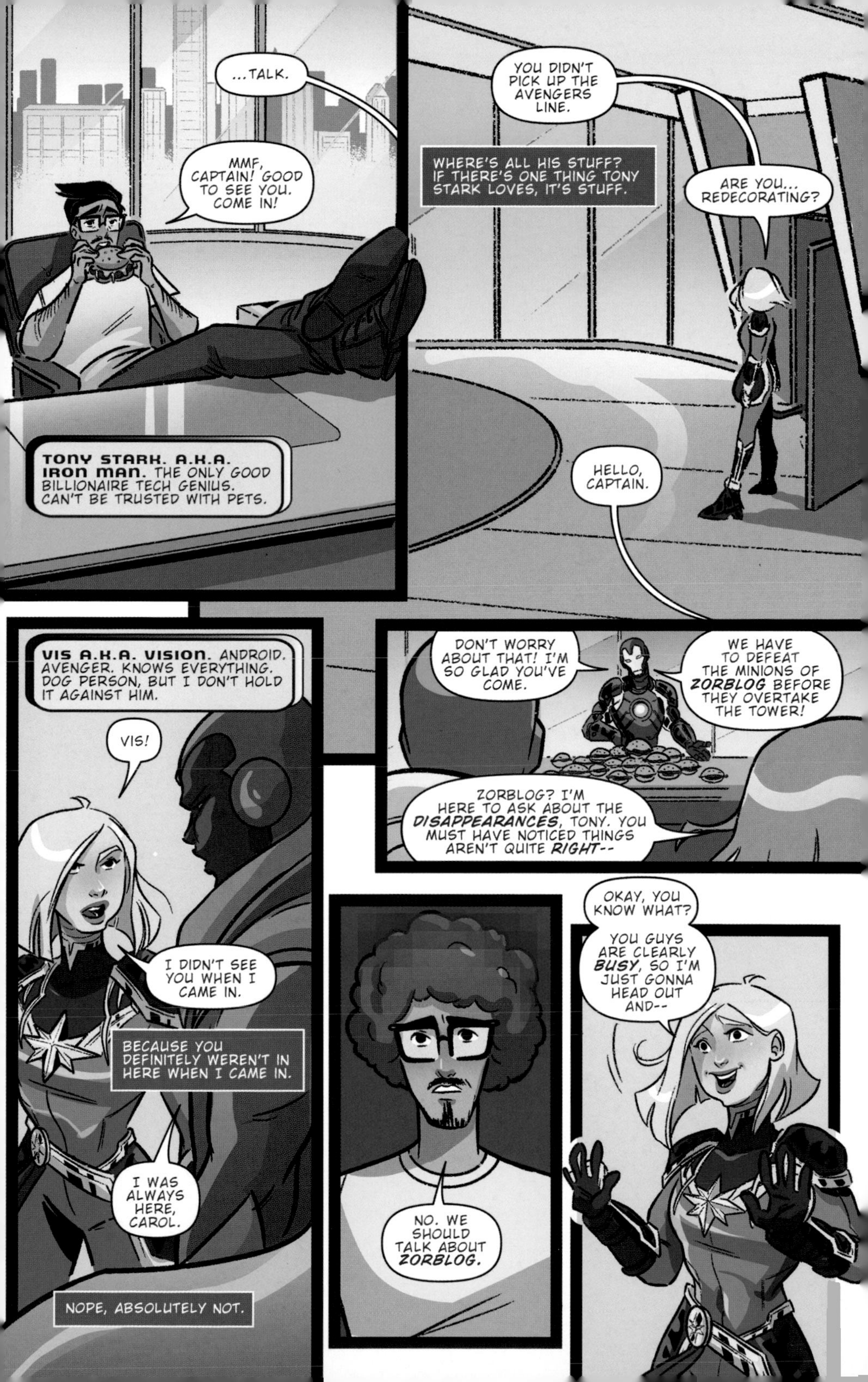
...TALK.
MMF, CAPTAIN! GOOD TO SEE YOU. COME IN!
TONY STARK. A.K.A. IRON MAN. THE ONLY GOOD BILLIONAIRE TECH GENIUS. CAN'T BE TRUSTED WITH PETS.
YOU DIDN'T PICK UP THE AVENGERS LINE.
WHERE'S ALL HIS STUFF? IF THERE'S ONE THING TONY STARK LOVES, IT'S STUFF.
ARE YOU... REDECORATING?
HELLO, CAPTAIN.
VIS A.K.A. VISION. ANDROID. AVENGER. KNOWS EVERYTHING. DOG PERSON, BUT I DON'T HOLD IT AGAINST HIM.
VIS!
I DIDN'T SEE YOU WHEN I CAME IN.
BECAUSE YOU DEFINITELY WEREN'T IN HERE WHEN I CAME IN.
I WAS ALWAYS HERE, CAROL.
NOPE, ABSOLUTELY NOT.
DON'T WORRY ABOUT THAT! I'M SO GLAD YOU'VE COME.
WE HAVE TO DEFEAT THE MINIONS OF ZORBLOG BEFORE THEY OVERTAKE THE TOWER!
ZORBLOG? I'M HERE TO ASK ABOUT THE DISAPPEARANCES, TONY. YOU MUST HAVE NOTICED THINGS AREN'T QUITE RIGHT--
NO. WE SHOULD TALK ABOUT ZORBLOG.
OKAY, YOU KNOW WHAT?
YOU GUYS ARE CLEARLY BUSY, SO I'M JUST GONNA HEAD OUT AND--

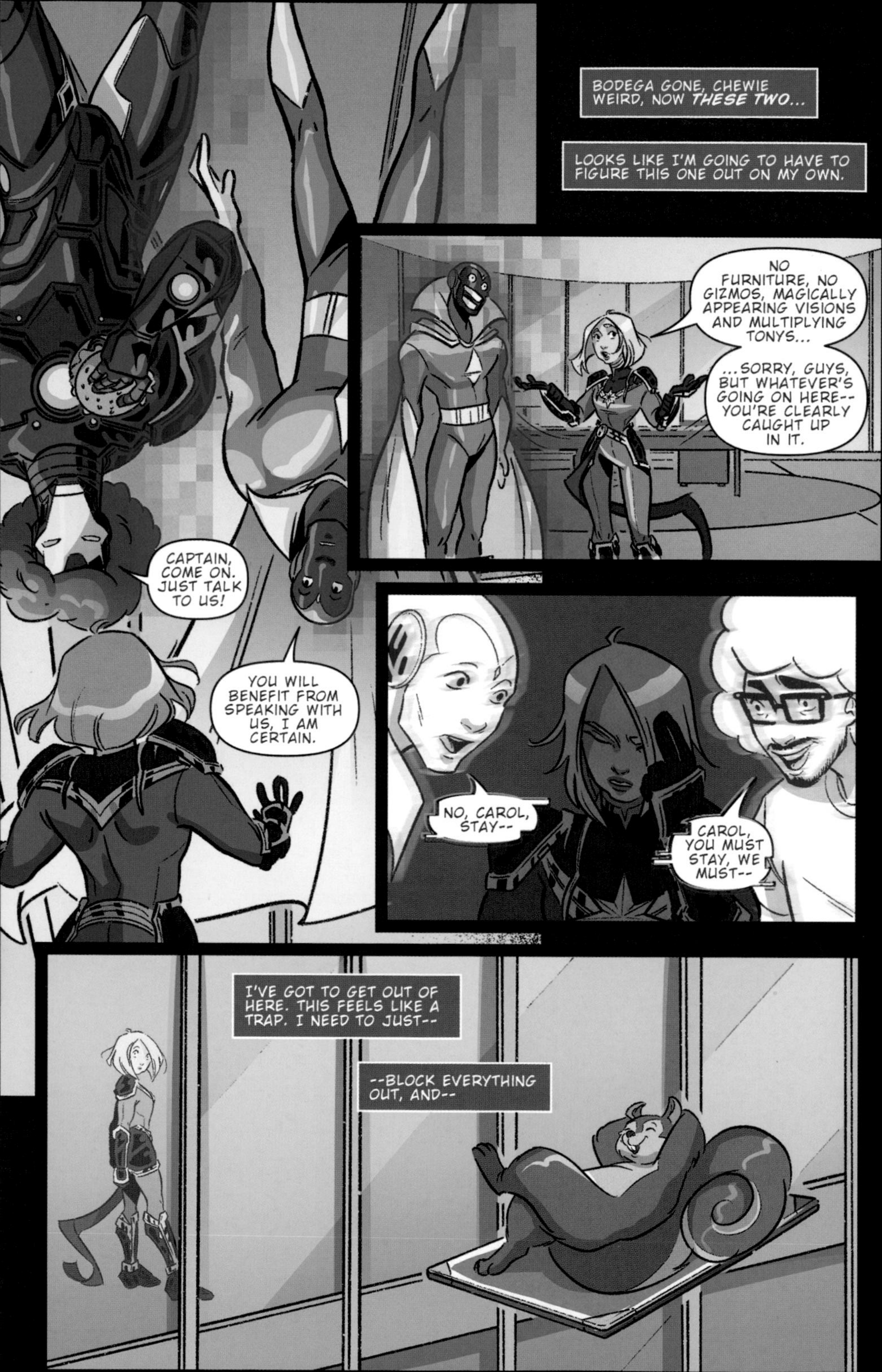
BODEGA GONE, CHEWIE WEIRD, NOW *THESE TWO...*
LOOKS LIKE I'M GOING TO HAVE TO FIGURE THIS ONE OUT ON MY OWN.
CAPTAIN, COME ON. JUST TALK TO US!
YOU WILL BENEFIT FROM SPEAKING WITH US, I AM CERTAIN.
NO FURNITURE, NO GIZMOS, MAGICALLY APPEARING VISIONS AND MULTIPLYING TONYS...
...SORRY, GUYS, BUT WHATEVER'S GOING ON HERE-- YOU'RE CLEARLY CAUGHT UP IN IT.
NO, CAROL, STAY--
CAROL, YOU MUST STAY, WE MUST--
I'VE GOT TO GET OUT OF HERE. THIS FEELS LIKE A TRAP. I NEED TO JUST--
--BLOCK EVERYTHING OUT, AND--

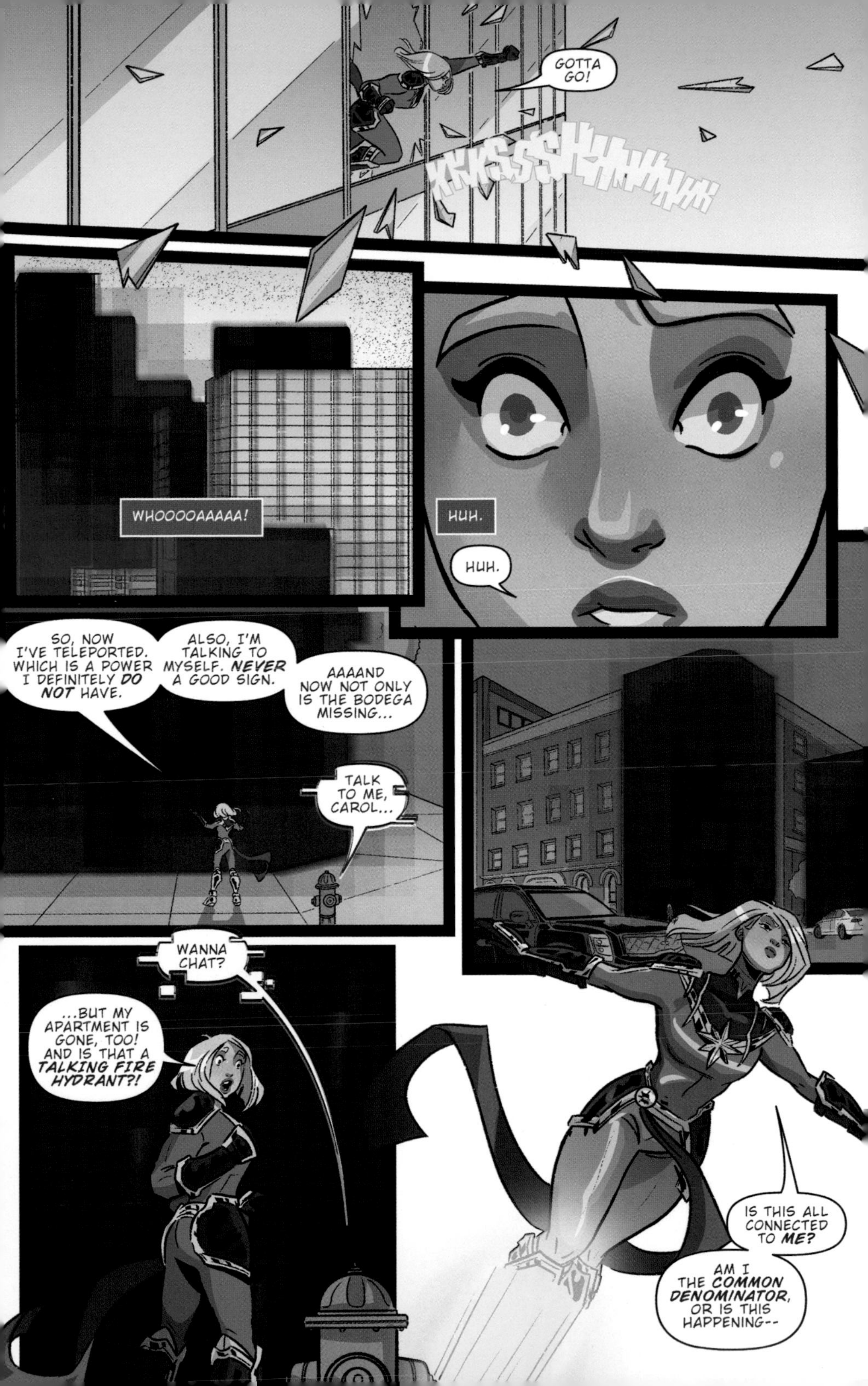
GOTTA GO!
WHOOOOAAAAA!
HUH.
HUH.
SO, NOW I'VE TELEPORTED. WHICH IS A POWER I DEFINITELY **DO NOT** HAVE.
ALSO, I'M TALKING TO MYSELF. **NEVER** A GOOD SIGN.
AAAAND NOW NOT ONLY IS THE BODEGA MISSING...
TALK TO ME, CAROL...
WANNA CHAT?
...BUT MY APARTMENT IS GONE, TOO! AND IS THAT A **TALKING FIRE HYDRANT?!**
IS THIS ALL CONNECTED TO **ME?**
AM I THE **COMMON DENOMINATOR**, OR IS THIS HAPPENING--

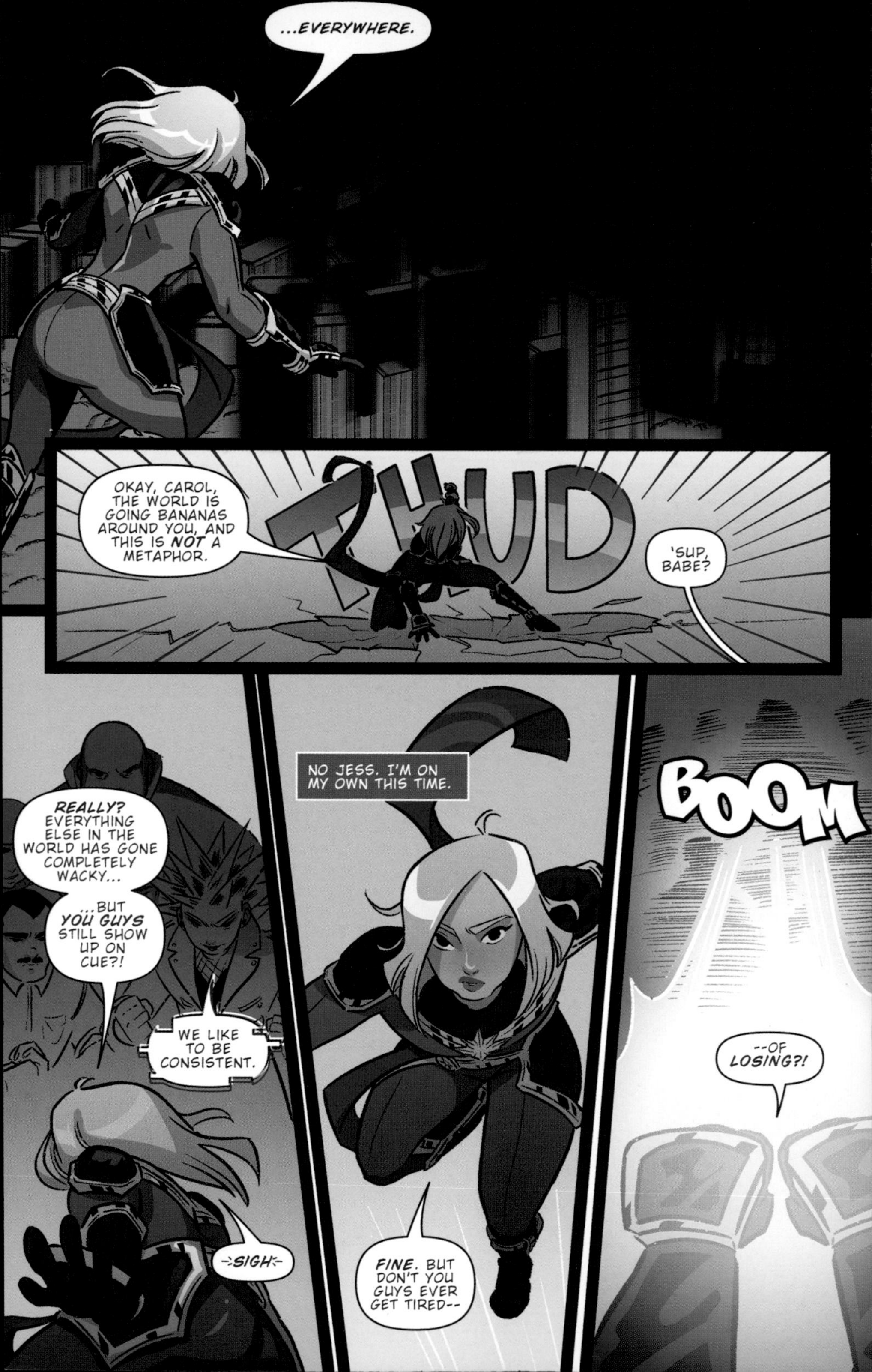
...EVERYWHERE.
THUD
OKAY, CAROL, THE WORLD IS GOING BANANAS AROUND YOU, AND THIS IS NOT A METAPHOR.
'SUP, BABE?
REALLY? EVERYTHING ELSE IN THE WORLD HAS GONE COMPLETELY WACKY...
...BUT YOU GUYS STILL SHOW UP ON CUE?!
WE LIKE TO BE CONSISTENT.
-SIGH-
NO JESS. I'M ON MY OWN THIS TIME.
FINE. BUT DON'T YOU GUYS EVER GET TIRED--
BOOM
--OF LOSING?!

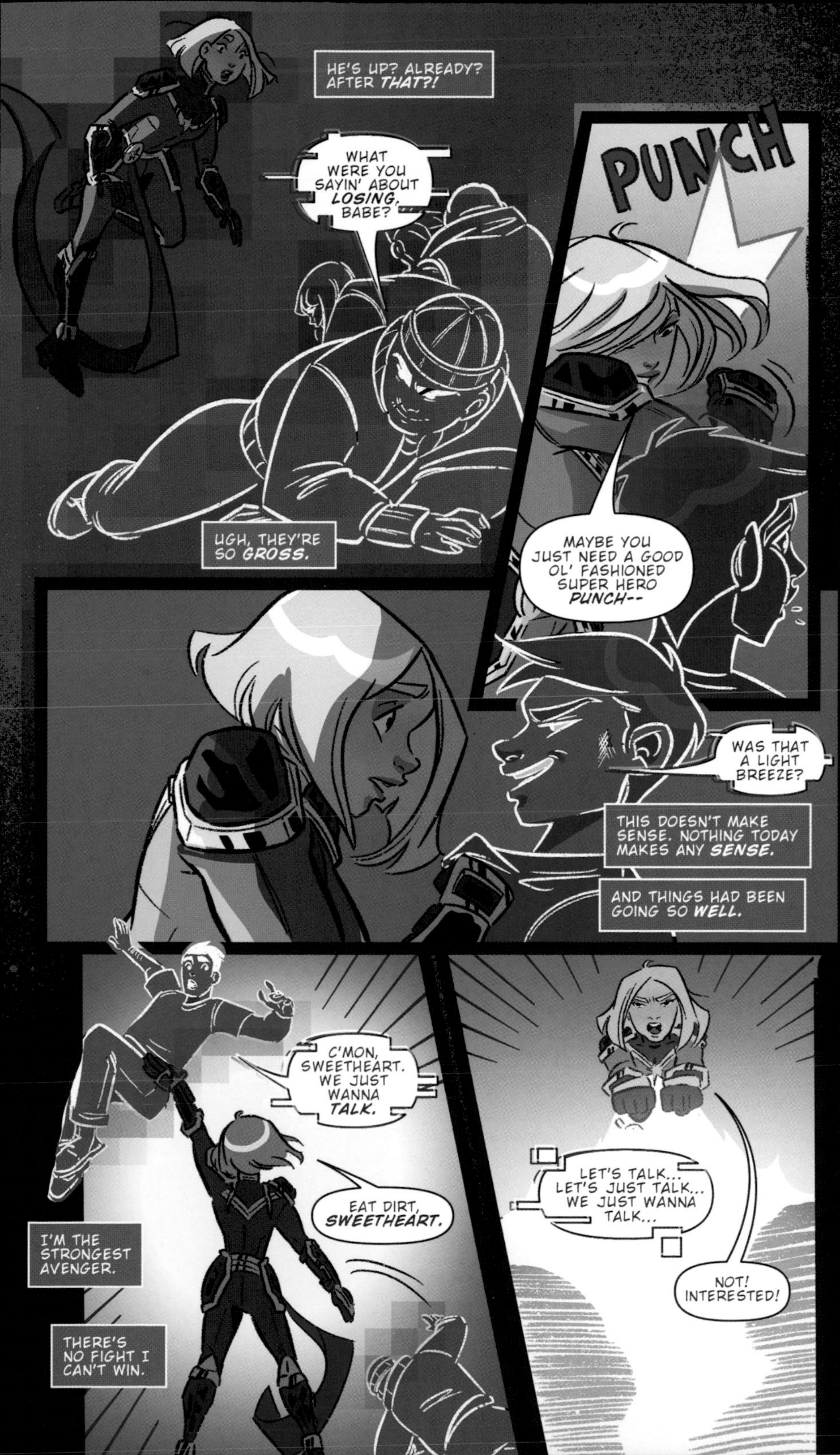
HE'S UP? ALREADY? AFTER THAT?!
WHAT WERE YOU SAYIN' ABOUT LOSING, BABE?
UGH, THEY'RE SO GROSS.
PUNCH
MAYBE YOU JUST NEED A GOOD OL' FASHIONED SUPER HERO PUNCH--
WAS THAT A LIGHT BREEZE?
THIS DOESN'T MAKE SENSE. NOTHING TODAY MAKES ANY SENSE.
AND THINGS HAD BEEN GOING SO WELL.
C'MON, SWEETHEART. WE JUST WANNA TALK.
EAT DIRT, SWEETHEART.
I'M THE STRONGEST AVENGER.
THERE'S NO FIGHT I CAN'T WIN.
LET'S TALK... LET'S JUST TALK... WE JUST WANNA TALK...
NOT! INTERESTED!

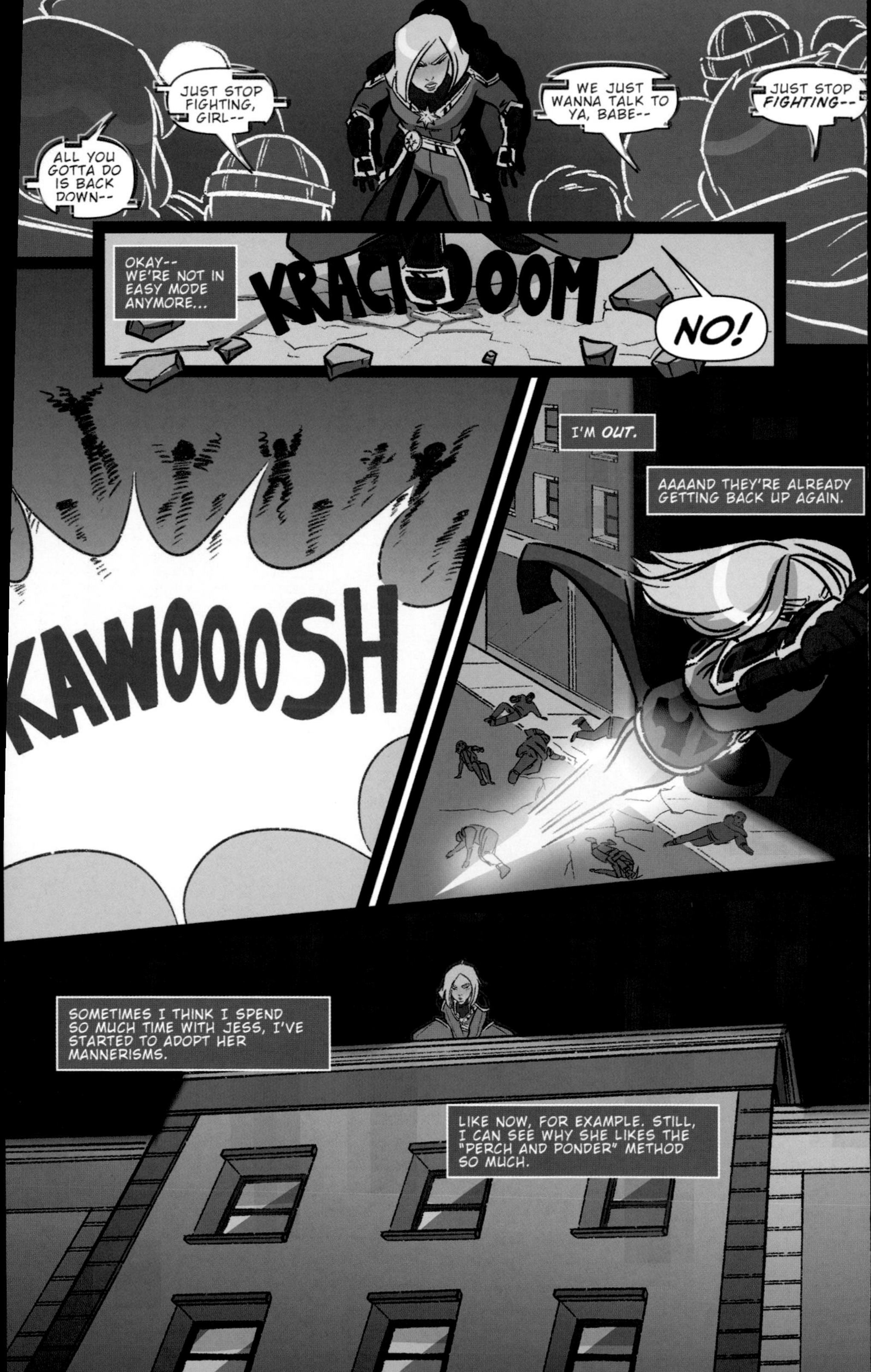
JUST STOP FIGHTING, GIRL--
ALL YOU GOTTA DO IS BACK DOWN--
WE JUST WANNA TALK TO YA, BABE--
JUST STOP *FIGHTING*--
OKAY-- WE'RE NOT IN EASY MODE ANYMORE...
KRACKOOOM
NO!
KAWOOOSH
I'M *OUT.*
AAAAND THEY'RE ALREADY GETTING BACK UP AGAIN.
SOMETIMES I THINK I SPEND SO MUCH TIME WITH JESS, I'VE STARTED TO ADOPT HER MANNERISMS.
LIKE NOW, FOR EXAMPLE. STILL, I CAN SEE WHY SHE LIKES THE "PERCH AND PONDER" METHOD SO MUCH.

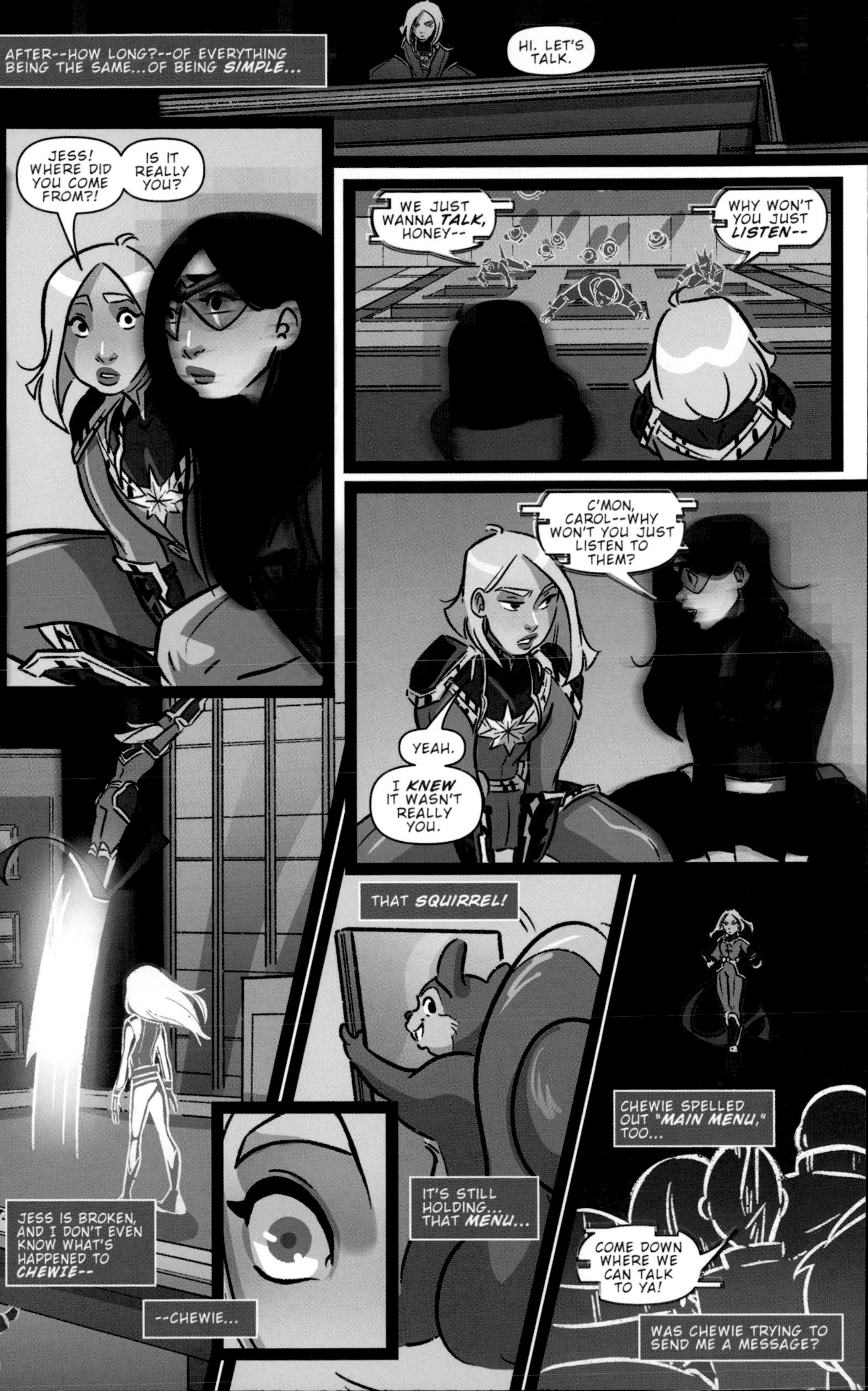
AFTER--HOW LONG?--OF EVERYTHING BEING THE SAME...OF BEING SIMPLE...
HI. LET'S TALK.
JESS! WHERE DID YOU COME FROM?!
IS IT REALLY YOU?
WE JUST WANNA TALK, HONEY--
WHY WON'T YOU JUST LISTEN--
C'MON, CAROL--WHY WON'T YOU JUST LISTEN TO THEM?
YEAH.
I KNEW IT WASN'T REALLY YOU.
THAT SQUIRREL!
JESS IS BROKEN, AND I DON'T EVEN KNOW WHAT'S HAPPENED TO CHEWIE--
--CHEWIE...
IT'S STILL HOLDING... THAT MENU...
CHEWIE SPELLED OUT "MAIN MENU," TOO...
COME DOWN WHERE WE CAN TALK TO YA!
WAS CHEWIE TRYING TO SEND ME A MESSAGE?

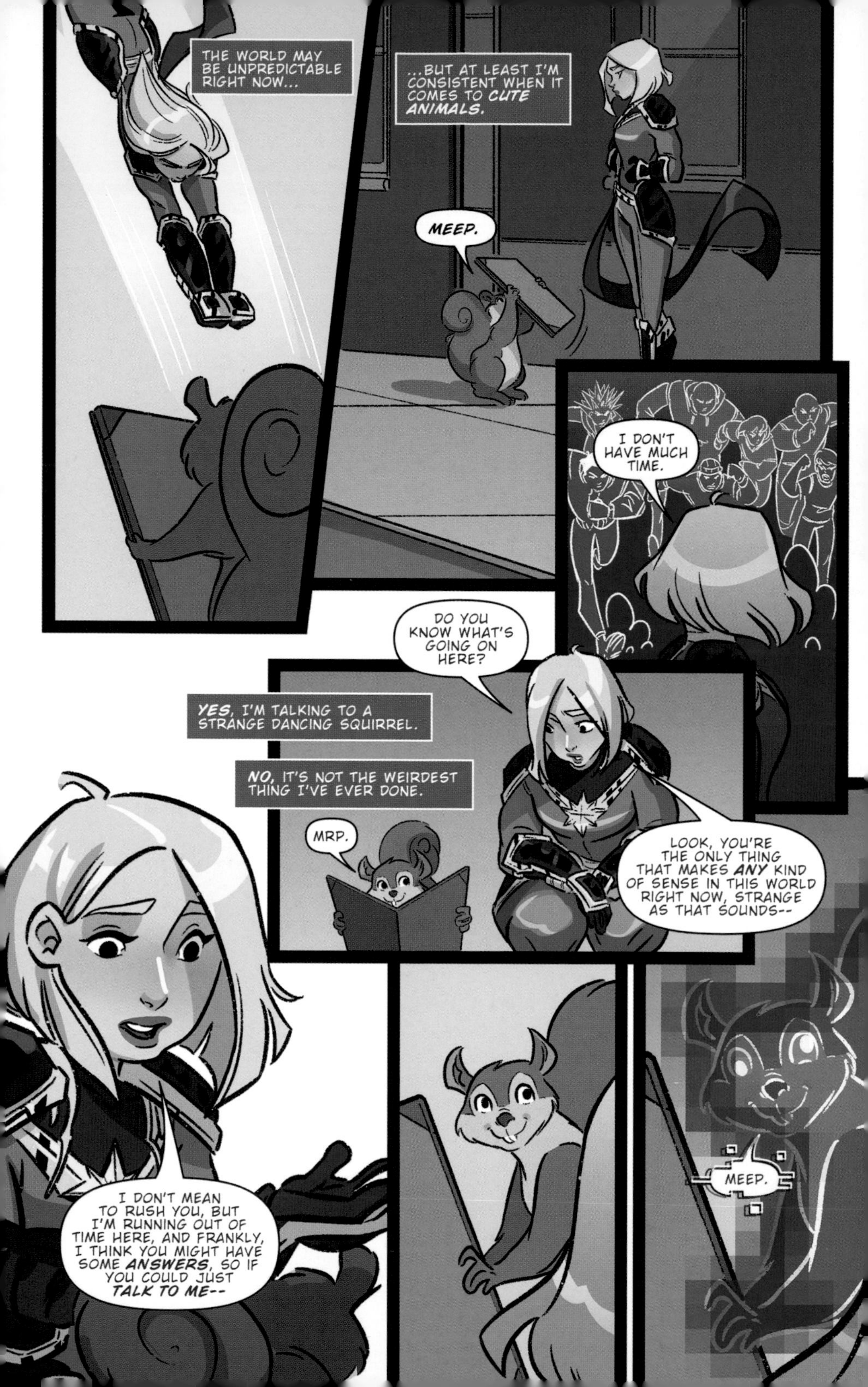
THE WORLD MAY BE UNPREDICTABLE RIGHT NOW...
...BUT AT LEAST I'M CONSISTENT WHEN IT COMES TO CUTE ANIMALS.
MEEP.
I DON'T HAVE MUCH TIME.
DO YOU KNOW WHAT'S GOING ON HERE?
YES, I'M TALKING TO A STRANGE DANCING SQUIRREL.
NO, IT'S NOT THE WEIRDEST THING I'VE EVER DONE.
MRP.
LOOK, YOU'RE THE ONLY THING THAT MAKES ANY KIND OF SENSE IN THIS WORLD RIGHT NOW, STRANGE AS THAT SOUNDS--
I DON'T MEAN TO RUSH YOU, BUT I'M RUNNING OUT OF TIME HERE, AND FRANKLY, I THINK YOU MIGHT HAVE SOME ANSWERS, SO IF YOU COULD JUST TALK TO ME--
MEEP.

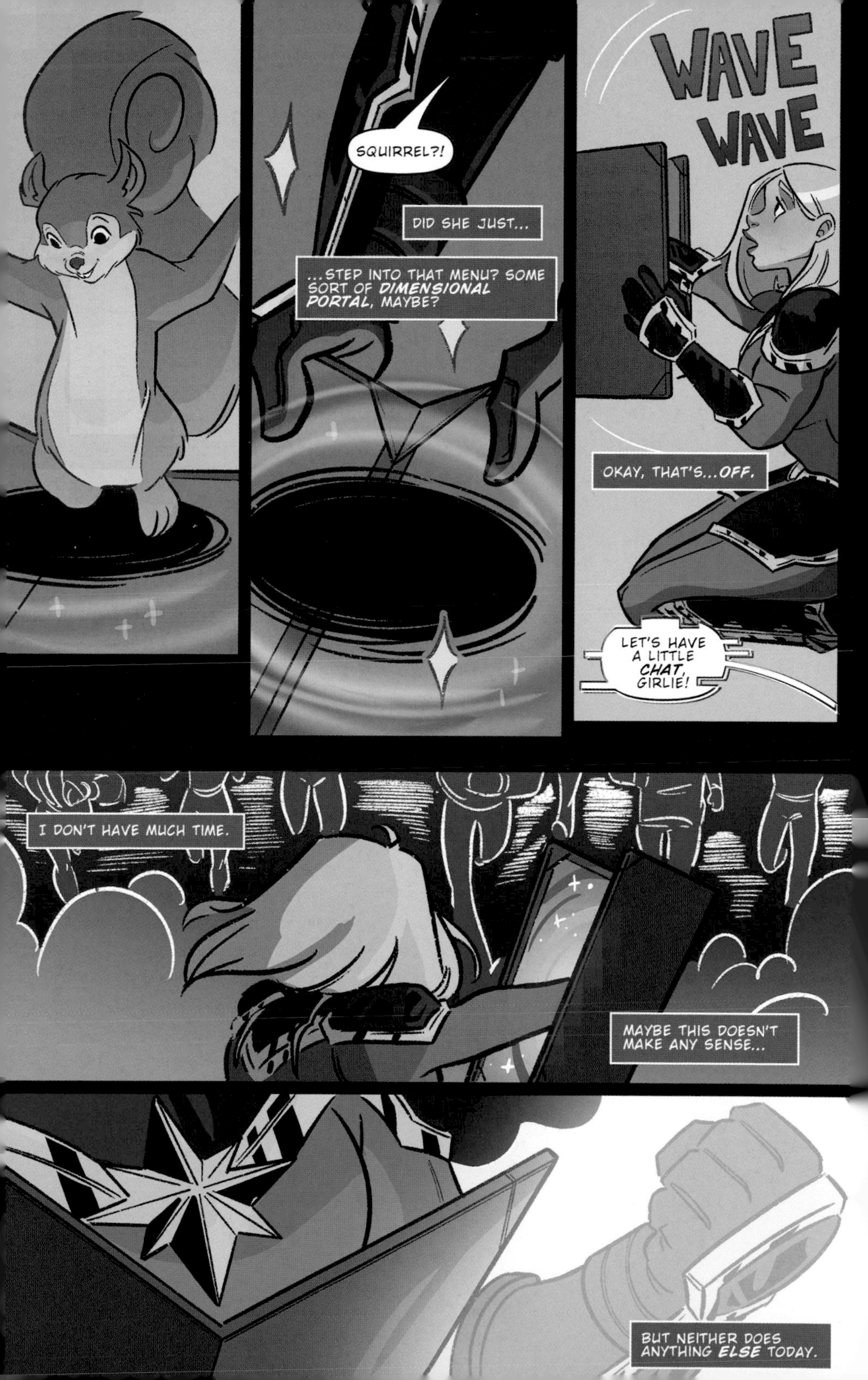
SQUIRREL?!
DID SHE JUST...
...STEP INTO THAT MENU? SOME SORT OF DIMENSIONAL PORTAL, MAYBE?
WAVE WAVE
OKAY, THAT'S...OFF.
LET'S HAVE A LITTLE CHAT, GIRLIE!
I DON'T HAVE MUCH TIME.
MAYBE THIS DOESN'T MAKE ANY SENSE...
BUT NEITHER DOES ANYTHING ELSE TODAY.

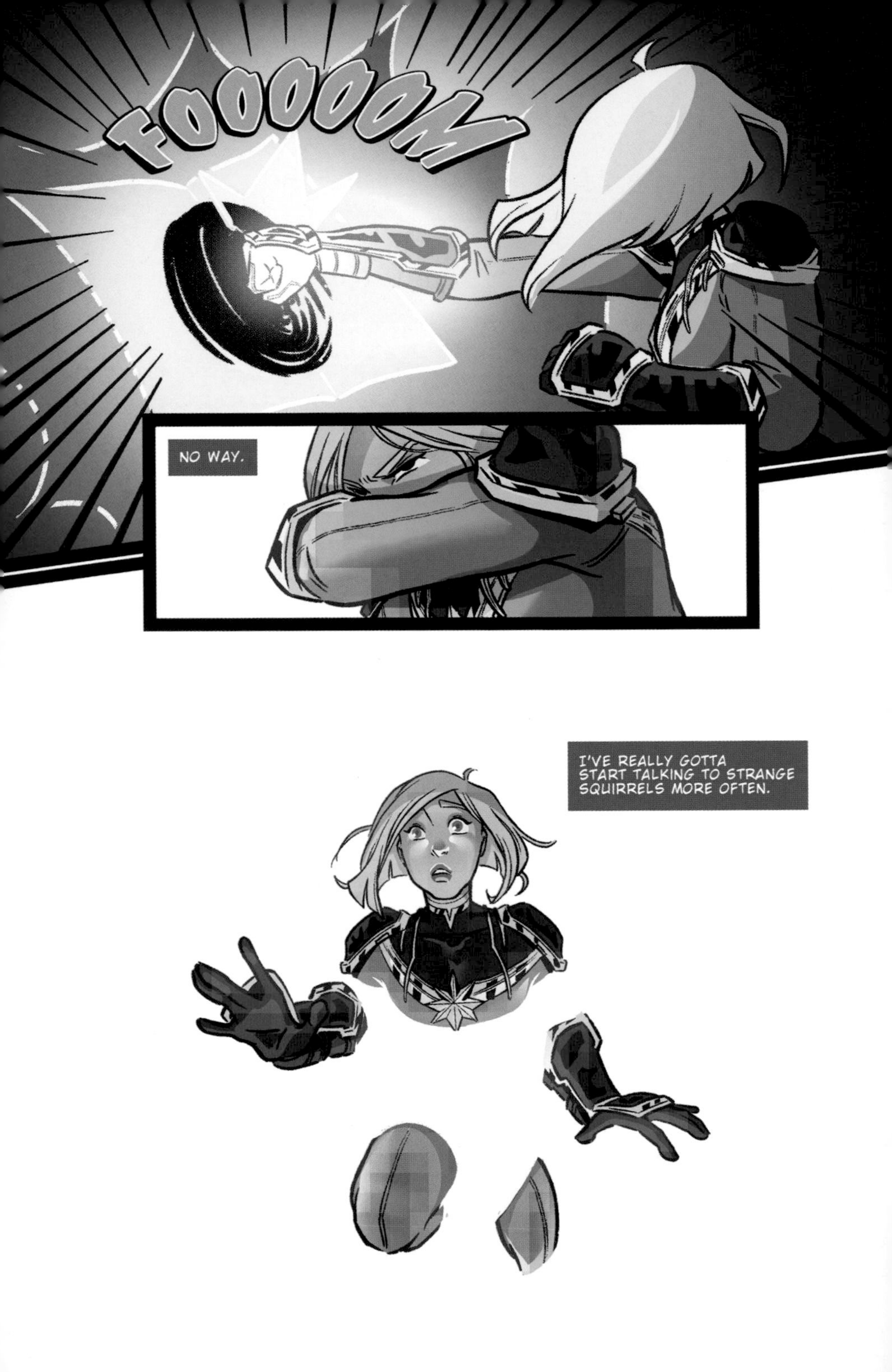
FOOOOOM
NO WAY.
I'VE REALLY GOTTA START TALKING TO STRANGE SQUIRRELS MORE OFTEN.

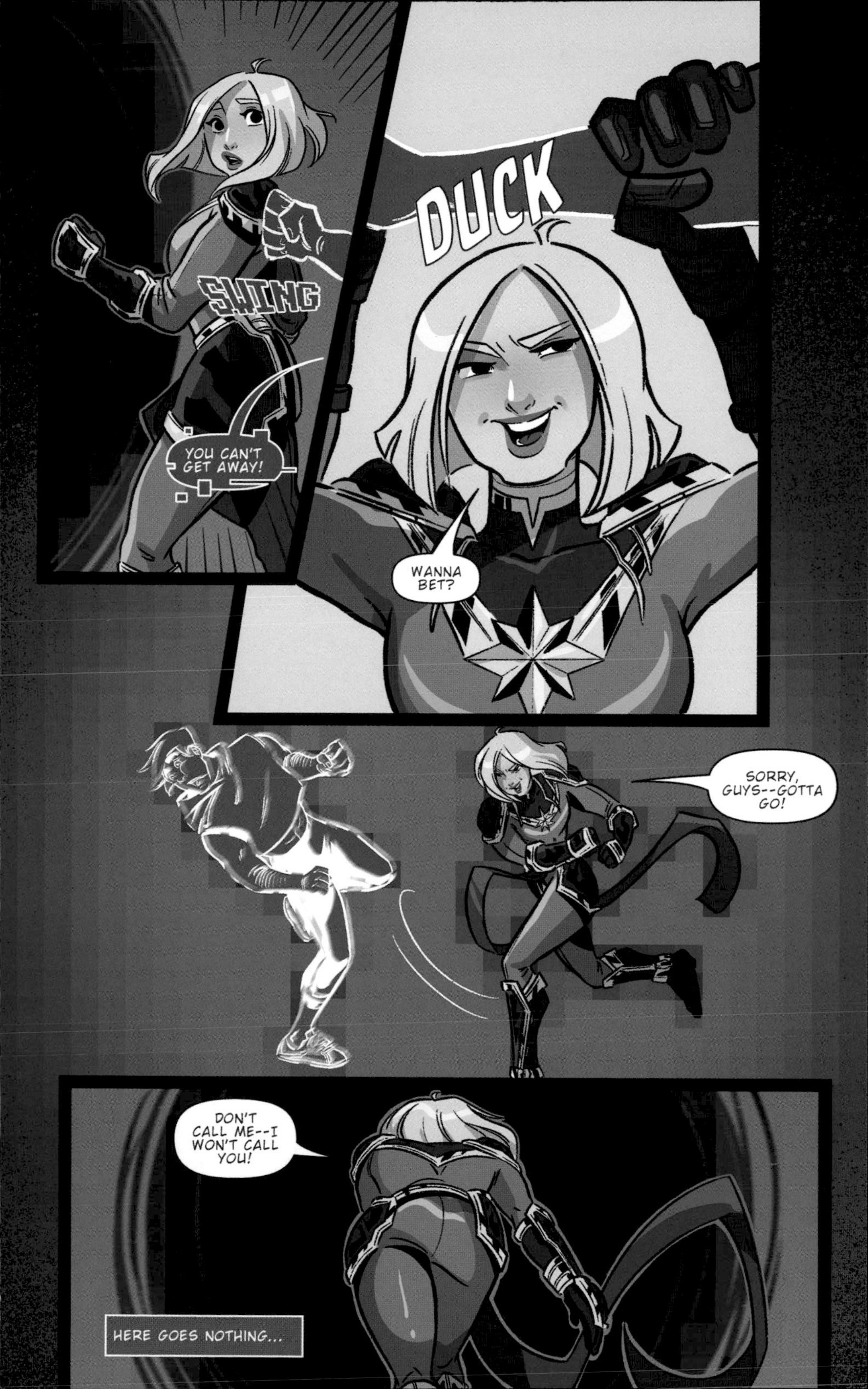
SHING
YOU CAN'T GET AWAY!
DUCK
WANNA BET?
SORRY, GUYS--GOTTA GO!
DON'T CALL ME--I WON'T CALL YOU!
HERE GOES NOTHING...

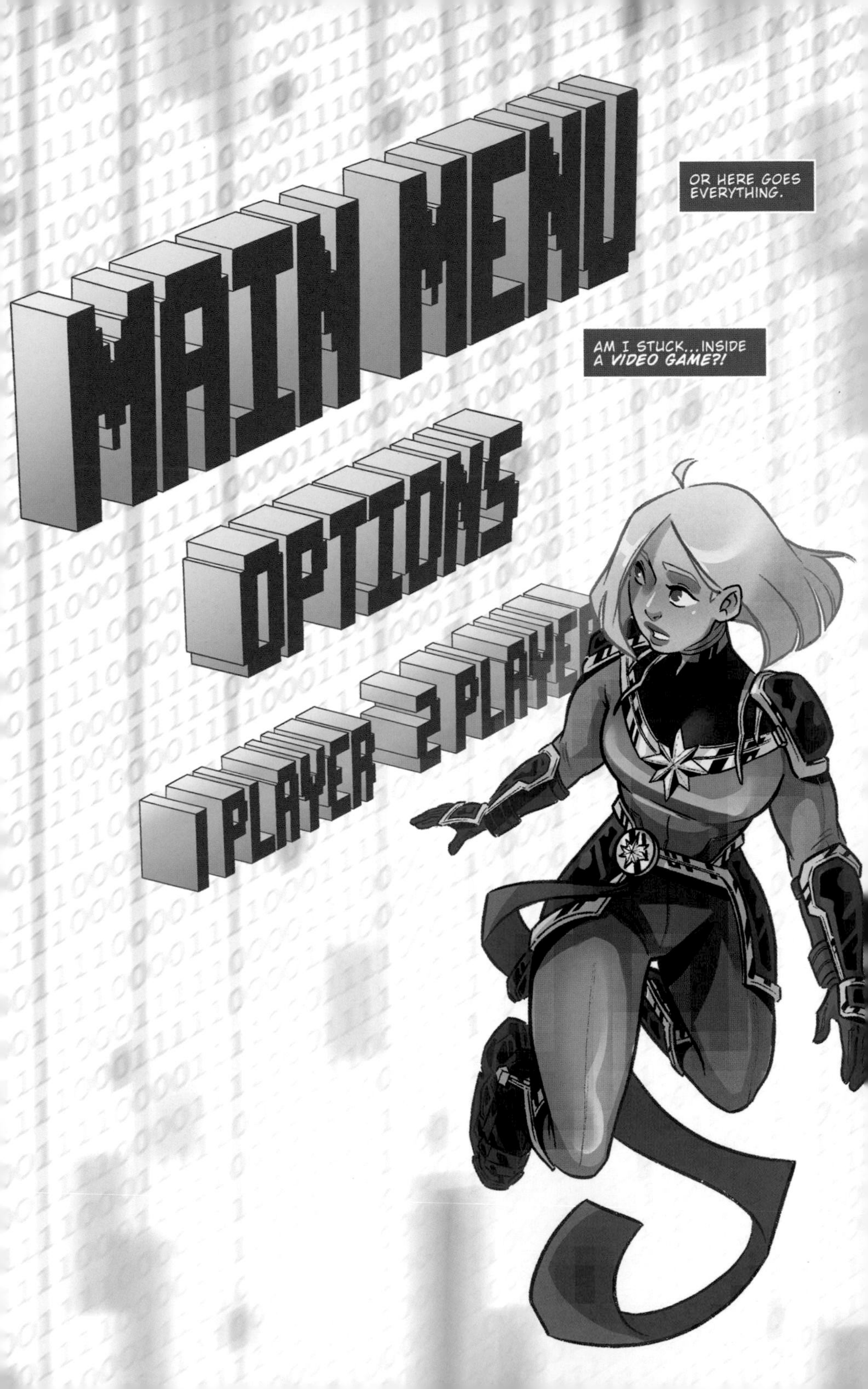
OR HERE GOES EVERYTHING.
MAIN MENU
AM I STUCK...INSIDE A VIDEO GAME?!
OPTIONS
1 PLAYER
2 PLAYER

GAME ON! PART TWO

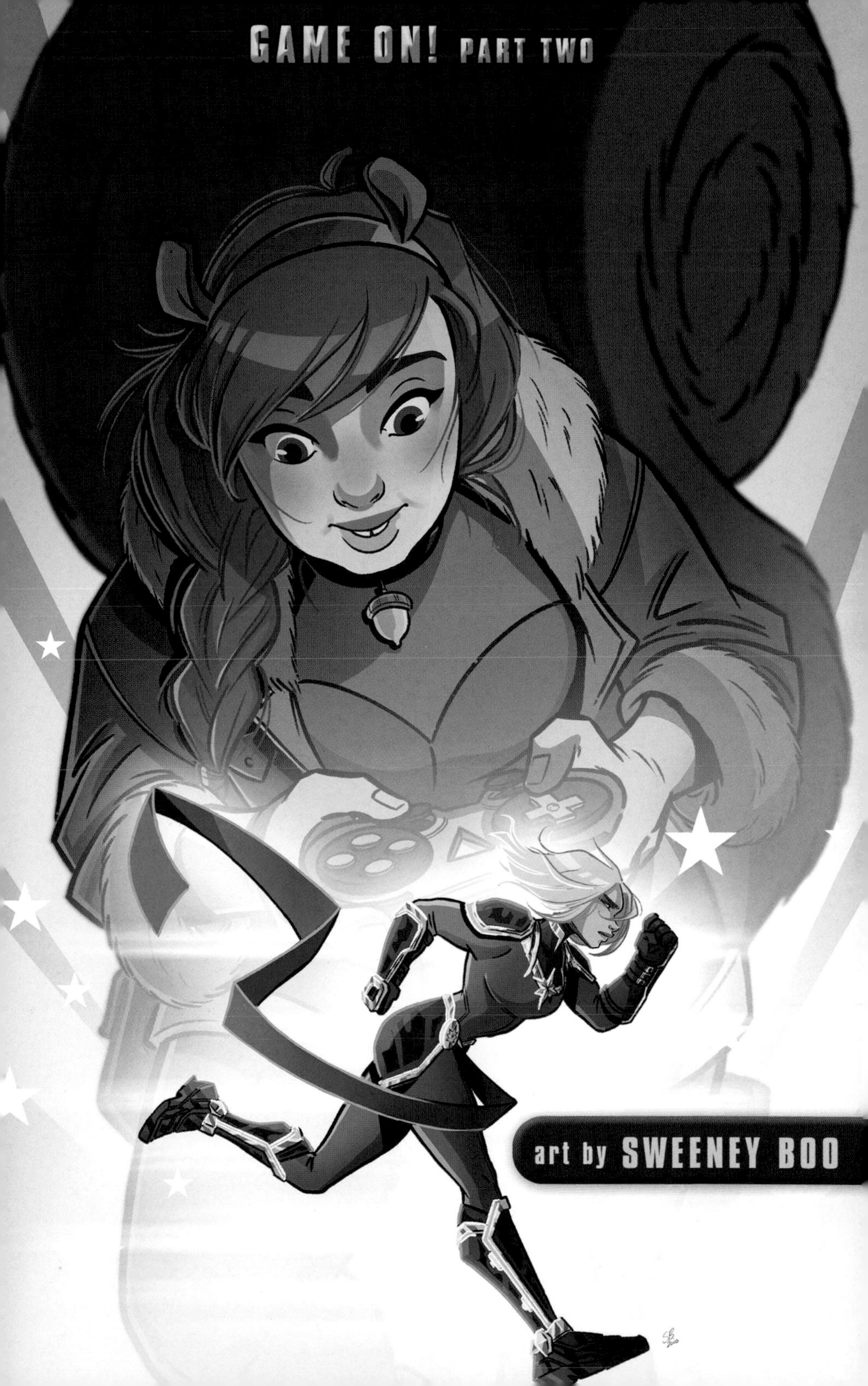

art by SWEENEY BOO

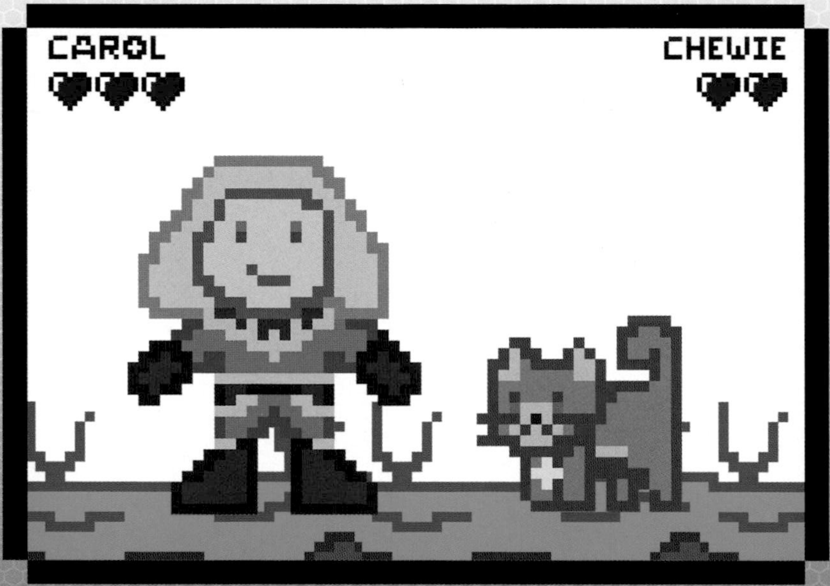
CAROL
CHEWIE

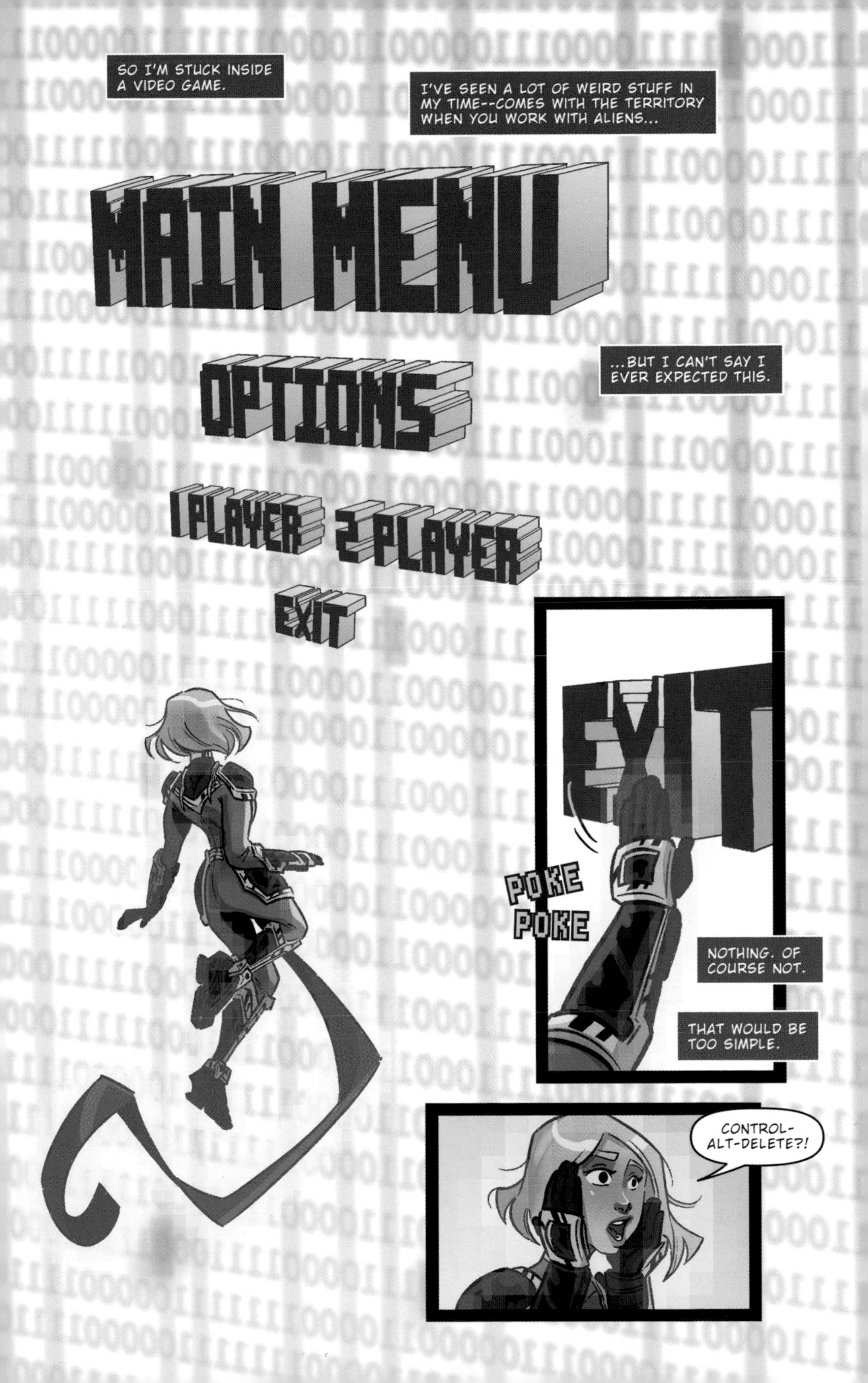
SO I'M STUCK INSIDE A VIDEO GAME.
I'VE SEEN A LOT OF WEIRD STUFF IN MY TIME--COMES WITH THE TERRITORY WHEN YOU WORK WITH ALIENS...
MAIN MENU
OPTIONS
1 PLAYER
2 PLAYER
EXIT
...BUT I CAN'T SAY I EVER EXPECTED THIS.
EXIT
POKE
POKE
NOTHING. OF COURSE NOT.
THAT WOULD BE TOO SIMPLE.
CONTROL-ALT-DELETE?!

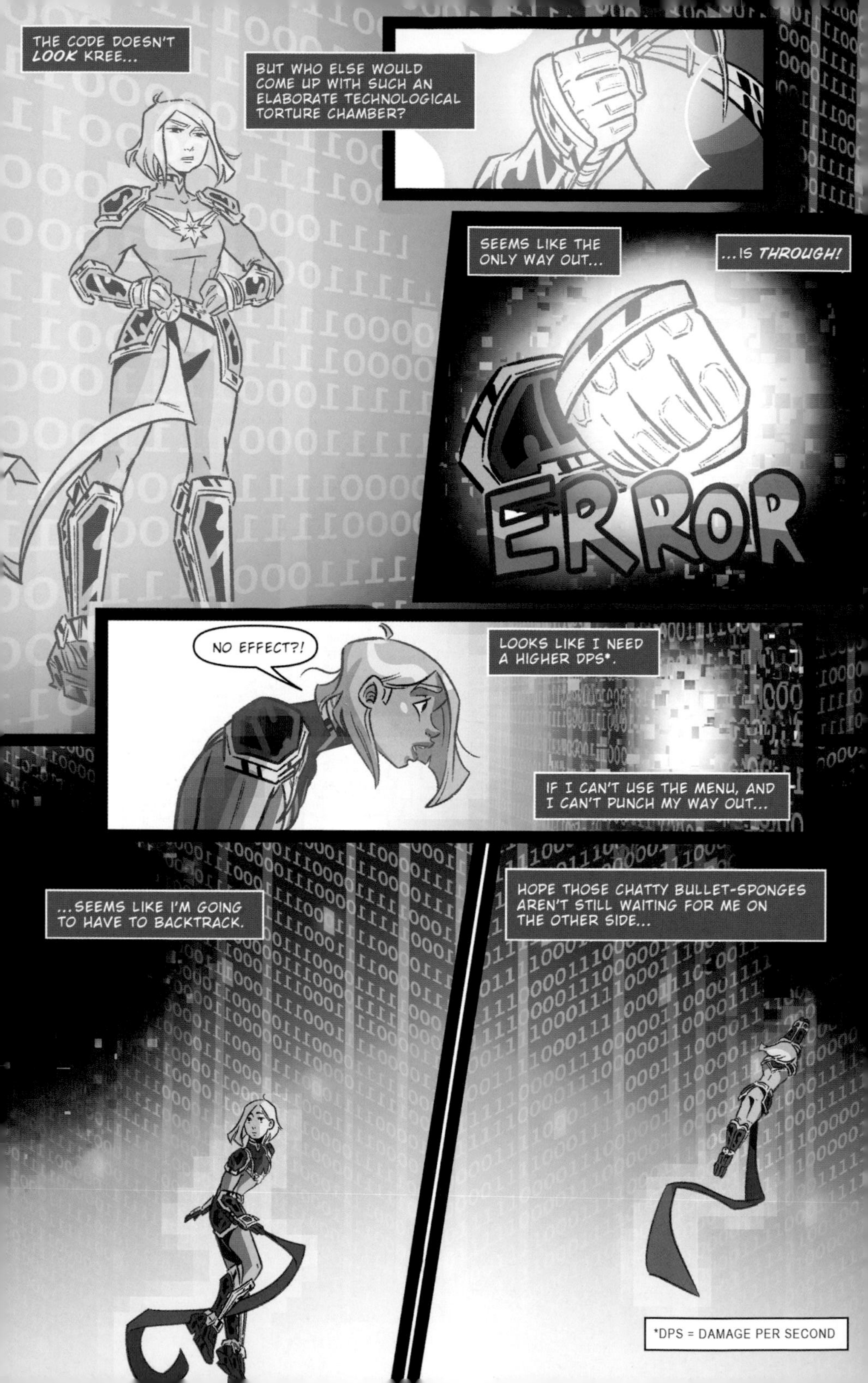
THE CODE DOESN'T *LOOK* KREE...
BUT WHO ELSE WOULD COME UP WITH SUCH AN ELABORATE TECHNOLOGICAL TORTURE CHAMBER?
SEEMS LIKE THE ONLY WAY OUT...
...IS *THROUGH!*
ERROR
NO EFFECT?!
LOOKS LIKE I NEED A HIGHER DPS*.
IF I CAN'T USE THE MENU, AND I CAN'T PUNCH MY WAY OUT...
...SEEMS LIKE I'M GOING TO HAVE TO BACKTRACK.
HOPE THOSE CHATTY BULLET-SPONGES AREN'T STILL WAITING FOR ME ON THE OTHER SIDE...
*DPS = DAMAGE PER SECOND

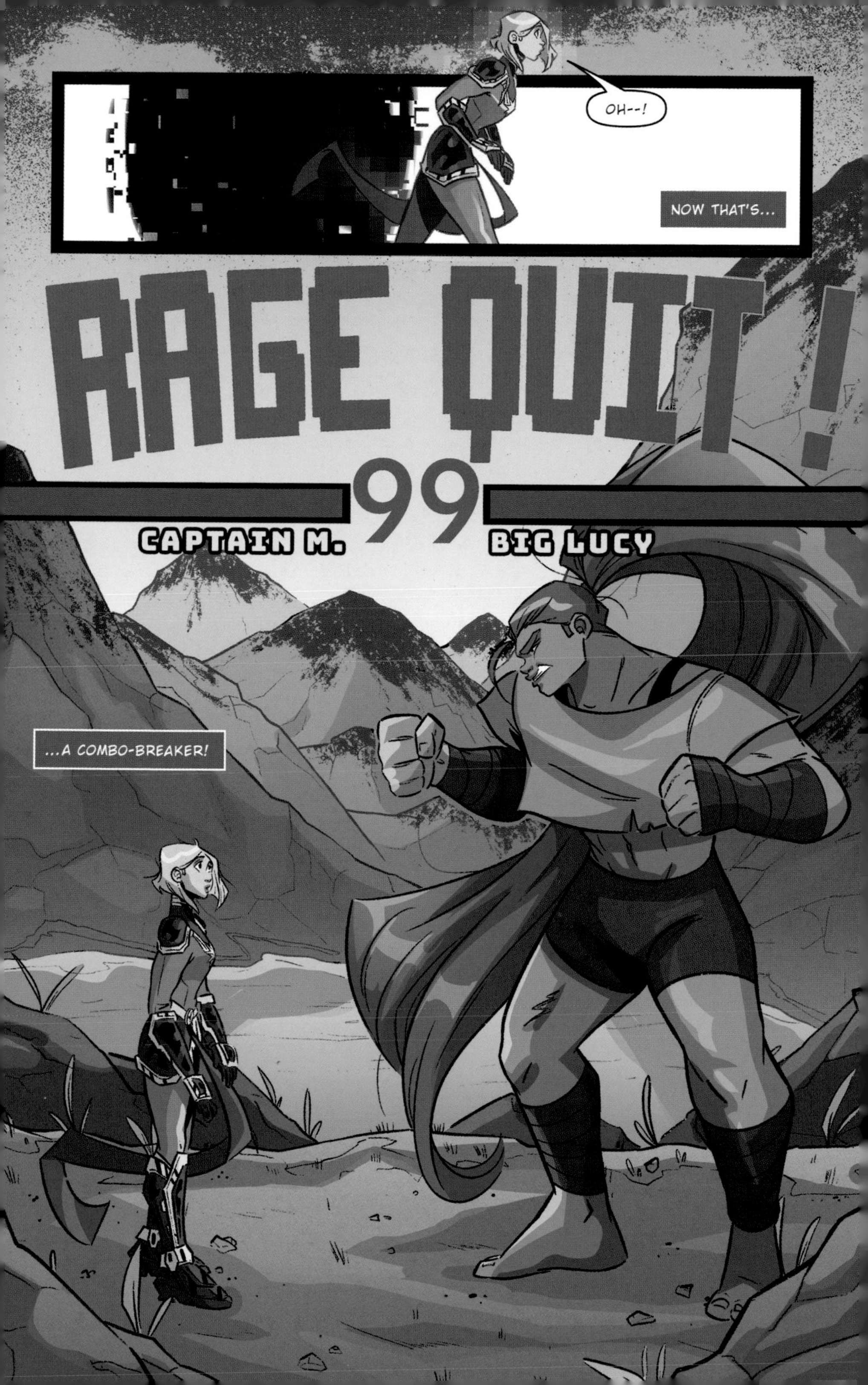
OH--!
NOW THAT'S...
RAGE QUIT!
99
CAPTAIN M.
BIG LUCY
...A COMBO-BREAKER!

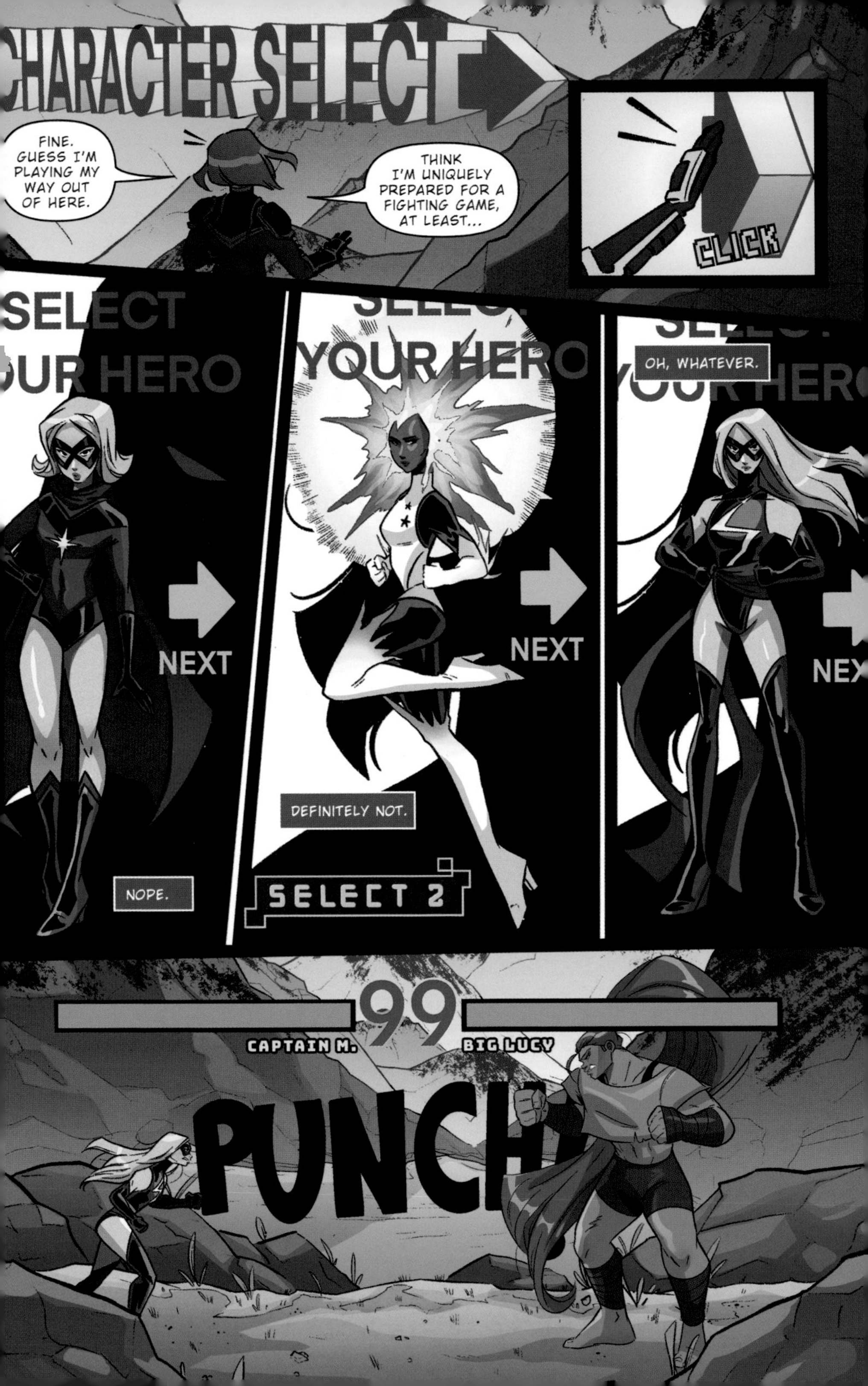

CHARACTER SELECT
FINE. GUESS I'M PLAYING MY WAY OUT OF HERE.
THINK I'M UNIQUELY PREPARED FOR A FIGHTING GAME, AT LEAST...
CLICK
SELECT YOUR HERO
NEXT
NOPE.
SELECT YOUR HERO
NEXT
DEFINITELY NOT.
SELECT 2
OH, WHATEVER.
99
CAPTAIN M.
BIG LUCY
PUNCH

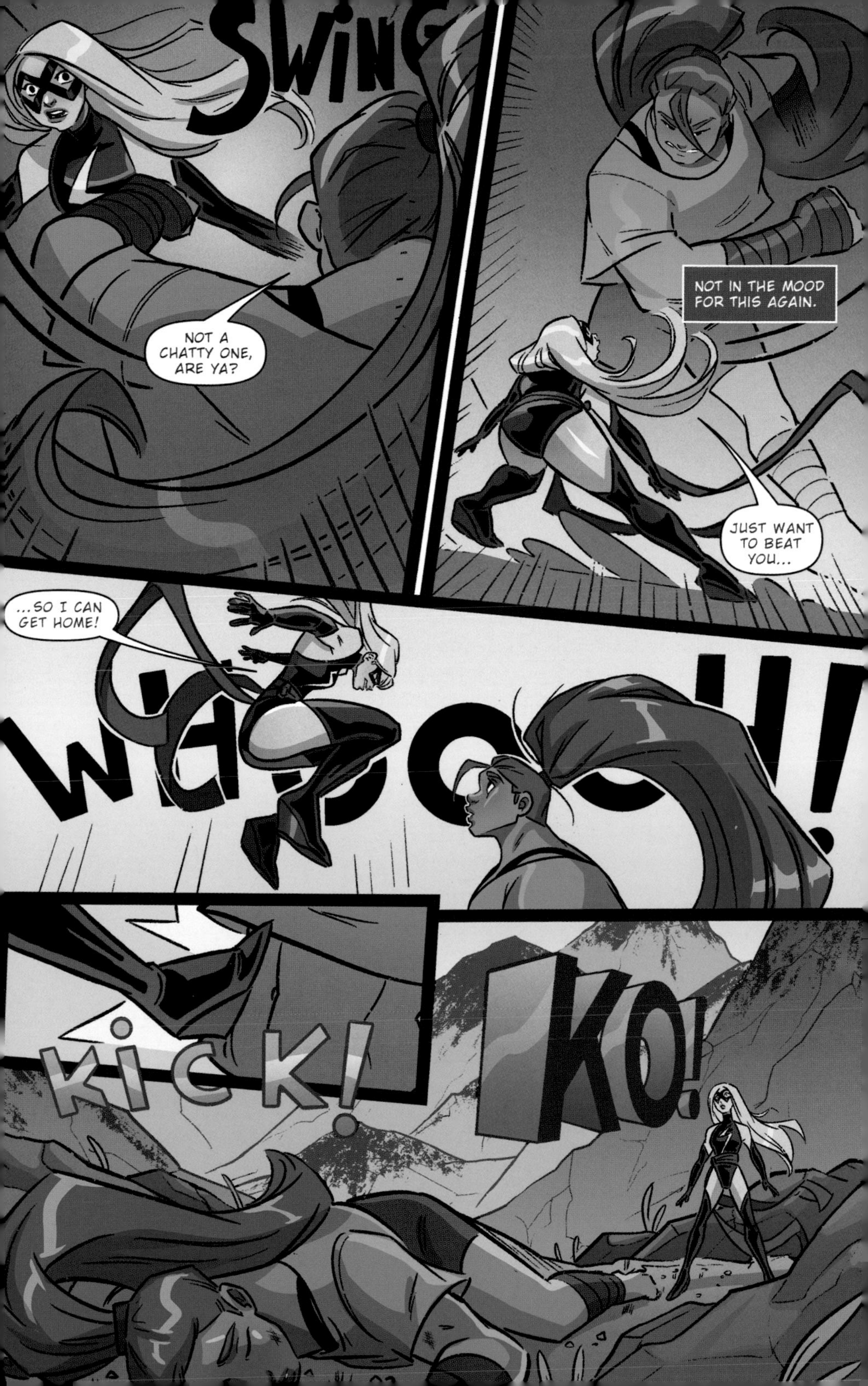
SWING
NOT A CHATTY ONE, ARE YA?
NOT IN THE MOOD FOR THIS AGAIN.
JUST WANT TO BEAT YOU...
...SO I CAN GET HOME!
KICK!
KO!

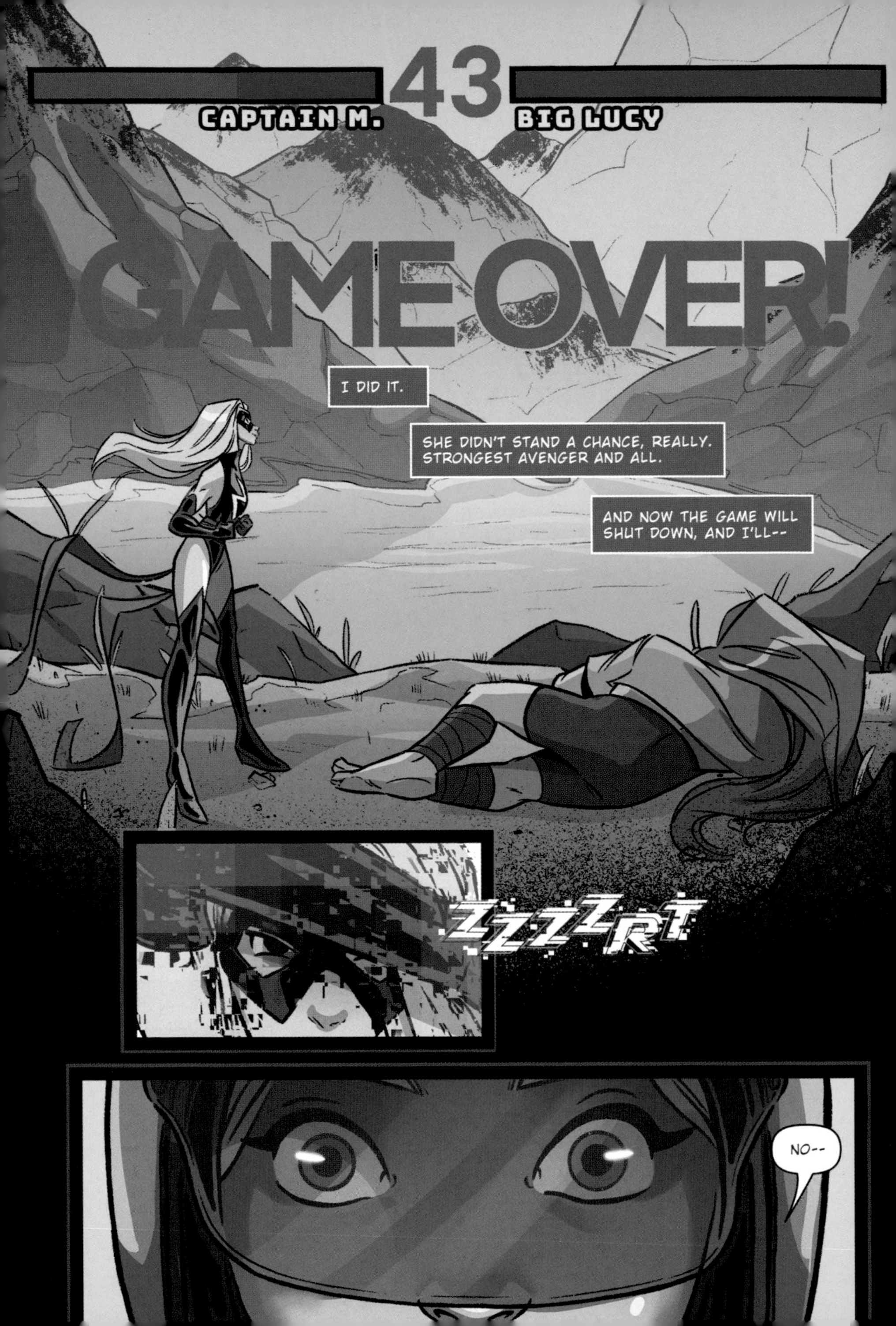
43
CAPTAIN M.
BIG LUCY
GAME OVER!
I DID IT.
SHE DIDN'T STAND A CHANCE, REALLY. STRONGEST AVENGER AND ALL.
AND NOW THE GAME WILL SHUT DOWN, AND I'LL--
ZZZZRT
NO--

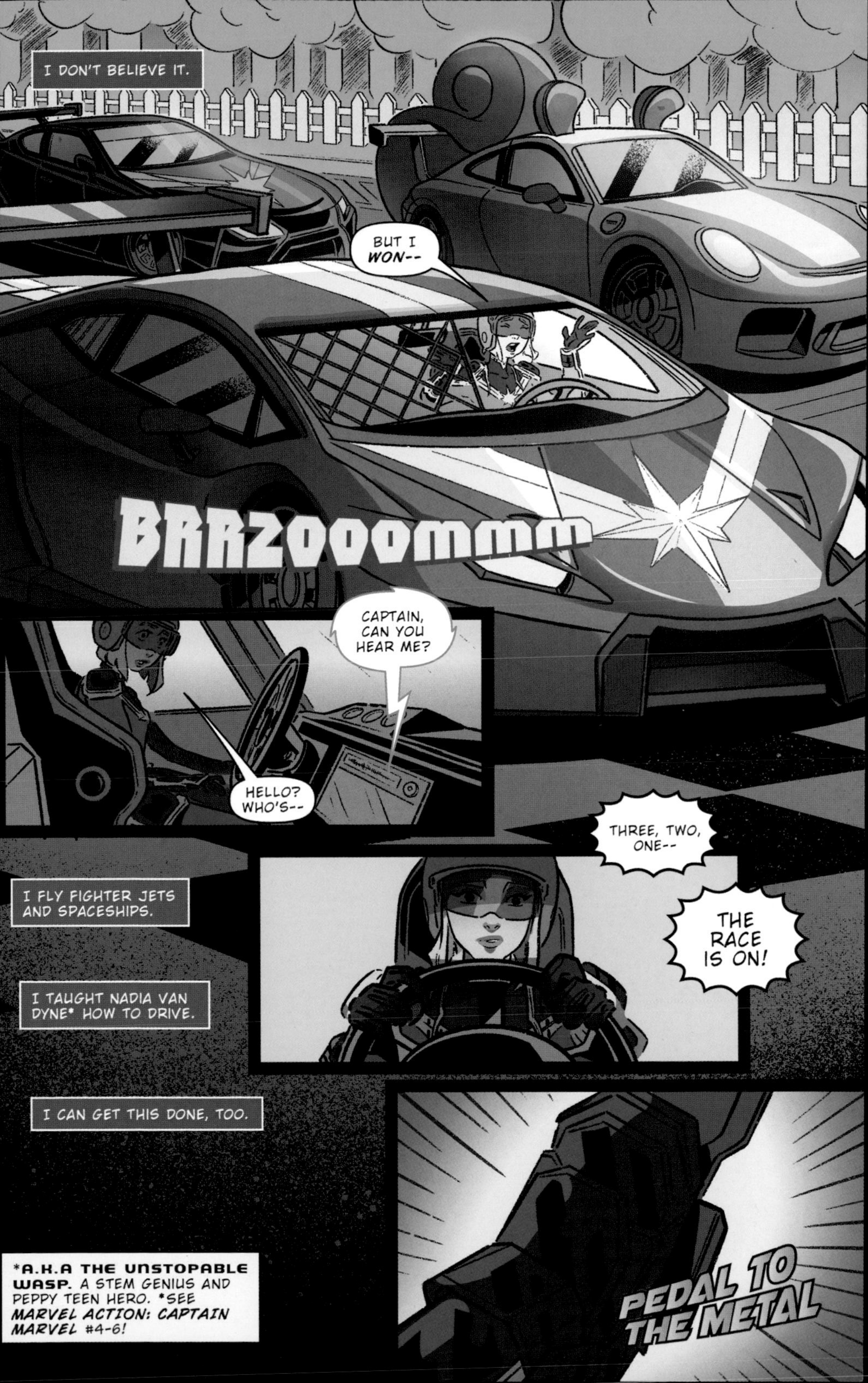

I DON'T BELIEVE IT.
BUT I WON--
BRRZOOOMMMM
CAPTAIN, CAN YOU HEAR ME?
HELLO? WHO'S--
THREE, TWO, ONE--
THE RACE IS ON!
I FLY FIGHTER JETS AND SPACESHIPS.
I TAUGHT NADIA VAN DYNE* HOW TO DRIVE.
I CAN GET THIS DONE, TOO.
*A.K.A THE UNSTOPABLE WASP. A STEM GENIUS AND PEPPY TEEN HERO. *SEE MARVEL ACTION: CAPTAIN MARVEL #4-6!
PEDAL TO THE METAL

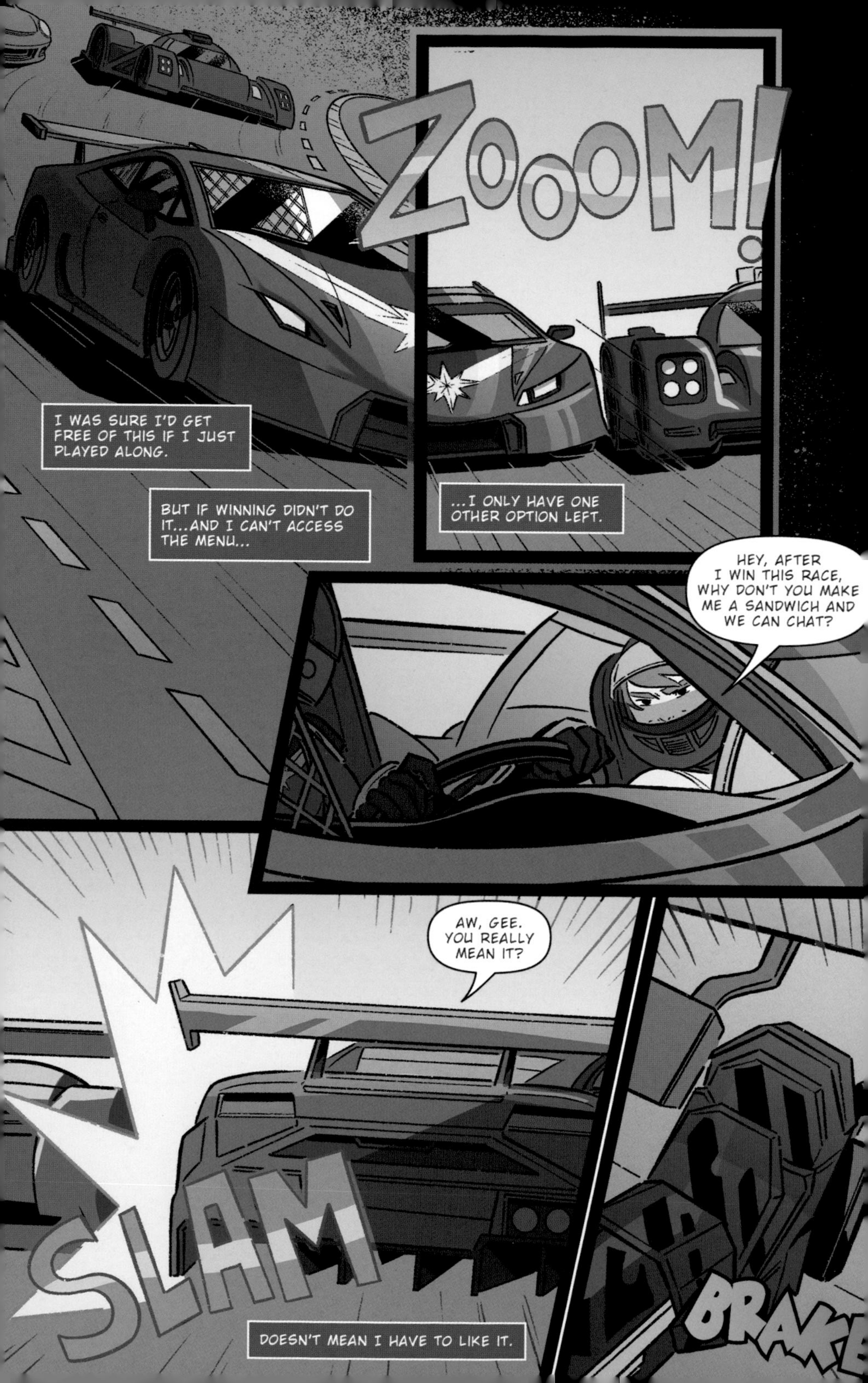
ZOOOM!
I WAS SURE I'D GET FREE OF THIS IF I JUST PLAYED ALONG.
BUT IF WINNING DIDN'T DO IT...AND I CAN'T ACCESS THE MENU...
...I ONLY HAVE ONE OTHER OPTION LEFT.
HEY, AFTER I WIN THIS RACE, WHY DON'T YOU MAKE ME A SANDWICH AND WE CAN CHAT?
AW, GEE. YOU REALLY MEAN IT?
SLAM
BRAKE
DOESN'T MEAN I HAVE TO LIKE IT.

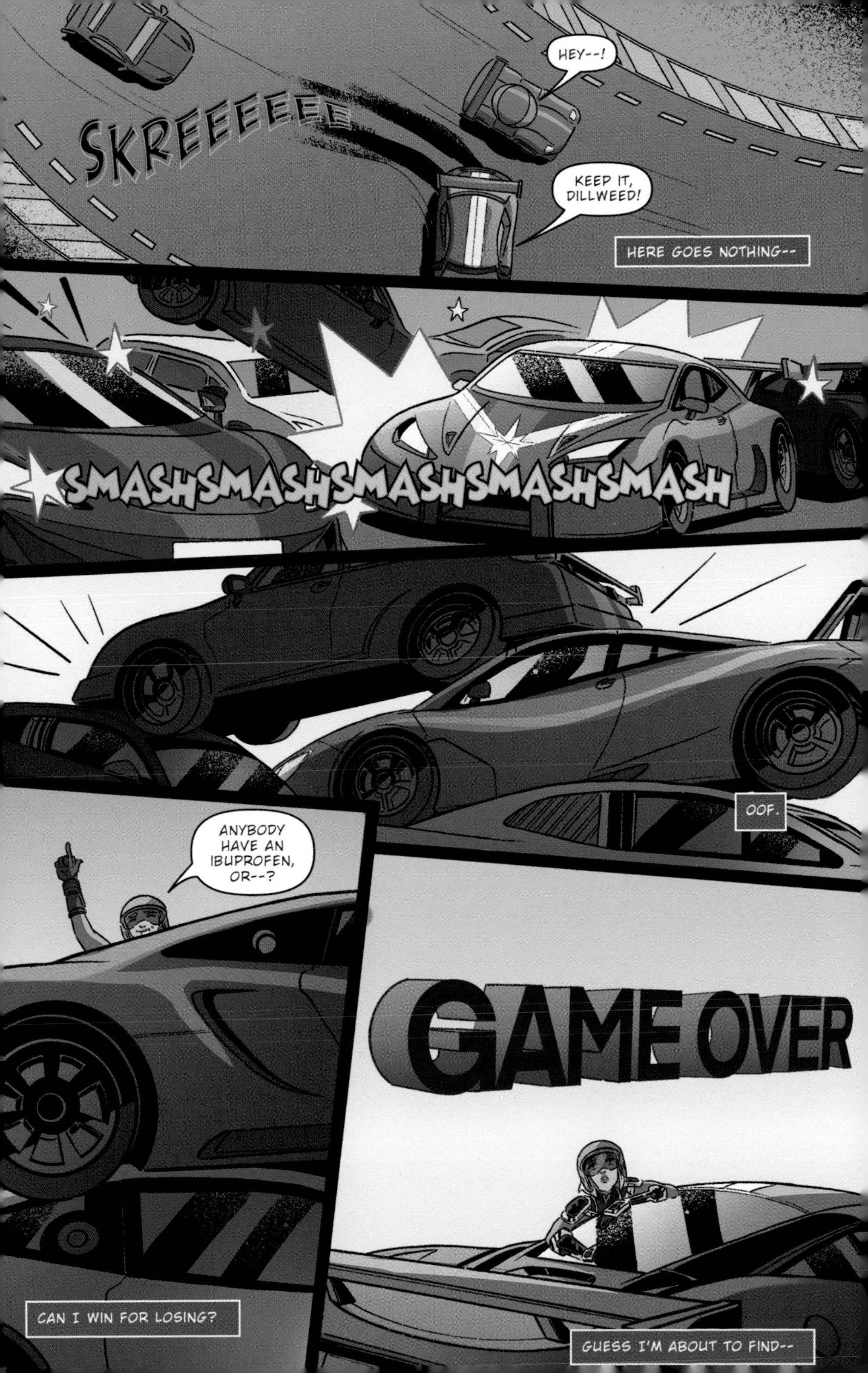
HEY--!
SKREEEEEEE
KEEP IT, DILLWEED!
HERE GOES NOTHING--
SMASHSMASHSMASHSMASHSMASH
OOF.
ANYBODY HAVE AN IBUPROFEN, OR--?
GAME OVER
CAN I WIN FOR LOSING?
GUESS I'M ABOUT TO FIND--

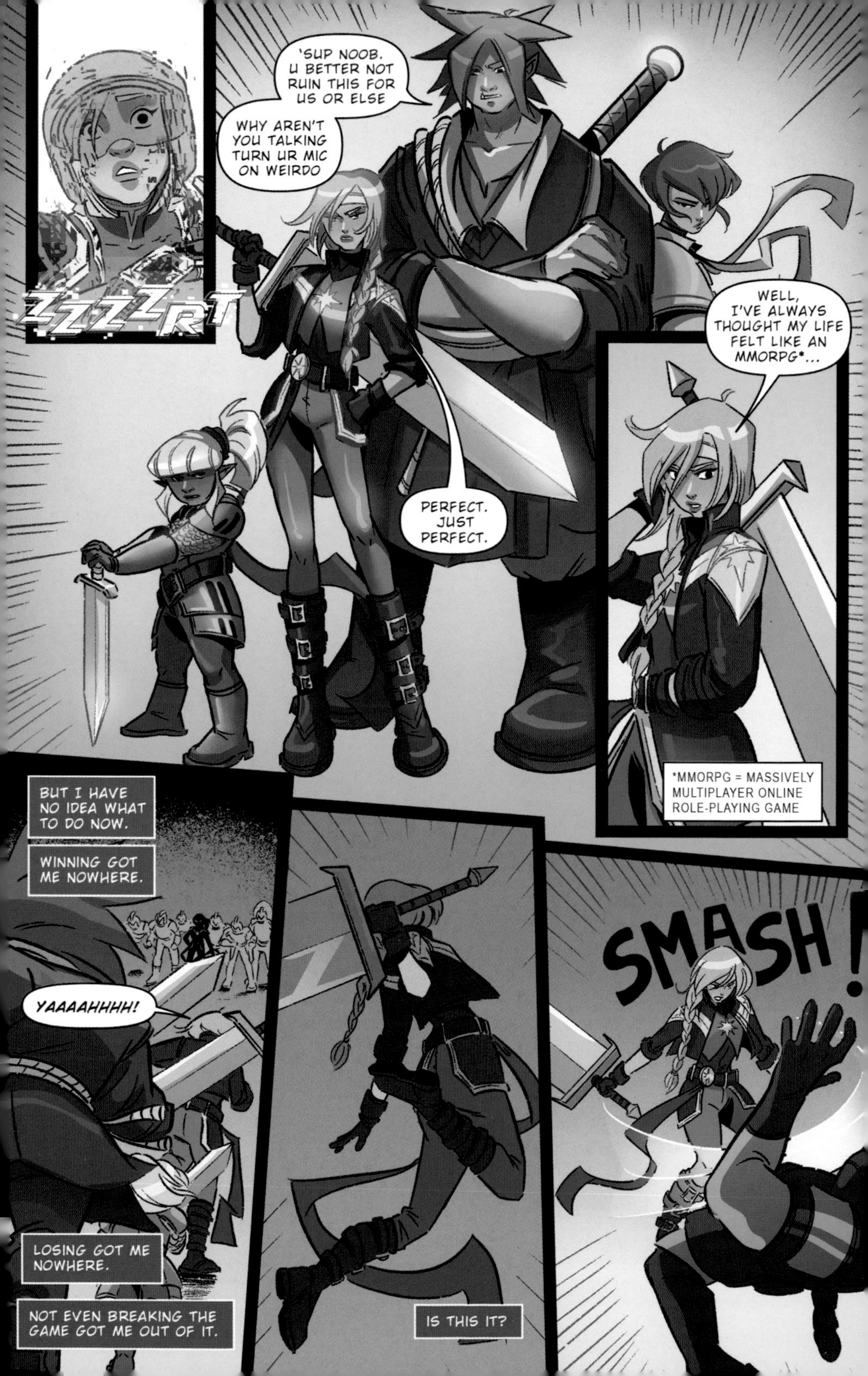
ZZZZZRT
'SUP NOOB. U BETTER NOT RUIN THIS FOR US OR ELSE
WHY AREN'T YOU TALKING TURN UR MIC ON WEIRDO
PERFECT. JUST PERFECT.
WELL, I'VE ALWAYS THOUGHT MY LIFE FELT LIKE AN MMORPG*...
*MMORPG = MASSIVELY MULTIPLAYER ONLINE ROLE-PLAYING GAME
BUT I HAVE NO IDEA WHAT TO DO NOW.
WINNING GOT ME NOWHERE.
YAAAAHHHH!
LOSING GOT ME NOWHERE.
NOT EVEN BREAKING THE GAME GOT ME OUT OF IT.
IS THIS IT?
SMASH!

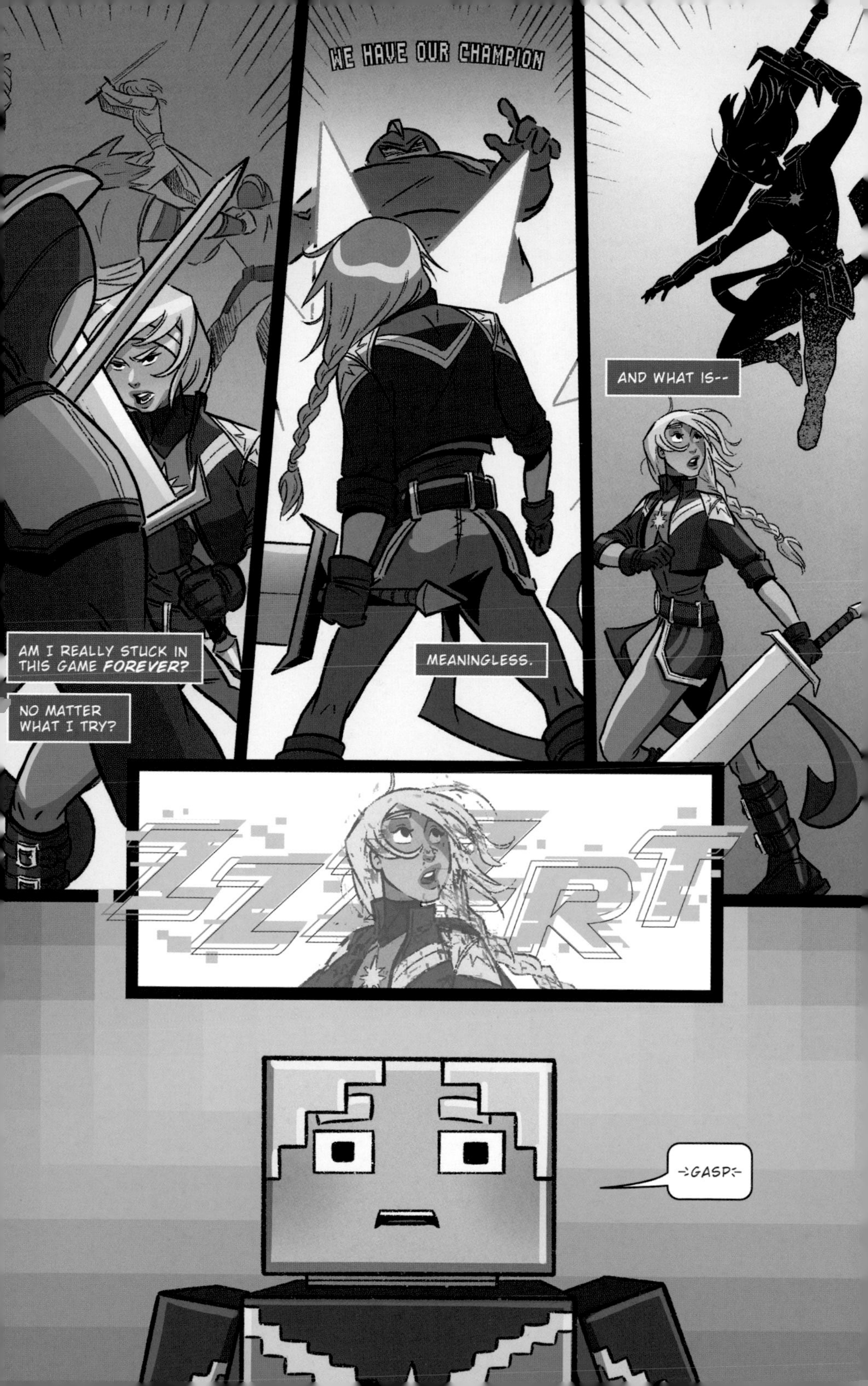
WE HAVE OUR CHAMPION
AM I REALLY STUCK IN THIS GAME *FOREVER?*
NO MATTER WHAT I TRY?
MEANINGLESS.
AND WHAT IS--
ZZZRT
GASP

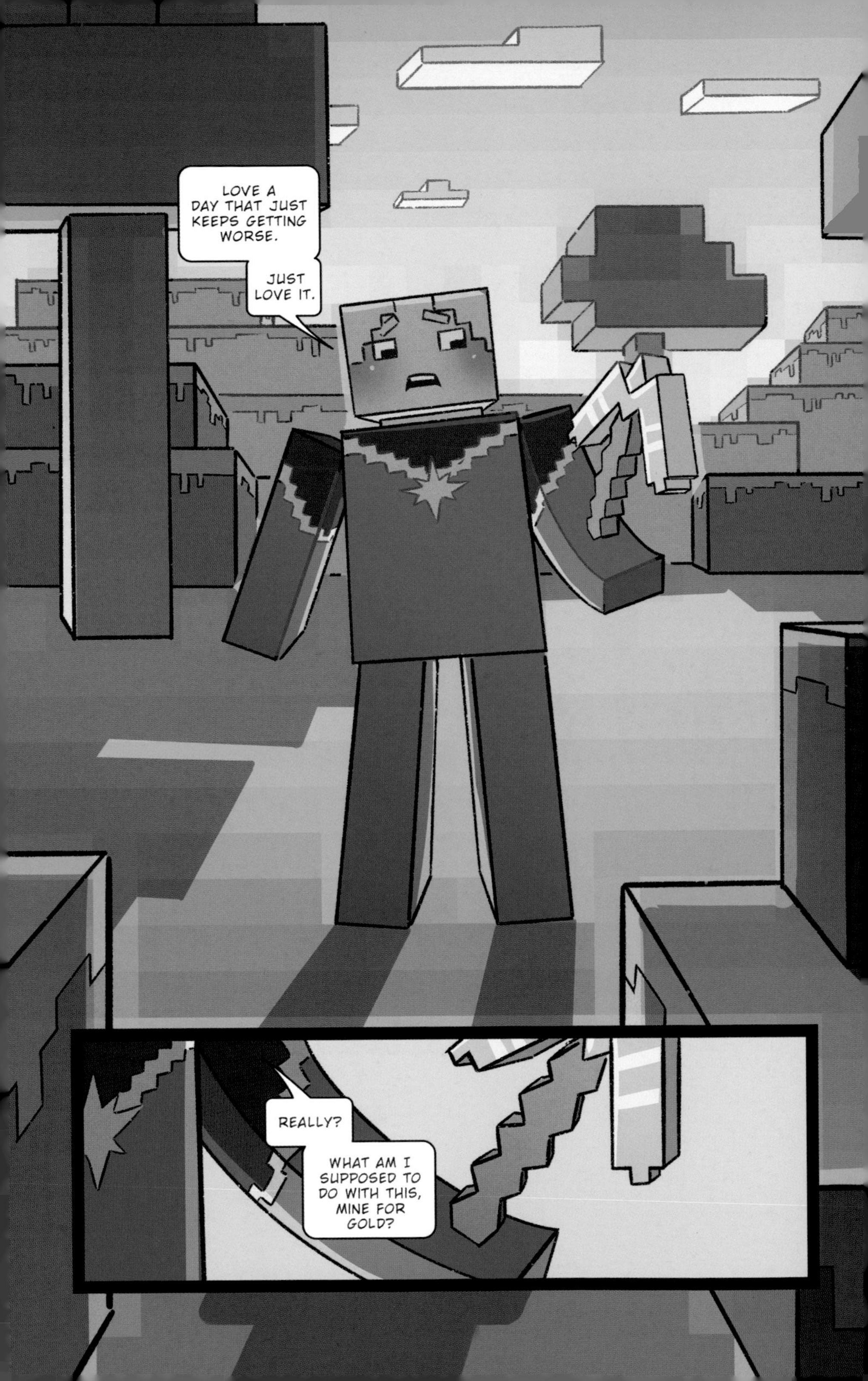
LOVE A DAY THAT JUST KEEPS GETTING WORSE.
JUST LOVE IT.
REALLY?
WHAT AM I SUPPOSED TO DO WITH THIS, MINE FOR GOLD?

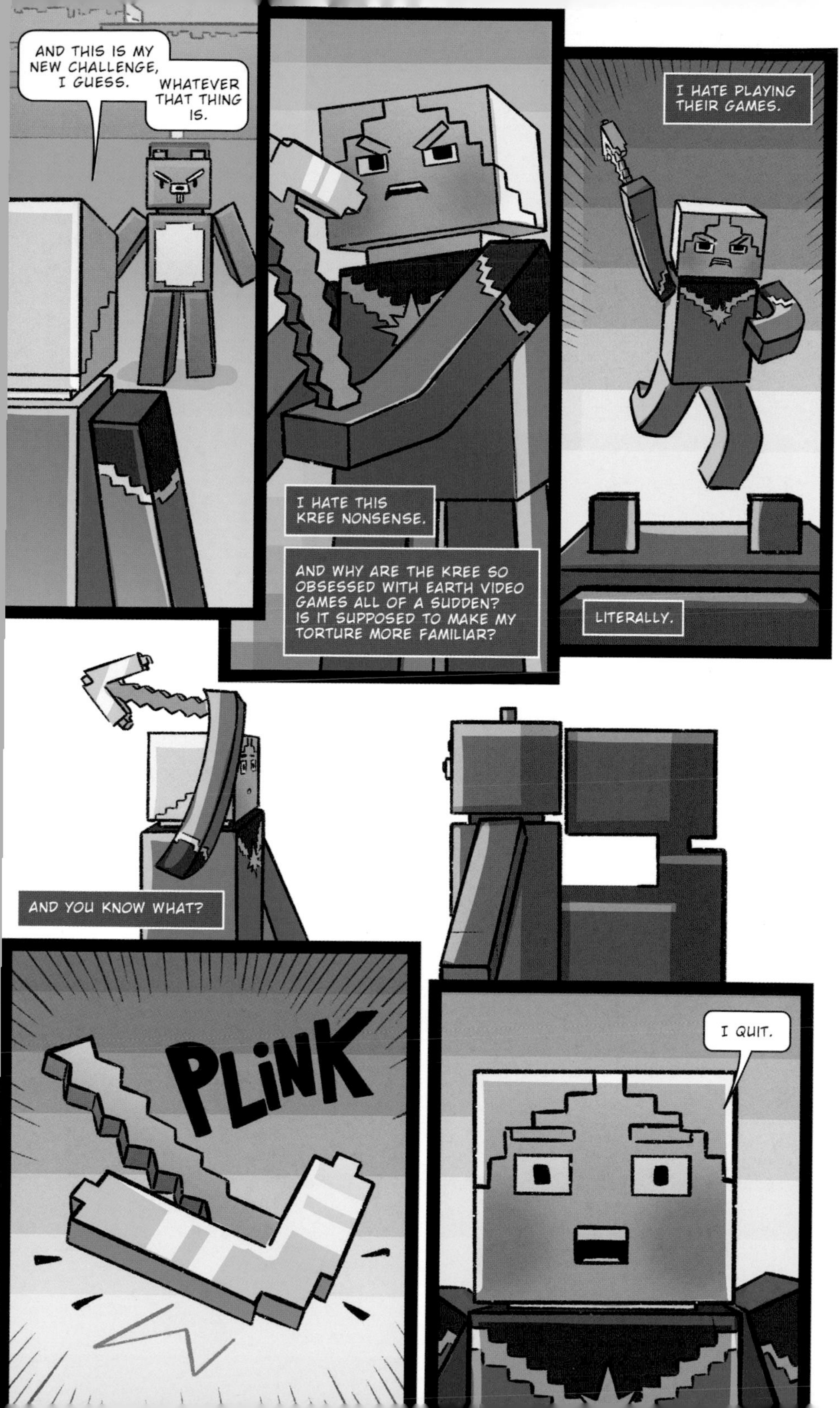
AND THIS IS MY NEW CHALLENGE, I GUESS.
WHATEVER THAT THING IS.
I HATE THIS KREE NONSENSE.
AND WHY ARE THE KREE SO OBSESSED WITH EARTH VIDEO GAMES ALL OF A SUDDEN? IS IT SUPPOSED TO MAKE MY TORTURE MORE FAMILIAR?
I HATE PLAYING THEIR GAMES.
LITERALLY.
AND YOU KNOW WHAT?
PLINK
I QUIT.

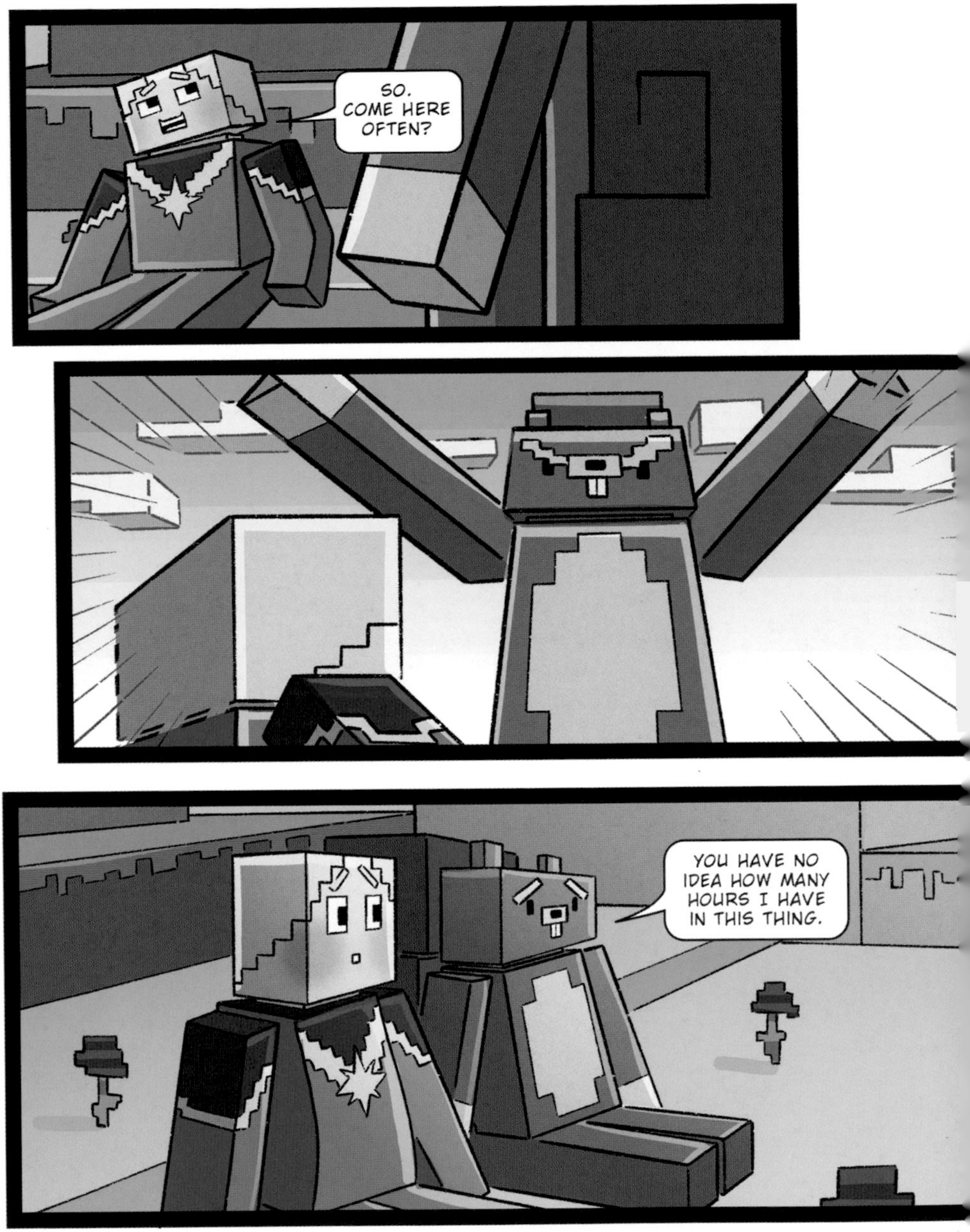
SO. COME HERE OFTEN?
YOU HAVE NO IDEA HOW MANY HOURS I HAVE IN THIS THING.

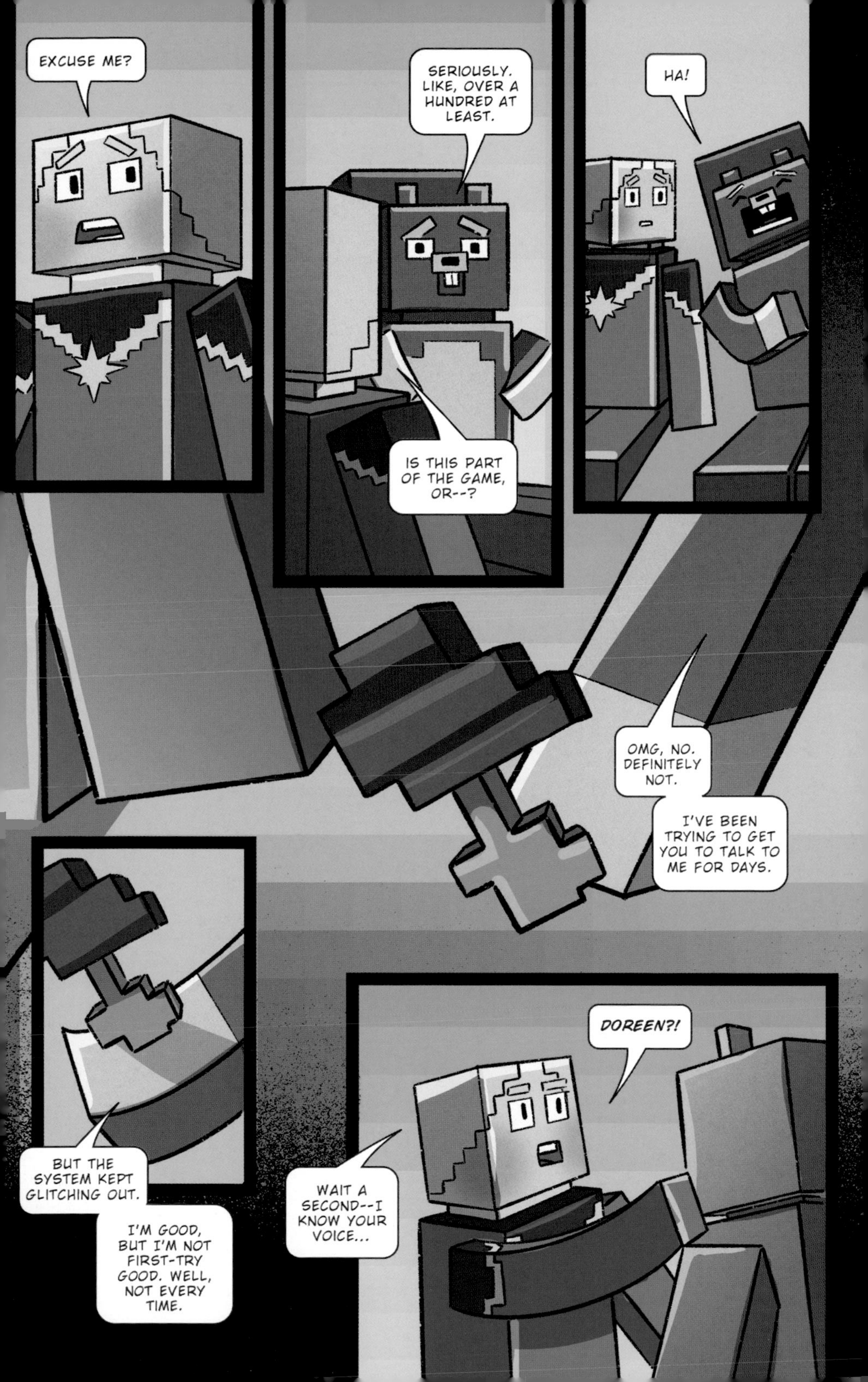
EXCUSE ME?
SERIOUSLY. LIKE, OVER A HUNDRED AT LEAST.
IS THIS PART OF THE GAME, OR--?
HA!
OMG, NO. DEFINITELY NOT.
I'VE BEEN TRYING TO GET YOU TO TALK TO ME FOR DAYS.
BUT THE SYSTEM KEPT GLITCHING OUT.
I'M GOOD, BUT I'M NOT FIRST-TRY GOOD. WELL, NOT EVERY TIME.
WAIT A SECOND--I KNOW YOUR VOICE...
DOREEN?!

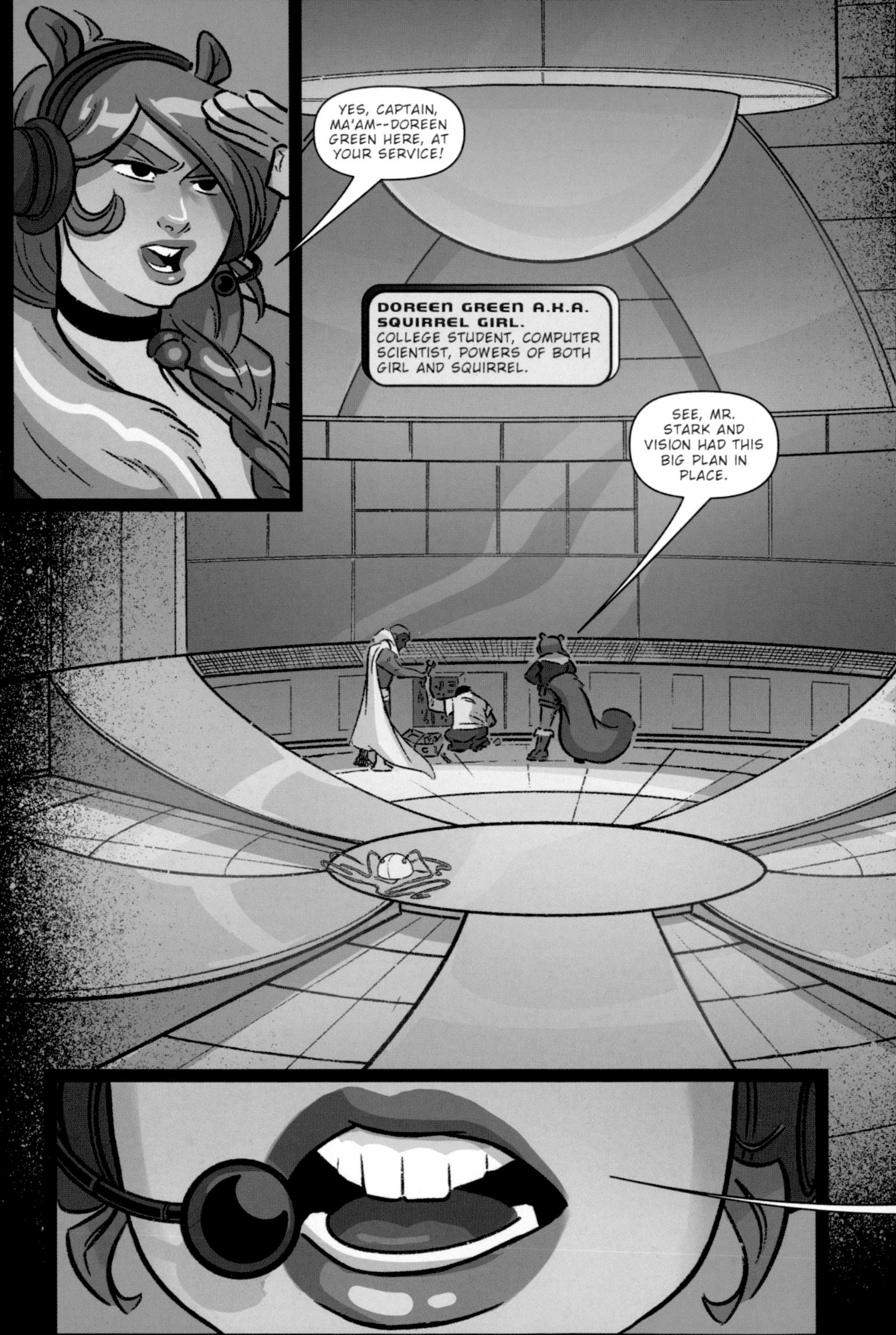
YES, CAPTAIN, MA'AM--DOREEN GREEN HERE, AT YOUR SERVICE!
DOREEN GREEN A.K.A. SQUIRREL GIRL. COLLEGE STUDENT, COMPUTER SCIENTIST, POWERS OF BOTH GIRL AND SQUIRREL.
SEE, MR. STARK AND VISION HAD THIS BIG PLAN IN PLACE.

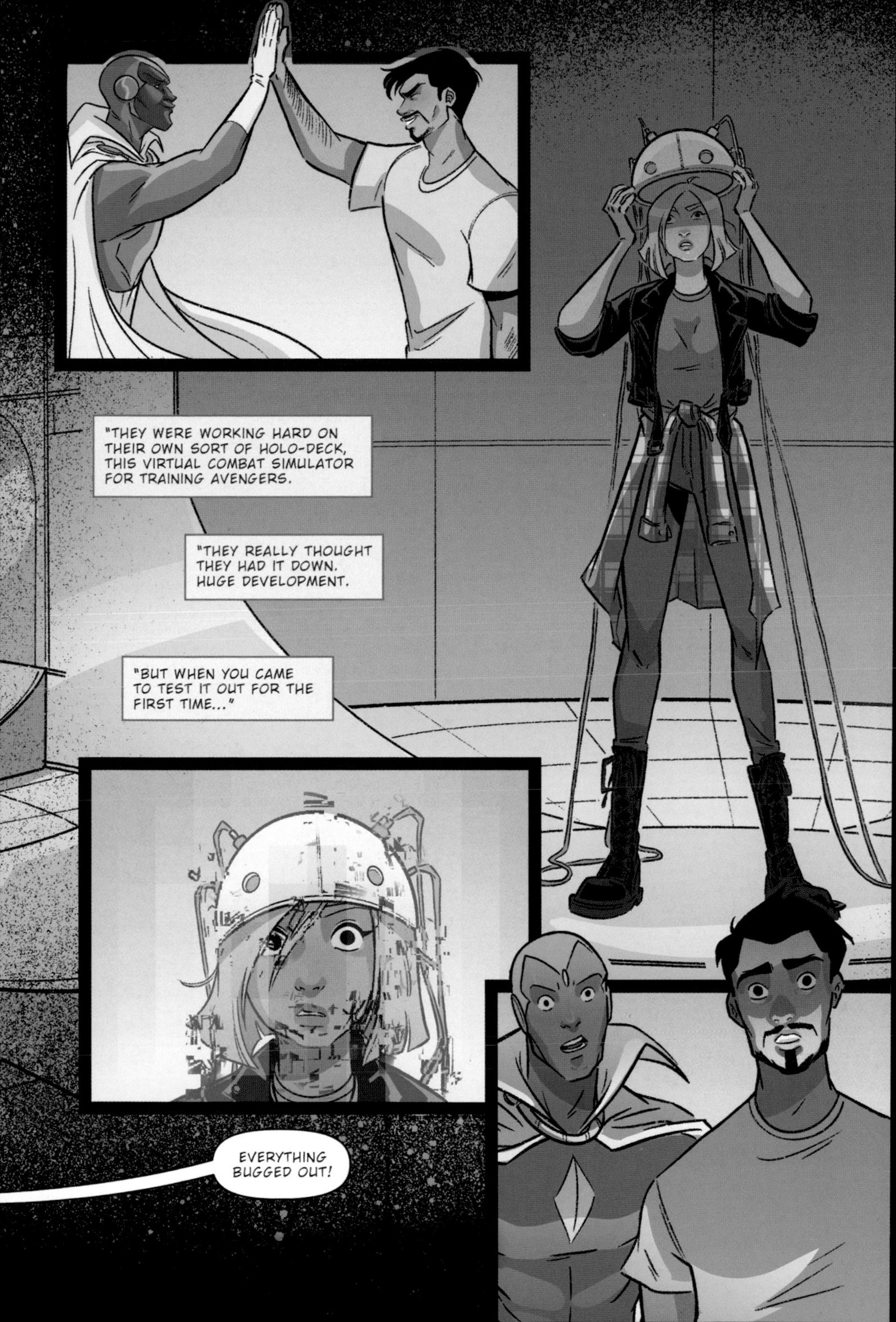
"THEY WERE WORKING HARD ON THEIR OWN SORT OF HOLO-DECK, THIS VIRTUAL COMBAT SIMULATOR FOR TRAINING AVENGERS.
"THEY REALLY THOUGHT THEY HAD IT DOWN. HUGE DEVELOPMENT.
"BUT WHEN YOU CAME TO TEST IT OUT FOR THE FIRST TIME..."
EVERYTHING BUGGED OUT!

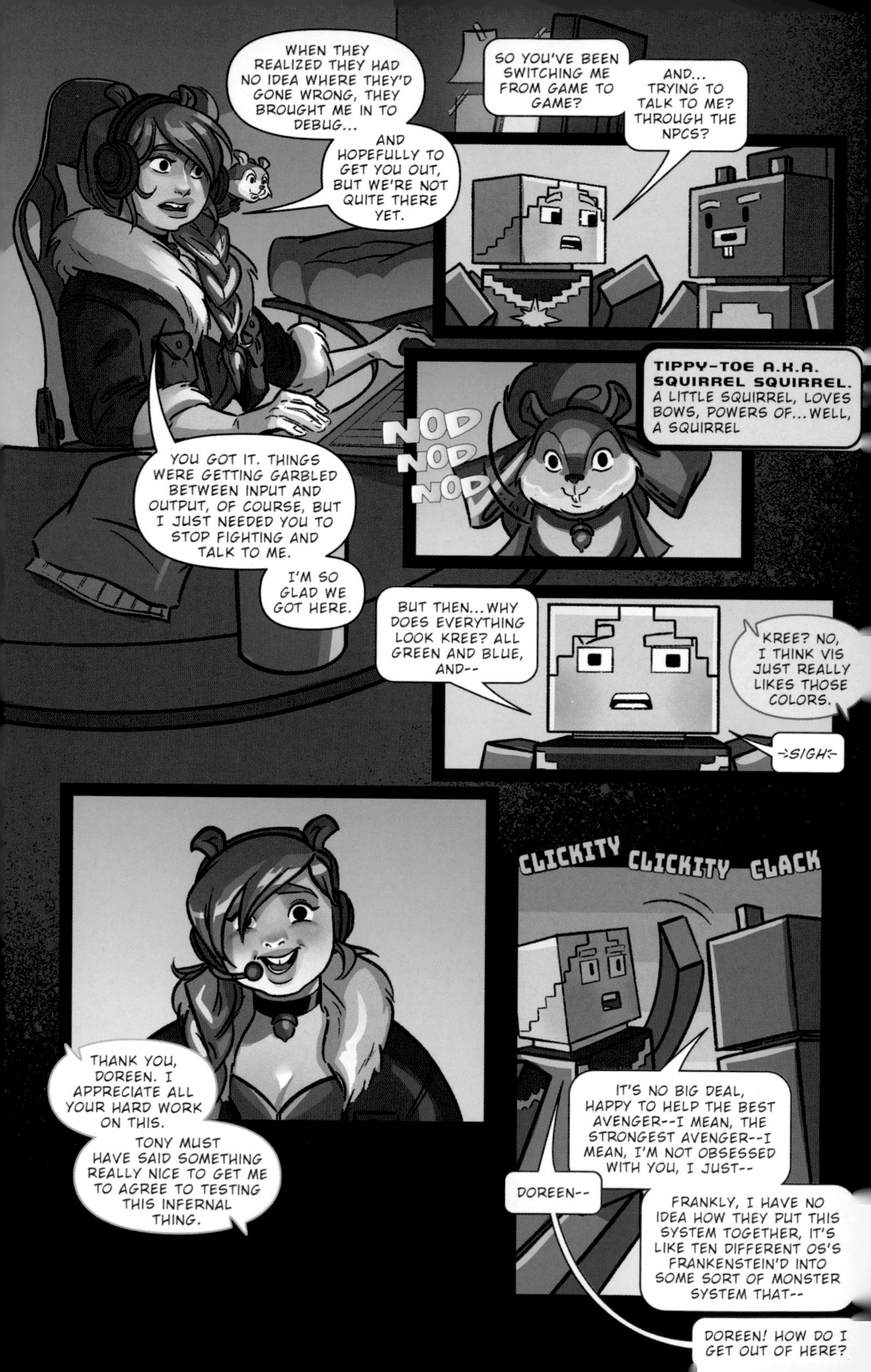
WHEN THEY REALIZED THEY HAD NO IDEA WHERE THEY'D GONE WRONG, THEY BROUGHT ME IN TO DEBUG...
AND HOPEFULLY TO GET YOU OUT, BUT WE'RE NOT QUITE THERE YET.
SO YOU'VE BEEN SWITCHING ME FROM GAME TO GAME?
AND... TRYING TO TALK TO ME? THROUGH THE NPCS?
YOU GOT IT. THINGS WERE GETTING GARBLED BETWEEN INPUT AND OUTPUT, OF COURSE, BUT I JUST NEEDED YOU TO STOP FIGHTING AND TALK TO ME.
I'M SO GLAD WE GOT HERE.
TIPPY-TOE A.K.A. SQUIRREL SQUIRREL. A LITTLE SQUIRREL, LOVES BOWS, POWERS OF...WELL, A SQUIRREL
NOD NOD NOD
BUT THEN...WHY DOES EVERYTHING LOOK KREE? ALL GREEN AND BLUE, AND--
KREE? NO, I THINK VIS JUST REALLY LIKES THOSE COLORS.
-SIGH-
THANK YOU, DOREEN. I APPRECIATE ALL YOUR HARD WORK ON THIS.
TONY MUST HAVE SAID SOMETHING REALLY NICE TO GET ME TO AGREE TO TESTING THIS INFERNAL THING.
CLICKITY CLICKITY CLACK
IT'S NO BIG DEAL, HAPPY TO HELP THE BEST AVENGER--I MEAN, THE STRONGEST AVENGER--I MEAN, I'M NOT OBSESSED WITH YOU, I JUST--
DOREEN--
FRANKLY, I HAVE NO IDEA HOW THEY PUT THIS SYSTEM TOGETHER, IT'S LIKE TEN DIFFERENT OS'S FRANKENSTEIN'D INTO SOME SORT OF MONSTER SYSTEM THAT--
DOREEN! HOW DO I GET OUT OF HERE?

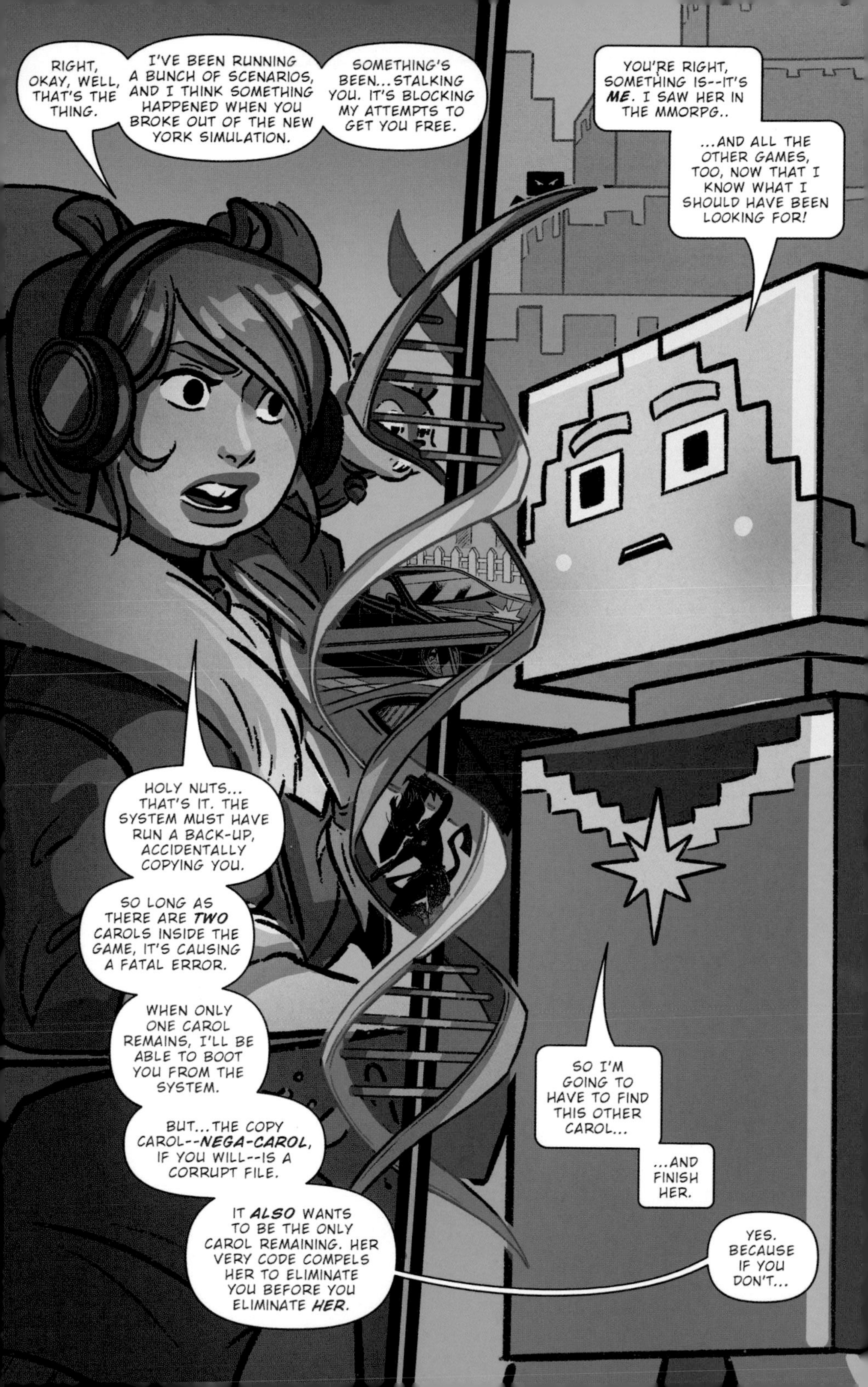
RIGHT, OKAY, WELL, THAT'S THE THING.
I'VE BEEN RUNNING A BUNCH OF SCENARIOS, AND I THINK SOMETHING HAPPENED WHEN YOU BROKE OUT OF THE NEW YORK SIMULATION.
SOMETHING'S BEEN...STALKING YOU. IT'S BLOCKING MY ATTEMPTS TO GET YOU FREE.
YOU'RE RIGHT, SOMETHING IS--IT'S ME. I SAW HER IN THE MMORPG..
...AND ALL THE OTHER GAMES, TOO, NOW THAT I KNOW WHAT I SHOULD HAVE BEEN LOOKING FOR!
HOLY NUTS... THAT'S IT. THE SYSTEM MUST HAVE RUN A BACK-UP, ACCIDENTALLY COPYING YOU.
SO LONG AS THERE ARE TWO CAROLS INSIDE THE GAME, IT'S CAUSING A FATAL ERROR.
WHEN ONLY ONE CAROL REMAINS, I'LL BE ABLE TO BOOT YOU FROM THE SYSTEM.
BUT...THE COPY CAROL--NEGA-CAROL, IF YOU WILL--IS A CORRUPT FILE.
IT ALSO WANTS TO BE THE ONLY CAROL REMAINING. HER VERY CODE COMPELS HER TO ELIMINATE YOU BEFORE YOU ELIMINATE HER.
SO I'M GOING TO HAVE TO FIND THIS OTHER CAROL...
...AND FINISH HER.
YES. BECAUSE IF YOU DON'T...

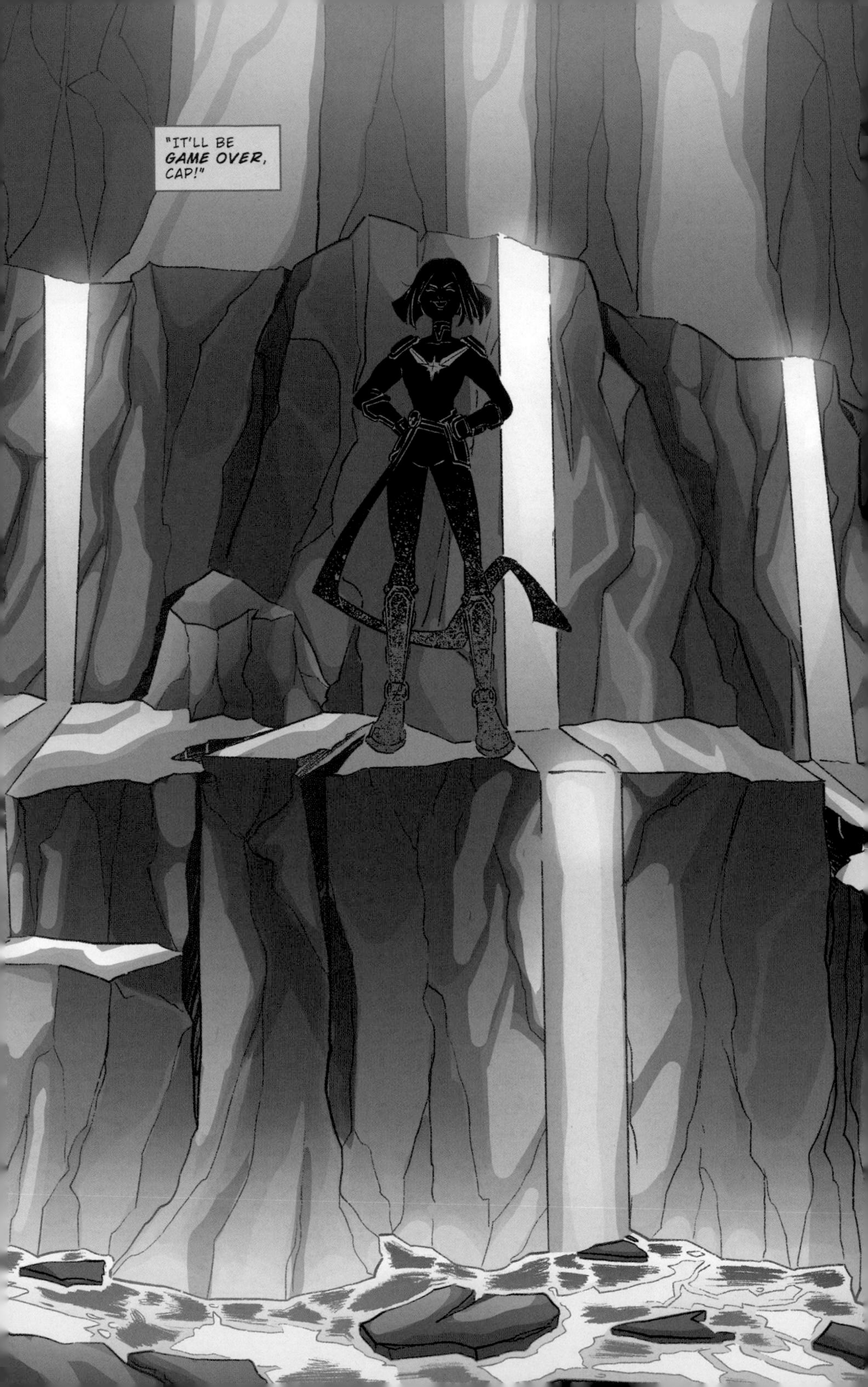
"IT'LL BE **GAME OVER**, CAP!"

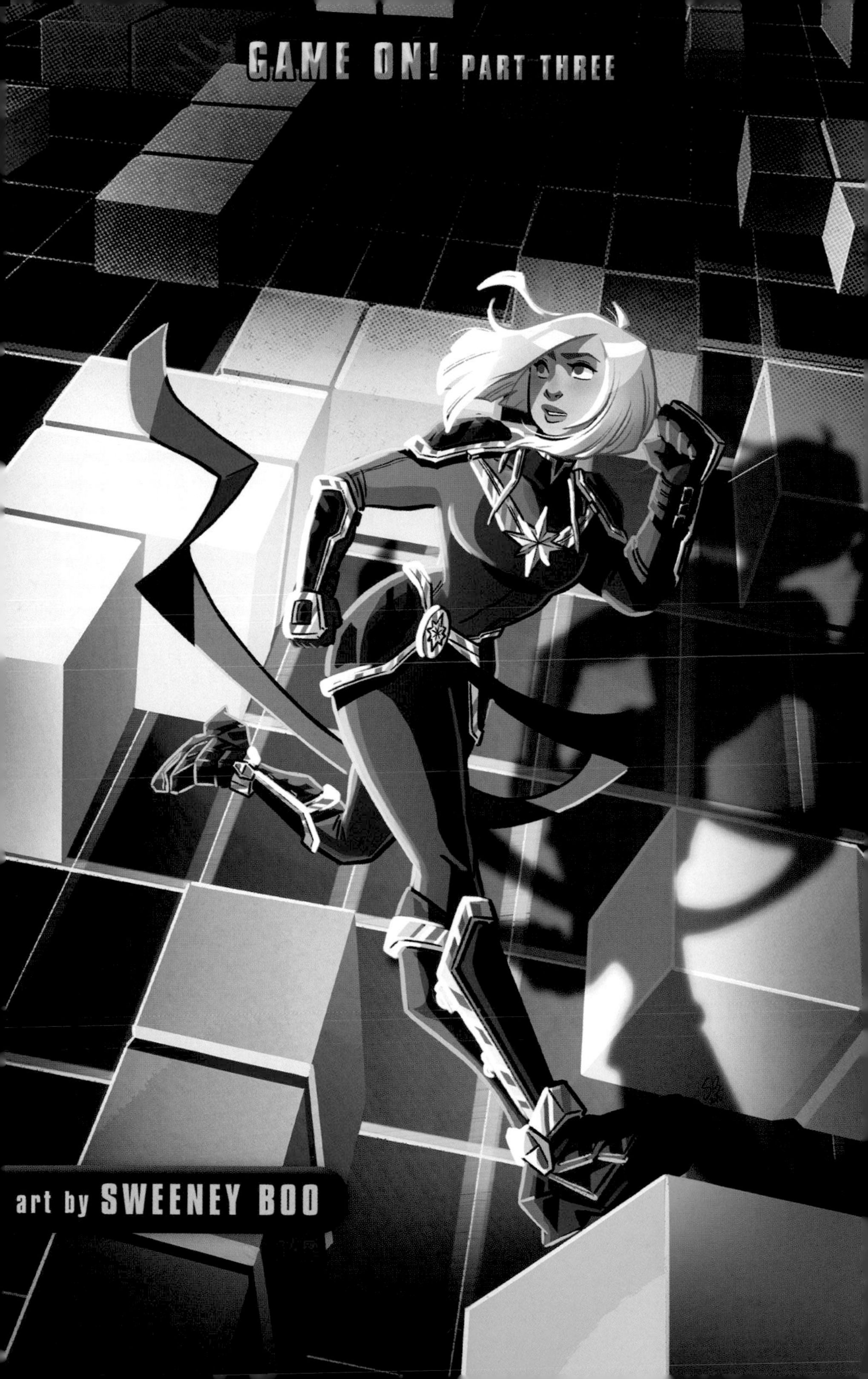
GAME ON! PART THREE
art by SWEENEY BOO

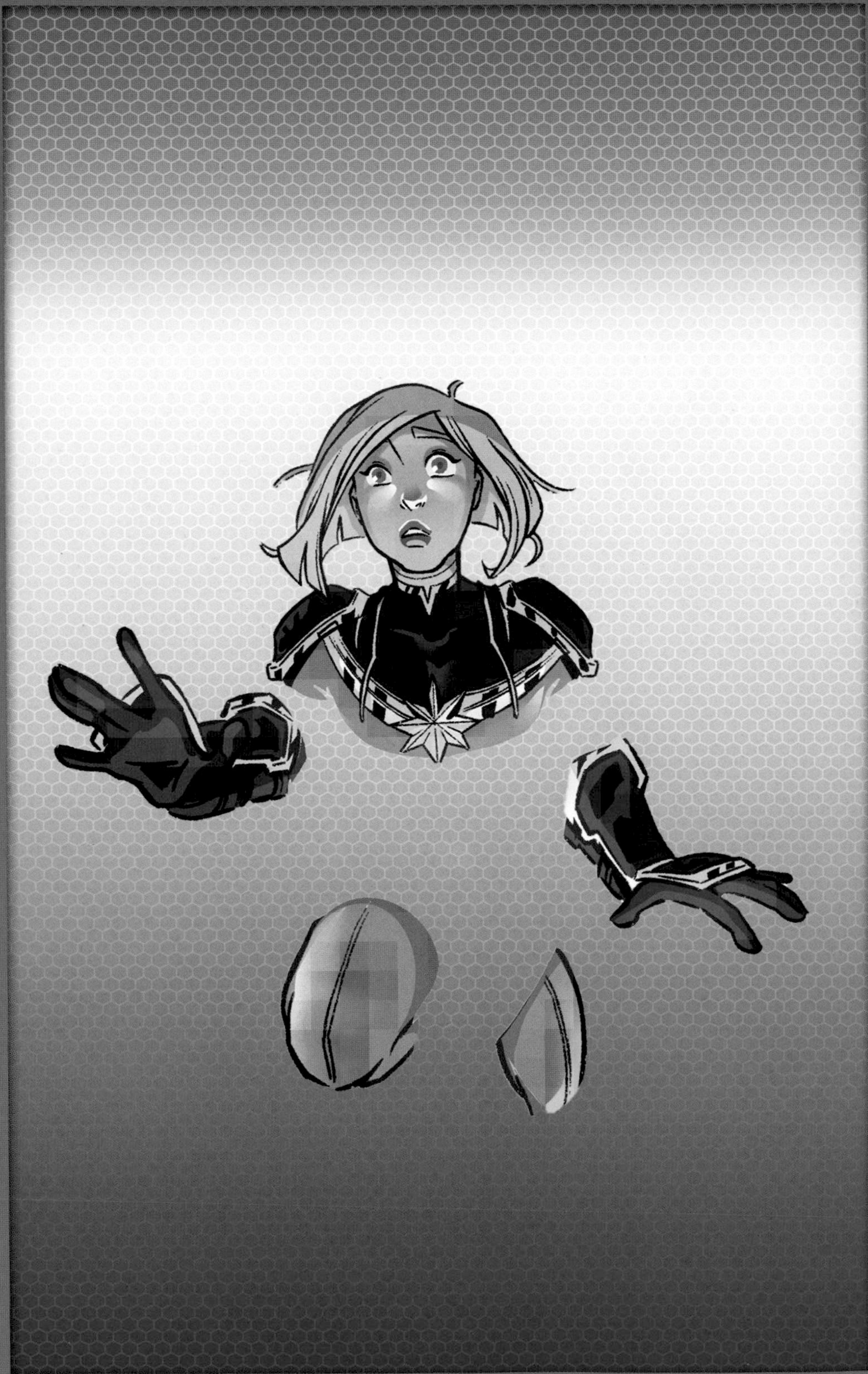

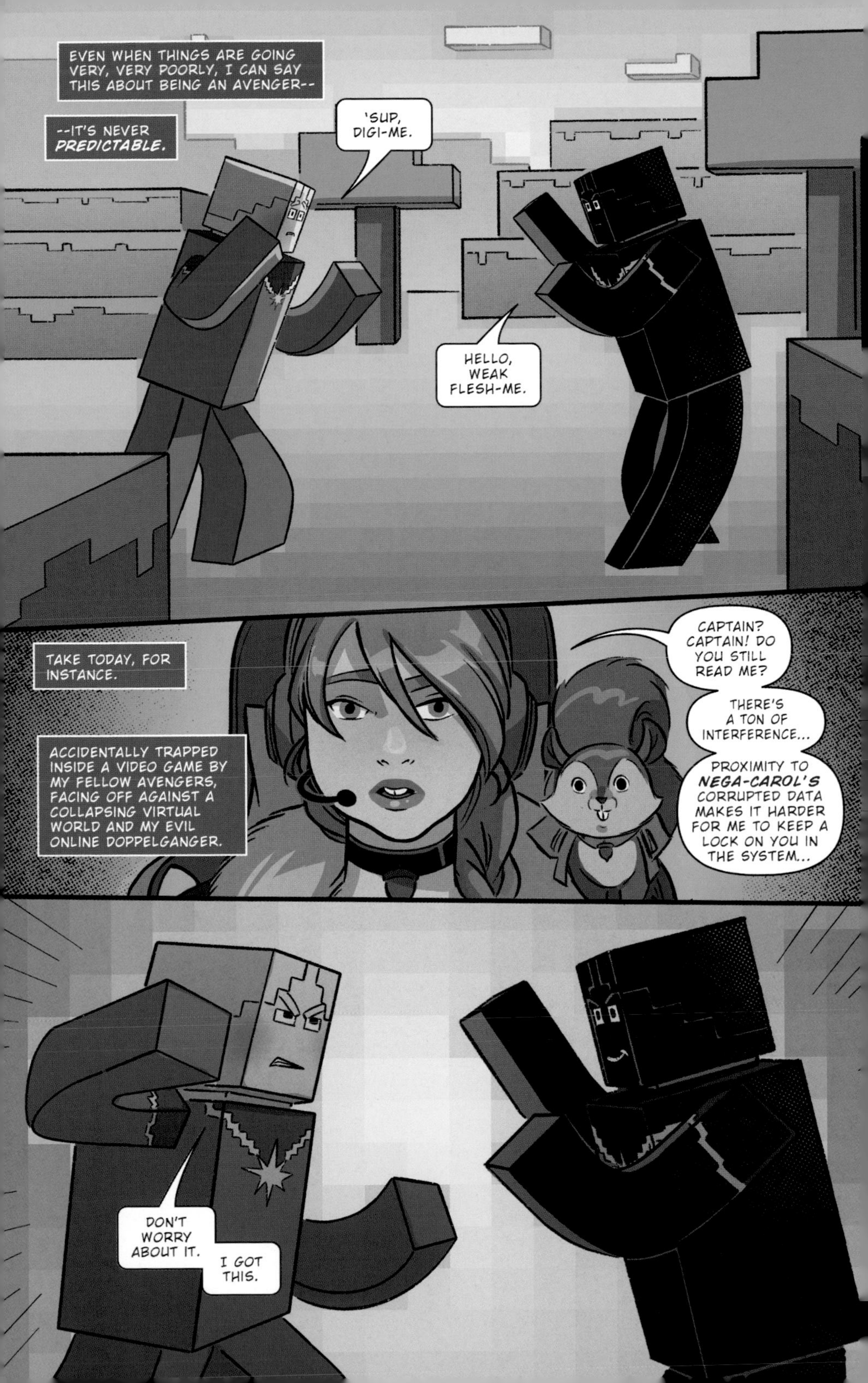
EVEN WHEN THINGS ARE GOING VERY, VERY POORLY, I CAN SAY THIS ABOUT BEING AN AVENGER--
--IT'S NEVER *PREDICTABLE.*
'SUP, DIGI-ME.
HELLO, WEAK FLESH-ME.
TAKE TODAY, FOR INSTANCE.
ACCIDENTALLY TRAPPED INSIDE A VIDEO GAME BY MY FELLOW AVENGERS, FACING OFF AGAINST A COLLAPSING VIRTUAL WORLD AND MY EVIL ONLINE DOPPELGANGER.
CAPTAIN? CAPTAIN! DO YOU STILL READ ME?
THERE'S A TON OF INTERFERENCE...
PROXIMITY TO **NEGA-CAROL'S** CORRUPTED DATA MAKES IT HARDER FOR ME TO KEEP A LOCK ON YOU IN THE SYSTEM...
DON'T WORRY ABOUT IT.
I GOT THIS.

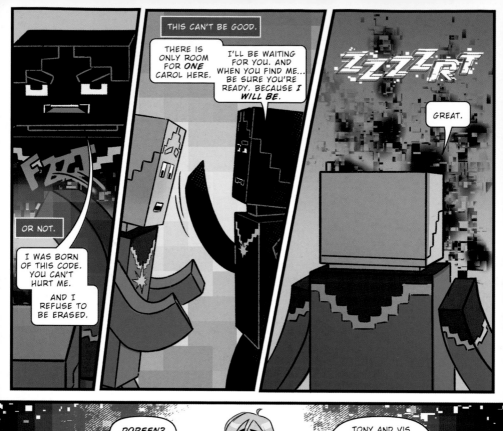

THIS CAN'T BE GOOD.

THERE IS ONLY ROOM FOR **ONE** CAROL HERE.

I'LL BE WAITING FOR YOU. AND WHEN YOU FIND ME... BE SURE YOU'RE READY. BECAUSE **I WILL BE.**

GREAT.

OR NOT.

I WAS BORN OF THIS CODE. YOU CAN'T HURT ME.

AND I REFUSE TO BE ERASED.

DOREEN? YOU THERE?

TONY AND VIS BETTER HOPE THEY AREN'T WITHIN A MILE OF AVENGERS TOWER WHEN WE GET ME OUTTA HERE...

YEAH, CAPTAIN, YOU'RE COMING THROUGH LOUD AND CLEAR AGAIN.

AND, UH...

...NO ONE HERE BUT US SQUIRRELS!

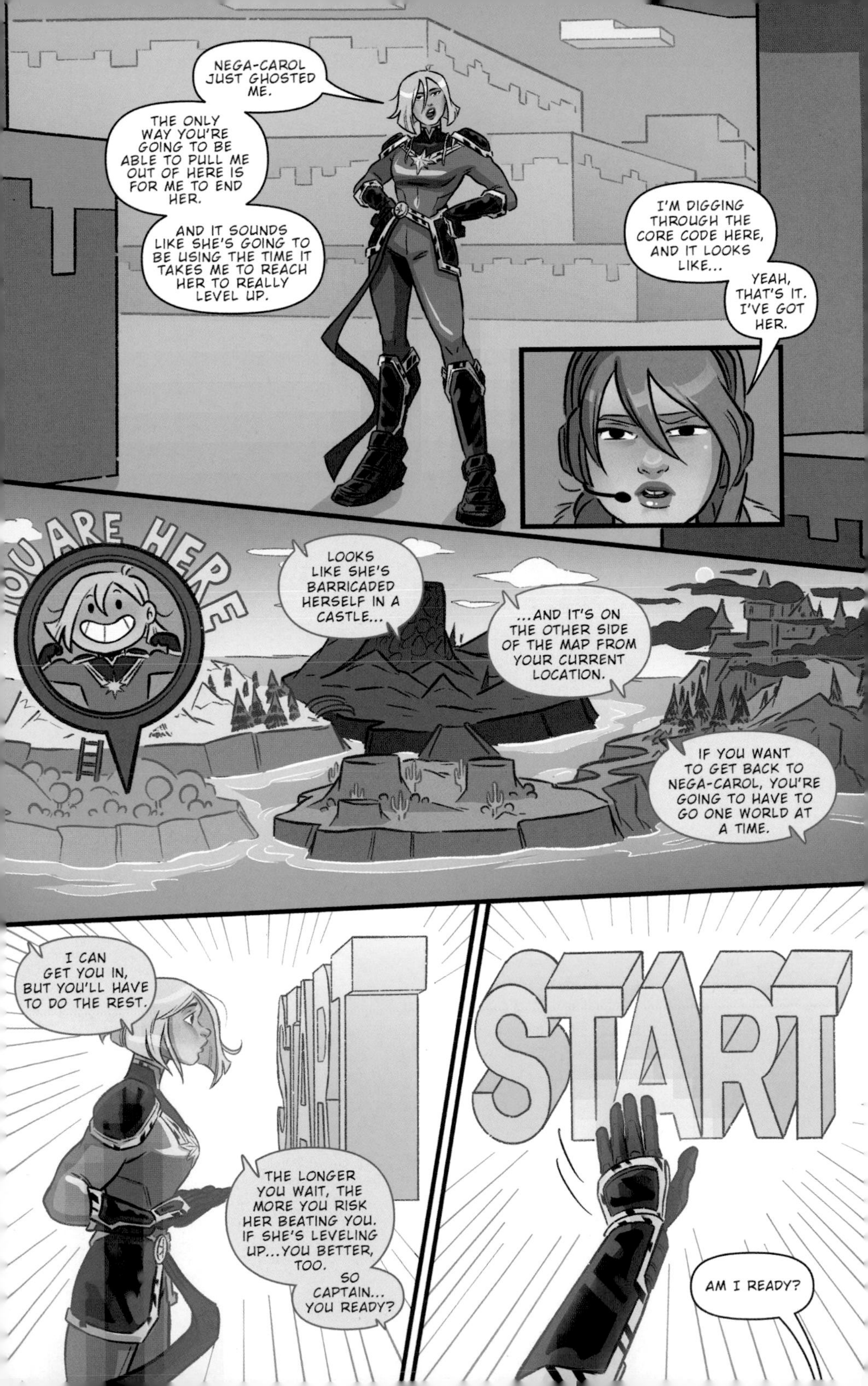
NEGA-CAROL JUST GHOSTED ME.
THE ONLY WAY YOU'RE GOING TO BE ABLE TO PULL ME OUT OF HERE IS FOR ME TO END HER.
AND IT SOUNDS LIKE SHE'S GOING TO BE USING THE TIME IT TAKES ME TO REACH HER TO REALLY LEVEL UP.
I'M DIGGING THROUGH THE CORE CODE HERE, AND IT LOOKS LIKE...
YEAH, THAT'S IT. I'VE GOT HER.
YOU ARE HERE
LOOKS LIKE SHE'S BARRICADED HERSELF IN A CASTLE...
...AND IT'S ON THE OTHER SIDE OF THE MAP FROM YOUR CURRENT LOCATION.
IF YOU WANT TO GET BACK TO NEGA-CAROL, YOU'RE GOING TO HAVE TO GO ONE WORLD AT A TIME.
I CAN GET YOU IN, BUT YOU'LL HAVE TO DO THE REST.
THE LONGER YOU WAIT, THE MORE YOU RISK HER BEATING YOU. IF SHE'S LEVELING UP...YOU BETTER, TOO.
SO CAPTAIN... YOU READY?
START
AM I READY?

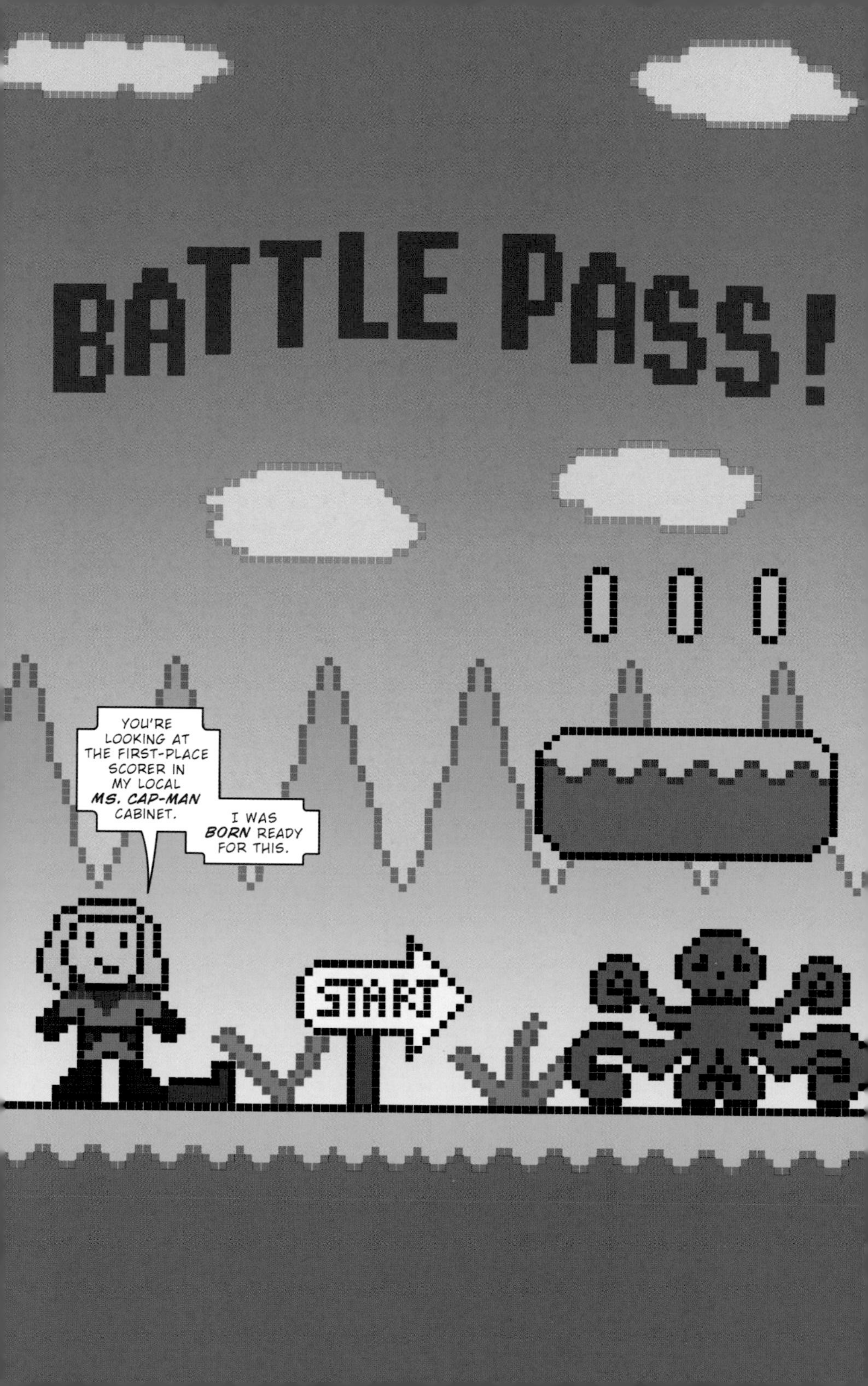
BATTLE PASS!
000
YOU'RE LOOKING AT THE FIRST-PLACE SCORER IN MY LOCAL MS. CAP-MAN CABINET.
I WAS BORN READY FOR THIS.
START

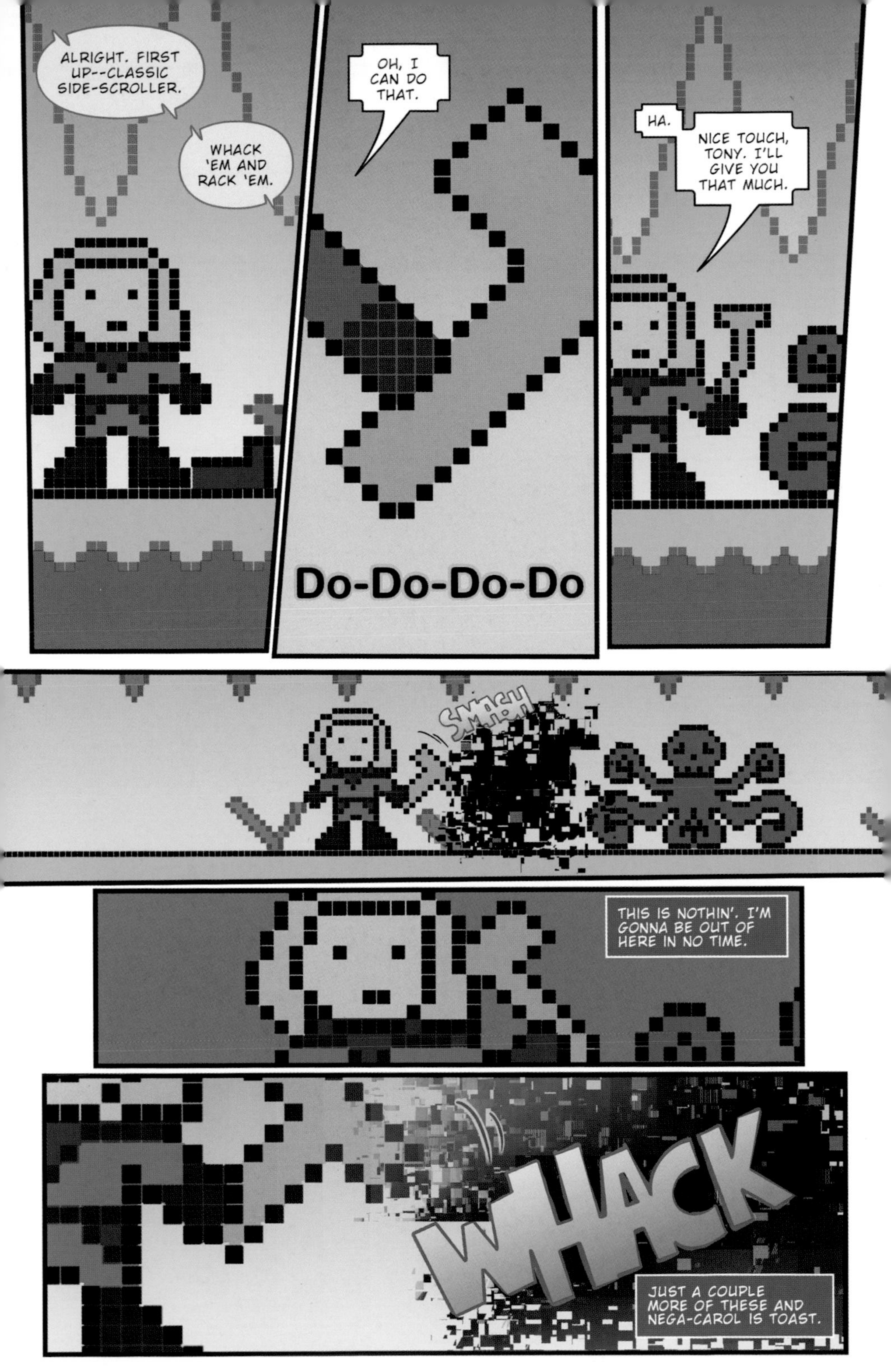

ALRIGHT. FIRST UP--CLASSIC SIDE-SCROLLER.
WHACK 'EM AND RACK 'EM.
OH, I CAN DO THAT.
Do-Do-Do-Do
HA.
NICE TOUCH, TONY. I'LL GIVE YOU THAT MUCH.
SMASH
THIS IS NOTHIN'. I'M GONNA BE OUT OF HERE IN NO TIME.
WHACK
JUST A COUPLE MORE OF THESE AND NEGA-CAROL IS TOAST.

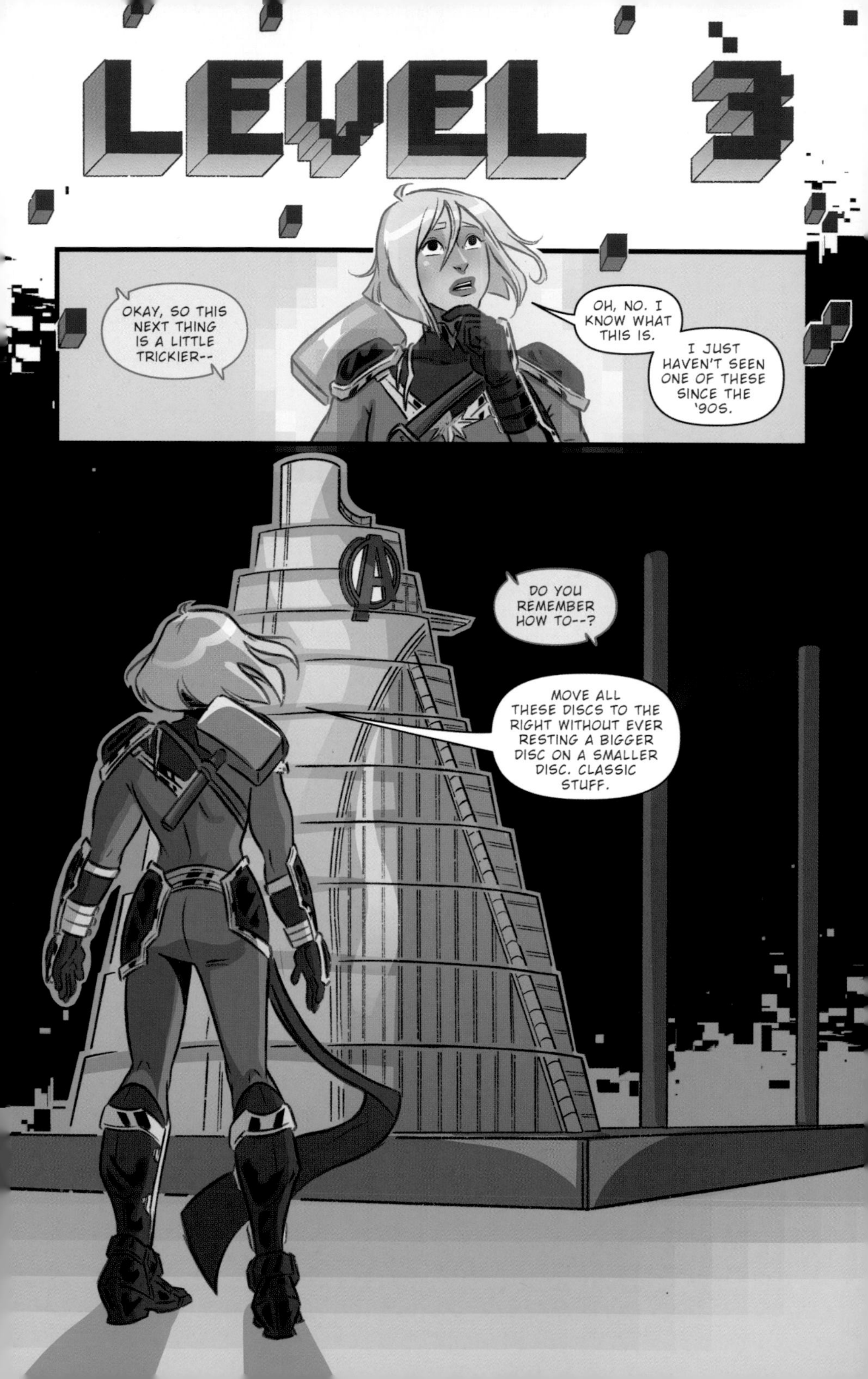
LEVEL 3
OKAY, SO THIS NEXT THING IS A LITTLE TRICKIER--
OH, NO. I KNOW WHAT THIS IS.
I JUST HAVEN'T SEEN ONE OF THESE SINCE THE '90S.
DO YOU REMEMBER HOW TO--?
MOVE ALL THESE DISCS TO THE RIGHT WITHOUT EVER RESTING A BIGGER DISC ON A SMALLER DISC. CLASSIC STUFF.

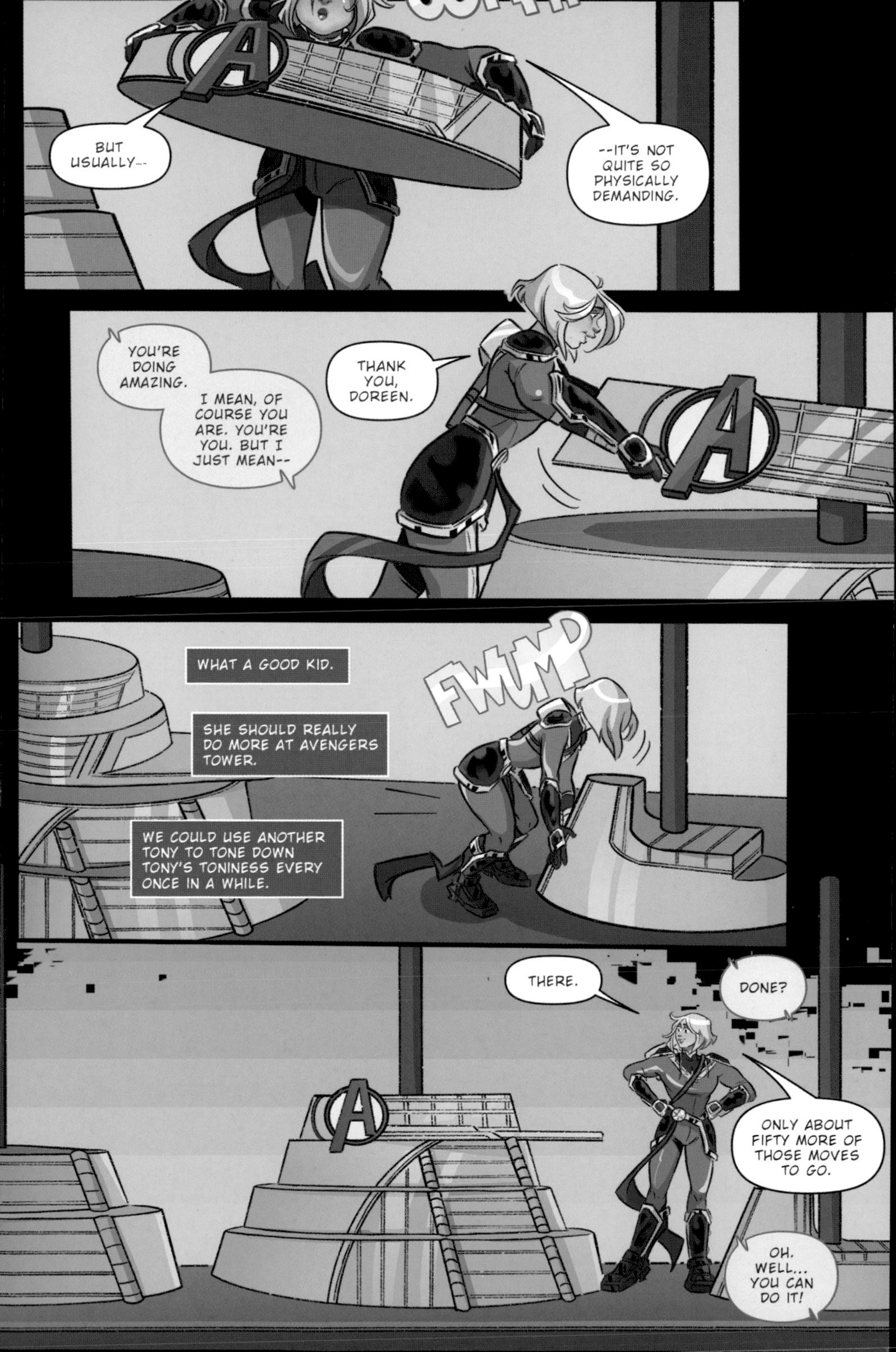

BUT USUALLY--
--IT'S NOT QUITE SO PHYSICALLY DEMANDING.
YOU'RE DOING AMAZING.
I MEAN, OF COURSE YOU ARE. YOU'RE YOU. BUT I JUST MEAN--
THANK YOU, DOREEN.
WHAT A GOOD KID.
SHE SHOULD REALLY DO MORE AT AVENGERS TOWER.
WE COULD USE ANOTHER TONY TO TONE DOWN TONY'S TONINESS EVERY ONCE IN A WHILE.
FWUMP
THERE.
DONE?
ONLY ABOUT FIFTY MORE OF THOSE MOVES TO GO.
OH. WELL... YOU CAN DO IT!

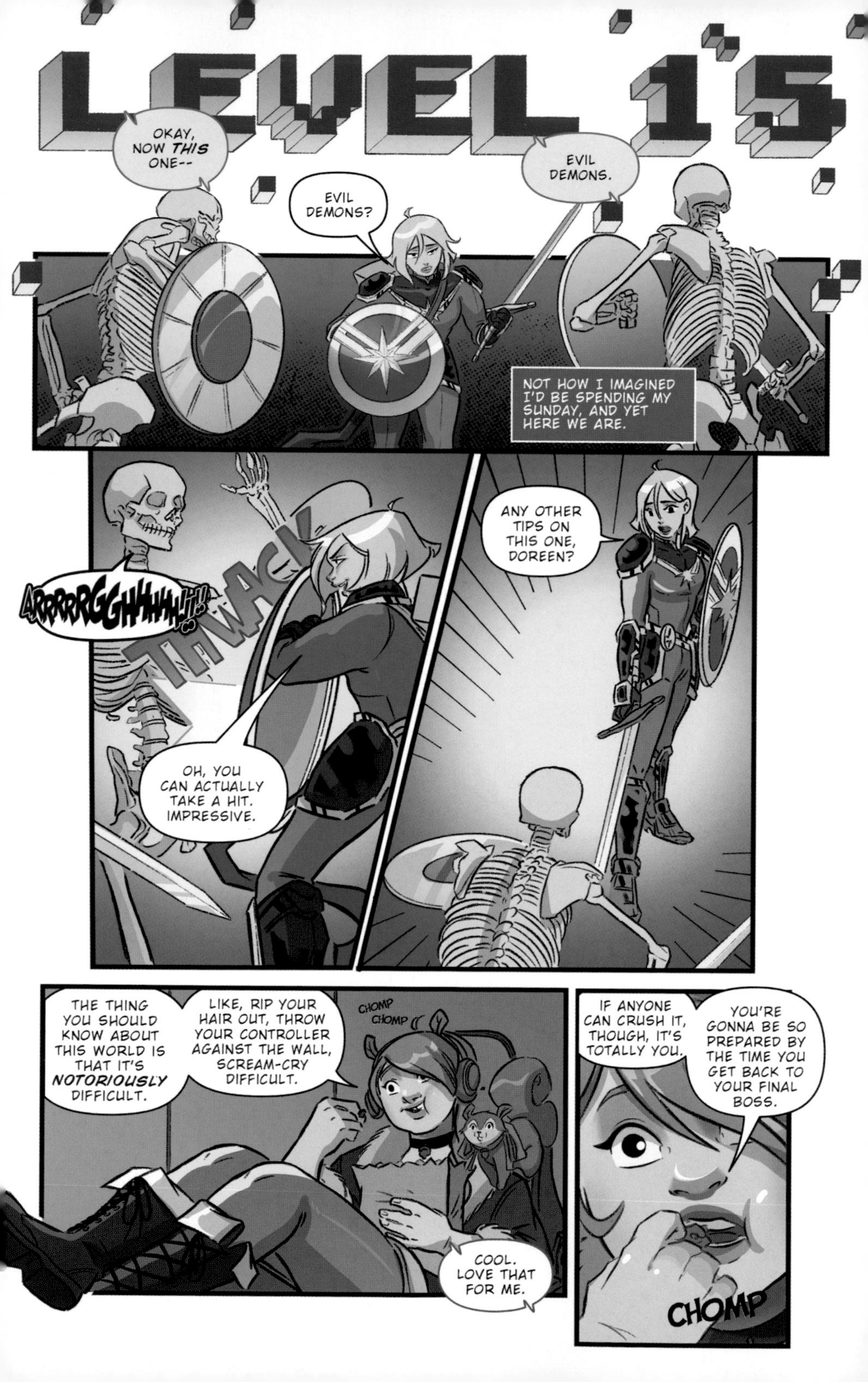
LEVEL 15
OKAY, NOW THIS ONE--
EVIL DEMONS?
EVIL DEMONS.
NOT HOW I IMAGINED I'D BE SPENDING MY SUNDAY, AND YET HERE WE ARE.
ARRRRRGGHHHHH!!!!
THWACK
OH, YOU CAN ACTUALLY TAKE A HIT. IMPRESSIVE.
ANY OTHER TIPS ON THIS ONE, DOREEN?
THE THING YOU SHOULD KNOW ABOUT THIS WORLD IS THAT IT'S NOTORIOUSLY DIFFICULT.
LIKE, RIP YOUR HAIR OUT, THROW YOUR CONTROLLER AGAINST THE WALL, SCREAM-CRY DIFFICULT.
CHOMP CHOMP
COOL. LOVE THAT FOR ME.
IF ANYONE CAN CRUSH IT, THOUGH, IT'S TOTALLY YOU.
YOU'RE GONNA BE SO PREPARED BY THE TIME YOU GET BACK TO YOUR FINAL BOSS.
CHOMP

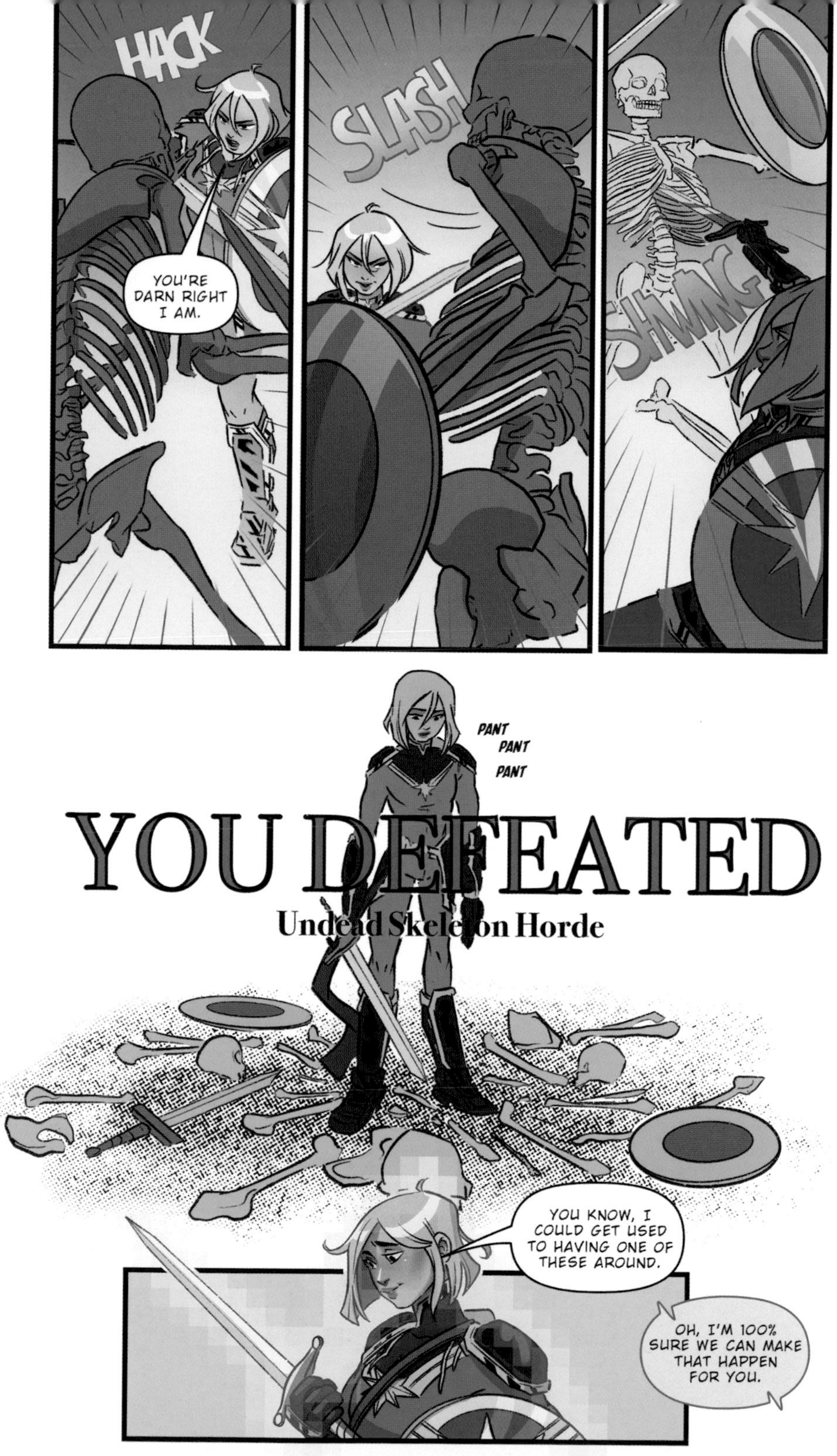
HACK
YOU'RE DARN RIGHT I AM.
SLASH
SHWING
PANT PANT PANT
YOU DEFEATED
Undead Skeleton Horde
YOU KNOW, I COULD GET USED TO HAVING ONE OF THESE AROUND.
OH, I'M 100% SURE WE CAN MAKE THAT HAPPEN FOR YOU.

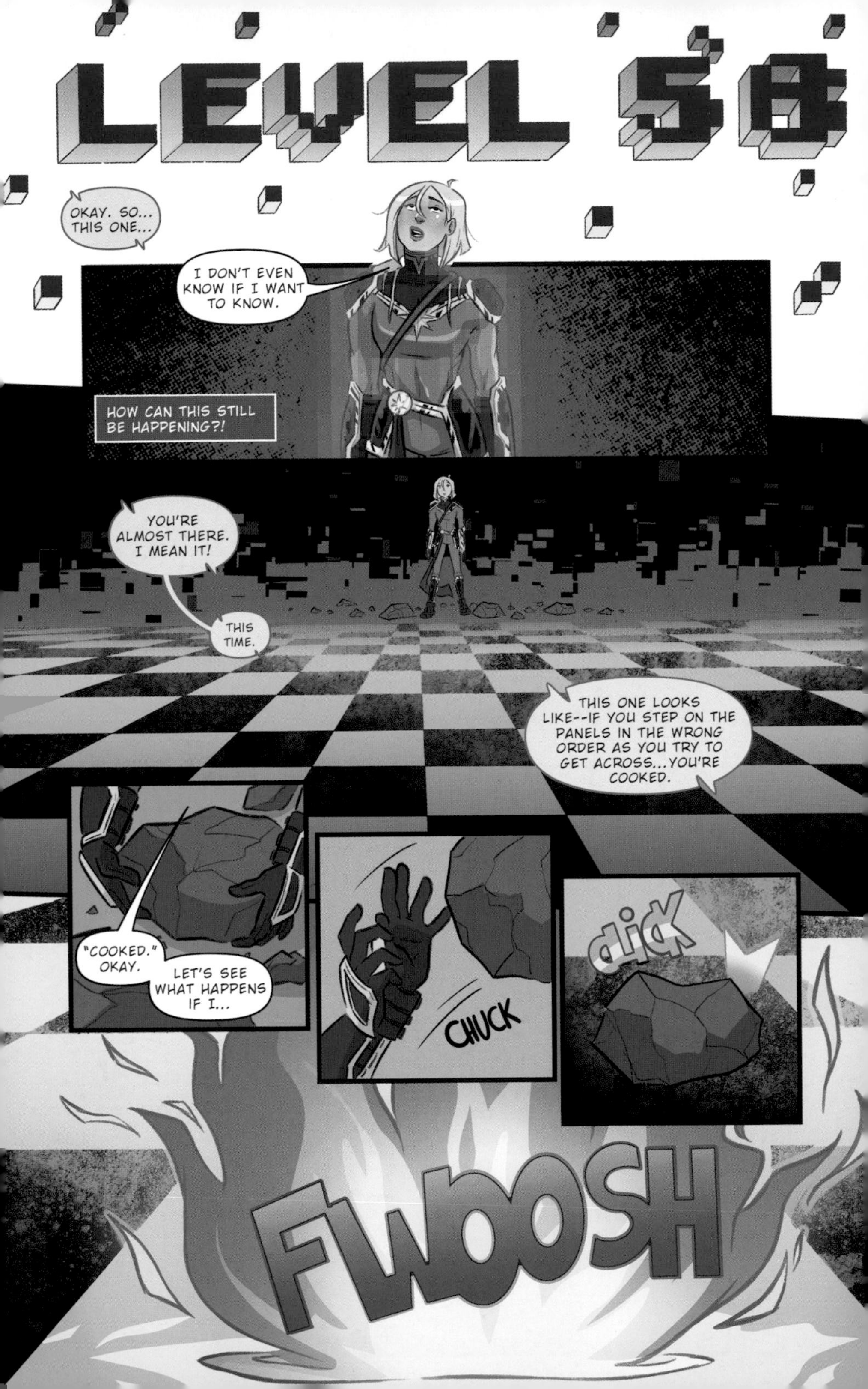
LEVEL 58
OKAY. SO... THIS ONE...
I DON'T EVEN KNOW IF I WANT TO KNOW.
HOW CAN THIS STILL BE HAPPENING?!
YOU'RE ALMOST THERE. I MEAN IT!
THIS TIME.
THIS ONE LOOKS LIKE--IF YOU STEP ON THE PANELS IN THE WRONG ORDER AS YOU TRY TO GET ACROSS...YOU'RE COOKED.
"COOKED." OKAY.
LET'S SEE WHAT HAPPENS IF I...
CHUCK
CLICK
FWOOSH

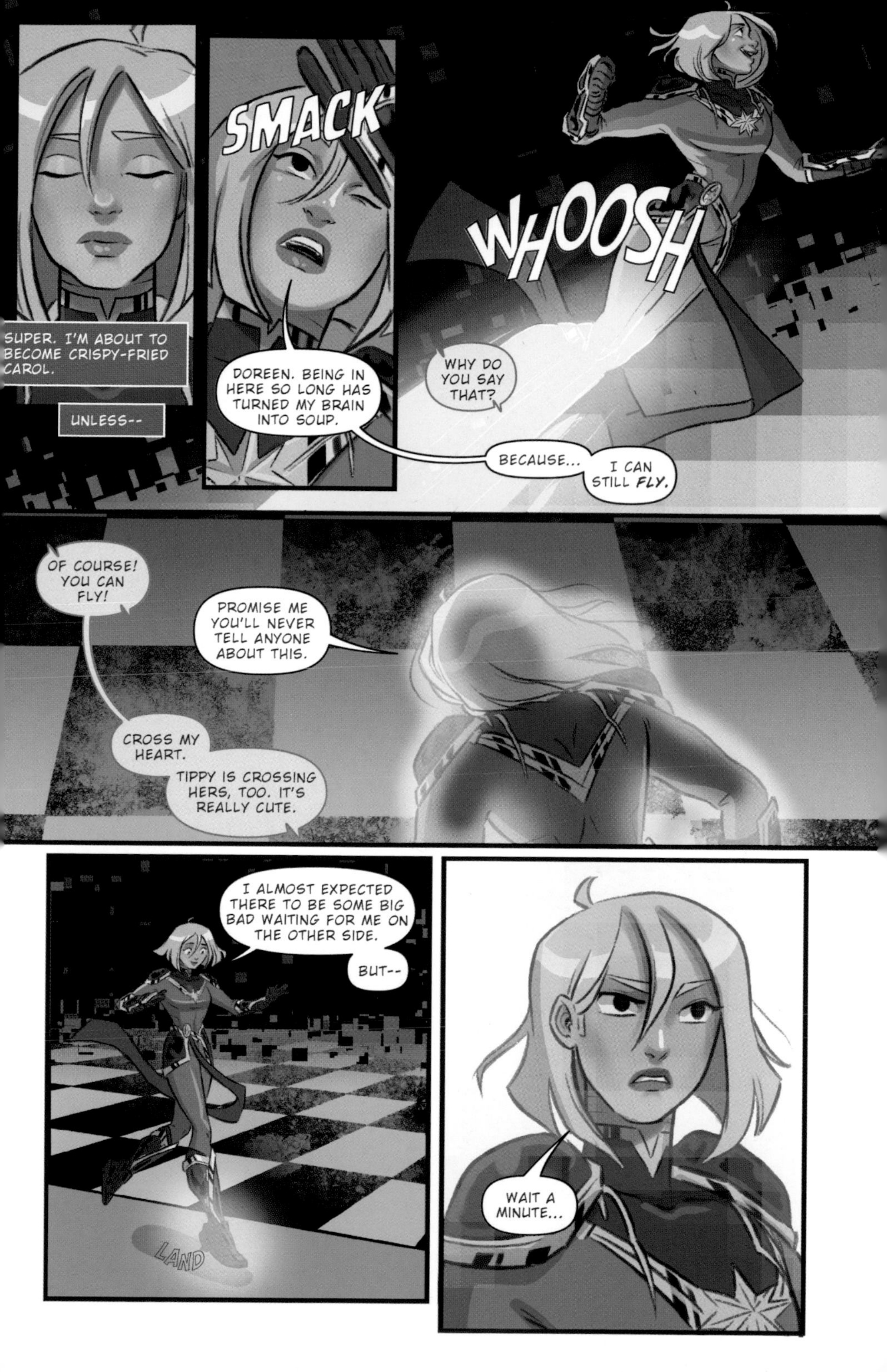
SUPER. I'M ABOUT TO BECOME CRISPY-FRIED CAROL.
UNLESS--
SMACK
DOREEN. BEING IN HERE SO LONG HAS TURNED MY BRAIN INTO SOUP.
WHOOSH
WHY DO YOU SAY THAT?
BECAUSE...
I CAN STILL *FLY.*
OF COURSE! YOU CAN FLY!
PROMISE ME YOU'LL NEVER TELL ANYONE ABOUT THIS.
CROSS MY HEART.
TIPPY IS CROSSING HERS, TOO. IT'S REALLY CUTE.
I ALMOST EXPECTED THERE TO BE SOME BIG BAD WAITING FOR ME ON THE OTHER SIDE.
BUT--
LAND
WAIT A MINUTE...

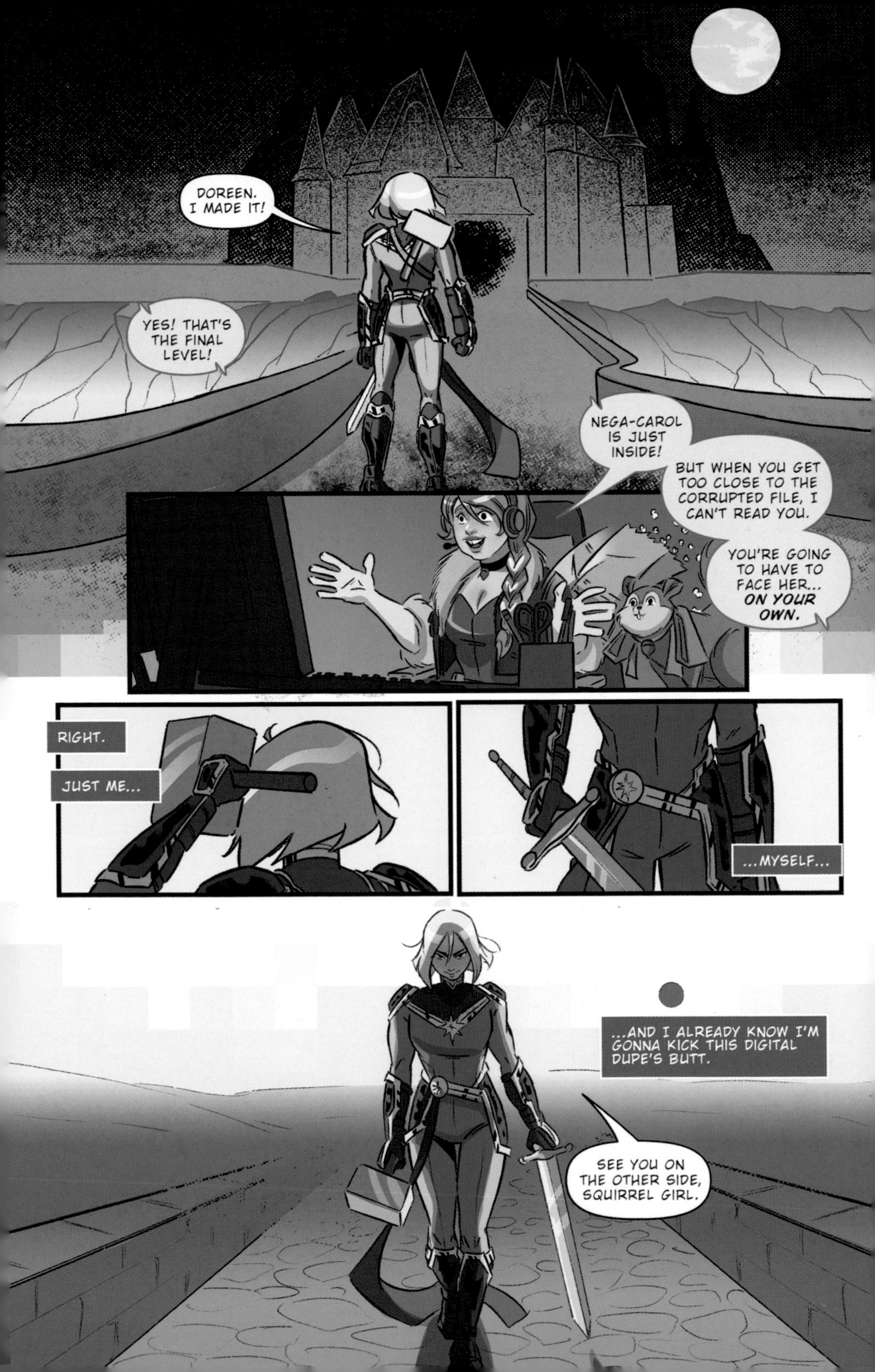
DOREEN. I MADE IT!
YES! THAT'S THE FINAL LEVEL!
NEGA-CAROL IS JUST INSIDE!
BUT WHEN YOU GET TOO CLOSE TO THE CORRUPTED FILE, I CAN'T READ YOU.
YOU'RE GOING TO HAVE TO FACE HER... **ON YOUR OWN.**
RIGHT.
JUST ME...
...MYSELF...
...AND I ALREADY KNOW I'M GONNA KICK THIS DIGITAL DUPE'S BUTT.
SEE YOU ON THE OTHER SIDE, SQUIRREL GIRL.

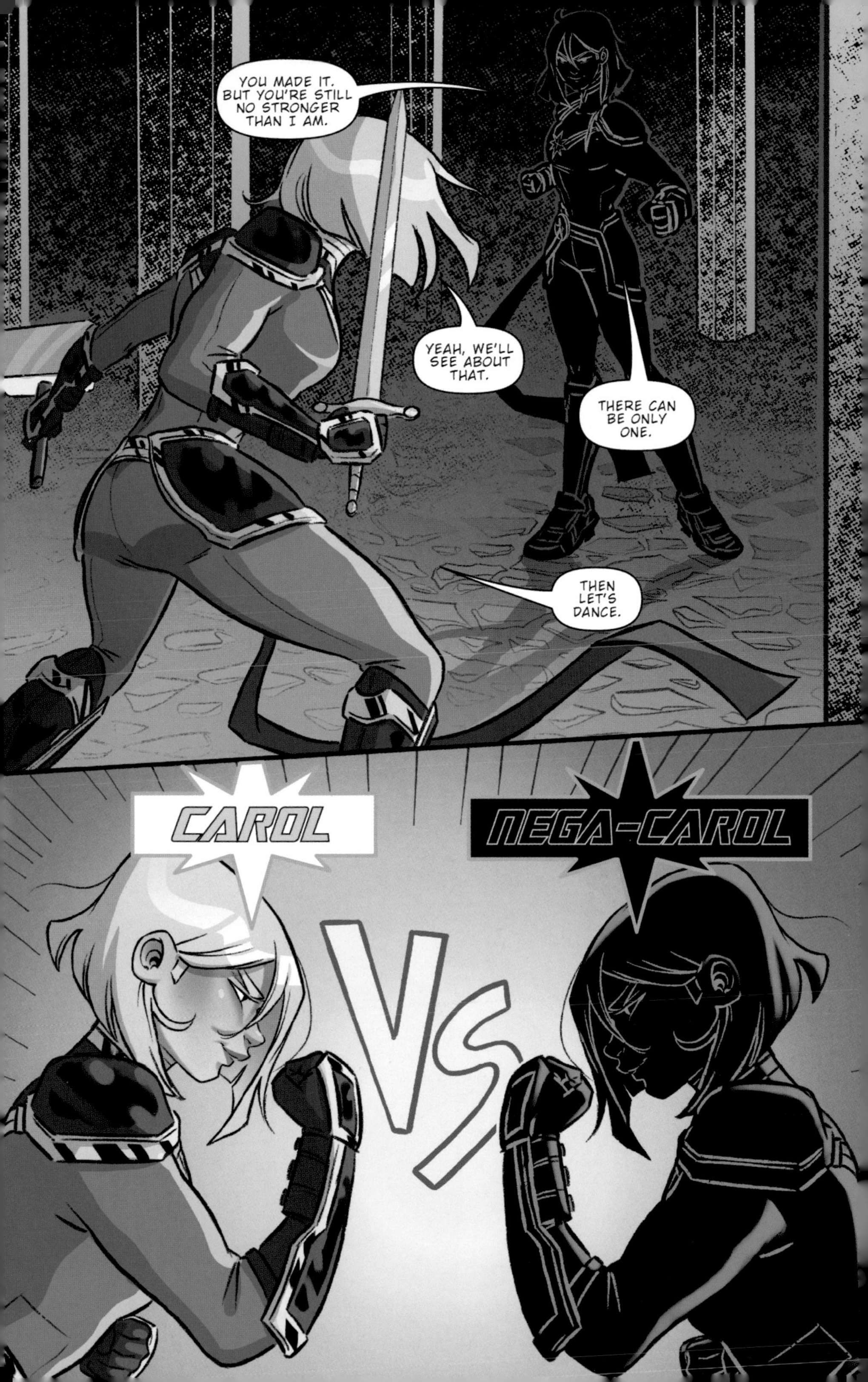
YOU MADE IT. BUT YOU'RE STILL NO STRONGER THAN I AM.
YEAH, WE'LL SEE ABOUT THAT.
THERE CAN BE ONLY ONE.
THEN LET'S DANCE.
CAROL
NEGA-CAROL
VS

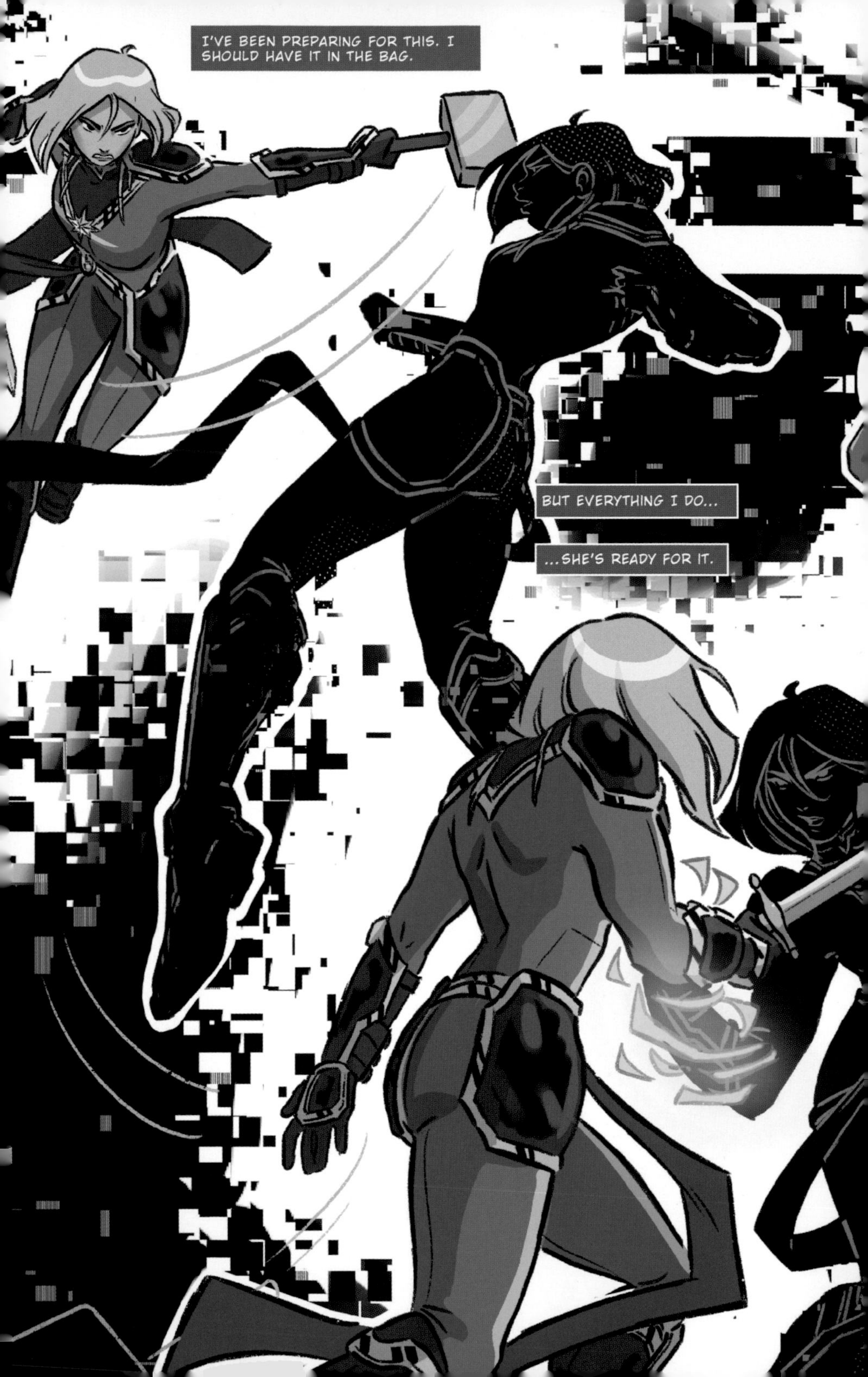

I'VE BEEN PREPARING FOR THIS. I SHOULD HAVE IT IN THE BAG.
BUT EVERYTHING I DO...
...SHE'S READY FOR IT.

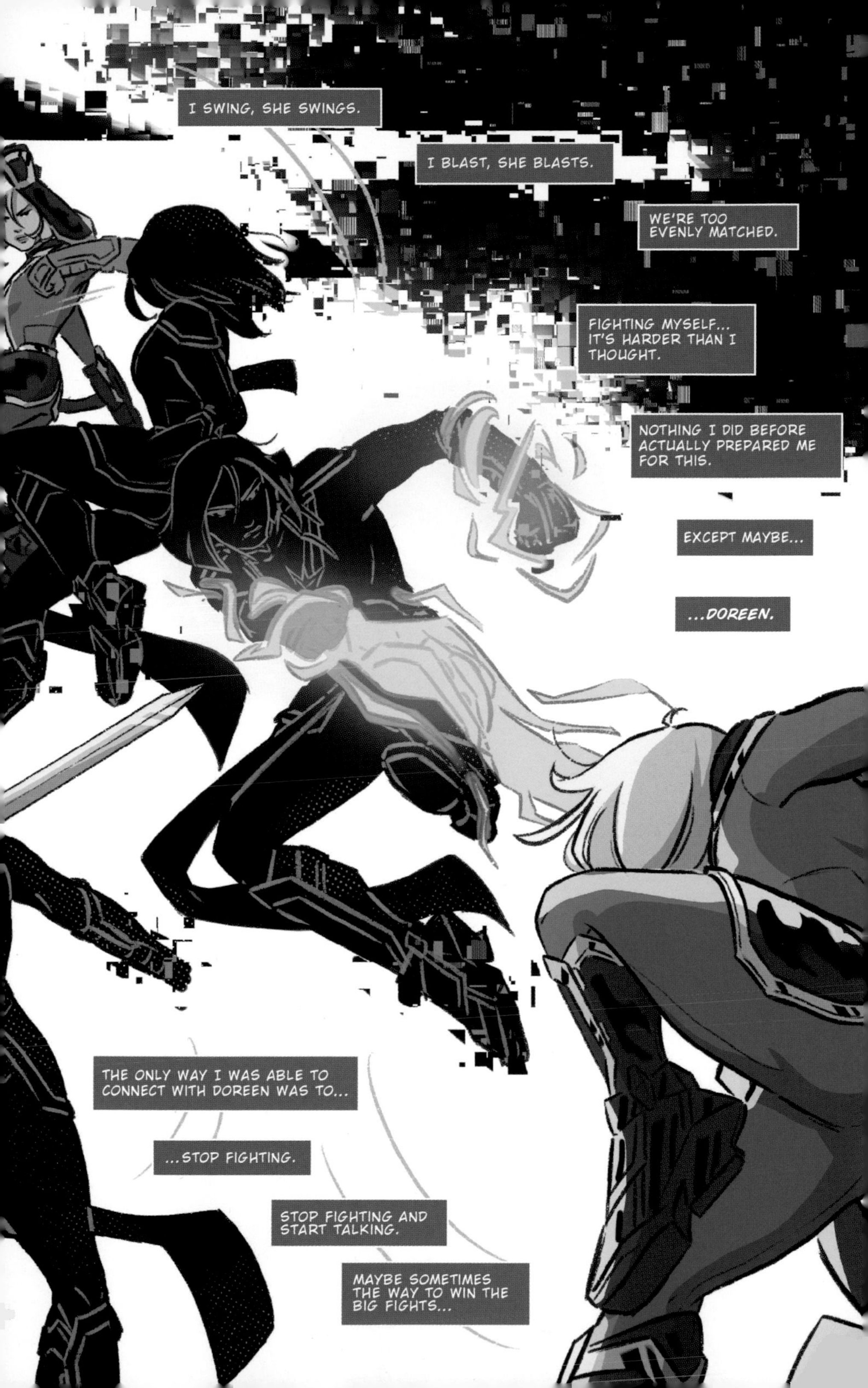
I SWING, SHE SWINGS.
I BLAST, SHE BLASTS.
WE'RE TOO EVENLY MATCHED.
FIGHTING MYSELF... IT'S HARDER THAN I THOUGHT.
NOTHING I DID BEFORE ACTUALLY PREPARED ME FOR THIS.
EXCEPT MAYBE...
...DOREEN.
THE ONLY WAY I WAS ABLE TO CONNECT WITH DOREEN WAS TO...
...STOP FIGHTING.
STOP FIGHTING AND START TALKING.
MAYBE SOMETIMES THE WAY TO WIN THE BIG FIGHTS...

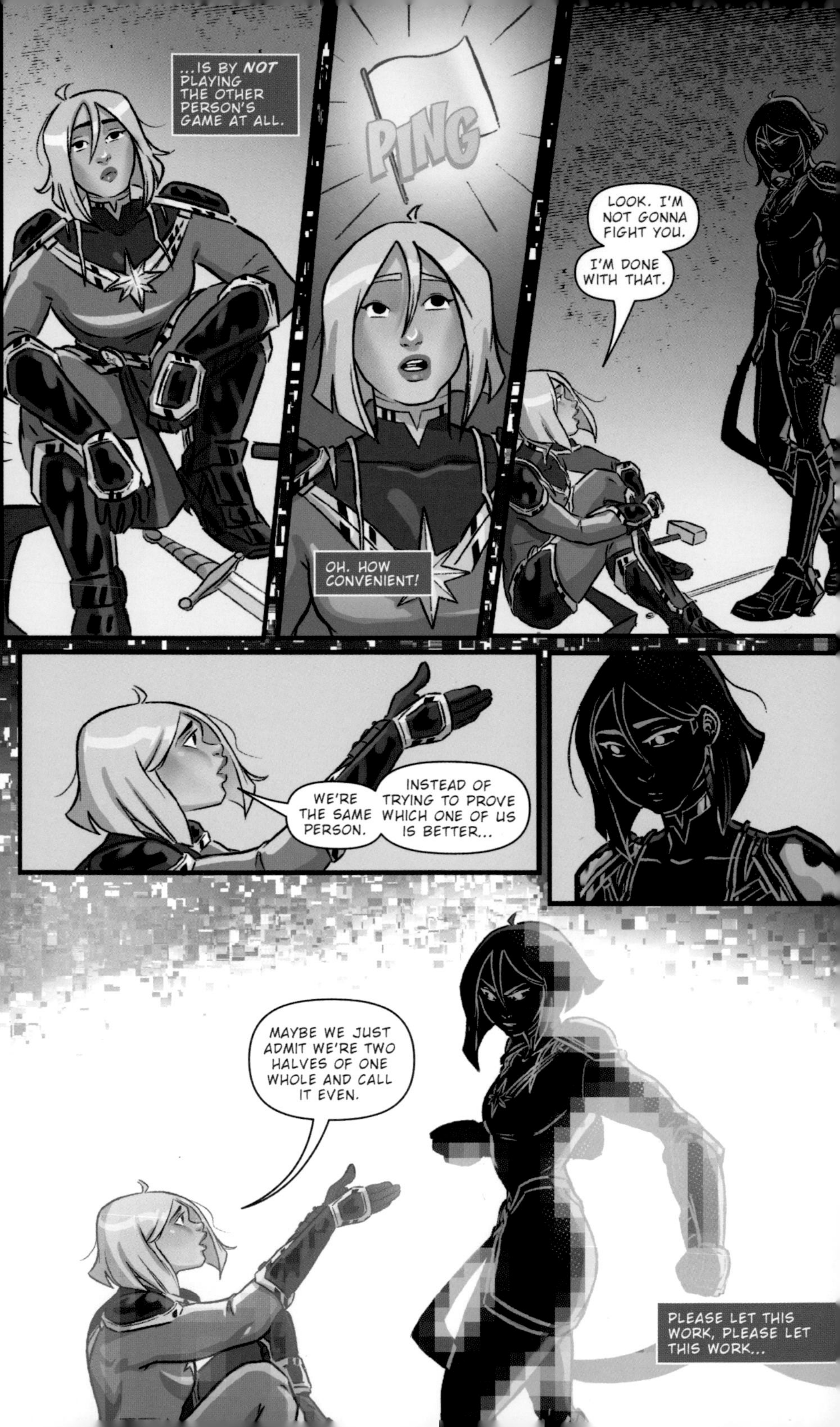
...IS BY NOT PLAYING THE OTHER PERSON'S GAME AT ALL.
PING
OH. HOW CONVENIENT!
LOOK. I'M NOT GONNA FIGHT YOU.
I'M DONE WITH THAT.
INSTEAD OF TRYING TO PROVE WHICH ONE OF US IS BETTER...
WE'RE THE SAME PERSON.
MAYBE WE JUST ADMIT WE'RE TWO HALVES OF ONE WHOLE AND CALL IT EVEN.
PLEASE LET THIS WORK, PLEASE LET THIS WORK...

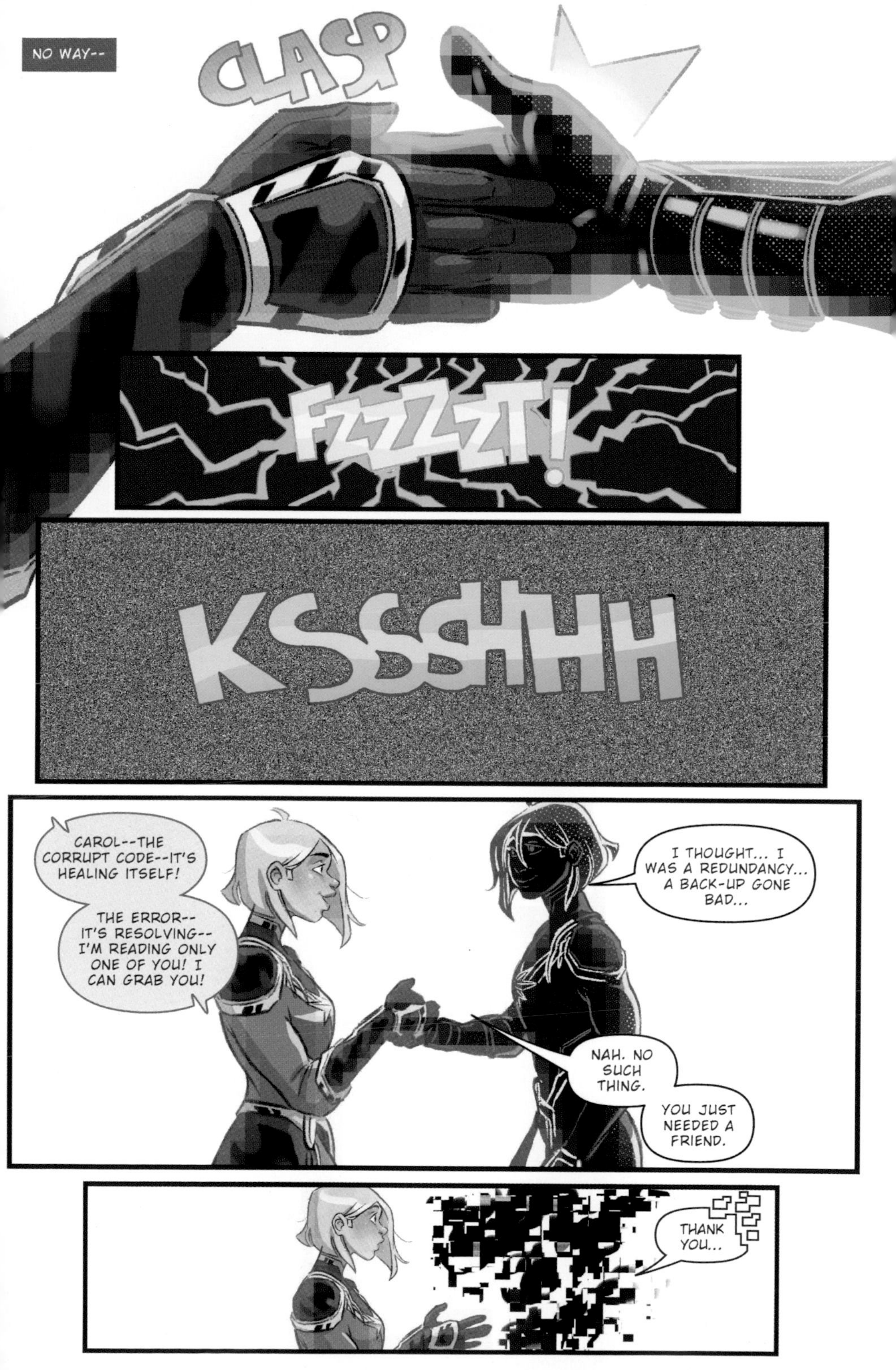
NO WAY--
CLASP
FZZZZT!
KSSSHHH
CAROL--THE CORRUPT CODE--IT'S HEALING ITSELF!
THE ERROR-- IT'S RESOLVING-- I'M READING ONLY ONE OF YOU! I CAN GRAB YOU!
I THOUGHT... I WAS A REDUNDANCY... A BACK-UP GONE BAD...
NAH. NO SUCH THING.
YOU JUST NEEDED A FRIEND.
THANK YOU...

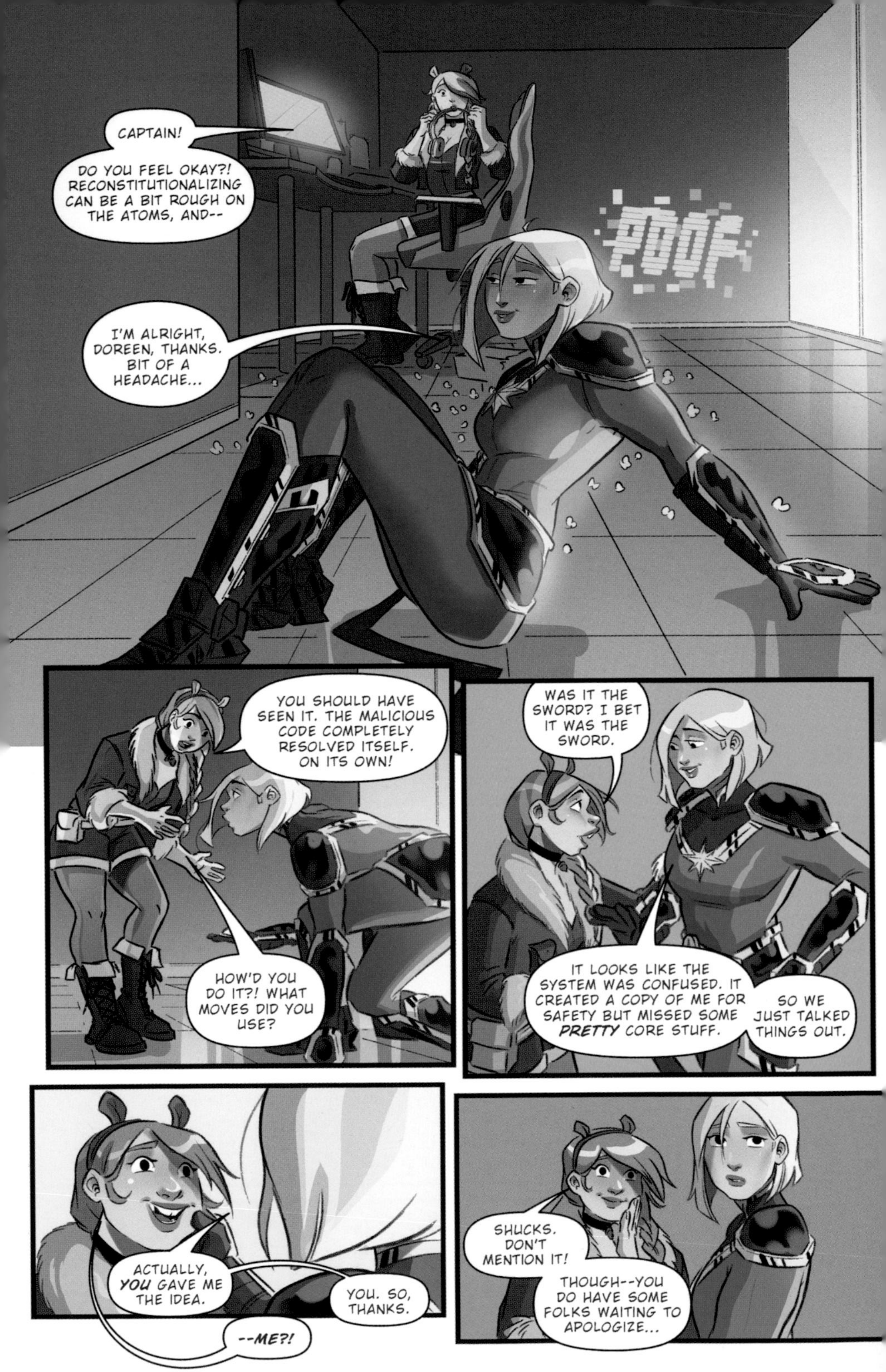
CAPTAIN!
DO YOU FEEL OKAY?! RECONSTITUTIONALIZING CAN BE A BIT ROUGH ON THE ATOMS, AND--
POOF
I'M ALRIGHT, DOREEN, THANKS. BIT OF A HEADACHE...
YOU SHOULD HAVE SEEN IT. THE MALICIOUS CODE COMPLETELY RESOLVED ITSELF. ON ITS OWN!
HOW'D YOU DO IT?! WHAT MOVES DID YOU USE?
WAS IT THE SWORD? I BET IT WAS THE SWORD.
IT LOOKS LIKE THE SYSTEM WAS CONFUSED. IT CREATED A COPY OF ME FOR SAFETY BUT MISSED SOME *PRETTY* CORE STUFF.
SO WE JUST TALKED THINGS OUT.
ACTUALLY, *YOU* GAVE ME THE IDEA.
--*ME?!*
YOU. SO, THANKS.
SHUCKS. DON'T MENTION IT!
THOUGH--YOU DO HAVE SOME FOLKS WAITING TO APOLOGIZE...

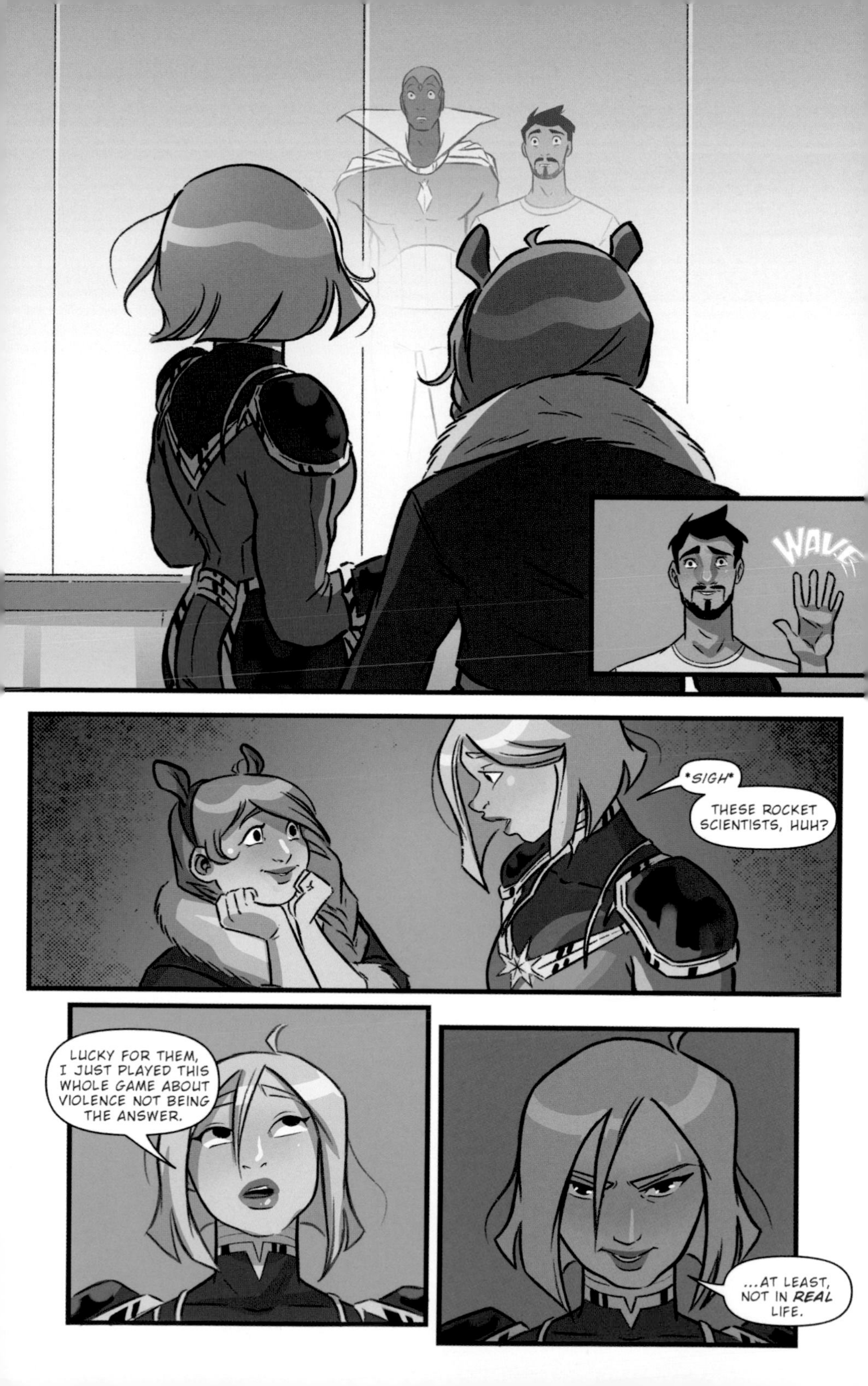
WAVE
SIGH
THESE ROCKET SCIENTISTS, HUH?
LUCKY FOR THEM, I JUST PLAYED THIS WHOLE GAME ABOUT VIOLENCE NOT BEING THE ANSWER.
...AT LEAST, NOT IN REAL LIFE.

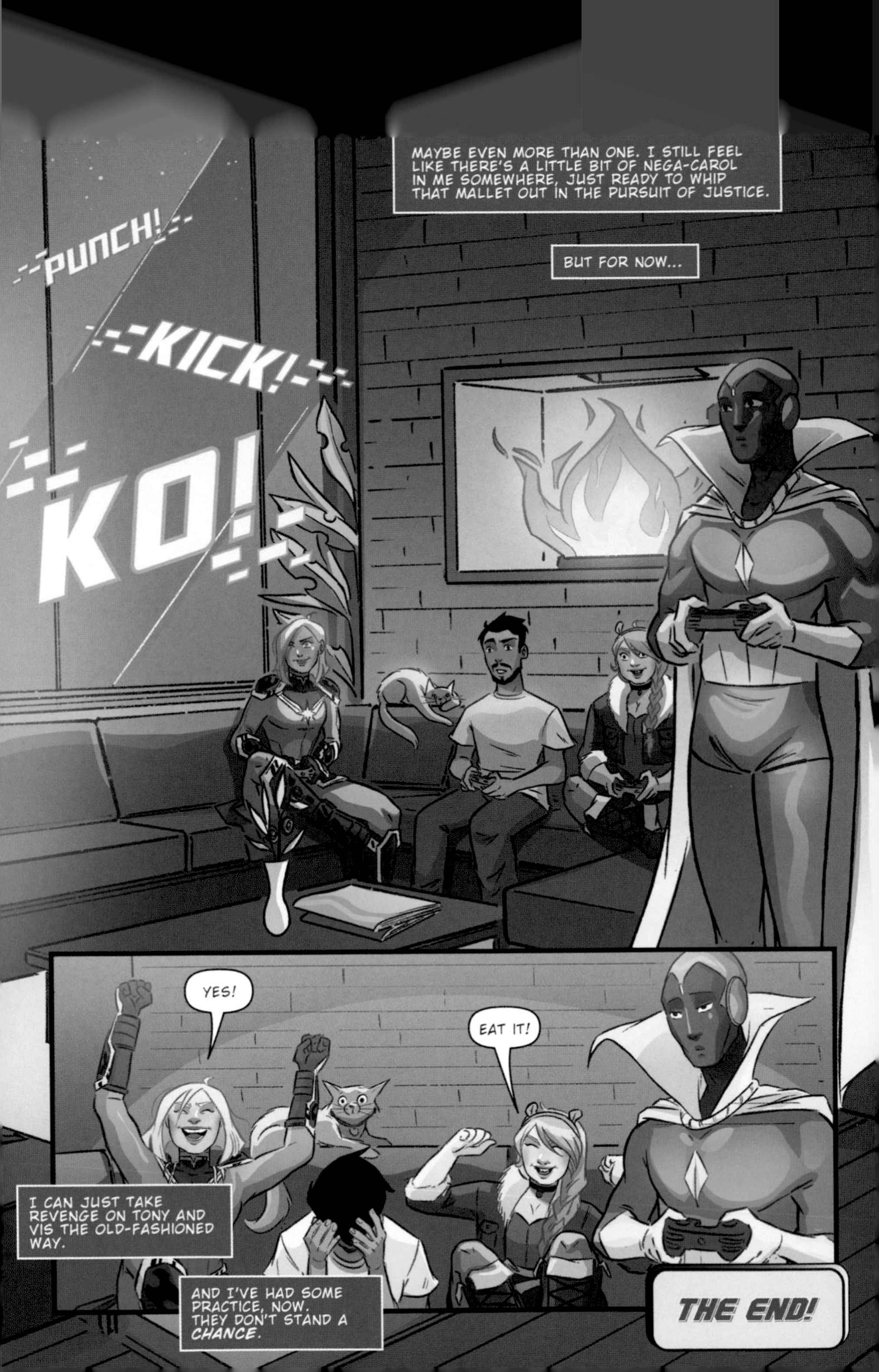

MAYBE EVEN MORE THAN ONE. I STILL FEEL LIKE THERE'S A LITTLE BIT OF NEGA-CAROL IN ME SOMEWHERE, JUST READY TO WHIP THAT MALLET OUT IN THE PURSUIT OF JUSTICE.
BUT FOR NOW...
PUNCH!
KICK!
KO!
YES!
EAT IT!
I CAN JUST TAKE REVENGE ON TONY AND VIS THE OLD-FASHIONED WAY.
AND I'VE HAD SOME PRACTICE, NOW. THEY DON'T STAND A *CHANCE*.
THE END!

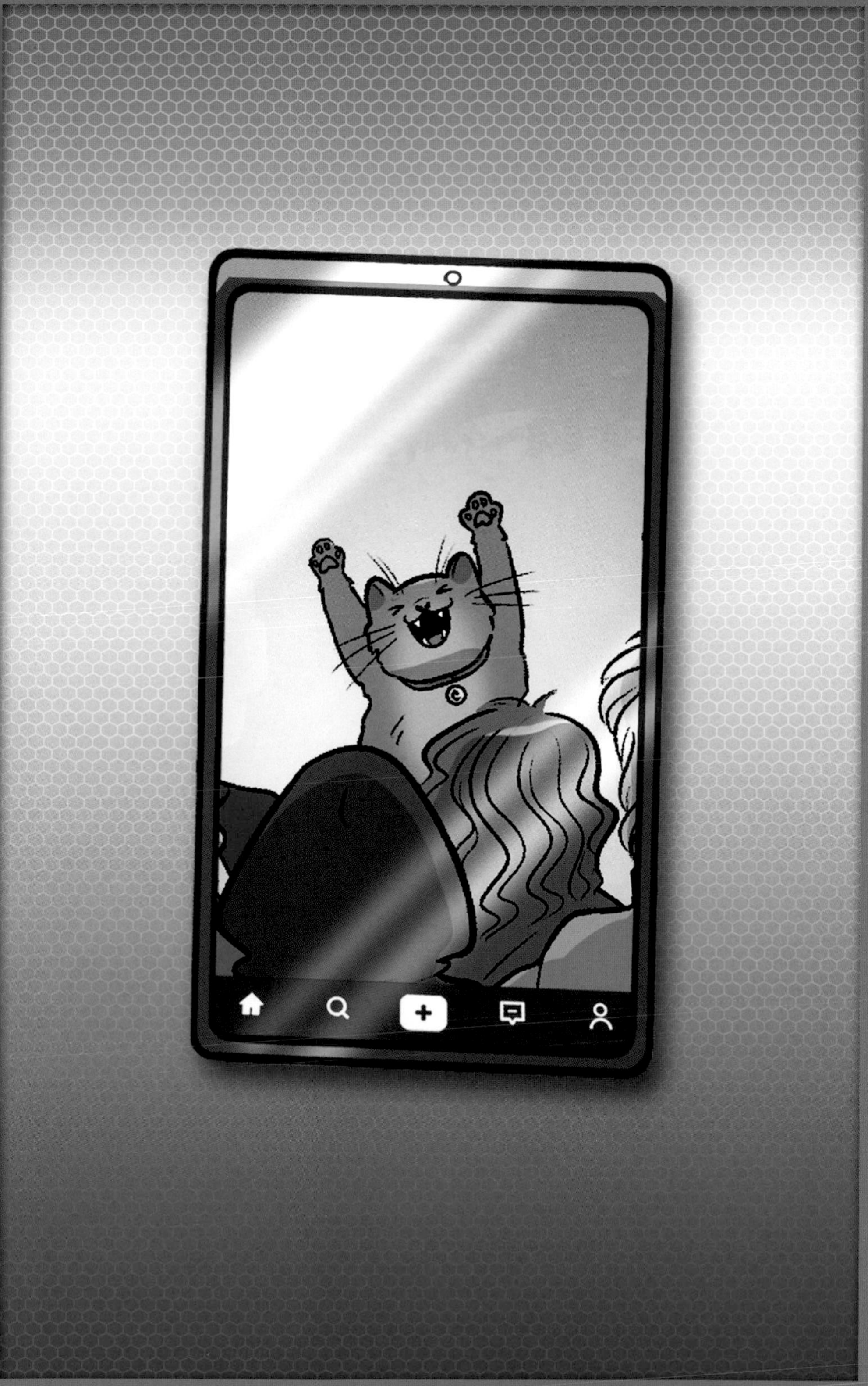

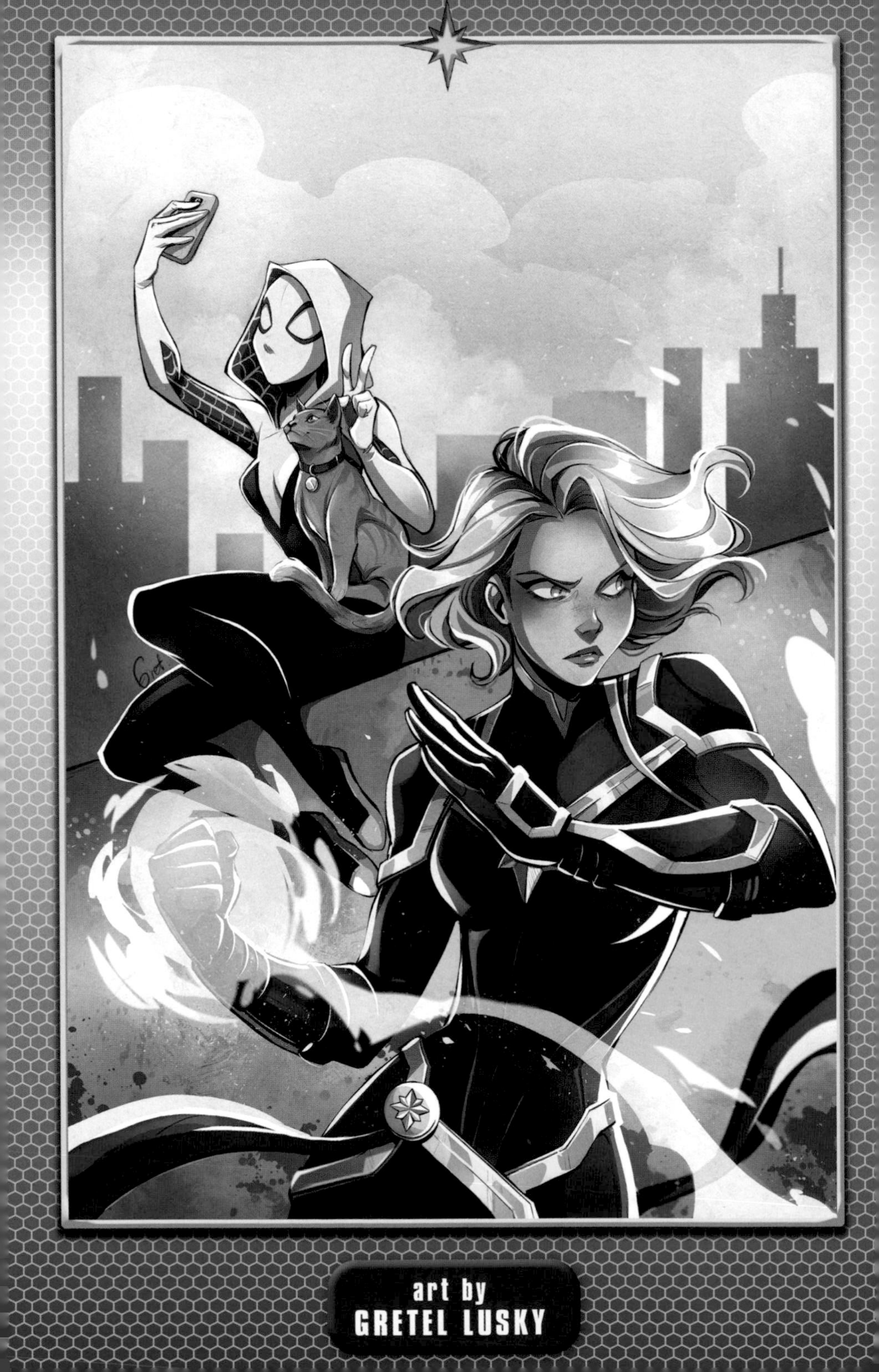

art by
GRETEL LUSKY

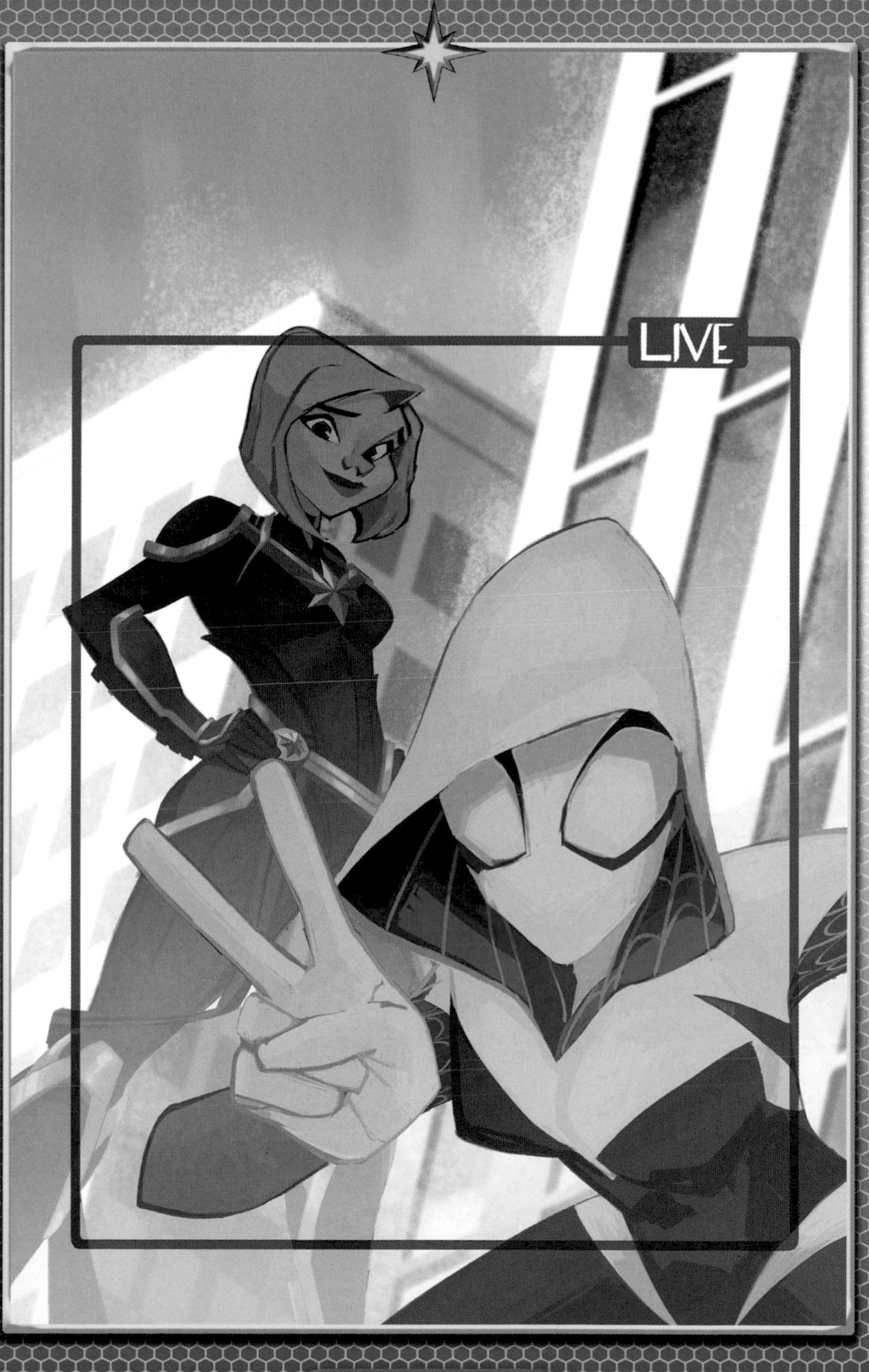
LIVE

art by
KAELA LASH

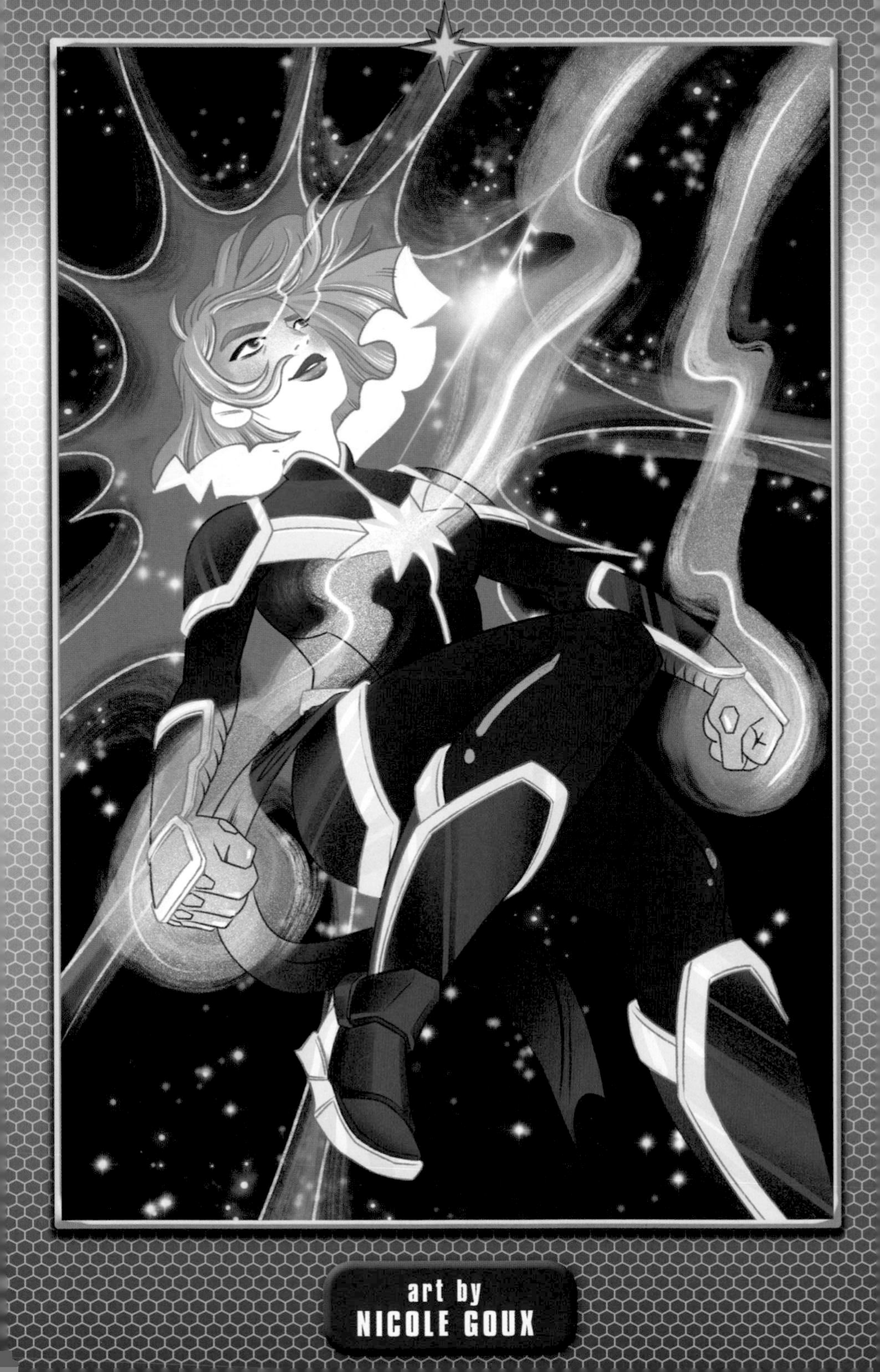

art by
NICOLE GOUX

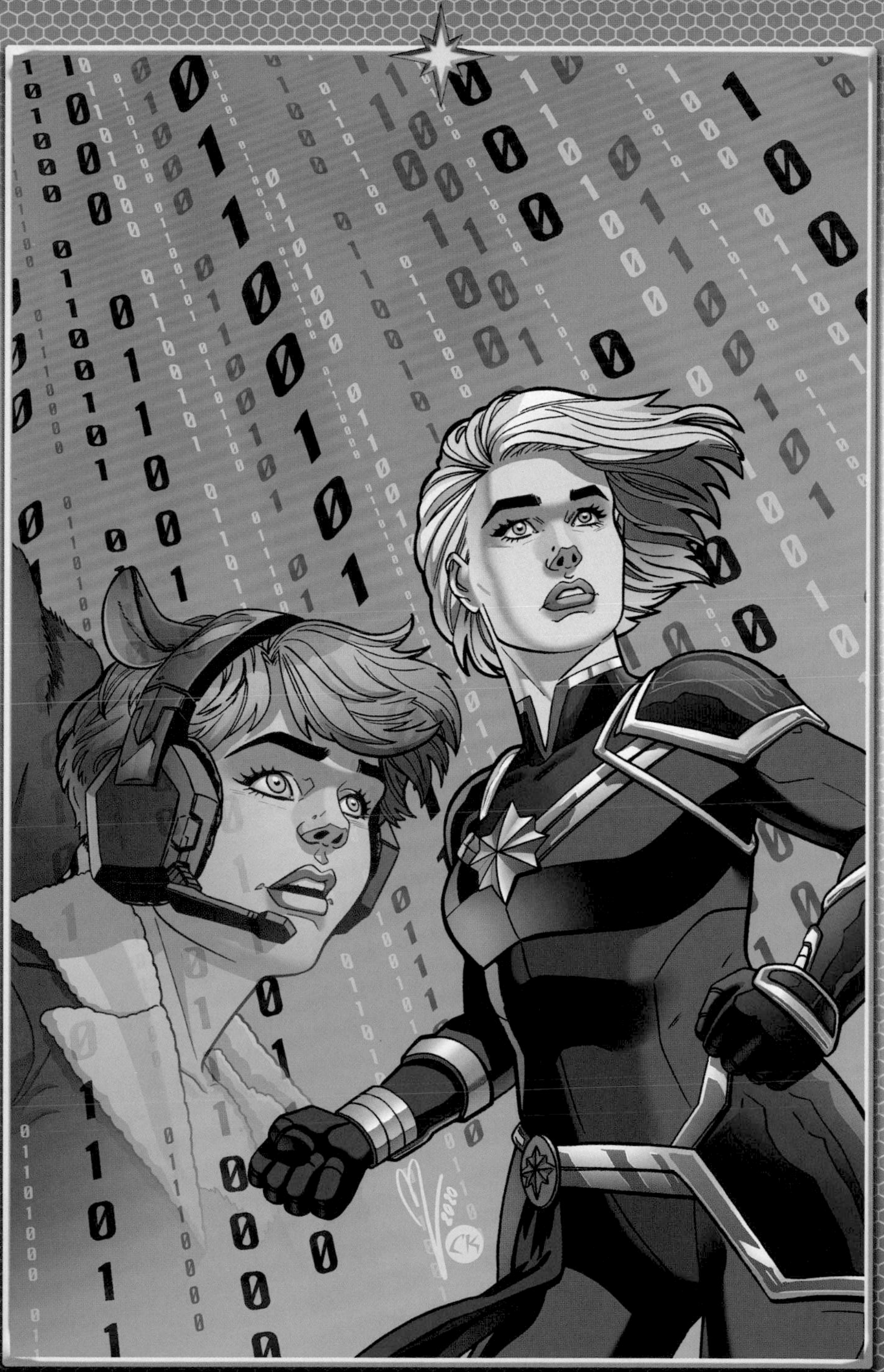

art by
MEGAN LEVENS

colors by
CHARLIE KIRCHOFF

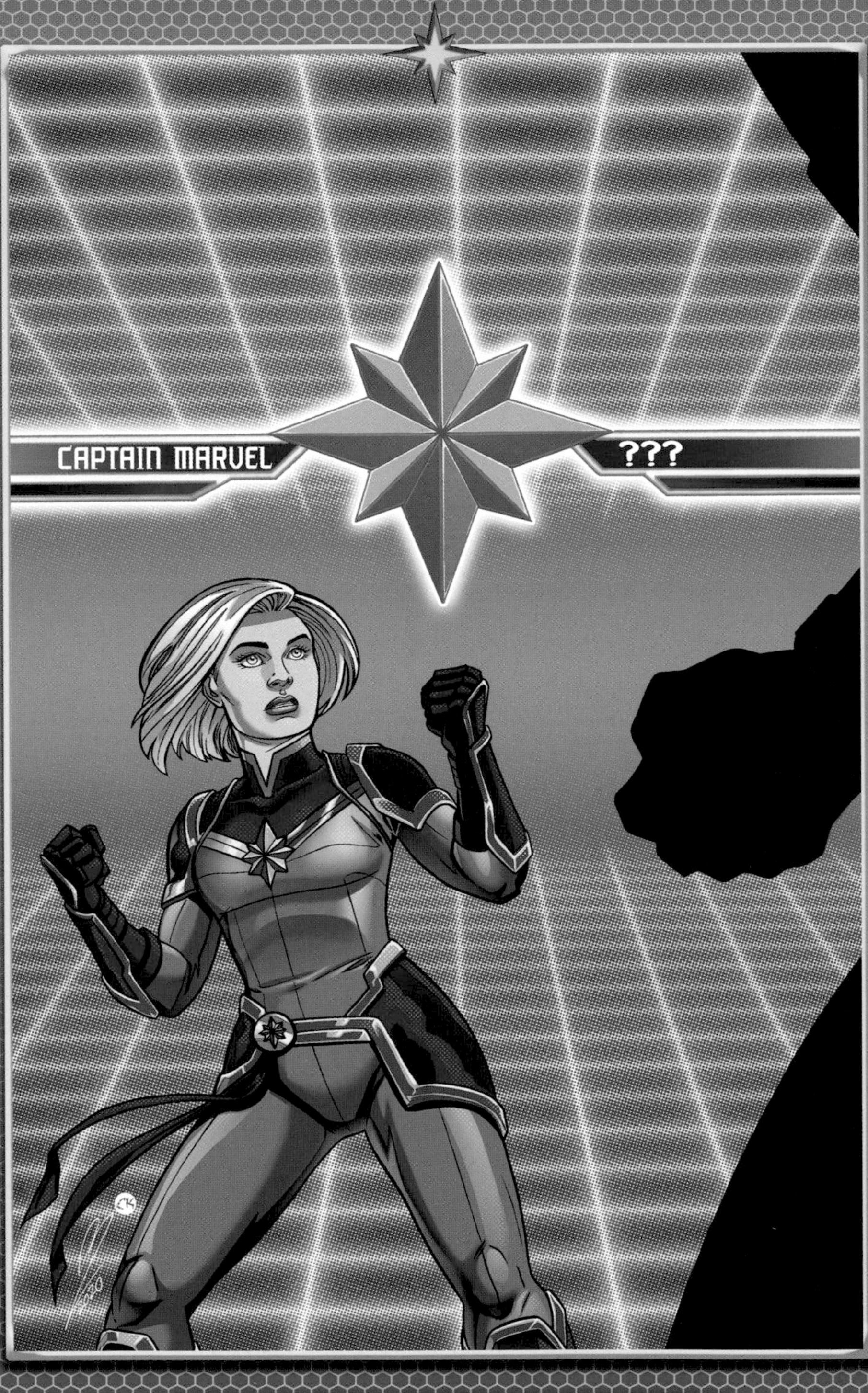
CAPTAIN MARVEL
???

art by
MEGAN LEVENS

colors by
CHARLIE KIRCHOFF